KEEPER OF THE DOVES

KEEPER OF THE DOVES

▼

Michael Ciardi

Writers Club Press
San Jose New York Lincoln Shanghai

Keeper of the Doves

Writers Club Press
an imprint of iUniverse.com, Inc.

For information address:
iUniverse.com, Inc.
5220 S 16th, Ste. 200
Lincoln, NE 68512
www.iuniverse.com

ISBN: 0-595-12655-3

Printed in the United States of America

This is for my wife, Laura, and our children, Brittney and Alyssa.

CONTENTS

CHAPTER ONE

A FUNERAL IN WAKELAND

A curtain of pewter-colored clouds cast a shadow over Wakeland's cemetery on the morning of Lawrence Dayton's funeral. As April's cool rain poured in misty bullets upon the hillside, a string of sparrows took shelter beneath the branches of a nearby pine tree. In addition to these flitting signs of life among the dead, an old priest marched toward the open grave.

Theodore Dayton stood beside his father's casket in a numb silence. No visible tear slid from the man's eyes, for the corpse lying within this coffin had been a stranger to him for most of his life. In truth, Lawrence's death marked a partial end to Theodore's agony, but it also reminded him of the hardships that he still endured.

As Theodore peered at his father's casket, he wondered where this man had been for the past forty-eight years. What degree of selfishness could have compelled any father to abandon his family when they most needed him? Sadly, the answer to this question would now be buried forever. Perhaps it was only fitting that Lawrence's life ended here, while the earth around him enshrouded itself in a cold, dense fog.

Lawrence did not venture to Wakeland by chance alone. The drifter spent his final weeks of life residing in a run-down motel on the rural edges of town. Although he had never before traveled to this small farming community in Pennsylvania, a part of him felt as though he had finally found a home. Before his death, Lawrence made one simple yet blunt request to his son. He wanted to be buried in Wakeland. Summoned by guilt but nothing more, Theodore reluctantly agreed to honor the man's final wish.

An exact cause for Lawrence's death remained a mystery that no one bothered to seriously investigate. A caretaker at the Sunset Motel told the county coroner that he didn't notice any visible signs of disease in the man. The coroner, who apparently had more essential work to consider, filed a death certificate without further interrogation.

"He just died in his sleep," the coroner told Theodore. "I'm guessing, but in such cases, it's usually the heart that's to blame."

Theodore may have done himself a service by accepting this confirmation and moving on with his already troubled life. But he still felt obligated to discover more information about his father, and this subconscious yearning no doubt brought him to the graveyard today. Maybe he was prepared to forgive Lawrence for his choices. In his own forty-eight years, Theodore learned how to appreciate how precious and fragile a life can be. Those bonds formed by blood and bone were important to him now. And as he stood upon this hillside, Theodore realized that a far greater sorrow loomed in the near future.

Thirteen years prior to this day, Theodore's life began to crumble. Up until this time he had been a virtually carefree man, far removed from the despair and loneliness that plagued the less fortunate. But as it so often went with much in life, all good things must be counterbalanced by its opposite.

Theodore's tailspin into darkness began in 1987. It was then that his wife, Claire, gave birth to their first child. The blissful promise of a new beginning for this family, however, was short-lived. Although Claire's pregnancy went to full term without any apparent complications, her body wasn't prepared for a backward birth. Shortly after delivery, she hemorrhaged. A team of dumbfounded obstetricians worked frantically to stop the bleeding, but she died before ever having a chance to cradle her infant daughter.

Those nearest to Theodore knew that he never truly recovered from the loss of his wife. For many years afterwards he clung to an imaginary notion that she still lived with him at home and presided over his affairs as if the pronouncement of her death had been a terrible mistake. A feeling of futility suffocated him, but he also realized that he had a child to love.

The role of fatherhood became clearer to Theodore while gazing into the violet-blue eyes of his daughter, Emily. In many respects, she saved her father's sanity in those bleak years. He often looked at her and saw Claire's face, and the thoughts of love and kindness slowly rekindled his spirit. As the years passed, the pain eventually subsided, but Theodore sensed a cruel turning point in his life once again.

When it seemed as though Theodore's life could only improve, things worsened. Two years ago, following Emily's eleventh birthday, Theodore brought his daughter to a doctor for treatment of a sickness that at first seemed no more critical than the flu. By the time Emily sought medical attention, the conspicuous symptoms of fatigue, a pallor complexion, and a sudden loss of weight were grossly apparent. She also experienced unprovoked nosebleeds and complained of various aches in her legs and arms.

A series of blood tests followed the initial examination. The results carried Theodore into his deepest state of anguish thus far. Despite the doctor's earnest attempt to remain optimistic, he diagnosed Emily with an incurable form of chronic leukemia. In most cases, the prognosis for Emily's type of blood cancer was three to six months, culminating in a painful death.

How much heartache could one man endure? Theodore dared to ask himself this question, but the answer was never close at hand. He didn't want to give up, and perhaps this in itself only reminded him of his futility as a man. Within a week after being informed of his daughter's terminal condition, Theodore quit his job as a magazine editor in order to dedicate all of his efforts toward finding a cure.

Specialists in New York and Philadelphia did little to alleviate his fears. With few other options to consider, doctors performed a bone marrow transplant in order to extend Emily's life. Following the surgery, the child's cancer went into remission. For the next eighteen months Emily's leukemia remained dormant. Theodore prematurely convinced himself that they had miraculously won this so often lost battle. But before any true celebration commenced, Emily's blood disorder returned with a vengeance.

In the last six months Emily's physical condition had deteriorated to a point where she could barely pull herself from bed. At present, she weighed no more than sixty pounds and spent the better portion of each day struggling to digest warm soup broth and breadcrumbs. With all conceivable avenues of medical treatment exhausted, Theodore readied himself for the inevitable outcome.

As Emily neared death, Theodore systematically eliminated all contact with those who offered hope or spiritual guidance. Even Father Quinn, Wakeland's only priest, had been rejected. Although Quinn attempted to dissuade Theodore from his choice to forsake the church, it did little good. Theodore convinced himself into believing that his prior devotion toward God had only rendered him more susceptible to this world's cruelties. He saw no reason to carry on with his blind faith, and was content with the present realization that God did not truly exist.

Being an optimist by nature, Quinn hoped that Theodore would pry the darkness from his mind, but he offered no evidence of change at this funeral. As Quinn recited the Twenty-third Psalm from memory, he felt the cold weight of Theodore's hand against his shoulder.

"Let's keep it simple today, Quinn," Theodore suggested in a grave tone. "We'll skip the eulogy, if you don't mind."

Quinn bowed his chin and inched away from the casket. "As you wish, Theodore," he whispered. "I thought maybe you had a change of heart."

Theodore smirked and turned away from the priest without further comment. He then descended the tombstone-dotted hillside toward his jeep. Quinn looked on silently as Theodore entered his vehicle and sped off down the mist-covered road.

While driving home, Theodore recalled the forlorn look in Quinn's eyes; it was the pitiful gaze of a betrayed friend. The gray sky swirled in his mind like an ominous sea as he thought of the priest and all that he signified submerging into a cesspool of blackness. This dire image followed him along Wakeland's country roads. He imagined the boiling clouds folding down upon his jeep, leaving him to accelerate blindly into a realm that was even grayer than the face of his dead father.

Quinn continued to watch Theodore's jeep until it disappeared behind the hills. Although the rain now fell at a considerable rate, the priest seemed oblivious to its presence. He allowed himself a few moments to inhale the dewy air that accompanied this shower. The first rains of spring always enhanced his mood and permitted him to sense the Lord he cherished with greater clarity.

Quinn may have stayed upon the hillside another few minutes, but he was distracted by the approaching footsteps of an older man and woman. They emerged in tandem from behind a sepulcher, and steadily navigated a narrow footpath toward Lawrence's gravesite. Quinn squinted between the droplets of rain, but he was fairly certain that neither of them were residents of Wakeland. He surmised that they were friends of the deceased. After watching the man and woman pause briefly in front of the casket, Quinn edged closer to them.

"Would you like me to finish the eulogy now?" Quinn asked in a solemn voice.

The man, who seemed unreasonably nervous, pivoted toward the priest and said, "I'd like that very much, Father, but it'd be much more helpful to us if you could answer a question."

Not knowing precisely how to respond, Quinn nodded his chin and peered at the man and woman with a growing curiosity working into his expression. "How do you two know the deceased?"

The woman, wearing a tattered black dress and veil, leaned forward and whispered, "He was dear, old friend. Extremely eccentric, you know, but we liked him very much."

"Well, I must confess," the priest replied, "I didn't know this fellow at all. But I'll try to help you if I can."

Quinn stood by awkwardly as the man and woman consulted in private. After a few moments, the woman stepped forward. "There was another man standing beside you a couple of minutes ago, Father. But he left before we had a chance to speak with him."

"Yes, that's true. He generally doesn't talk to anyone nowadays."

The older man motioned to the casket before saying, "Was that man Lawrence's son, Father?"

Quinn nodded his chin once and replied sheepishly, "By blood alone, I suppose. But I'm afraid Theodore didn't know his father very well."

At this point, Quinn sensed a hint of intrigue igniting in the woman's eyes. She offered her male friend an encouraging gesture before refocusing her attention toward the priest.

"We've rambled on for far too many miles and years," she declared. "Lawrence always seemed to keep one step ahead of us. He was quite good at being alone. But I didn't want it to end like this—not when we were so close to finding the truth."

Quinn attempted to remain empathetic to the strangers' plight, but his perplexity only deepened. "As I said, Ma'am, I'm really not in any position to answer for Lawrence Dayton."

The woman smiled and gently patted the priest's hand with her own. "But you do know his son, don't you?"

"That all depends," Quinn responded, somewhat despondently. "We were once very close, but I'm afraid that's not the case anymore. Theodore has some serious issues to resolve."

At this point the woman removed a white cloth and pencil from her handbag and, using her purse as a prop, scribbled her name and a phone number onto the napkin. She then folded the napkin in half and placed it firmly into Quinn's hand.

"My name is Belinda Willinger," she announced, "and my gentleman friend, Mr. Gibbon, and I will be staying at the Sunset Motel for the next few days. Theodore will be able to get in touch with us there."

"I still don't know if I can do this for you, Miss Willinger," Quinn said, trying to stuff the napkin into his coat's pocket. "This is an extremely difficult time in Theodore's life right now."

"Just see to it that Theodore calls me within the next forty-eight hours," Belinda pleaded. "We'll handle the details from there."

Quinn conceded to the probability that Belinda was not going to accept any refusal on his part, so he reluctantly agreed to at least deliver her message to Theodore in good faith.

Before any further discourse passed between them, the two strangers turned away from the priest and started back down the hill. Suddenly, the storm, which seemed as if it might endure for hours, began to dissipate. Slivers of sunlight squirted through the dark clouds and fell upon the cemetery's headstones. In another instant the gray sky opened, exposing its azure color to the fresh winds of spring.

Quinn tilted his head to the air to watch the sparrows take flight from the trees. In these brief moments, all of nature seemed settled in a state of tranquility once again.

CHAPTER TWO

▼

THE JOURNAL'S ARRIVAL

Regina Hopewell waited all winter for the snowfall to melt from the field behind the Dayton's farmhouse. But as the last traces of frost surrendered to nature's rebirth, she found herself struggling to appreciate the significance of new life forming in an otherwise frigid time. It was too easy for her to find fault with this seasonal change, especially when the forthcoming spring only afforded a promise of death to an innocent child.

After dedicating nearly twenty years of her life to the profession of nursing, Regina refused to accept the idea that a child's demise could be classified as a natural occurrence. Granted, she had tended to her share of terminally sick patients over the course of her career without becoming emotionally attached, but she couldn't separate herself from all of them—especially the young ones. Perhaps this was the driving force behind her decision to care for Emily.

Six months ago, just after Emily's leukemia relapsed, Regina graciously volunteered her services to Theodore in his home. She of course realized that Theodore was in no mental condition to care for his daughter, so the responsibilities would be extraordinarily difficult, even for a seasoned professional like herself. Yet, sensing that the child required someone like herself to fulfill her basic needs, Regina made the choice to temporarily leave her job at the hospital and work under Theodore's roof—free of charge.

Soon after Regina arrived in Wakeland she learned that Theodore's depression had intensified. In a matter of three months, she watched his dark hair fade to silver, and his skin appeared excessively wrinkled and gray. His mouth dipped at each corner. Even on his best days, he barely managed to fake a halfhearted smile. In many ways, Regina equated his condition as being as ravaging to his mind as Emily's cancer was to her body.

Despite Theodore's unpredictability, Regina remained tolerant to his inner-discord, for she suspected that few men would have reacted differently if challenged with a similar level of turmoil. No matter what his mood, she had already promised herself that she was not going to leave the Dayton's farmhouse until her duty toward Emily had been thoroughly satisfied.

Most of Regina's colleagues were not as enthusiastic about her decision to undertake Emily's treatment alone, especially after assessing Theodore's current mental stability. Before relocating to Wakeland, Regina prepared herself for many of the pitfalls that might occur, but she was not quite ready to examine her own feelings with any depth.

Although Regina had not planned for such diversions, she found herself becoming increasingly closer to Theodore. While interludes of this nature were not entirely unusual, Regina spent an inordinate amount of energy trying to repress her feelings. She was not prepared to adore such a man, and he certainly could not develop feelings for her at this tragic point in his life.

At the age of forty-one, Regina suspected that she had squandered the best days of her life searching for a soul mate. Up until a few years ago, she occupied her thoughts with work, but suddenly—and for reasons she couldn't perceive with any clarity—she felt strangely alone.

While lying in bed at night, she gazed at the ceiling of her room, piercing the shadows with her thoughts. Then, in the midst of a fantasy, she brushed her bare legs across the cool bed sheets. A feeling of emptiness struck her, for the bed was cold where it should have been warm.

Regina waited most of the morning in front of the kitchen window for Theodore to return home. She had been intensely worried about him ever since he learned of his father's arrival in Wakeland two weeks ago. Lawrence's subsequent funeral, as Theodore explained it, would at least permit him to concentrate on Emily's malady without any further distractions. Still, as callous as Theodore sounded, Regina realized that more healing needed to be rendered.

As Theodore's jeep approached the house, Regina's attention swayed to the kitchen table, where she had earlier placed a single package. She then gazed out the window toward the circular driveway, focusing her eyes along a brick pathway that served as a centerpiece to the landscape. Theodore ambled across the yard, pausing briefly to admire the budding leaves of a weeping cherry tree.

At this point, Regina stood up from the table and took hold of the package. It was wrapped in a brown mailing envelope and appeared to be about the size and shape of a book of some kind. None of these details were conspicuous, save for the writing scribbled in the left corner of the package's mailing paper. It read: To Emily, from L. Dayton.

Theodore may have not uttered too much about his father to Regina, but he did mention his first name to her in more than one conversation. She concluded that Lawrence must have mailed this package to Emily shortly before he died. This act in itself gave Regina pause because, according to Emily and Theodore, Lawrence had never established a true relationship with either one of them.

Regina decided that Theodore was entitled to view the package first, and even examine the contents before delivering it to his daughter. As she stepped outside with the package tucked beneath her arm, she noticed Theodore crouched beside a rock-edged flowerbed in the backyard. She often found him puttering around this area, waiting for the first blossoms of spring to sprout through the soil.

The perennials' green stems had just crept through the earth last week. Theodore's mind reeled with memories of his wife as he traced his fingers through the cool dirt. He remembered how Claire loved gardening, and took particular pride in the tulips' scarlet-colored bulbs each April. As he pondered about their lost time together, he noticed Regina's shadow pressing over his left shoulder. She waited for him to speak.

"How's Emily?" He asked faintly, wincing each time the answer came back to him, and fearing the day when Regina would respond with only silence.

"She's sleeping now," Regina said. "If you're busy, I can come back later."

Theodore rose to his feet and muttered, "It's okay. I was just out here thinking things over."

Regina hesitated before asking her next question, but deemed it to be impractical to avoid the subject closest to both their thoughts at the moment. "I hope everything went well today. I was thinking about how hard this must've been for you right now."

Theodore pivoted toward Regina and shrugged his shoulders. "Life's a bag of mysteries, I suppose. It just seems kind of weird to feel like a stranger at your own father's funeral."

"Was anyone there who knew your father?"

Theodore shook his head and brushed the dirt from his hands against his dungarees. "Apparently, the man kept few ties, Regina. Now that I've had time to think about it, I know it's really not important."

"I wish things could've been different for you and him. I really think he was trying to reach out to you and Emily in the end."

"Even before he died, it was way too late for that," Theodore snapped. "He had forty-eight years to think about why he left me. Now I have the rest of my life to try and forget him."

Regina exhaled a deep breath before revealing the package. "I don't know if you're ready to forget him, but I think you might want to take a look inside this envelope before making your final decision."

Regina held the package out in front of herself so Theodore could clearly see the writing. Theodore glanced quickly at the package and huffed, "What's that?"

"It came in the mail this morning. Actually, it's addressed to Emily."

"So why are you showing it to me? Emily can still open her own mail, can't she?"

"I wanted to check with you first before giving it to her," Regina said, pointing to the writing on the package. Theodore noticed Regina's hands trembling as he tried to decipher the print. After reading the words, he gradually retreated from his position. He suddenly he found himself looking away from Regina, as if trying to shield a tear from his eye.

After a moment of deliberation, Theodore blurted out a question that seemed appropriate. "Why would my father send Emily anything?" He then moved toward Regina and snatched the package from her hands.

"Maybe it's a gift," Regina suggested.

"A gift," Theodore snarled. "He barely knew her. He doesn't have a right to offer her a damn thing."

Regina hesitated with her next thought, for she sensed that Theodore's temper was about to get the best of him again. "He did know that Emily was very sick," she finally offered, "he was probably trying to make her feel better." As she spoke these words, she watched Theodore's hands trace over the package.

"It feels like a book or something," Theodore said, referring to the proportions of the package. "Do you think it's important?"

"Well," Regina said gently, "it couldn't hurt to find out."

"What do you think it could be?"

Instead of debating the matter any further, Theodore tore open the package with his fingers. Regina kept silent as he shoved his hand inside the envelope's sleeve and pulled out a notebook of yellow paper. After examining the contents briefly, Theodore determined that each of the hundred or so pages had been written longhand in black ink. The only identification as to the author remained on the outside of the package.

"It looks like a bunch of notes," Theodore said, holding up the papers for Regina to inspect.

"Not just notes," Regina surmised. "This appears to be your father's memoirs."

"Like a journal of some kind?"

"Most likely," Regina deduced, while flipping through several of the wire-bound pages. "This paper doesn't appear to be very old, though. He must have written this just before he died."

"That doesn't make any sense, Regina. Why would my father feel a need to explain his life to my daughter? He never even told me a damn thing about himself."

"Well, he's telling you now, Theodore. Maybe he felt too ashamed to give this journal to you personally, or maybe he thought you wouldn't bother reading it in the first place. Whatever his reason, at least he left something behind for you to consider."

Theodore was tempted to read the notes, but he resisted for now. During the next few seconds he lifted his chin to the sky, as if to inhale the scent of this morning's fading rain. In the distance, he admired a trail of clouds drifting over the barnyards and silos. His eyes suddenly dipped to the window of his daughter's bedroom. A dark feeling stirred in his mind as he thought about Emily's frail body slowly withering behind that glass.

Regina stood motionless at his side, watching the sullen man with a secret tenderness. "I'll leave you alone for a while," she said softly. "I'm sure you'll do the right thing."

"I know what to do, Regina," Theodore muttered. "If my father intended for Emily to see these notes before me, then so be it. I don't know if I want to read it anyway."

Regina watched him step gingerly toward the house. She sensed resistance in his stride as he made his way inside. No matter what his decision, she only hoped that his spirit was strong enough to prepare him for whatever loomed in the days and months ahead.

▼

CHAPTER THREE

THEODORE'S LAMENT

Despite enduring a feeling of emptiness each time he walked through the front door of his house, Theodore could not bring himself to sell the home and six acres of pristine property to another family. Ironically, his wife's untimely death only intensified his desire to remain in the home she had personally selected. The two-story colonial farmhouse always served as a reminder to what he and Claire loved most about the country—its pure simplicity and hidden grandeur.

Although the clapboard residence was modestly sized, it possessed a distinct charm and craftsmanship not readily found in the newer homes throughout Wakeland. Theodore was deliberate in his choice to keep the interior exactly as Claire had decorated it nearly fourteen years ago. Most of the rooms remained unchanged, including the gold and blue hues flanking the home's lower level.

Perhaps Theodore's greatest peculiarity was his choice to keep the door to his master bedroom locked at all times. He permitted no one other than himself to enter this room, not even Emily. Upon her arrival, Regina wondered why he chose to shield this room from all the others. She eventually gathered that Theodore sought to preserve the intimacy that had existed between him and his wife. Although his odd behavior concerned her at some level, Regina found his devotion toward Claire endearing. But she also understood that he might never push himself far enough away from his past to entertain the affections of another woman.

On this morning, Theodore paced through the corridor outside of Emily's bedroom with a growing distress. As he neared her bedroom door, sweat collected on his forehead and spilled over his eyes. He dreaded the thought of his daughter lying in her bed, trying to hide her agony. She wanted to be brave, but Theodore suspected that her illness had already began to chip away at her once impervious will to survive.

As Theodore entered the room, he momentarily stood in the door's thin shadow. The room's interior was dappled in sunlight. The rays sprayed through the window and across the bed, where Emily sat reading. Theodore despised the daylight, especially when the light shone directly into Emily's room, illuminating the decline of her physical being. He no longer detected his precious child's beauty. The process of disease had whitened her skin, and her eyes, once as blue as sapphire, now appeared dull and rimmed with charcoal-colored circles.

Despite her ailment and the inevitable consequences that she no doubt faced, Emily refused to surrender her passion for reading. Her bedroom resembled a treasure box of old and new books. An entire wall of shelving was laden with novels from every period of American and British literature. The collection stood like a fortress, guarding her imagination from the strains of reality. If nothing else, this pastime permitted an escape from her bedroom's confinement—if only for a short while.

Ironically, Theodore approached his daughter's bedside with another book in hand. He paused briefly in front of the Victorian, four-post bed, noticing—perhaps for the first time—the butterfly-speckled wallpaper adorning her walls. Emily, who busied herself with a volume of poetry, placed the book on her nightstand. Since her father rarely entered her room without knocking, she guessed that he had something important weighing on his mind.

After pulling a wooden chair away from her desk, Theodore sat down and made himself as comfortable as possible next to the bed. He then motioned to the book and remarked, "Still chipping away at all these novels, I see. Who's the author of choice for today—Twain or Milton?"

"Neither," Emily said, smiling as she brushed her straw-blonde hair away from her eyes with a swipe of her hand. "Did you ever read Dickinson's poetry? In a way, it's all kind of sad. She was a very lonely woman, you know."

"Well, it's been a while since I brushed up on my literature. I'll have to take your word for it."

Once sensing Theodore's discomfort intensifying, Emily grew sheepish as she noticed the notebook in her father's lap. "What's on your mind, Dad?"

Theodore cleared his throat and gently placed his hand on his daughter's shoulder. "I just came in here to check on you, honey. How are you feeling today?"

"Same as always, I guess," Emily murmured, "but I should be asking you the same question—how'd the funeral go?"

Theodore tilted his head toward the ceiling and groaned slightly before saying, "Let's just say it's over, and maybe that's the best thing that could have happened at this point."

"Were you scared?"

"I don't think that's the right word. Confused, maybe."

Emily repositioned herself atop the bed by fluffing out the bed pillows behind the headboard. As she shifted to an upright position, Theodore noticed her cringe with pain. "Are you sure you're okay?"

"Dad," she moaned, perturbed by the question. "We go through this almost everyday. All things considered, I'm fine. Now, since you're confused about the funeral, do you want to talk about something else?"

Theodore now saw that his daughter's eyes were trained on the notebook he was holding. Instead of fidgeting with the papers any longer, he tossed it on the bed in a casual manner.

"Apparently, this came in the mail for you today while I was gone. Regina wanted me to give it to you."

Emily peered at the ruffled notebook before picking it up. She flipped through the pages once and asked, "What is this all about?"

"It's from my father," Theodore huffed. "I'm guessing, but I think it's a diary of some kind."

"A diary?" Emily questioned. "Why would he send me something so personal? I only met the man once."

"I know, I know," Theodore sighed, "but the envelope was clearly addressed to you. For whatever reason, Lawrence must have wanted you to see it first."

Feeling awkward by this untimely offering, Emily immediately tried to hand the notebook back to her father. "Dad, you know I can't read this diary before you do. It wouldn't be fair. He was your father."

Theodore refused the notebook by holding out his hands. "I've already made up my mind about this. Lawrence Dayton was no more a father to me than he was a grandfather to you. Besides, I don't even know if I want to read about the man's life at this point."

"Then you are scared," Emily chided. "You really don't want to learn about your own family's history?"

"Emily, what's left of my family lives right here in this house with me." As Theodore spoke these words, he stood up from his chair and paced over to the window. His eyes squinted as he gazed out across the sun-streaked yard toward the tulip garden.

While Theodore paused to recollect his thoughts, Emily tried to establish a valid reason as to why Lawrence chose her to be the benefactor of his memoirs. "He must've noticed my collection," Emily said, glancing at the shelves of books. "I bet he figured I had nothing better to do with my time."

Theodore's voice trembled when he declared, "I should've never let that man into our home. It would've been so much easier on the both of us if I just turned him away."

"I know this might sound weird, but I'm glad that I had a chance to see Lawrence before he died."

Startled by this confession, Theodore turned his head slightly away from the window. He then uttered, "What did that old man say to you, anyway?"

"Nothing, really," Emily admitted. "He was very kind, just like a grandfather should be, or so I'm told." Emily sensed an agitation burning into her father's expression as he sidled closer to her bed.

Theodore's voice lowered to a whisper before he spoke again. "Did he mention me at all?"

Emily pressed the notebook snugly against her pink sweater and closed her eyes, as if in a mode of remembrance. "I can't recall his exact words," she said, "but I think he wanted to let you know that he was very sorry for the choices that he made. He also said that everything will make sense to you in the end, whenever that may be."

Emily's insight into her father's turmoil permitted her to recognize his feelings with more compassion than most. She understood that the pleasures in his life had been unfairly consumed by an ongoing presence of suffering and death. She also realized that his current lack of faith in God had left him vulnerable to impure thoughts.

"I'll read the diary, Dad, but not for myself. Just promise me that you'll listen to what I have to say when I'm done."

Emily waited for a reply for several seconds before she realized that Theodore had no answer to offer. As he leaned against the wall, Emily noticed teardrops trickling across his cheeks. She remained as silent as her father during these seconds.

"You know I don't mean to be like this," Theodore sobbed. "There's just so much that I don't understand. I wish I could change everything about my life."

"You can't change any of it," Emily said, reaching across her bed to open the desk drawer. Theodore tentatively watched as his daughter pulled her Bible from the drawer. "I don't want you to be afraid," she continued, holding out the Bible for him to observe. "Maybe you can take some time to read this."

"Let's not get into this argument again," Theodore admonished. "You know how I feel about that subject."

"Are you afraid to believe in God?"

"Is that what you think?" Theodore asked, glumly.

"I think you're too scared to remember how you once were," Emily said, setting the Bible on her bed. "Before I got sick, you were different— you still believed in God, but more importantly, you still had hope."

Theodore bowed his chin against his chest in shame as he listened to his daughter's recollection. "I didn't want to bring this up today, Dad, but do you want to know what my first memory of you is? It's when we were in church together, holding hands at the altar. I don't think I was much older than five, but I remember how we listened to the choir on that day—I remember the beautiful music, and how we talked about mom being safe in God's hands."

Theodore wiped the tears from his cheeks and glared with stone-cold eyes at his daughter. "That was a long time ago, Emily. I don't even recall being that person."

"Deny it if you want to, but you once believed in God. It's not too late to change."

Theodore stumbled away from Emily's bed like a frightened boy lost in the chaos of a nightmare. When he turned toward his daughter again, his voice cracked with anger. "Do you think it's that easy? Do you think I want to feel the way I do? I just can't go back to what I was before. Too much has happened since then. Can't you understand?"

Emily remained quiet while staring at Theodore. She couldn't help but to feel sorry for the man. Despite her empathy, she refused to accept the notion that his faith in God had simply faded into nothing. For now, though, she decided to let him stew in his hostilities.

Theodore retreated from Emily's room without uttering another word. After he had gone, she sighed deeply and returned her attention toward the sunlight pouring between the window's sheer curtains. For a moment, she listened as a bird chirped its melody from a pine tree outside. Once settled into her thoughts, she placed Lawrence's journal on her lap and opened the book to its first page.

Chapter Four

▼

Journal Entry One

My Youth in Orefield

As I near death I've determined that my life's journey mustn't be kept a secret any longer. For years I've debated on whether or not it would serve any meaningful purpose to reveal what I've learned in seventy years. Now, with the evidence disclosed, I've come to Wakeland with a hope that my message is not read in vain. Undoubtedly, those who review this tale will have formed an opinion of my character when they are done, but that is not my sole intention. Before the last page of this journal is turned, I want all those who might read my words to know that I'm recording these observations for them as much as I am for my own peace of mind.

In order to tell my story most accurately, I must take you back to the beginning, where my earliest misadventures linger in my memory as vividly as the most recent. In 1941, I was an eleven-year-old boy struggling to survive poverty amid the squalid backdrop of a small, Pennsylvania mining town. They referred to our insignificant community as Orefield, home to a dreary band of half-illiterate souls, who toiled with pickaxes and spades beneath the green fields and tree-dotted hillsides.

Make no mistake, mining ore for a living was a dirty, thankless chore, reserved for men who had convinced themselves at an early age that it was far more noble to work with brawn rather than brain. My father, Samuel Dayton, was one of these profitless puppets to the industrial empires of the north. Yet despite his false pride, I sensed that he wasn't truly satisfied with the life he had made for himself and family.

As a child I remember sitting around the breakfast table of our three-room shanty, casually viewing the shafts, where the disheartened laborers descended into their cubicles of darkness. At dawn, they'd march out across the muddy trails in tandem. Fully garbed in their crusty overalls and hardhats, they looked like an infantry of mercenaries assigned to an unenviable task. The tools of their trade glimmered beneath a canopy of orange sunlight. But beneath the veneer of warmth and unity, I suspected that each man would have sold his dying soul if offered a fair wage at some other work.

Admittedly, I didn't know much about the business of mining back then. My recollections were based on the impressions left to me by my father. Of course, he never articulated his anguish to me, but I saw the sadness well in his eyes each night when he came home. He often slumped into the house blackened with soot. His eyes were as dim as the chasms in which he descended. In all the years I knew this man, he never offered me a smile, save for an occasional curl of his upper lip. Although I can't say for certain, I believe he left a little part of himself down in those filthy pits upon the passing of each day.

Had it not been for my mother's unrealistic expectations, I think Samuel would've had an easier time accepting his job. In truth, my mother, Lily, was a physically stunning woman, but ruthlessly vicious to those who she deemed inferior. As a matter of recreation, she belittled my father on a daily basis, and used her own mother, Beatrice, as a weapon in the war that their marriage had become.

Shortly before my eleventh birthday, Samuel turned to whiskey in order to subdue his sorrow. In hindsight, I wish that I'd been old and wise enough to help the man. As a boy, I always wondered when he would ask me what I really expected from a father. I would've simply told him that I sought nothing more or less than to be his friend. But as fate would have it, I never had a chance to speak those words. Sometimes the passage of time beats a tad faster than a heart's intention.

In the summer of 1941, my father made his final journey into Orefield's mineshaft. Apparently a collapse in the main shaft buried several men beneath tons of jagged rock. Miraculously, the other men in his company managed to escape the mishap unharmed, but my father had been crushed. As a consolation to his demise, we were assured that his suffocation came quickly and without pain.

Sadly, Samuel Dayton never looked more at peace with himself than on the day of his own funeral. I remembered the faces of those few who came to watch his pine box being lowered into the earth. A couple of men from his union actually had teardrops forming in their eyes. I'd like to say that I cried, too, but I honestly can't remember. But I do know that my father died with many regrets, and despite his addictions, he deserved something better than what he ended up with.

As for my mother, she made her obligatory appearance at the cemetery, offering tears of grief on cue. Even during the procession, she announced her new status of eligibility to the suitors in town. A vain streak ran through that woman's soul as wide and deep as a ravine. Lily flaunted her sexuality like a harlot on parade. Blessed with a mane of fiery red hair, and flesh as smooth as buttermilk, she possessed an ability to entice men with a single glance. Now, with my father gone, I suspected that her emerald eyes would be set upon new prey without haste.

Apart from this early indifference with my mother, I felt equally troubled by Beatrice. Although she was my maternal grandmother by blood, I found it impossible to believe that we shared a similar gene pool. In many ways, I blamed this cantankerous woman for the destruction of my parents' marriage.

Before my father's death, Beatrice fueled my mother's discontent with her bitter tirades. Eventually, Beatrice persuaded her daughter to adopt the notion that my father wasn't good enough to be her husband. Tormented by the thought that Lily had actually accepted Beatrice's hatred as sound knowledge, I learned to cringe whenever hearing her voice.

The months following my father's funeral should have included a period of grieving. This loss, however, was a burden for me to bear alone. If Lily ever shed a tear in the aftermath of my father's death, it must've slipped from her eye when no one was looking. Neither she nor Beatrice concealed their jubilation any longer than necessary. Apparently, my father was worth far more money dead than alive.

Following the accident, which Beatrice referred to a blessing in disguise, the Orefield Mining Company agreed to pay a hefty settlement to my mother. As it turned out, Lily didn't unleash her long-repressed rapture until the money fell into her lap. To remedy her thus-far impoverished existence, she immediately bought herself a closet full of gaudy clothes and expensive jewelry. In fairness, she certainly looked like a gem stone mixed between pieces of coal, but as a rule of nature, the prettiest creatures were often the most venomous.

As a middle-aged, semi-rich widow, Lily quickly became the envy of Orefield, especially in the eyes of the men she so desperately sought to seduce. Although I tried to comprehend her selfish desires for a while, I soon resented her flamboyancy and disregard for family. When I say family, I'm really talking about me, because I had become virtually invisible in the woman's eyes. Even before my father died, I suspected that Lily had no inclination to be a mother.

On some evenings, I reluctantly witnessed my mother sneaking strange men into her bedroom. Evidently, Lily found the company of her nameless lovers more essential than her own son's welfare. Since she seemed to have no preference on the men she bed in the beginning, most of the fellows crept home before morning, well before their wives became suspicious of their carnal activity.

Before the year ended, however, Lily had set her sights on a young, virile man from out of town. Being ten years her junior, with a physique like Adonis, my mother quickly abandoned her wanton ways in exchange for his affections. His name was Jack, and he came packaged with more promises than my father ever had the gumption to utter in nearly fifteen years of marriage.

Within a month, he had convinced my mother into believing that he loved her. I don't know why, but I felt uneasy with Jack. Perhaps I wasn't giving the man a fair chance. He wasn't abusive, and rarely drank in our home. Still, I think I despised this man simply because my mother gazed at him with all the tenderness and adoration that I still yearned to know.

In order to confirm my fears of pending isolation, I approached Beatrice one evening with a question that, until this point, had only stewed in my mind. By now, Beatrice was a gaunt, sixty-five year old spinster who squandered most of her sober hours by meddling in my mother's affairs. As always, I found her hunkered in a rocking chair in front of a window, periodically swigging vodka straight from a bottle.

"Grandma," I asked lowly, clenching my teeth to hide my disgust, "may I ask you something?"

After glancing at a wall clock in the corner of her sitting room, Beatrice groaned, "It's a little late for questions, Lawrence. What do you want?"

"It's about my mother."

"Don't fret about my Lily, do you understand? She's finally making some smart choices in her life. Jack's gonna make that woman happy, I just know it."

"I don't want to talk about Jack," I said. "I just wanted to know if my mother ever really loved my father. I need to know the truth."

Beatrice paused to gulp the last traces of vodka from her bottle. She then snickered hoarsely and tittered, "What difference does that make? Your daddy's dead, and I can't say I'm sorry that he's gone. Your mother's got a decent man in her life right now. She can't live in the past, and neither should you."

"But that still doesn't answer my question," I persisted.

At this point, Beatrice stopped rocking in her chair and narrowed her eyes. I listened to the woman's voice simmer with fiendish delight as she replied, "Oh, I think you've got a pretty good idea how she felt about that man."

"She must have loved him at one time."

Beatrice smirked at my ignorance, before dropping her empty bottle to the floorboards. "Let me tell you something," she hissed, "Lily never loved your father. In fact, had he not had the good sense to die when he did, I believe she would've left him within the year."

"Then I guess she never loved me either, huh?" I sulked.

"Go to bed, Lawrence. And stop asking questions to which you already know the answer."

Though I tried to desensitize myself from Beatrice's callousness, in my heart I knew that she had not lied. It was safe to assume that my mother didn't loathe me as much as she did my father. After all, she fed me three meals a day and kept me in clothes. What more could a son expect from a mother? How could I find fault with a woman for wanting to manufacture some semblance of passion in her life? Maybe Beatrice was right; perhaps I just didn't understand, or was simply too preoccupied with being a child that I had no conception on what truly mattered in life.

Six weeks after they met, Lily announced her engagement to Jack. Unlike her previous ceremony, my mother planned to be married in a way that was befitting of her pride. She arranged a lavish church wedding for herself and new beau, which included the purchase of a virgin-white gown, garnished with lace and pearls. I can't presume to guess how she ever managed to persuade a clergyman to lend his pulpit to such a farce, but Lily had forged some rather close connections in Orefield's Christian community.

As for Jack, he was a fellow who seemed more adept at freeloading off my mother's good fortune than he did on earning any money of his own. Of course Jack played the role of a gentleman quite well, and had a knack at getting my mother to believe anything he said. For a while, he showered my mother and Beatrice with expensive gifts, usually with funds derived from an unknown source. Had the women suspected that they paid for these luxuries out of their own savings, Jack's descent into mediocrity would've come much sooner.

I wondered how many months would elapse before Jack's golden image began to tarnish in my mother's eyes. Despite his lackadaisical nature, Lily was truly misguided by her blind devotion toward this charlatan. As it turned out, Jack wasn't anything close to being the chivalrous knight that Beatrice claimed him to be. He was just another unemployed miner prospecting for work in town, and a warm bed to tuck his shoes under each night. To his credit, he possessed what my father sorely lacked—the craft of being a persuasive conversationalist. Looking back, I really can't fault Jack for pretending to be worth more than he was. He had nothing to lose, and a widow's small fortune to gain.

Much to my surprise, Lily lived with her second mistake better than her first. Maybe she really did love Jack, or maybe she knew that he wouldn't have left our home even if she insisted. At least her new husband was prettier to stare at in the morning. In the meantime, Beatrice adjusted to the grim notion that the road leading out of Orefield was never going to be hinged to the coattail of her daughter's husband. In order to dull her pangs of disappointment, the old woman retreated to her bottled vodka in pursuit of an unprecedented assault upon her own liver.

In the midst of all this heartache, I learned to ponder cruel thoughts. I also came to understand that not every boy has a chance to be a child. Sometimes, while lying in bed at night, I'd gaze up at the stars and wished for some celestial force to fire down from the heavens and transport me to another world—a world where loneliness and isolation did not exist. As I soon discovered, a boy can only hide from his agonies for a short while. Eventually, whatever his age may be, he must turn and face his unknown tormentor. He must fight to stay alive.

CHAPTER FIVE

▼

JOURNAL ENTRY TWO

THE CAUSE OF DISEASE

By the winter of 1942, I had settled into my role as the neglected son quite nicely. While my mother and Jack learned to accept each other's inadequacies, I retreated to my journal in a bid to escape boredom and misery. Despite the disinterest of those who surrounded me, I began writing in my diary at an early age. No one ever thought to ask me what I wrote about, but I'm grateful that I relied on my own intuition in this regard, rather than the shortsighted opinions of a disconnected family.

Before age twelve, I had it firmly rooted in my mind that I wouldn't end up loading coal for any mining company. Even though death had divided us, I aimed to make my father proud of me. I didn't think he would've preferred to see his only son following his footsteps into Orefield's shafts. Above all, it was my secret wish to leave this town forever and forget everything in my life that had delivered me to this degree of shame.

Though I never spoke of my discontent aloud, I soon discovered that such bitterness, no matter how unspoken, ferments in the soul like a poison. It was only a matter of time before the venom churning within my brain began its merciless assault upon my senses.

One day, while ambling along a snowy trail on my way to school, I felt a sensation building inside my head. At first the pain was only minimal, but it gradually worsened to a point where my vision blurred. This was the initial sign of my disease. By the following evening, I became overcome by the intensity of these headaches. It felt as though a sharp instrument had been bored into each of my eyeballs and then etched methodically through the deepest regions of my brain.

After three days of this ongoing torture, I went to my mother for help. She ignored my complaints and accused me of trying to compete for Jack's attention. Up until this time, I had only a slight inclination on how heartless this woman had become. Feeling betrayed and strangely forlorn, I learned to muffle my cries in my pillow until falling unconscious.

My sickness never gained any credibility until a phone call from my school prompted my mother and Beatrice to reconsider their diagnosis. After being informed that I blacked-out in a pool of vomit, Lily forced a teardrop to materialize from her eye. Beatrice did her part by drowning her senses in a bottle of brandy.

After my spell of vertigo ended at school, I was carried directly across the street to Orefield's lone physician. Dr. Harris treated everything from head colds to fractured limbs. Although I never imagined myself being examined by any doctor, I knew that my condition needed to be rectified.

Within five minutes after entering his office, Dr. Harris and a nurse had stripped away my sweat-soaked clothing and set me down on a steel table, matted with a piece of thin paper. The elderly doctor peered at me through his bifocals like a man determined to find something wrong. He then directed a powerful strobe of light into each of my open eyes. His cold fingertips proceeded to press on specific areas of my spine, shoulders, and neck.

After ten minutes of probing and poking at my body, Dr. Harris ambushed me with an onslaught of questions. My revealed symptoms of dizziness, blurred vision, nausea, and migraine headaches induced a timid glare from the doctor. Finally, he traced his hands across my skull, before releasing a disheartened sigh in the direction of his nurse.

"What's the matter?" I cried groggily. "Do I got to get a shot or something?"

Dr. Harris shook his head gently and handed me my shirt. "It's not that simple, Lawrence." He then opened a folder and quickly scribbled something in his notes.

"What's wrong with me?" I asked frightfully, this time looking to the nurse for a response. Neither of them offered an immediate reply, but I detected urgency magnifying through his eyeglasses. For several seconds we all quivered beneath the room's fluorescent light. Every inch of my skin began to speckle with goose bumps.

Without warning and with a faraway iciness, Dr. Harris instructed me to get dressed. He then left the room with the nurse, leaving me to stew alone between the coldness of those walls for several terrifying minutes. I remember the room's numbing quietness being almost as unbearable as the headaches that brought me here.

When Dr. Harris reentered the examining room, my mother lurched beside him. After she embraced me with a halfhearted hug, I suspected that I required more than an aspirin to remedy my condition.

"What's wrong with my son?" my mother sniffled.

Dr. Harris lowered his head, momentarily exposing his balding crown to us before straightening his chin. When his eyes reconnected with my own, I experienced a peculiar flashback to my father's funeral. During the eulogy, the priest had a similar gaze of despondency seeping from his eyes. He then turned toward my mother and guided her to a chair near the door.

In his most humble voice, the doctor stated, "I think we may need to do more extensive testing on your son, Lily. This is a potentially serious condition."

"Serious?" my mother screeched, "how serious?"

"Well," Dr. Harris offered, "I can't diagnose Lawrence adequately without having a full X-ray done on his skull."

My mother's voice became more grim when she said, "Doctor, I really don't think it's that serious. Boys his age get headaches all the time—don't they?"

"Lily, believe me, I wouldn't recommend such a procedure unless I thought it was necessary. Besides, it's really not as complicated as it sounds. Unfortunately, we don't have a radiologist here in Orefield. You'll have to go to Pittsburgh with your son."

"We can't go to Pittsburgh," my mother yelped, before pushing the doctor's hand away from her shoulder. "Can't you give him some medicine or something to perk him up?"

Dr. Harris shook his head insistently before replying, "Lawrence needs to see a specialist. I know an excellent neurologist at the Children's Center in Pittsburgh. If anything shows up on your son's X-ray, Doctor Cain may be able to help."

At this point, my mother jabbed her finger into Dr. Harris's chest and screamed, "I don't have time for this nonsense right now, Doctor."

"We're talking about your son, Lily," Dr. Harris whispered, taken aback by the woman's blatant cruelty. I, however, was already numb to her frigidness. The doctor then shifted away from my mother and patted me on my head, as if to say farewell to an old sick dog.

Truthfully, I was grateful for Dr. Harris's candidness, although I didn't know exactly what to expect from this moment forward. Over the next couple days, the gravity of my illness had still not been confirmed. I of course knew that something was causing me intolerable levels of pain, but Dr. Harris refused to speculate on the precise nature of my malady.

By the end of the week, after it was inarguably clear to my mother that my symptoms weren't simply going to vanish, she agreed to schedule an appointment with Dr. Cain in Pittsburgh. Predictably, my mother's procrastination in making this decision was linked to Jack. He refused to become emotionally attached to a boy who was not his own son.

Meanwhile, Beatrice used her sober hours tallying up the potential expenses of an extended hospital stay for me. With no medical insurance to speak of, any treatment that I received would have to be garnished directly from my mother's settlement. Unfortunately, most of that money had been squandered by the time my condition became apparent.

On the night before our train ride into Pittsburgh, I remember how ravaged my mother's face appeared. With swollen eyes and clenched teeth, she perched in front of her bedroom mirror and cried at her own reflection. Although my next thought may have been a selfish notion, I wanted to believe that her tears were shed for my pending agony. Her show of emotion, however, remained shallow and self-inspired.

As my mother readied herself to leave for Pittsburgh with me, Jack busied himself by packing a canvas bag with everything he had brought into their relationship. Evidently, Jack had figured that my disease would eventually slash too deep a gash into my mother's dwindling bank account. Since destitution seemed inevitable in his eyes, Jack said his goodbye rather hastily. Though my mother cried like a stood-up schoolgirl, I was glad to see him go. I likened his presence to that of a leech being plucked from a bloodless limb. With potentially nothing left to suck from my mother, Jack simply moved away to feast in riper pastures.

We left for Pittsburgh aboard the passenger wagon of a coal-burning train. Neither my mother nor I had ever ventured outside of Orefield before this day. Had we not made this journey under such bleak circumstances, I think the transport would've been a bit more bearable. But these moments were uncertain and cruel. I felt a chill akin to death creeping into my flesh.

As it turned out, the train's iron wheels caused me to cringe at every curve in the steel track. Adding to this annoyance, the train's few instances of steady movement was frequently disrupted by clanging brakes and pealing whistles that seemed to split the air into fragments.

During our three-hour train ride, I sensed resentment gathering behind my mother's eyes like a foreboding storm. She simply stared into nothingness, never once inquiring as to how or what I was feeling. Though I partially understood her disappointment, I resented the pitiful fact that she could not look beyond her own desires in order to attain happiness.

As the city of Pittsburgh drew closer, I watched through the train's windows as the emerald farmlands slowly disappeared. Sprawling concrete barriers gradually replaced the vast countryside. Suddenly, my world had turned as dark as the sky overhead.

As the train slowed into its final miles, I remember studying the countless steel structures that silhouetted the cityscape. Columns of brick chimney pipe erected against the sky, overshadowing an endless corridor of warehouses and industrial wasteland. Black smoke belched into the firmament from the pipe's hollow stacks, smothering the air with an oily film. This strange, bustling habitat stored an unnatural frigidity deep within its crevices. In disgust, I tilted my head against the train's window.

Nothing between these walls of stone and steel could have saved me from whatever loomed within my head. Then, with my forehead still firmly pressed against the train's window, my eyes were suddenly drawn to a light more dazzling than the sun. This burning sphere of energy illuminated an otherwise dark sky. For several seconds, I watched the scintillating ball hover over the city. After several seconds, the light dissolved into the billowing factory smoke, but not before captivating my imagination.

After evaluating this occurrence as an unexplainable phenomenon, I looked around the passenger cart to see if anyone else had shared in my experience. Most of their faces appeared as cold and detached as the city's backdrop. I guessed that this light was somehow invisible to their eyes. My mother, who had not glanced at me since we departed Orefield's train station, remained as cold as stone. In any event, I settled into my seat in silent wonder for the remainder of our journey.

After we arrived in Pittsburgh, I realized how small and insignificant a single life can be in the grander scope of urban life, especially when contrasted against the Children Center's immense tower of concrete and glass. Upon entering the hospital, I sensed myself instinctually reaching for my mother's hand. In hindsight, I believe this was my last desperate effort to generate some compassion from this woman.

Sadly, Lily was still a stranger to me after all these years. As our hands joined, I sensed the icy texture of her flesh. It would've served me better to clasp hands with the dead. Perhaps she had already predicted my fate and now sought to sever whatever remained of our fragile connection as mother and son. Whatever the source of her callousness, I realized that neither of us could ever truly forgive each other. In light of this breakdown, I prepared for a test of endurance and faith that would soon change my perception of this world forever.

CHAPTER SIX

▼

FATHER QUINN'S PLEA

Upon hearing the sound of an idling engine outside her window, Emily closed the journal and placed it on her pillow. After listening to the noise for a moment, she determined that a guest had arrived. Just six months ago, a visitor would not have stimulated her interest, but that was before Theodore's current restrictions disconnected her from Wakeland's residents. Now any chance of company at their residence seemed like a long overdue blessing.

Emily exerted more energy than usual, but she managed to pull herself from bed and walk gingerly across the carpet toward the window. Once looking outside, she saw Father Quinn's car parked in the circular driveway. She smiled after he emerged from his sky-blue Pinto. Although she had not been to his church in nearly a year, she missed the priest's sermons and still considered him to be an influential friend throughout her family's crisis.

Quinn almost decided against returning to the Dayton's farmhouse unannounced. He had been waiting for the right opportunity for months. At least the two strangers at Lawrence's funeral provided him with a legitimate reason to come back. With any luck, he might even get a chance to see Emily again.

As Quinn glanced up at the restored farmhouse, he fondly recalled when Theodore and Claire first bought the deserted home at auction. The previous owner had left the property's seven acres in near ruins, but nothing was beyond repair when placed in the hands of a diligent couple. In a matter of months, the Dayton's refurbished the entire home. It now stood as a testament to the enduring craftsmanship from nearly three generations of men.

Builders may have taken credit for the house's restoration, but Quinn was privileged to the fact that Claire had served as the vocal blueprint throughout every meticulous detail of construction. She alone selected the ocher tones bordering white clapboard on the home's exterior. The placement of each garden, stone wall, and tree had been prearranged in her imagination as well. It was her wish to make the house and all of its surrounding hills more enchanting than it had ever been before. Anyone who had since set eyes upon the residence realized that Claire's dream had exceeded all expectations.

As Quinn limped up the driveway, he admired a grove of pine trees veering off an embankment's left side. Some of the trees' green buds had already decorated the stark branches. Adding to a promise of an early spring, a nest of robins flitted between pines, almost in sequence to a breeze rushing over the landscape like an invisible wave. The old priest paused and inhaled the mid-morning air, savoring the dewy remnants of rain.

Although partially blinded by cataracts and hampered by arthritis, Quinn refused to let his own disabilities pilfer life's pleasantries from him. He counterbalanced his awkward gait with a cane of polished maple, and he had become quite efficient at traversing Wakeland's steepest inclines. Despite his minor aches, he remained thankful that he was approaching his seventy-fifth year, nearly fifty of which were solely dedicated to the clergy. As he neared the front walkway, he remembered that everyone was not as fortunate. Even after thirteen years, the memory of Claire's unexpected death struck him with a sense of regret.

After Quinn knocked on the front door, his thoughts turned to a grouping of songbirds singing in a nearby thicket. He removed his felt derby and smiled at the inviting tune. Then, in the midst of his deepest recollections, he recalled how melodic Claire's voice had been. Though the woman possessed a radiance and genuine love for humanity that few people shared, many of Wakeland's residents referred to her voice as being a true source of divine inspiration.

Quinn never disputed such praise for the woman, for he had recognized Claire's talent soon after she joined his church. Within a month, Claire earned a spot at the center of the church's choir. Without the intermission of a single Sunday, she remained there until her death.

Even today, Quinn envisioned Claire's final performance at his church with great clarity. Just before the birth of her child, she stood solo at the altar in a yellow gown. Sunlight reflected off her shoulders like a spotlight recast by the kaleidoscopic glass from a row of oblong windows. Her flaxen hair was bound in a halo of crisp light. Then, as the congregation raised in prayer, her angelic syllables echoed through the overhead rafters.

Claire's songs filled the church with grace and hope on this day. Those in company closed their eyes while listening to her voice. For at least a short while, their heartache softened, and their flightless spirits soared with notions of kindness toward each neighbor. Quinn likened the experience to that of being swept away into a realm of complete tranquility. Whatever the mood had been, not a person within that room could have forecasted the level of despair that soon besieged Claire Dayton and her husband.

In the beginning, Quinn understood Theodore's depression. Though the priest grieved along with the whole town after Claire died, he imagined the loss being far more devastating for the man who shared her love. But Quinn also realized that faith had enabled him to continue. Theodore chose the opposite path, one that unconsciously led him away from what his wife would have ultimately wanted for their family.

Before this thought escaped Quinn's mind, the front door to the Dayton's home edged open. Regina stood stiffly in the doorway. Quinn had met this woman only twice before, but he remembered that she normally tied her shoulder-length hair up in a bun. Today, she let her chestnut locks fall across her shoulders, concealing a portion of her oval face.

Quinn greeted Regina with a wide grin, but her discomfort with this situation was obvious. "Hello, Miss Hopewell," he chimed. "It's good to see you again."

"Father Quinn," she replied, trying to sound pleasantly surprised. Caution invaded her tone when she stated, "Theodore didn't mention that you'd be stopping by today."

"Forgive me, I don't usually drop by without phoning first, but I didn't think Theodore would accept my call."

Regina didn't wish to make Quinn feel like an intruder, but Theodore had already expressed himself in matters of this regard. "You know I don't want to be rude, Father," she said, pausing to check the foyer behind herself. Her eyes then anxiously darted between the stairwell and alcove leading into the living room.

"Please relax," Quinn remarked. "I don't want to cause any trouble around here. But, I'd really like to know how Emily is doing."

Regina did not respond. She felt uncomfortable with the prospect of being untruthful to the priest, and equally troubled by divulging the child's rapidly deteriorating health. She decided to remain silent so that Quinn could study the anguish pouring openly from her eyes. Being a keen observer, he bowed his chin against his collar and muttered a soft prayer.

"Maybe you should come back another day to see Emily," Regina advised, still monitoring the tone of her own voice. "She's sleeping now."

"At least that explains your whispering, Miss Hopewell," Quinn said. "However, as you probably already guessed, I didn't come out here today just to check on Emily. I would like to talk to Theodore, too. Is he at home?"

Regina nodded her head once in agreement as Quinn trained his eyes on her face. The swarthy flesh beneath the woman's eyes told a tale of many sleepless nights. Quinn knew that she had been working intently to keep Emily comfortable, but he also surmised that a deeper degree of motivation had enabled her to withstand Theodore's unpredictable temperament.

"I give you a lot of credit, Miss Hopewell," he commended. "Taking care of a sick child is no easy task, especially under these circumstances."

"It's what I do, Father."

"Yes, of course. But don't be afraid to take a bit of advice from an old man, Miss Hopewell, even if he is just a farsighted priest. Everyone needs to take a little break now and again. It's good for your soul."

Not knowing exactly how to respond, Regina said, "Father, you didn't drive all the way out here to ask me to take it easy— "

"No, no, no," Quinn interrupted. "You look exhausted, that's all. I don't want to see you get sick from all of this."

"It's a little too late for that," Regina sighed. "Besides, I can't walk away now. I think Emily and Theodore need me more now than ever."

"I believe you're right," Quinn agreed. "That's partly the reason why I'm here to see Theodore."

"It's really not a good time," Regina confessed, almost shamefaced. "Theodore seems to be taking his father's death very hard. You know how he tries to hide his feelings. I don't want him to say anything to you that he'll regret later on."

"Trust me, Miss Hopewell," Quinn tittered, while gesturing to his ears. "There's nothing that Theodore can say to me that these old ears haven't heard a thousand times before."

Without another immediate thought to convey, Regina leaned against the door's frame. Her posture now appeared as listless as her expression. She was tempted to let Quinn come inside, but the presence of footsteps caused her to retreat from the door.

Theodore then stepped in line with the door. He leered out at Quinn as if he was nothing more than peddler. At first, Theodore's expression did not indicate contempt, but a hollowness embedded itself deep in the core of both his eyes. After Regina disappeared into the adjoining room, Quinn quietly folded his arms across his chest and waited for Theodore's reprimand.

"I thought we had an agreement, Quinn—no visitors. I wasn't kidding," Theodore fumed.

"You left the funeral so quickly this morning," Quinn explained. "I didn't have a chance to talk to you about your father."

Theodore smirked at Quinn and said, "I don't think there's anything for us to discuss. Lawrence is dead now. Let's just leave it alone, okay?"

Sensing that Theodore was one breath short from slamming the door in his face, Quinn reached inside his jacket to fetch the napkin given to him earlier.

"I won't take up much of your time," Quinn promised, while holding the crumpled paper in his hand. "After you left the cemetery, an older man and woman approached me. They seemed very surprised that you were Lawrence's son. The woman wrote her name down—here."

Theodore accepted the napkin from Quinn's hand. He then scanned the penciled name—Belinda Willinger—and the phone number scrawled beneath it. After a moment of halfhearted concentration, Theodore said, "This name means nothing to me. I never met anyone by the name of Belinda Willinger in my life."

"I was under the impression that she knew your father."

"So what? That's got nothing to do with me."

"On the contrary," Quinn countered, referring to the paper. "That woman must've had some reason for wanting to see you. I think you should give her a call."

"Didn't you explain to the old lady that I never knew my father?" Theodore questioned.

"She's still very adamant about meeting with you. Why not hear what she has to say? Who knows—you might even learn something about your father worth remembering."

Theodore looked at the paper again, hoping that his memory might provide a hint as to what this woman wanted. After raising his eyes from the napkin, he still cast a blank stare at Quinn.

"I can't do this," Theodore murmured, trying to hand the paper back to Quinn.

Quinn refused to accept the note; he instead nudged the tip of his walking cane between the door's opening to prevent Theodore from closing it. "Theodore, please don't be stubborn about this. I'm only trying to help you."

"Then help me by not mentioning my father's name. You know, now that Lawrence is dead, he's suddenly become a thorn in my side."

"Don't fool yourself," Quinn persisted. "I know what it's like for a boy to grow up without a father. My own father died when I was quite young. For many years, I was bitter, too. But I turned my life around, Theodore. I let God save me. And He can do the same for you."

"Spare me the trite rhetoric," Theodore groaned, rolling his eyes. "I'm not in the mood for any long-winded sermon."

"Just hear me out for a minute," Quinn pleaded. "There's a lot of people in this town who want to help you, Theodore. We remember the man you once were. I've seen what fear can do to a man's soul. Without a defense, it'll eat you up inside. I beg you, don't let your own bitterness destroy you."

"You still don't get it," Theodore whispered. "I can't be the person I was before, Quinn. Can't you understand that I've lost too much?"

"What will it take to restore your faith?"

Theodore's eyes pinched shut and his voice shuddered when he replied, "A miracle—nothing less. Ask your god to spare my daughter's life. If there really is a god, let him give me something back for a change. Haven't I been dealt enough punishment?"

"Be realistic," Quinn said, "I can't promise miracles. I can only help you accept reality. You know I've always prayed for your family. No one was more saddened by Claire's death than me, and Emily's sickness has struck the members of our community just as hard."

"But nothing has changed," Theodore muttered. "Despite all your prayers, my daughter is still dying."

"We must continue to believe that people die for a reason. That's what makes us different from the animals, Theodore—we understand that death marks only the beginning of our relationship with God."

Despite Quinn's sincerity, the darkness bloomed in Theodore's eyes as if droplets of black iodine had spread over both pupils. All reflection of hope suffocated beneath this gloom. In defeat, Quinn removed his cane from the door and turned away from Theodore.

"I'll leave you to your thoughts for now," Quinn said as he hobbled off the front porch. "Maybe you'll listen to me as your friend some day, rather than just an old, sanctimonious priest."

Theodore remained firmly pressed against the door as Quinn stepped down the driveway toward his car. While watching Quinn drive away, he clutched the napkin tighter in his hand. Then, after warding off an unexplainable urge to cry, he folded the paper in half and stuffed it in his shirt's pocket. From the stairwell, Regina watched Theodore in silence as he turned away from the door.

Meanwhile, Emily had returned to her bed by now. She listened as the melody of songbirds filled her room with the sounds of spring. Though the morning was merely half over, she already felt tired again. Sensing sleep coming on, she reached across the night table for her Bible. Instead of reading a verse or two from the book—as she had normally done before resting—she removed a gold crucifix from between its pages.

This Christian cross, which was beautifully ornamented with braided gold, glimmered in her hand. She held the crucifix in front of herself for a moment, allowing the sunlight to reflect off its burnished edges. For a fleeting second, she watched her bedroom door, hoping that Father Quinn would open it.

Save for a tepid breeze, the room quickly became silent again. Emily's eyes then swayed to the journal, which lay on her pillow. With the cross in one hand, and the open notebook in the other, she resumed reading Lawrence's diary.

CHAPTER SEVEN

▼

JOURNAL ENTRY THREE

CAIN'S CONFIRMATION

Before taking one step into the hospital's sprawling lobby, I knew that this was not a place for me. The sanitized air and shining corridors frightened me. I wanted to believe that my presence here had been a mistake. In order to tame my own fear, I kept telling my mother not to fret over anything. Her pathetic demeanor did nothing to comfort me. Apparently she was already resigned to losing me. Though I wished my mother and I had no biological connection to bind us in the shadow of this pending crisis, I truly needed for someone to treat me like a boy.

Soon after arriving at the Children's Center, Dr. Cain introduced himself as the chief neurosurgeon. Upon meeting the man, I was mildly impressed by his clean, navy-blue suit, scarlet tie, and polished black shoes. What remained of his thinning silver hair was swept back from a protruding forehead and cemented against his scalp with an oily tonic. His jaw and sideburns were carpeted with a beard of white whiskers, and his eyes remained half-hidden behind plastic eyeglasses.

As Cain guided me by my hand through the facility, I became willfully blinded by his renowned reputation. It must've provided him with an incredible sense of satisfaction to know that my life—among others—hinged on his commitment to the medical profession. For the first few hours, I felt in safe hands.

Following my four-hour examination, which included a series of cranium X-rays and blood tests, my mother and I were escorted into a small office. Cain's office reminded me of a dank lair, which seemed far removed from the white corridors of the rest of this perfectly disguised prison. The room was absent of all natural light; a metal desk lamp provided the sole source of illumination.

For such an organized man, Cain's office seemed littered with a lifetime of debris. Atop his mahogany desk, a collage of family photographs mixed with stacks of medical papers and reference manuals. Books and certificate credentials tattooed the walls, and a smell of stale coffee clashed with cigar smoke. The most prominent feature in the room, a beautifully ornate grandfather clock, was located in the corner. I immediately focused my attention on the ticking of this decorative treasure.

After my mother and I were seated comfortably on a leather couch near the clock, Cain entered the office holding a folder full of my test results. I tried not to stare at the doctor's face. Even before he uttered a word, I was petrified. If any spark of hope still flickered in my eyes, Cain quickly snuffed out the flame with his diagnosis.

Cain's voice cracked when he said, "I've been a surgeon at this hospital for almost twenty years now, but this part of my job never gets any easier."

My heart quickened in my chest. I felt the beat throbbing in my neck as my fingers and toes curled into knots. Pleading to my mother's eyes, Cain continued, "I'm afraid Lawrence's tests have revealed an inoperable condition."

"What the hell does that mean, Doctor?" my mother asked.

"We've discovered a tumor at the center of your son's brain. It appears to be fiercely malignant."

For a moment I sensed my mother's eyes widening. She then settled deeper into the couch and asked, "Are you telling me that Lawrence has brain cancer?"

Cain shuffled through the X-rays and placed his hands flat on his desk. "I wish I had better news," he uttered softly.

"There's nothing you can do for him?" my mother gasped.

"Based on the location of the tumor, an operation would be far too risky. I'm sorry that I must be so blunt. Please, forgive me, Lawrence."

Sorry? I repeated Cain's apology ten times over in my mind, before concluding that nothing was made better by the utterance of such an empty statement. I sensed the finality of his words as clearly as if a death sentence had been handed down. Suddenly, the clock's methodical ticking exploded against my temples with a bomb's force. I wanted to leap from the couch and shatter that confounded clock. It seemed to mock me with its insidious ticking. It drowned all other sound or thought from my diseased brain. Now the message was clear to me. It was my time—a time limited by the circumference of these dreary walls.

My first inclination was to call Dr. Cain a liar, but it soon occurred to me that this man truly cared about his work and the suffering children who came under his watch. In truth, he may have become somewhat numb to his obligations, but what else could I expect from a man who gazed into the eyes of so many dying children?

My mother did her best to spout forth her misdirected rage, but I was not fooled by her contrived outburst. Everything she shouted at the doctor sounded scripted, as if she had written an epilogue to my death weeks in advance. After ten minutes of listening to her yammer on about nothing relevant to my fate, Cain attempted to explain my immediate future in simple terms. All through this, I thought about my father. Maybe he was-n't so unfortunate after all. At least no one ever told him when he was going to die.

When the air cleared, Lily dried her crocodile tears and waited patiently for my prognosis. Cain estimated that I had about three months to live, maybe less. Being that my symptoms would only worsen over time, Cain suggested that I remain at the Children's Center under the constant influence of medication. The conversation quickly deteriorated into a question of money and time, neither of which my mother wanted to squander on me.

If given the choice in advance, Lily may have sent me off into the woods to die alone. Despite her deplorable nature, even she had to have possessed some compassion for the fruit of her labor. I know that she never loved me more than she did herself, but I hoped that she would at least make the right choice on this occasion.

After a long debate with Dr. Cain, Lily arrived at a decision that worked out for the both of us. I was going to remain at the hospital, but she was not. Being abandoned here like an unwanted package shouldn't have been a revelation to me. I often wondered if she ever had an inten-tion of returning to Orefield with me at her side.

On the evening before my transport to the children's ward, my mother sat beside my bed like a stranger sharing space on a train. Our eyes did not meet. Her presence offered me no company. She had already shut me out of her mind, just as she'd done to my father so many years ago. Perhaps it was better that we parted without the burden of a coerced love.

Before fading into the first of many shadows in my memory, Lily turned and stared at me with a tenderness that I longed to know. Genuine teardrops flooded her eyes and trickled paths through the makeup cover-ing her face.

"I want you to know something," she wept. "I'm sorry that every-thing turned out like this. I never wanted anything bad to happen to you, Lawrence."

"It doesn't matter now," I replied. "Nothing matters. You can go home now."

"I just don't know what else to do for you," she sobbed. "I know I haven't been a good mother. I just hope that you'll be able to forgive me some day."

Perhaps it was a wise choice for me to simply close my eyes and let Lily slip away like a shadow shrinking in the sunlight. Before leaving me to my sorrows, she touched my scalp with her hands. Her fingertips felt like sickles of ice. I loathed her in these seconds. I prayed that she would go, taking the coldness with her as she made a retreat toward the door. At last I'd be alone to stew in my misery, wondering about the final days of my life.

The beginning of the end for me started in the children's ward, located in another section of the hospital. Despite its sky-blue wallpaper and lemon-yellow tiled floor, the ward struck me with a frigidness that I had seldom felt before. Aside from a feeble attempt to manufacture some bliss into this otherwise solemn atmosphere, one significant difference presented itself here. All sense of privacy had been stripped away.

Eight other beds beside my own were pressed up along the walls of this ward. As my eyes drifted from bed to bed, I noticed several of the children, ranging in age from six to thirteen, staring at me with sad, listless eyes. Though I didn't yet know the extent of the children's various diseases, everyone in here appeared physically sicker than me.

One boy around my age, bedded directly to my left, wore a red baseball cap and busied himself by reading a comic book. Since he was closest to me, I tried to initiate conversation into this thus far silent room. He casually ignored my attempts by rustling the pages of his comic book. After it became rather obvious that he was trying to snub me, I became more insistent.

"What's the matter?" I asked jokingly, "doesn't anybody around this place like to talk?"

Finally, the boy dropped the comic book into his lap and sighed heavily. He then glared at me as if I should've known not to disturb him.

"Another newcomer," he huffed. "Look, kid, none of us got much to talk about. So let's just keep it quiet, okay?"

As the boy projected a disgruntled look in my direction, I tilted my head back against my pillow. Although I had it in my mind not to speak to this kid again, I sensed that he needed somebody to talk to almost as much as I did.

When the silence became too distracting for me to bear, I turned back to the boy and asked, "How'd you end up in this place?"

"None of your business," he answered miserably.

"My name is Lawrence Dayton," I went on, "and the doctor says I got some kind of brain tumor."

Now perturbed by my stubbornness, the boy leaned forward in his bed and pointed an index finger within inches of my nose. "Since you're new in here, kid, I'm gonna cut you some slack, but this is the last time I'm gonna warn you—shut your mouth."

"I don't get it," I said, "why are you so angry?"

"We got certain rules around this place," the boy explained. "Rule number one—never try to get to know any kid who comes in here."

My immediate expression must've been one of disbelief because I was not convinced that all the other children were as unsociable as he was. Then, after shifting my stare in a circle from boy to girl around the ward, I noticed that none of them were conversing. Granted, many of them appeared too ill to speak, but others chose to remain mute, while gazing off into blank spaces throughout the room.

"I don't understand," I said. "Why do you have such a stupid rule?"

Using the same index finger that he nearly rammed up my nostril a moment ago, the boy pointed to the floor next to my bed. Actually, he directed my eyes to the metal wheels attached to each leg of my bed's frame.

"You see those rollers," he said, casually pivoting his eyes to where I looked. "It's all a matter of mobility in here, kid. Those wheels are there to remind us that no one stays around this place for too long. They roll us in, and then they roll us out—real quietly."

"Where do they bring us?" I asked, revealing my ignorance to our shared misfortune.

"Notice how this ward doesn't have any windows," the boy continued. "They keep us closer to the basement, next to the morgue."

Frightened by the boy's lurid observation, I said, "That's a rotten way to look at things."

"You can look at it any way you please, but that won't change the truth. No one likes seeing a small body being carted through the halls upstairs. We're kind of used to it down here, though. Besides, it's usually late at night when they take the dead ones away. They think we're sleeping and won't notice the change."

"That's terrible," I sulked.

"Trust me," the boy grumbled, "you won't even care after a couple of weeks. Heck, just three days ago some other kid was in your spot, but he's gone now."

"So that's it," I deduced, before pausing to consider the boy's grim confession. "Since you all think everybody is gonna die in here, nobody wants to get involved—is that right?"

The boy then held out his arms as if acting as a ringmaster to a band of helpless souls. "As I said, kid, we all got wheels, and we know what's coming. It's now just a matter of waiting for the time when they roll us away."

Although I was the one stricken with brain cancer, it soon occurred to me that this boy's mind was far more infected. In spite of the fact that no doctor had fed me any false hope that I would survive my disease, I still possessed something that wasn't within any doctor's power to predict—a sheer desire to live. Contrarily, this boy and my seven other roommates had already resigned themselves to dying. Suddenly, and for reasons not yet apparent to me, I felt compelled to change the mood of this abominable setting.

"I know we don't got much to be happy about," I declared, "but sitting around this place—waiting to roll out of here—as you put it, isn't a good plan. We're not dead yet, so why give up?"

The boy smirked at my optimism, which bordered on blatant stupidity as far as he was concerned. His voice poured with sarcasm when he spoke again. "You think you're so different from us? Well, I guess you're better off than Franky, Sally, and Ben. Of course let's not forget about Sara, Nicky, Joe, and Bob. We all must look pretty stupid to you, huh?"

After the boy defiantly introduced me to each patient, he poked his finger into his own chest through the paper vest of a comic book. He then told me his name in a whisper. "I'm Danny Gibbon. They say that my liver won't last another month."

Before Danny had a chance to turn inhospitable toward me again, I extended my hand and attempted to initiate a handshake. Danny smugly pushed my arm away and resumed reading his comic book. Embarrassed, I tucked my arm back against my body and shifted onto my backside.

"I'm sorry if I bothered you," I said. "I just thought it'd be a lot easier on everyone in here if we tried to take our minds off of things."

"You sound like my mother," Danny chided. After a pause, he said, "You know, I can't figure you newcomers out half the time."

"What do you mean?"

"I mean, you're sick and dying, just like the rest of us, but you don't want to accept reality. You can't face the fact that death eventually takes us all. It doesn't matter that we're only kids, or that we've never had a chance to really live. None of this phases you, Lawrence, because you're still convinced that you're in control, and that's not the way it works."

"You don't know me well enough to say that, Danny."

"Well, tell us what your big secret is," Danny shouted. "How do we wake up happy each morning knowing that it might be our last day?"

For now, I turned away from Danny and shut my eyes. I don't know if I was wise enough to give him the answer that he sought. Maybe I didn't even understand my own feelings. Whatever the reason for my silence, I decided to wait until another time to resume our conversation. Something told me that Danny Gibbon would be around to hear it.

Chapter Eight

▼

Journal Entry Four

A Harvester Among Us

My first evening in this ward provided me with some time to consider our plight more thoroughly. I didn't blame Danny or any of the other children for the way they felt. Despite my young age, I suspected that no child—no matter how ill—could've plunged to such a level of despondency on his own. At some point, these patients had been exposed to a cruel source within this hospital, and I aimed to find out where and from whom it was coming.

On the following morning, Danny had asked one of the nurses to relocate his bed to the opposite side of the ward. I guess he didn't want to hear my answer to his question. Franky Miller, a lanky, freckle-faced twelve-year-old, gladly assumed Danny's place on the floor next to mine. Franky appeared sicker than the other children in the ward did, but I sensed that he was my best chance at finding out what was going on.

"Don't worry about Danny," he whispered to me. "He wasn't always so negative. I don't think he means half the things he says."

"What about you?" I asked. "Do you feel like there's no hope for any of us, too?"

Franky thought for a moment before saying, "I've been in here three months now—that's two weeks longer than anybody else. In the beginning, I sort of felt like you did. But lately, I've started to accept my disease."

"Accepting your sickness is one thing, giving in to it is another."

Franky sighed heavily and confessed, "Lawrence, nobody leaves this room alive. I think this hospital is cursed."

"Cursed? Why do you think that?"

"Because," Franky said, leaning closer to my bed. "Weird things happen around here. I think it has something to do with one of the doctors."

"Not Doctor Cain," I said, "he seems like a good man to me."

"It's not him who you got to worry about," Franky explained. "There's another doctor who works in this ward. He looks after us most of the time."

My voice became timorous when I asked, "What's wrong with him?"

Franky shrugged his shoulders and said, "I'm not exactly sure, but he's very cold to us—not directly, but in a sly way that I can't explain."

"What's his name?"

"You'll meet him later," Franky told me before settling into his bed. "He usually works the nightshift."

On that same evening, I became acquainted to the culprit of Franky's apprehension. His name was Dr. Kross, and he was primarily in charge of the children's ward, especially since Dr. Cain had taken on additional responsibilities. I distinctly remember the first time Kross sauntered into the ward. Though I was immediately unnerved by Kross's arrogance, I sensed something more unsettling stirring beneath his flashy smile.

While staring at Kross, I determined that he lacked an intangible quality that I was still too unseasoned to identify. Unlike the other physicians

I had encountered since my diagnosis, Kross did not exhibit an altruistic persona. When gazing into his ink-black eyes in search of compassion, I found none. These were the eyes of a very deceptive man—a man who seemed to have more than one motive on his mind.

Being a tall, lean man, Kross possessed an aura of sophistication that belied his youth. I guessed him to be no older than thirty-five. He sported a head full of onyx-black hair, swarthy, unblemished skin, and a finely tuned physique. Many of the nurses in our ward found it difficult to withhold their flirtations when he approached them. Even the most hard-nosed personalities became as malleable as clay under his command.

Of course none of these reactions were nearly as important to me than the way he related to the children. As Kross ambled by their beds, the kids shuddered beneath their cotton sheets. On this occasion, he gently touched the feet or hands of some, others he passed over with an artificial smile. I may not have had any definite evidence to confirm my suspicion, but I sensed that Kross played a vital part in planting and sowing the seeds of contamination in this ward.

My first encounter with Dr. Kross occurred on the next evening, well after the nurses had retired from their rounds. Most of the children were sleeping peacefully at this late hour. Being drowsy and half-asleep myself, I slipped into a momentary dream. Suddenly, a shadow pressed across the walls of the faintly lit corridor. From my place in bed, I distinguished a human silhouette progressing into the room. Soon, this image developed into a definite shape—it was Kross.

Kross skulked into our ward like a ghost garbed in a white overcoat, with latex gloves covering his hands. His stealthy movement seemed deliberately animated, as if he tried to draw attention to himself as he crept by my bed. Admittedly, I was only brave enough to open one eye. I followed his footsteps to Franky's bedside. At first, I assumed that Franky was resting quietly, but then a terrible possibility caused a surge of adrenaline to race through my body. I nearly leapt from my bed, as my fear became a reality.

For a moment, Kross hovered over Franky's motionless body. Then, as if conducting a ritualistic chore, Kross pulled a sheet over Franky's gray face. Though I couldn't swear to my next thought as fact, I saw a wicked smile curve into the man's thin lips.

In the stillness of this moment, I listened to the squeaking wheels of Franky's bed being pushed across the tiled floor. Kross stood behind the bed's steel frame, purposely leaning his weight down upon the bed's chirping axial. Now, being petrified by disbelief, I closed my eyes and wished for this horrible sound to fade away.

Kross stopped his progress and stood at the foot of my bed. Despite my attempt to muffle my face in a pillow and fake sleep, I sensed a pair of coal-black eyes penetrating the space between us. As I turned to inspect the situation more clearly, I noticed that Kross had directed his stare upon me. Finally, when I could no longer bear his taunting presence, I lifted my head off the pillow and glared at him through the folds of darkness.

Kross skillfully detected my distress, and then took full advantage of his authority. "You must be the new boy that I've heard so much about," he said, trying to keep his voice mellow. "I'm very sorry to hear about your cancer."

I ignored Kross's statement and presented him with a question of my own. "Where are you taking Franky?"

"Oh," Kross chimed innocently, "I'm afraid that Franky Miller's time has expired."

"He's dead?" I gasped, peering at the sheet that covered his stiff body. "That's impossible. I was just talking to him yesterday," I pouted.

"Well, things of this nature happen very quickly around here, Lawrence. But I'm sure the other children have already told you that."

Just as Franky and I had anticipated, Kross seemed unnaturally prepared for this grim task. I sensed that he relished this chore more than any man should have been allowed.

"Where are you taking him?" I cried.

"To the morgue, of course," Kross replied. "That's where we bring all of our dead. It helps keep the nurses happy."

"You don't seem too upset," I grimaced, "don't you like kids?"

Kross snickered at my audacity and answered, "Lawrence, what makes you ask such a question? Could it be that some little bird was whispering woeful thoughts into your ear?"

"Maybe," I said, watching Kross slide his hands up the length of Franky's body.

"Well, for the record, let it be known that I adore children. Some might even say that I live for them. But even I can't stop death."

"Just stay away from me," I sneered.

"You know I can't do that, Lawrence," Kross said, using an eerie monotone to frighten me into submission. "Go to sleep now. I'll see to it that your friend is put in his proper place."

Kross then lifted the sheet covering Franky's face. A bluish-gray hue had already discolored his skin. After Kross was certain that I had examined the dead body, he covered him and continued across the corridor. Kross made no effort to look back at me. Long after the bed's squeaking wheels quieted, I remained awake in my bed. Even though I had only known Franky for less than a day, I felt an urge to cry for him. I think I may have even uttered a prayer in his memory.

By morning, all of the children noticed the vacant bed next to mine. Surprisingly, Franky's death didn't seem suspicious to anyone besides me. Even Dr. Cain, who I trusted more than anyone since arriving at this hospital, informed me that the boy's death was inevitable. Apparently, Franky had acquired an incurable blood disease. Of course I wasn't so easily satisfied, especially after getting a small taste of Dr. Kross's bedside manner firsthand.

By the end of my first week in the ward, I determined that Dr. Kross was a menace to us all. I brought this matter to Dr. Cain's attention, but he tactfully explained that my judgment of Kross was premature. Adding to my troubles, none of the other children or nurses in the ward supported my accusations against Kross. Without any concrete evidence and a tumor roughly the size of a golf ball hindering the clarity of my thoughts, I could do little else but submit to the consensus of those around me.

Subsequently, my reservations toward Kross had alienated me from everyone else in the ward. Even the nurses turned on me, displaying their outrage by randomly delaying my medication. Sometimes when my pain became too intense, I cried myself to sleep. I knew, however, that it served no purpose for me to whine now. Nobody was listening.

With no one to speak to other than a chorus of vague voices trailing through my mind, I resumed writing my journal in a quest to ease the tension. In the meantime, Kross continued to badger me with his casual banter and disarming patience. All the while, I refused to let him do to me what he had already done to the others. In the process, I unwittingly made myself an enemy who would haunt me for the rest of my life.

According to Dr. Cain, Kross arrived at the Children's Center six months before I did. Kross had come to Pittsburgh with an impeccable reputation; even rumored to be a more accomplished surgeon than Dr. Cain. Soon after Kross's appointment to the ward, however, the hospital's pediatric division experienced a rash increase in its number of deaths. Most conspicuously, none of the terminally sick children left in Kross's care had recovered from their illnesses.

In a series of private conversations with Dr. Cain, I articulated my rather harsh opinions of Kross. In my own mind, I felt that Kross was toying with our infirmities, making us feel unworthy of life. As suffering children, we were deprived of all the pleasures that most take for granted. We needed strong, positive men and women to guide us through our maladies. Whether intentional or not, Kross had ultimately become a burden to his patients' welfare.

Shortly after I made my observations known, Dr. Cain began to scrutinize Kross's motives more closely. Cain knew that it was foolhardy to accuse his colleague of moral crimes without any real evidence, but he certainly couldn't let such a blemished record go unchallenged. Within a week after Franky's death, Cain removed Kross from the children's ward, pending an investigation. I expected that Kross would not accept the deliverance of his demotion in good faith.

Before submitting his resignation to Cain, Kross decided that he owed me at least one more unannounced visit. As I anticipated, Kross waited until after dark to confront me. He came to my bedside dressed in a dark suit; his face was enshrouded by the room's shadows. Not even the blackest night could've hidden the fire blazing behind his eyes. On this occasion, he made no effort to conceal the fury that stirred deep within his twisted mind.

Whispering in my ear, he said, "You've managed to create quite a stir around here in the last few weeks, Lawrence. Why do you waste so much of your energy trying to ruin my name?"

"You don't belong here," I murmured.

"I'm amused by your ignorance, little boy. Yet I fear you're not nearly as naïve as you'd like me to believe. I keep reminding myself that you're only a child, albeit—a very meddlesome one."

"I just want you to go away. You're not helping any of us."

Kross edged his mouth closer to my ear and hissed, "What is it that you truly hope to accomplish, Lawrence? Are you merely trying to save yourself, or is your plan more elaborate?"

Before I uttered another word, Kross's fingers snapped forward like the bite of a virulent creature. His icy fingertips dug into the bone in my wrist. I winced beneath the pressure of his bloodless grasp, but refused to cry out for assistance.

"Listen to me, Lawrence Dayton," Kross sneered, shifting his hollow eyes closer to my own. "It is not yet clear to me who you are or what pertinence you hold to me beyond this night. But know this—neither you nor Doctor Cain can stop what must be fulfilled. Accept your fate, and take your hostility to the grave, as the children here will continue to do long after I'm gone from here."

With those words, Kross released my arm and turned away from my bed. For many hours after his departure, I reflected upon his admonition. I eventually concluded that Kross had devised a demented scheme to strip the children of their desire to live. Many of them had already succumbed to his devious spell, but I had no intention of proving him right at this point.

Within the silence of the darkened ward, shadows soon slithered across the walls. Between these serpentine patterns, I envisioned the formation of godless creatures. Even with Kross gone, I felt his eyes hovering about the room like a nocturnal beast hunting its prey. In an effort to thwart this illusion, I closed my eyes and wished for the blackness to dissolve.

After opening my eyes again, I sensed the shadows being lifted away, almost as if a vacuum of unknown energy had imprisoned the darkness and carried it off into a cylinder of burning light. And it was toward this same light that my eyes now focused. I was more intrigued than I was terrified. I'd seen such a glow before. It had crossed the midnight sky while I was en route to Pittsburgh. Only this time, the light was more resplendent. Within seconds, I felt myself welcoming to its presence. It gyrated across the room's ceiling, before slowly descending in front of my bed. A warm breeze filled the ward, followed by a glistening mist that seemed to invigorate every cell in my body.

Suddenly it was if the night had turned to day. I sat upright in my bed, stretching to feel the radiance as it sifted between my fingertips and settled onto the floor. And in this designated spot I discerned the image of a lone man, only this man was unlike any other I had ever set eyes on before. His narrow face, although young and untested, projected a light more powerful than the energy that enveloped his body.

The flaxen-hair man hovered in front of my bed for several seconds, but I envisioned his face as clearly as if he was standing before me now. Though he was only a stranger to me, I felt compelled to reach out to him. When peering into his azure-colored eyes, I sensed that he understood the secrets about this world that I would never live to comprehend. And then, when it seemed at though my illusion would intensify, the mist vanished, leaving behind this apparition in its place.

As I mentioned, he was not like other men. When looking directly at him, I could see through his body as if he was made of crystal. Was he a ghost? Or was he something far stranger? Before I had a chance to draw any conclusions regarding this man's identity or intentions, he placed both his hands upon my shoulder. I immediately leaned backwards in my bed, completely mesmerized by his touch.

"Who are you?" I asked, through hazy eyes.

"I'm here to help you," the man replied. "My name is Jonathan."

An amber glow emanated from Jonathan's hands as he spoke. "Tonight is only the beginning for you, Lawrence Dayton. You must prepare yourself to leave this hospital soon."

"I—I can't leave," I stammered, "I'm dying…"

"No," Jonathan corrected, "You must continue to live."

Jonathan uttered nothing more to me on this evening. He turned to leave as quickly as he had arrived. "Don't go," I pleaded. "I don't even know what you're talking about."

Despite my cries, the phantom named Jonathan faded into the darkness of the ceiling. By now I had inadvertently drawn unwanted attention to myself. Several of the other children in the ward, including Danny, were staring at me from their beds. Judging by their perplexed expressions, I guessed that they could not see what I had just witnessed.

"Didn't you see him?" I asked, pointing excitedly toward the ceiling. "He was amazing!"

"See who?" Danny asked, glancing nonchalantly toward where I waggled my finger."

"Jonathan," I exclaimed. "He was standing right in front of my bed a few seconds ago."

"There's no one there now," Danny remarked. "You must've been dreaming again."

"No, Danny," I insisted. "This wasn't a dream—this was real. I felt him touch my shoulder. I heard him speak to me."

"Nobody was in here," Danny said. "Now quit making so much noise. Some of us in here are trying to get some sleep."

I figured that Danny and the others were a long way off from accepting anything I said as foolproof. Many of them were still bickering about Dr. Kross's departure, but I'd let them thank me later for helping cleanse our souls from this fiend's company. Since I had already caused too much upset in my brief stay, I decided to keep my thoughts private for now. Inwardly, I knew that Jonathan was not merely a figment of my diseased brain; he was more real to me than anything or anyone I had ever encountered in my lifetime. Though I didn't yet know it, I would soon reap the benefits of his kindness.

CHAPTER NINE

▼

JOURNAL ENTRY FIVE

MEDICINE OF FAITH

I spent the next several days trying to decipher Jonathan's intentions in the pages of my journal. Regrettably, by the end of the first week, it became clear to me that Jonathan was not coming back to this hospital. I concluded that his work here was done, and it was now up to me to make sense out of it all, whether I wanted to or not.

Up until this point, my stay at the Children's Center had been made bearable by a daily consumption of medication. Soon after Jonathan's visit, however, I discovered that my cocktail of painkillers was no longer necessary. Miraculously, the mind-numbing headaches and nausea quickly subsided. In addition, my appetite returned to what it was before I fell ill.

Soon thereafter, I felt strong enough to get out of bed and walk around the room for the first time in weeks.

These minor feats only marked the onset of my convalescence. I read and dreamt peacefully without the slightest indication of sickness. After two weeks, I was fairly certain that my supposed terminal cancer no longer existed within my brain. For whatever reason, no one wanted to believe me at first. Even Dr. Cain refused to lend credence to my claim until I revealed my collection of undigested medication.

When my reversal of fortune could no longer be explained or ignored, Dr. Cain supervised a new set of X-rays on my skull. Being a skeptical doctor by nature, I expected him to be suspicious, especially after comparing the new X-rays with those photographed previously.

"There must be some kind of mistake," Cain said, mulling over the transparencies of my brain. His eyes shifted neurotically between the two exposures. After taking my new tests in hand he announced, "I don't see any trace of malignancy. The cancer has completely dissolved, almost as if it was never even there."

"I've been trying to tell you that for the last week now," I said.

Cain stared at me as if I was withholding information. His expression remained half-twisted as he recounted everything that I had told him. He then turned back to the first set of X-rays and said, "Unquestionably, there's a growth here. It's medically impossible for a tumor of such density and size to simply disappear."

I shrugged my shoulders and said, "Well, you've got the proof right in your hands. I feel fine, Doctor Cain. In fact, I've never felt better."

My doctor sounded like he was trying to convince himself otherwise when he muttered, "A logical answer exists for every problem. We need to do more tests to confirm your remission."

"No more tests," I refused. "No offense, Doctor Cain, but I don't like hospitals. I just want to get out of here, even if it means going back home to Orefield."

"Lawrence, if these new tests are correct, then I need to study how an event like this could have occurred. We may be on the verge of a breakthrough in our treatment of cancer."

Now perturbed by Cain's stubbornness I said, "Maybe this isn't about science or anything else that you'll find in your books."

"Please," Cain said, "I've heard all of your stories about this so-called visitor named Jonathan. As I told you before, no one on our staff or security has that name. You must've been dreaming."

"It was no dream, Doctor Cain. It's hard for me to describe him, but Jonathan was real. I'm sure he's the reason that I'm no longer sick."

Cain shoved his chair away from his desk and sighed heavily. Judging by the tightness in his jaw, I sensed that he had become as aggravated as I had. After a moment, he kneeled down in front of me and stared into my eyes.

"Lawrence, you know I don't think of you as a liar. Sometimes, especially when children become ill, their minds can make them see things that aren't really there. They're called hallucinations. Now, isn't it reasonable to suggest that Jonathan may have been visible to you for a short time, but in fact was never there at all?"

"Hallucinations don't talk to you," I argued. "I may have had brain cancer, Doctor Cain, but I'm not crazy. I know what I saw. Jonathan told me that I would survive, and I believed him."

"Okay," Cain conceded, "let's say that a man named Jonathan somehow managed to sneak into the children's ward. Why would he make himself known only to you? There are many other sick children in this hospital. Don't you think it would've been fair of Jonathan to do the same for them as you claim he has done for you?"

"He didn't take time to explain himself," I said. "I don't know why he chose me. Maybe it was God's will."

"Excuse me," Cain questioned, leaning his face closer to mine. "Do you think God cured you of this disease?"

"I don't know," I answered honestly. "I mean, I never believed in miracles before, but who knows? Maybe Jonathan was a messenger from heaven or something."

Cain snickered before saying, "You mean like an angel?"

"Do you got any better ideas?"

Cain paused for a moment and massaged his fingers across his brow. He continued to speak to me in a gentle monotone. "Lawrence, I appreciate your belief in God, but as your doctor, you must realize that I need scientific evidence to support whatever I write into your files. It's simply not practical for me to report that my patient was cured by God, or any other supernatural creation for that matter."

Although I admired Dr. Cain's commitment to the medical profession, it troubled me to witness him deliberating these circumstances from a defensive standpoint. In my mind, there was little else to debate. Of course what can be measured on a graph or mapped beneath the lens of a microscope can only satisfy educated men like Cain.

Though the comparison seemed unwarranted, I imagined how my father might have reacted to a similar confrontation. Being a simpleminded man, Samuel Dayton would've never questioned his own spirituality. I once thought that my father was incredibly ignorant for not wanting to know more about the world. Now I know differently. My father, despite his flaws, realized that the mysteries of faith were essential components to every man's disposition, perhaps just as substantial as Cain's medicinal skills.

After a moment of contemplation, I decided to ask Cain a question of my own. "Do you believe in God?"

He paused again, scratching at his temple as if my inquiry baffled him in some way. Finally, he remarked, "I don't know how to answer that truthfully, Lawrence."

"That's what I thought," I sulked. "You really don't believe in anything that you can't see or understand."

"I suppose I'm like most people. I want to believe that a god exists, but it's not my job to convince my patients of this. I must help them with the skills I possess. I must continue to do what I know is best."

"Me, too," I said. "And right now I think it's best that we learn to believe each other. Jonathan saved my life, Doctor Cain, and I'll try to prove that to you some day."

Once realizing that my opinion into this matter was firm, Dr. Cain decided to accept my X-rays as documentation to a miraculous recovery. No further tests would be needed. He of course never admitted that God or any of His angels were connected to my welfare, but he ordered my discharge within the week.

In the meantime, I was mindful to the fact that the other children in the ward weren't nearly as fortunate. Unlike me, their death sentences hadn't been reprieved. On the evening before I left Pittsburgh, I went to Danny's bedside to say goodbye. A dampened comic book lay crumpled in his lap. As I glanced into his tear-speckled eyes, I saw fear mixing with traces of happiness.

"I know we never got a chance to become friends," I offered, "but you can make it out of here, too. Don't give up—no matter what."

Danny sniffled and rubbed his eyes before saying, "I was wrong about you, Lawrence. Maybe you are different from the rest of us."

"I don't think so, Danny. We're all the same."

"That can't be true," Danny rationalized, "because if we were, then I'd be leaving with you, rather than lying around here in this rotten place."

At that moment the tears vanished from Danny's eyes. He then sat upright in his bed and extended his arm toward me. "I owe you a handshake," he said, gesturing for me to take his hand. "Where do you live, anyway?"

I took Danny's hand into my own and said, "Orefield. It's a small town, but it's the only home I've ever really known. I'm gonna be staying with my grandmother for a while, at least last time I heard."

"Where are your parents?"

I hesitated before answering, "Gone." I immediately thought about the phone call that Dr. Cain had made to Beatrice earlier in the week. Apparently, soon after returning from Pittsburgh, my mother met and ran off with another man half her age. She didn't leave her old, destitute mother any money to offset her poverty, but the house served as a final payment for her abandonment.

My attention swiftly reverted to Danny. I still clasped his hand, and in these seconds I recognized how short-lived all life's relationships could be. There was too little time to resent those who had wronged me in the past. A second chance at life afforded me an opportunity to become a better person. I'd only become such a person after I learned to accept the flaws in all of humanity, specifically from those who I loved and lost in my early years.

Upon my return to Orefield, I discovered that Beatrice had found a new passion to occupy herself with during the hours of loneliness. Thankfully, she had discarded her last bottle of vodka weeks ago and replaced her inebriation with the wisdom of Scripture. Though this could be rated as a miracle in its own right, Beatrice had found God in the pages where infidels had failed to look before. To her credit, she was no longer a contemptible hag bent on sullying my father's name. The Bible had changed her into a woman who finally realized that the best people in this world are those who stick beside you when all others have gone.

I didn't learn of my mother's fate until two years after returning home. Admittedly, I waited for her to come back to us, if only to offer an apology for her selfish endeavors. Before my fourteenth birthday, however, a state police officer delivered a telegram confirming Lily Dayton's sad demise. While courting yet another lover somewhere between the seedy barrooms of Ohio, Lily was murdered. They found her bludgeoned body mixed with the remnants of back-alley trash.

Beatrice forbade me to mention this incident to anyone in town, especially to our church's pastor. Later on, Beatrice requested that my mother's body be planted beside my father in Orefield's cemetery. I never fully understood this gesture, and it made me sorrowful to think that my father's unrequited love was never pure enough until now.

Over the years, I remembered visiting the tiny churchyard where my parents lay buried. In truth, the neglected cemetery did little to honor the memories of these forgotten corpses. Generations of crumbling headstones served as crude markers. Weeds and tall grass crept over a rusted, wrought iron fence. Yet even in the midst of this decay, I felt an odd satisfaction in my parents' eternal placement. Never before now had either of them been so close to one another. Maybe I wanted to believe that Samuel and Lily were united in death and all the misery and unfound wishes of their living years would be cast aside, enabling a new hope to flourish from the dust of their remains.

Years later, during what turned out to be my last visit to Orefield's cemetery, my attention was drawn to a peculiarity on my parents' graves. Despite the churchyard's muddy terrain, the area surrounding their headstones seemed recently gardened. A cluster of white poppies bloomed over the plotted soil. No other flowers grew elsewhere in the entire graveyard. I initially suspected that Beatrice had ventured here by herself to adorn the graves, but she was an invalid at this point in time.

After returning home, Beatrice assured me that she made no attempt to plant poppies on their gravesites. She also suggested that these flowers represented a sign from God. Such an explanation may have sounded like hogwash a few years ago, but now I considered this evaluation quite reasonable, or at least possible. Whatever I believed previously, Beatrice's newfound faith actually made sense to me now.

Following my nineteenth birthday in 1949, Beatrice summoned me to her bedside. Ravaged by arthritis and liver disease, I watched this jaundice-faced woman slowly wither and die. On this occasion, she muttered gentle prayers into the fabric of her pillow. At the time of her death, she nestled a Bible against her chest in the same manner that a stuffed toy pacified a child. When staring at her lifeless body, a realization of solitude struck me harder than ever before.

Months before Beatrice's suffering ended, I had been planning to leave Orefield in pursuit of a career as a journalist. Admittedly, I had little experience in writing and even less formal education to speak of, but ignorance to protocol permitted me to take chances. Following her funeral, I sold our house and property to the mining company for $1500. The transaction provided me with enough money to purchase a satchel full of new clothes and a one-way train ticket to Philadelphia.

CHAPTER TEN

▼

BEDSIDE OBSERVATIONS

Since arriving at the Dayton's home, Regina had voluntarily shouldered many of the household responsibilities that Theodore neglected to perform. Although she may have been slightly embarrassed of her duties, Regina took it upon herself to prepare Emily's meals each evening. Over a span of several months, she noticed how Emily's appetite had steadily diminished. Tonight, Regina served warm chicken broth, applesauce, and a slice of Italian bread.

With this meal in hand, Regina approached Emily's bedroom door at 5:30 P.M. Emily had spent most of the day reading and almost didn't hear Regina's knock on the door. After realizing that it was time for supper, Emily closed the journal and invited Regina into her room. As Regina entered the room with a plate and saucer balanced on a plastic tray, Emily laid the journal on the nightstand and sat upright in her bed.

Before Regina set the tray of food on the bed, Emily asked, "Regina, I was wondering when you're planning to go back to the hospital in Kindred Woods?"

Regina's eyes sparked with surprise at this question. Kindred Woods Hospital, in northern Pennsylvania, was the last place Regina had worked before moving to Wakeland with Emily and Theodore. After her discharge, Regina never heard Emily mention anything remotely connected to the hospital.

"What makes you ask?" Regina questioned, stirring the chicken broth with a spoon. As she situated the tray in front of Emily, Regina noticed the notebook on her nightstand.

"I was hoping that maybe we could go back there," Emily suggested. Emily's voice quavered slightly when she continued, "I started to think about all those kids there. It'd be nice to spend some time with some of them."

Now perplexed by Emily's request, Regina sat on the bed's edge and watched her sip soup from the spoon. "If you really want to go, Emily, I suppose I can arrange something with Doctor Garrison."

"Good. And could you do that by tomorrow?"

Regina appeared flushed before saying, "That's rather short notice, don't you think?"

"I know," Emily said, placing her spoon on the tray, "But it's important to me. If you can get Doctor Garrison to agree, I think my father will drive us."

"I'll see what I can do," Regina said, shifting her eyes to the journal once again. By now it was clear to Emily that Regina's attention was conflicted between her request and the progress she had made in Lawrence's journal.

Emily smiled pleasantly as she inspected the food placed before her lap. She felt unusually hungry tonight, and appeased her appetite by quickly nibbling on the bread. After consuming the bread's crust and three spoonfuls of applesauce, Emily reclined against her bed's headboard.

"Thank you, Regina," Emily sighed, referring to the food and agreement to call Dr. Garrison at Kindred Woods. "You've been such a help to me lately. My father could've never taken care of me by himself. He wasn't always so angry, you know?"

As Emily spoke, her eyes drifted to a photograph on the wall beside her closet. This particular photo was Emily's only remembrance of her mother. It depicted Claire standing on a moonlit beach near the ocean, wearing a summer frock. Although Regina had noticed this photograph many times before this night, she never spoke a word about it.

At times, Emily wished to hurl herself into that photograph and join her mother on the sand. She often thought about the ocean, too, and how continuously its dark waves lapped against the shoreline, dissolving the footprints of a thousand lovers. She imagined the tide's undulating force being unchallenged by those who found pleasure within its path. These waves rolled on without mercy, and all Emily could do was dream of a day when life was less imperfect, and the world was as silently blissful as the one preserved in that haunting photograph.

"She was very beautiful," Emily whispered, motioning toward the photograph. She then continued in monotone, "That photo is the only one I've ever seen of my mother. I guess my father didn't take many pictures back then."

Feeling insecure with the direction and tone of this conversation, Regina said, "I'm sure he wants to remember her in his own special way."

"Maybe. But I still worry about him, Regina. My mother's been dead for over twelve years now. I think it's about time that he at least tried to love another woman, don't you?"

Regina fell silent as she sensed her throat swelling shut. Although her next thought was difficult to express, she blurted it out in one breath. "I may have thought that once—" Before finishing, she stopped herself and swallowed the remainder of her confession like a sour pill.

Emily then leaned forward and stared at Regina more intensely before saying, "You know, my mother's picture has been hanging on that wall since I was a little girl. I've always tried to imagine what she might've been like, and how she would've treated me, even after I got sick."

"I'm sure she would've been wonderful to you, Emily."

"Yeah," Emily replied sheepishly, "but I'll never know for sure. If you really think about it, you've been like a mother to me over these last six months—the only mother I've ever known. I'm sure my father sees it, too."

Now clearly unnerved by this comparison, Regina said, "I'm flattered that you feel that way, but I can't replace your mother, Emily, especially in your father's mind."

"But you do love him," Emily declared confidently. Had Emily's estimation been incorrect, Regina may have been offended, but she remained mute for a moment, struggling with her bottled emotions. Up until now, Regina had carefully meandered between the lines of conversation that might've pushed her into exploring such feelings. Now, Emily forced her to examine her desires with greater sincerity.

"Your father needs more healing before he can begin a new relationship with a woman," Regina explained.

"How much healing?"

"That depends," Regina replied faintly, almost stalling to recollect her thoughts. "People grieve differently. You're father is probably too afraid to be in love right now."

"Why don't you just go and tell him how you feel?"

"Emily, I'm not sure what I feel. It's not easy for me to sort through this now. I care about this family, and at times I feel like I'm part of this home." Regina's eyes turned toward Claire's photograph before she said, "But there are many levels to romantic relationships, and these must be met by two people at the right time."

"It all seems so foolish," Emily pouted. "You're here in this house for a reason besides me. I wouldn't be telling you this unless I thought that my father loved you, too."

Regina stood up from the bed and paced across the floor toward the window. She placed both of her quivering hands on the sill and huffed, "Please, I'd rather not talk about this right now. Besides, even if what you say is true, I can't get involved."

"Why not?" Emily persisted. "I see the way that you two look at each other."

"I sort of promised myself a long time ago that I'd never let my personal life mix with work."

Emily cringed at Regina's unconvincing pledge before saying, "That's a silly promise to make to yourself. How can you plan on who to love and who not to love? Isn't falling in love something that just happens—like death? That's what makes life so exciting—and scary."

Regina became silent again. She permitted her eyes to methodically shift back to the journal lying upon the night table. A dewy breeze sprung through the half-open window, rustling the white curtains. Emily felt the air strike against her skin. She grimaced as a chill seeped beneath the fabric of her nightgown.

"I'll be gone from here soon," Emily mumbled. "I sense it as clearly as the wind."

"I hope that's not true," Regina uttered softly, moving back toward Emily's bed. She then took Emily's warm hand into her own and whispered, "You've been so courageous through all of this. I've never before met a child as brave as you."

"It's okay," Emily assured. "I'm not afraid to die, Regina. Why should I be scared when I know that my soul will go to heaven?"

Regina bit her bottom lip, withholding a confession that she may have regretted later. Perhaps their conversation should have ended here, but Emily had little to gain by prolonging what had been troubling her for weeks. Sensing that she would have few other opportunities to speak to Regina alone, Emily decided to use this time to her advantage.

"Before I die," Emily started, "I wanted to know if you could make a promise?"

Regina reclaimed her seat on the edge of Emily's mattress before inquiring with some reservation. "What would you like me to do for you?" she asked.

"Nothing for me," Emily clarified. "I just want you to promise to tell my father how you feel about him. He needs to know the truth."

Regina rolled her eyes in frustration and sighed, "This is an impossible situation. Emily, you know I care for you and your father, but you're asking me to make a promise that I might not be able to keep."

"You do love him," Emily insisted. "I haven't heard you deny it yet."

Now frazzled and breathless, Regina swept the hair off the back of her neck and cupped her hands over her face. Inwardly, she may have had ardent feelings toward Theodore, but a fear of being compared to his deceased wife—especially during moments of intimacy—kept her from disclosing her emotions.

"I'm sorry," Regina declared. "It's just not the right time for either of us."

"How long will you continue to allow yourself to be alone? Can't you see what's happening to the both of you?"

Emily's questions pounded against Regina's ears with a certain veracity, for in her heart—a place she seldom searched—she realized that Emily was right. Neither of them uttered a word in the seconds that followed. Their discourse had pushed them both to the brink of an argument. For now, Regina debated, it was better to stew in silence.

Before excusing herself from the room, Regina reminded Emily that she still planned to arrange a meeting for tomorrow with Dr. Garrison in Kindred Woods. This promise seemed more like a consolation to what Emily truly wanted, but she said nothing else to expose her disappointment. After Regina exited her room, Emily sighed in frustration. She then placed her hand on Lawrence's journal and decided to occupy the rest of her evening by reading his memoirs.

Immediately after opening the notebook, a loud crash, similar to shattering glass, caused Emily to jump with fright. She then heard the sound of footsteps rushing by her closed bedroom door.

Regina sprinted down the corridor to investigate the disturbance. The single door at the hallway's end was ajar. She knew this to be the master bedroom's doorway. Had it been any other room in the house, her apprehension would not have peaked, but she lived in this home long enough to know that Theodore rarely left this door unlocked.

Theodore seldom entered this bedroom, but he was the only other person in the house outside of Emily's room. As Regina approached the door, she raised her hands to protect herself from an unwarranted attack. With an extension of one arm, she tentatively shoved the door open. A tiny stream of light gradually illuminated the bedroom's interior. For a moment, she allowed her eyes to adjust to the bending shadows. Once her vision cleared, she noticed Theodore hunched next to a mahogany dressing table.

Wearing only a towel knotted around his waist, he appeared puzzled by his own surroundings. As Regina stepped into the bedroom, her eyes immediately settled upon a dark maroon substance dripping from Theodore's fingertips. His chest and bare feet were splattered with blood.

Seeing that Theodore stood among shards of broken glass, Regina rushed over to him. Then she noticed a twisted picture frame lying on the floor. Theodore sensed Regina hovering over his shoulder, but he remained strangely quiet. As Regina edged closer to him to inspect his wounds, he mumbled something inaudible under his breath. Then, as she touched his shoulder, his voice became more distinct.

"You're not supposed to come in here, Regina."

Regina withdrew her shaking hand and stammered, "I—I heard something break." The source to Theodore's injury had already revealed itself in the remnants of what was once a framed photograph of Claire—not unlike the one Emily had hanging in her own bedroom.

"I'm okay," Theodore whispered, dispassionately.

"Your hands," Regina murmured, pointing to his fresh cuts, "they're bleeding pretty badly."

Theodore held up his hands into the light framing the ceiling. For a moment, he permitted the blood to trickle up his forearms and fall in dollops upon the rose-colored carpet. He then gestured innocently to the shattered glass gathered around his toes.

"I had a little accident," he grimaced. "Let's not make a big deal about this, okay."

Regina nodded her chin once, confirming only that she planned to obey his admonition, but not that she believed he had destroyed the photograph by mistake. Theodore then stood up, wiping the blood on the towel as he sidled by her in the doorway. She tried not to look in his eyes as he passed.

Once in the corridor, Theodore called back to her, "Are you coming, Regina?"

"I'll clean up this mess in here first," she suggested. "Don't worry, I'll lock the door when I'm finished."

Theodore did not respond with words. His eyes remained fixated down the hallway, where he distinguished his daughter's voice calling for him or Regina.

Realizing that he was in no condition to be seen by Emily, Regina rushed out into the hall and took hold of Theodore's arm. "Make sure you clean yourself up," she advised, "then go and talk to Emily. She wants all of us to go back to Kindred Woods tomorrow. I told her that I'd have to ask you first."

"Of course," Theodore responded listlessly. "I guess it can't be avoided any longer."

As Theodore uttered these words, Regina sensed the last traces of hope plummeting from his voice. The man's demise was readily clear to her while watching him lurch through the corridor. With a growing sadness, she observed the dark shadows pressing across his naked torso. He seemed to be lost in his movement, even while progressing across this familiar pathway toward the bathroom. She imagined him being swallowed by this blackness and the farther he moved away from her eyes, the more distant his silhouette became.

Regina turned back into the master bedroom and recast her gaze upon the floor, where the target of Theodore's rage laid in ruins. As she crouched on the floor, she carefully removed the shredded glass from the photo's surface. After creasing her hand across the crumpled photo, she recognized the picture.

At first glance, Regina unintentionally reacquainted herself to Claire's image, clad here in a white summer dress. Just as in Emily's photo, Claire appeared playful and sweet, bantering for the camera's lens like a would-be starlet fawning for her first role. Regina wondered why Theodore had decimated this photo, especially since it was—by her observations—one of only a handful of photographs he still possessed of his wife.

While staring intently at the photo's torn surface, Regina detected a far more different woman than she had envisioned. At close range, Regina noticed a series of scars scaling up the entire left side of Claire's body. Her skin appeared burnt and grossly discolored in places. These crude marks tracked up her left leg, then angled across her shoulders, before finally stopping beneath her throat.

At first Regina thought that this photo simply withered over time. Upon closer inspection, however, she realized that the color print revealed no other obvious defects. The imperfections belonged to Claire alone. Claire's hideous scars were real, but never discussed by anyone. Now stricken by this unsettling discovery, she shamefully lowered the photo to the floor.

As her hands trembled, Regina considered how brave Claire must have been throughout her short lifetime. Despite her disfigurements, Claire exhibited the courage to show herself in a way that mocked society's shallow compulsion to judge one's worth solely by physical beauty. This remarkable woman loved life, her husband, and endured the world's hardships with a refreshing and often unappreciated giddiness.

After removing the last bits of glass and droplets of blood from the carpet, Regina exited the bedroom and locked the door. At the corridor's far end, she saw a sliver of light creeping out from beneath the bathroom door. She listened to a sound of water methodically spraying against a porcelain surface. Beneath that shower, she imagined, stood a once-proud man, who desperately tried to wash the intolerable memories from his mind. She wondered if any man could cleanse himself from such pain. Did he really stand a chance to love again? For now, the answer to her thoughts seemed buried within the echoes of Theodore's past.

Meanwhile, Emily became comforted by the silence. Once her thoughts eased into a familiar mode, she reopened Lawrence's journal and continued to read well into the night.

CHAPTER ELEVEN

▼

JOURNAL ENTRY SIX

REPORTING A MIRACLE

In the summer of 1949 I became entangled within the concrete and steel labyrinths of a city celebrated for its brotherly love. Somewhere between this network of sidewalks and skyscrapers, I planned to forge a reputation for myself in the newspaper business. I may have entered this urban environment without a friend or viable source of income, but good fortune was well within my grasp—or so I presumed.

As an upstart, I sought to chisel my way to the top of this trade. Soon enough, the ingratitude and destitution, which had served to squelch my father's unrealized dreams, would become a distant memory in my past. I quickly learned that my vision of achieving the American Dream resembled a fantasy better reserved for a child's storybook. My first error in judgment was to make the assumption that someone in this city actually cared as much about my dreams as I did.

Editor after editor demonstrated a maniacal pleasure in dissecting my writing portfolio. In truth, I might've been more receptive to their criticism if they had shown a shred of tact. Regrettably, more than one potential employer informed me that it was neither their duty nor desire to secure a would-be writer's fragile ego.

No doubt, such words rang harshly in a young man's ears, but I cannot fault them for their honesty. In fairness to them, I went to some of the most respected and circulated publications in Philadelphia. Perhaps it was to my benefit that I eventually accepted their rejections as sound evidence of my inexperience. Without a reference or employment history to speak of, I unknowingly set myself up for failure.

Undaunted by these initial setbacks, I restructured my portfolio and devised a more attainable plan. My mission to find work resumed on the city's outskirts. A stamp-sized advertisement in a local trade paper indicated that a weekly publication was searching for a journalist. With my money and ambition running dry, I swiftly ventured to a pint-sized fishing community adjacent to the Delaware River.

South Port was home to a harbor of iron vessels and dilapidated shanties. Boats of every size, shape, and state of decay were anchored along a ribbon of ink-black water. An odor of dead fish lingered in the humid, summer air. Soon after arriving in town, I discerned that South Port was primarily home to a band of briny-skinned fisherman and their families. The men and women laboring on these docks twelve hours a day, peddled their scaly wares to vendors throughout the northeast. Though at first glance it was difficult for me to imagine my future commencing here, South Port afforded me with a chance to finally become a journalist.

South Port's only periodic newspaper—The Port Chronicle—was wedged between two fish markets on a dead-end street. A rancid aroma of unsold or shucked fish simmered under July's sun. Had I not been utterly desperate for employment, I may have reconsidered my decision to enter this cinderblock hovel.

The editor-in-chief to The Port Chronicle was named Artie Jenkins. A crude sign pinned to Jenkins's office door provided me with an immediate indication of what he expected from his fledgling employees. The sign read: Sensationalism Sells. Those two words alone best summarized Jenkins's editorial philosophy.

Being a businessman by heredity, I presumed that Jenkins's possessed an innate—or at least inherited—understanding of what sold newspapers in this town. He contended that people, especially those of the working class, skimmed the morning headlines for scathing details. In theory, Jenkins was convinced that everyone in society was tantalized by the misery of his or her fellow man. As Jenkins explained it to me, random carnage, famine, and scandalous deeds excited and terrified the average intellect.

Personally, I journeyed many miles from my home and had already been dealt and undeserved portion of displeasure in my life. Writing for a newspaper that actually supported itself through the misfortune of others almost frightened me away. But, as I said, I was a young, callow man with no other opportunities to entertain. Whether I agreed with Jenkins's perverted wisdom or not, I owed it to myself to at least try and make a difference.

When I first met Jenkins, he looked more like a downtrodden mariner than an editor. He was burly, unshaven man, with tawny-colored teeth and sweaty jowls. Though I guessed personal hygiene was not high on his list of priorities, Jenkins's addiction to cigarette tobacco proved to be his worst foe.

Upon entering his office, the smoky air singed my eyes and throat. Everything within this habitat had suffered the fallout of his pungent compulsion to smoke. The desks, chairs, ceiling, and wallpaper were lacquered with a mustard-colored haze.

Jenkins peered at me through a bubble of gray smoke, which hovered around his head like a storm cloud. His voice wheezed and crackled between every syllable. Before I introduced myself, Jenkins extended a moist, meaty hand over his desk. He then squeezed my palm with enough force to pop my knuckles.

After glimpsing at my portfolio, he chuckled and invited me to sit down. Although the smoke he emitted already impaired my vision, I eventually crouched into a vinyl chair near a half-open window. Jenkins flicked his smoldering cigarette into a cup of coffee before settling into conversation with me.

"Where does a kid like you get off thinking that he can be a journalist for a newspaper like mine?" Jenkins asked.

"Well, Mr. Jenkins, I saw your advertisement. It said that you were looking for a reporter. I figured I'd take a chance. So here I am. "

"Call me Artie," he replied, still flipping through my portfolio with a disinterested scowl. Evidently, he had assessed everything that I'd written in a matter of two minutes. "I'm gonna be honest with you, kid. Judging by what I'm looking at here, you've never had any professional training in writing for a newspaper."

"That's true, sir—I mean, Artie."

"I've been in this business long enough to weed out the pretenders from the contenders, kid," Jenkins grunted. "So why are you wasting my time?"

Jenkins tossed my portfolio on his desk and reclined backwards in his chair. Sensing that he was waiting for me to do something out of the ordinary, I stood up from my chair and assumed a confident posture. Then, in my boldest voice, I said, "Look, Artie, we can sit here for a few minutes and talk about the experience I don't have, but that's not helping either of us. I need this job, and if you have room on your staff for a person who doesn't accept failure, then I think you could do far worst than by hiring a fellow like me."

While reclining in his chair, Jenkins pulled another cigarette from his shirt's pocket. He crammed the white tube between his thin lips and snickered at my show of enthusiasm. After sparking his cigarette with a match, he huffed, "Sit down, kid. You just earned yourself five minutes."

After puffing deeply on his cigarette, Jenkins continued. "Here's the deal. Right now I'm searching for a young man to take under my wing as an apprentice. You know, kid, being a good journalist doesn't necessarily mean that you have to write like Dickens. In fact, after browsing at some of your material, I'd say that you've sacrificed clarity and substance for a shit load of purple prose."

"It's just my style, Artie," I said, somewhat listlessly.

"Well," Jenkins fumed, "part of being a stylist is to know who you're writing for. The boy I intend to hire has to be quick-witted and have an ability to breathe life into an otherwise dead story. Remember, kid, most folks nowadays don't give a crap if you can write an epic poem or not. They just want to be entertained and informed. Does that sound like something you can handle?"

After I assured Jenkins that I wouldn't disappoint him, he offered me an opportunity to prove him wrong. "I have a little test for you, kid," he stated. "Maybe it'll give me an idea on how to evaluate your potential."

"What kind of test do you have in mind?" I asked, my voice now perking with excitement.

"Keep your britches on, kid," Jenkins admonished. "What I have in mind for you is field work. Normally, you'd be responsible for finding your own leads, but I got a rare opportunity staring me in the face."

"Is this a real assignment, Artie?"

Jenkins nodded his chin and cleared his throat before saying, "If you're worth anything to this business, it'll be clear to me after just one day. So I'm offering you a chance to grab a front-page headline. Do you think you're up to it, kid?"

The idea of being treated like a potential journalist caused me to reconsider my initial impression of Jenkins. Without being prompted, I removed a small pad of paper and pen from an inner pocket in my suit coat.

"I'm ready for anything, Artie," I said. "What do you want me to do?"

"Being new to the Philadelphia area, you've probably never heard of a man named Walter Willinger, am I right?"

I shook my head and scribbled the unfamiliar name into my notepad. Jenkins continued to speak as I wrote. "Willinger has established quite a name for himself in the newspaper business over the last three months. His success, I'm almost embarrassed to admit, is due in large part because of his lack of ethics."

"Is Mr. Willinger a friend of yours, Artie?"

"Competitors can never be friends, kid—remember that. But in this case, I don't think I'd be a friend to this man even if he were peeling bananas for a bunch of monkeys. In my opinion, Willinger has crossed the line that separates fine journalism from pure trash."

"What's he done to upset you?" I asked, dropping my pen to listen more intently.

"Well, for starters, he's outselling my newspaper about five to one. Now, I don't hold grudges against men for being successful, but I do take offense by the means in which they choose to attain it."

"Has Mr. Willinger broken any laws?"

"Technically, no," Jenkins complained. "But he has broken many spirits."

"What do you mean?" I asked, picking up my pen again.

"Every man in this business should have a boundary," Jenkins said, exhaling from his cigarette. "As far as I'm concerned, Willinger has poisoned the minds of thousands of youngsters by using his editorial as a pulpit to promote atheism."

"I'm sorry," I paused, "did you say atheism?"

"That's right, kid. It seems that Willinger has carved a niche for himself in the underground. Too bad that he's creating a society full of God-less freaks in the process. Hey, I may not go to church as often as I should, but I'm not about to turn my livelihood into an anti-religious rag sheet."

"I don't blame you, Artie. I can't believe the public is actually buying his publication, much less adopting it."

"That was my first impression, too," Jenkins admitted. "I never thought that so many folks would embrace this heathen's message. I've since learned that there are a lot of people in this city who are searching for quick answers to their hardship. They're looking for something new to believe in, and God can't offer them the instant gratification they want."

When I finished jotting down Jenkins's story, I almost felt ashamed. "I suppose you want me to try and talk to Mr. Willinger—maybe get him to change his mind, or at least his editorial?"

Jenkins chortled at my initiative, but his tone was intensely sharper when he spoke again. "I'm afraid it's not that uncomplicated, kid." I detected a slight pause in Jenkins speech as he extinguished his cigarette into an ashtray. He then motioned to the pen that I held loosely between my fingers. "For your notes, understand that Walter Willinger will never change his mind."

"Then what can I do to help?" I asked, still trying to sound eager.

"Your test involves getting next to the one person who this tyrant still cares about—his teenage daughter. Her name is Belinda."

Before I asked another question, Jenkins stood up and moved out from behind his desk. The cloud of gray smoke followed him like a foul shadow as he paced across the floor. "Ten days ago, Willinger's daughter and a couple of her friends from Philadelphia went for a boat ride off the Jersey coast. Apparently at some point during their excursion, the boat caught fire."

I scribbled Jenkins's report into my notepad verbatim before saying, "Was anyone injured?"

Jenkins waddled closer to me and said, "An explosion followed—the entire boat was engulfed in flames. According to the Coastguard, the boat's captain and Belinda's two friends were killed instantly..."

"And what happened to Mr. Willinger's daughter?"

A spark of mischief ignited in Jenkins's eye as he took a seat behind his desk again. He then said, "Here's where my story gets interesting. You see, kid, although Walter tried to keep the details of his daughter's accident out of the local press, a couple of rumors leaked."

"What kind of rumors?"

"Well," Jenkins mulled. "In my opinion, Belinda should've never survived this tragedy. Consider this: when the Coastguard plucked her from the waves, they discovered that over eighty percent of her body was burnt beyond recognition. Though Belinda's flesh was entirely incinerated from her face, she was still breathing. But it was essentially a delayed death sentence for this young lady."

I sat motionless for a moment, sensing that Jenkins hadn't yet revealed his point to me. As he continued, his voice became increasingly sonorous. "Thanks to a very reliable source, I've managed to obtain a copy of the medical report filed by the attending paramedics. Their accounts confirmed that a teenage girl was in fact admitted into a burn clinic outside of Camden ten days ago."

Not knowing exactly how to react, I displayed my interest by nodding my head repeatedly. I still, however, remained perplexed toward the relevance that I might play in any of this. "Artie, it sounds to me that Mr. Willinger is trying to maintain his daughter's privacy."

"Yes, of course," Jenkins agreed. "Being a public figure, I can almost understand Walter's desire to protect his daughter. But something strange is going on in that clinic, kid. Walter's literally shut the door on the press—he's not letting anybody unauthorized in or out of the confines. He also refuses to release any information regarding his daughter's present condition."

"Do you think she's still alive?"

"You know as well as I do that injuries of this nature are almost impossible to survive. According to one nurse at the burn center, Belinda was dead on arrival, but they managed to revive her. Even so, no one thought she'd live through the night, much less ten full days."

"Why do you think Mr. Willinger is trying to hide his daughter's injuries from the press? I mean, it sounds to me like she's making progress."

"That's where you come in, kid," Jenkins said. "As we sit here, Walter's already stationed enough security guards around that clinic to oversee a small prison population. He's hired men from his own organization to ensure that the press is kept at bay. Your job is to find a way inside that clinic and figure out what the hell is going on."

"In all due respect, Artie," I asked, "how do you expect me to get past Mr. Willinger's security?"

"Kid, the best and only thing you've got going for you right now is your anonymity. Since nobody there has seen your face before, I figured that you'd have an easier time getting next to Belinda. Of course, you're gonna have to exercise a little common sense, maybe even break a few rules."

Before Jenkins had an inclination to change his mind or spark up another cigarette, I accepted the task. Within the hour, I boarded a ferry and crossed the harbor between Philadelphia and Camden. For a variety of reasons, I was both saddened and inspired by the challenge of Jenkins's assignment. During my brief transport into the Garden State, I reminisced about my own childhood, particularly focusing upon the miracle that happened to me in Pittsburgh nearly eight years prior to this day.

CHAPTER TWELVE

▼

JOURNAL ENTRY SEVEN

BELINDA'S REVELATION

Camden's Medical Clinic was a two-story structure sandwiched in the downtown business district. Its facade of white plaster and rectangular windows stood out among a hedgerow of conventional redbrick domiciles along Central Avenue. Upon my arrival, my eyes were immediately drawn to the street's center square, where a bronze statue, commemorating the Archangel Michael, gleamed in the afternoon sunlight. I paused briefly in my tracks, marveling at the angelic warrior's heroic image.

My first order of business was to preview the clinic's exterior for a possible opening. After my initial inspection, I counted six armed guards patrolling the front and back entrances. At least one dozen reporters had already been marshaled off into a designated area in an adjacent parking lot. Rather than join them in an exercise of futility, I proceeded to the building's rear loading zone in quest of an alternate passage inside. As Jenkins correctly estimated, I'd have to resort to stealth if I even had a slim hope of sharing company with Belinda Willinger on this day.

Despite the seemingly insurmountable odds unfolding before me, I was emotionally primed for this challenge. I maneuvered with relative ease to the clinic's rear and concealed myself between a convoy of trailer trucks. A mere fifty yards now separated me from the clinic's loading docks. To my advantage, only two guards watched over the shipping area. I managed to slip between them without so much as missing a step. In truth, Mr. Willinger's barricade proved to be a laughable line of defense.

I eventually made my way inside by masquerading as a member of the kitchen's staff. A simple disguise consisting of a white smock, shoes, and a carriage of meal trays afforded me with unrestricted access through the clinic's corridors. While pushing the steel cart through a web of hallways in search of Belinda's room, I realized that this venture marked my first return to a hospital since I was a boy. This notion frightened me more than I anticipated.

The polished glow of the white-tiled walls and floors rattled a chain of detestable memories within my mind. While progressing farther into the clinic, I sensed a cold sweat gathering on my neck. For a moment, I imagined the walls enclosing around my body. Fortunately, my disorientation subsided before it became too overbearing. With a revitalized urgency, I continued to pursue the girl in question.

The clinic's burn unit was located on the second floor. Since Belinda's injuries seemed too severe, I at first assumed that she was being monitored in intensive care. After my search here proved fruitless, I eventually made my way over to the recovery ward. When noticing an inordinate number of armed guards in sections A and B, I realized that her room was close. Once bypassing the last line of security in Wing C, I approached a door safeguarded by two professionally dressed men.

Judging by their tailored suits, I assumed that these guards worked for Mr. Willinger. Being hulk-like in size, I gathered that they would be the final impediments before reaching Belinda's bedside. My plan to get inside her room was insanely simple. I casually strolled up to the burly duo and informed them that Mr. Willinger had specifically ordered lunch for his daughter. Fortunately, Mr. Willinger was not inside the room, so my lie went undetected. The guards quickly inspected the contents of my food carriage before stepping aside.

I didn't really know what to expect when first walking into that airy room. Initially, I imagined seeing a young girl bandaged and horribly disfigured. My hands trembled upon the steel cart as I edged around a blue nylon curtain encircling her bed. Astonishingly, after peeling back the curtain to observe the girl, I detected no visible signs of injury on her body. In fact this raven-haired teenager, with chocolate-colored eyes and dimpled cheeks, hadn't even been issued a standard hospital gown. She was fully clothed in an ankle-length skirt, white blouse, and a pair of shiny black shoes. Her ivory skin glowed with a youthful radiance.

"I'm sorry," I said to her, "I think I'm looking for someone else."

The girl didn't reply at first, but directed her stare at the food cart. "My father never orders lunch for me," she sighed. I then watched her lift herself off the bed and defiantly stride across the floor to summon the guards.

"Wait," I pleaded. "Is your name Belinda Willinger?"

She turned and smirked at me knowingly before saying, "You don't work at this clinic, do you?" Before I had a chance to answer, she continued, "I bet you're just another reporter. Why can't you all just leave me alone?"

"You're right," I confessed, being mindful to keep my voice close to a whisper. "I am a reporter, and I was sent here to talk to you. All I'm asking for is a minute of your time—okay?"

Belinda suddenly stopped and turned away from the door. As she walked closer toward me, I sensed that she was at least partially confused by the turn of events. Instead of calling for the suited brutes, she sat in a vinyl chair beside the bed. I watched her eyes pivot to a column of windows aligning the opposite wall. She now seemed subdued by my presence. Her eyes fixated on the rays of sunlight filtering through the windows.

Realizing that she might resort to an outburst at any moment, I quickly tried to engage her in conversation. "I know a lot has happened in the last week or so, and I don't expect you to remember everything."

"I wish I could do that," Belinda said, cupping her hands beneath her chin as if in a mode of remembrance. She leaned forward in the chair, before asking me for my name and the newspaper that I represented. After I answered her truthfully, she rolled her eyes and smiled beneath the fingers of her hand.

"My father thinks that people like you are trying to ruin him. I'm surprised that you made it this far."

"I didn't come here to talk about your father, Belinda. I'm here because of you."

"I know why you're here, but I want you to understand that I don't share my father's beliefs—at least not the ones he's most known for."

I decided to take a seat on the hospital bed before saying anything further. Once situated on the mattress with my notepad in hand, I cautiously suggested, "Maybe it would be better if we talked about the accident."

"How'd I know that you were gonna ask me that?"

"I'd really appreciate it if you could tell me what happened on the boat."

Belinda's eyes pooled with tears as she hurled herself backward against the chair. After clamping her hands over her cheeks, she pushed a few strands of dark hair behind her ears. As she did this, I studied her smooth, unblemished features. Even while staring at the girl at close range, I couldn't discern any evidence to suggest that she had been recently injured.

As I marked my observations in my notes, Belinda continued in a frightful tone. "Everything was burning," she whimpered. "I—I heard screaming. My friends were crying for help, but I couldn't save them. I must've passed out after that because I really can't remember anything else too clearly."

"Do you recall being rescued from the boat at all?"

Belinda closed her eyes momentarily before offering a response. "I felt a burning sensation all over my body. I remember the flashing lights—red and yellow, maybe even blue, but I don't know who saved me. They told me it was men from the Coastguard."

I paused to compose my thoughts before asking, "Have any of the doctors explained to you what happened?"

"My friends are dead," she replied, nodding her chin once and wiping her eyes. "I don't know how I survived. I don't even know how I got in this place."

At the risk of intimidating the girl I remarked, "There were some witnesses to your accident, Belinda. They said that you were burnt very badly in the explosion, but I don't see it. Do you have memory of anything that happened after you saw the flashing lights—maybe when you fell into the water?"

Belinda shrugged her shoulders, straightened from her slouch, and then stood up from the chair. Fearing that her movement might rouse the suspicion of the men outside, I promptly stood between her and the door. She continued to pace across the tiled floor, avoiding my attempt to make direct eye contact.

"I overheard a couple of doctors talking to my father," she sobbed. "They said it was impossible for anyone to heal from third-degree burns so quickly. My father, of course, hasn't asked me what happened. It's like he's waiting for a doctor to come up with some kind of explanation, but I'm convinced that they had nothing to do with it."

A possibility that this entire medical staff had no impact on Belinda's convalescence caused me to shiver. Was it possible that they were all truly ignorant to her miraculous recovery? Realizing that my time was limited, I hurried her back into conversation.

"Belinda," I implored, "try to tell me something specific that happened after the accident. What was the first thing you saw when you opened your eyes?"

Belinda peered at me blank-faced. She struggled to extract some sense of order from the chaos in less time than I would have been able to duplicate. Her cooperation, however, was not only to offer me peace of mind; she needed to understand the truth more than I could've ever imagined.

While engrossed in a furious contest with the blurred fragments of her ordeal, Belinda's memory gradually cleared. With her fists now clenched and eyes squinted, she stammered through the agony—and then the wonderment.

"There's something else," she murmured, massaging both of her temples with her fingers. "At first I wasn't sure if it was a dream or not."

"Just say exactly what's on your mind," I advised, empathetically.

"Two nights ago, after I woke up, I saw someone standing over my bed. I think it was a man."

"A doctor?" I interjected. "Or maybe your father?"

Belinda shook her head and replied, "No. This person was a stranger. He wasn't dressed like a doctor. There was something very odd about him—almost as if he wasn't a real man."

"But you weren't dreaming, Belinda, were you?"

"I'm not positive. I remember seeing a bright light—it filled the whole room. Then, without saying a word, he touched me. I felt his hands moving across my arms and legs."

As Belinda uttered these words, I sensed my own thoughts being dragged back to an earlier time in my own life—a time when I was as innocent as this young girl was now. Did her encounter somehow interlock with my own childhood experience? Although I had little evidence to satisfy my lingering suspicion, she had no reason to misdirect me with lies. When she spoke, I fully believed that her words were as true to her today as mine had once been to me. Yet in order to convince myself that neither of us had gone insane, I needed to know more.

"Tell me," I beseeched her, "did this stranger speak to you—did he tell you his name?"

Belinda lowered her chin and closed both eyes. Forcing herself to probe deeper into the misty regions of her brain proved to be a tiresome and almost futile task.

"I can't remember, Mr. Dayton. He may have, but I'm not sure."

"It's vital that you try to remember, Belinda, otherwise I won't be able to help tell your story as it really happened."

"My God," she cried, now completely exasperated by my persistence. "I want to tell you, but I can't think right now. Everything is still muddled inside my head. I need more time."

I was sorely reminded of the one luxury that had almost expired on me—time. In order to calm her mood, I chose a less forward approach with my questioning. "Let's talk about this clinic. When did you first realize that you were here?"

Without hesitation Belinda said, "The morning after I saw the stranger. When I woke up, I felt fine—like I'd just taken a long nap. Then I noticed that my entire body was covered in gauze and tape, and they had tubes running into my arms and nose."

"But you didn't feel any pain?"

"None whatsoever. I figured someone was playing a bad joke on me. After that, I started to get mad—then I panicked."

"And it never crossed your mind that you might really be injured?"

Belinda shook her head confidently and replied, "I just kept unraveling the bandages. As I unrolled the cloth and tape from my body, I couldn't find anything wrong." She then hiked her skirt up to the top of her knees, revealing the smooth, white skin on her legs. "You see—I don't have burns anywhere on my body and no one can explain it."

Before having an opportunity to proceed any further with my inquiry, I heard the footsteps of several men entering the room. As I anticipated, our conversation was about to abruptly end. Belinda's face collapsed into a frown as her father strutted into the room with the two guards at his side.

Physically, Walter Willinger was a puny, emaciated man, and not at all what I expected from someone with such a notorious reputation. Although he tried to shroud his gaunt stature beneath a baggy suit, his recessed cheeks and bulging eyes were telltale signs of malnutrition. Yet whatever he lacked in brawn or beauty he counterbalanced with a natural flare to command his followers at will.

Within seconds upon entering the room, Willinger ordered his guards to seize me. They sprung upon me like salivating dogs. As their brooding master glared at me, I suspected that he had the room under surveillance the whole time I was here. To her credit and my surprise, Belinda made no attempt to blow my cover.

"What do you want us to do with this one, Mr. Willinger?" one guard muttered, pulling at my arms as if I was a toy.

"Nothing just yet," Willinger replied. "I'd first like to hear why our unannounced guest feels as though he's above the law."

While struggling to break free from Willinger's henchmen, I questioned, "Law? Since when is it against the law to investigate an accident?"

Willinger moved closer to me before sneering, "You should understand that I make the rules in this place. It makes me very angry when insignificant individuals like you try to capitalize in this industry at the expense of my daughter's privacy."

Rather than defy Willinger's authority with a tirade of my own, I decided to remain humble. "I apologize," I said, ruefully. "I didn't mean to violate you or your daughter's privacy. I was just trying to find out what happened—I mean, the facts, as I understand them, simply don't make any sense."

"My daughter's accident is not your concern, Mr. Dayton. I suggest that you go back to Artie Jenkins and inform him that his information was incorrect. As you can plainly see, Belinda is not injured. There is no news here, other than the fact that she is a very fortunate young lady."

"I don't mean to offend you, Mr. Willinger, but your daughter has told me a different story. Maybe we should ask her how she feels about this situation."

I must've touched a hot nerve somewhere in Willinger's brain, for he suddenly possessed the facial contortions of a lunatic. His eyes pinched into vertical slots, displaying nothing but depth and darkness as he stared at my face. With his guards still restraining my arms, I could do little else but gag as his hand swung upward, clenching my throat. Shockingly, this externally feeble man carried the grip of a constrictor. He applied enough pressure to nearly collapse my windpipe.

"Understand me," Willinger grunted, squeezing his jagged fingernails into my neck. "We don't have anything left to discuss. You will never whisper a word about what my daughter said—is that clear?"

Willinger eased his grip so that I could respond to his threat. Gasping, I said, "It's your obligation to report the truth. Whatever happened to your daughter won't remain a secret forever. People witnessed the accident, Mr. Willinger. It's now just a matter of collecting the facts."

Willinger laughed boisterously at my ignorance before saying, "Oh, Jenkins must be getting very desperate for help nowadays. Look, Mr. Dayton, I don't really want to get into this conversation with you, but didn't your boss explain to you who I am and what kind of influence I hold over this city?"

My disgust with Willinger was unmistakable when I said, "I'm aware of your atheistic beliefs, if that's what you mean."

"And how does that make you feel?"

"I don't normally judge people," I responded. "But if you must know, I think you're wrong. And I also believe that you're afraid of something—something that you can't understand. A miracle may have taken place in this room, Mr. Willinger, and that possibility scares you more than anything else in this world."

Clearly amused by what he regarded as prattle, Willinger gaily chuckled at my observation. He then instructed both of his guards to release me. After they obeyed, I stood petting at the raw finger marks imprinted on my throat. I still refused to resort to anger, if only because I knew that's what Willinger expected from me. I intently watched the man's actions in these seconds, resenting his pompousness as he sauntered beside his daughter.

"Men like you are so hopelessly lost," Willinger gloated. "I have seen far too much misery to lend my thoughts to the Biblical myths that are instilled in us as children. Don't you see, Mr. Dayton, I'm doing this city a service by redirecting their thoughts away from the notion of a god existing. They need to be enlightened, and so do you."

"How do you explain your daughter's recovery?" I countered, causing Willinger to pause in his thoughts. "The truth is, Mr. Willinger—you can't. That's why you're keeping your daughter locked up in this clinic. But you can't shield her from the spotlight forever, you know. Eventually, Belinda's miracle will be known by everyone."

A fire sparked in Willinger's eyes again; blood flowed like lava from his tainted heart. "Are you trying to make a fool out of me?" he asked, gnashing his teeth. Then he gestured to my bruised neck and said, "Haven't I made a deep enough impression on you yet?"

"This isn't about you," I said. "Look, I didn't come here to be a spokesman for God's work, but I'm willing to keep an open mind. You can deny God's miracles if you wish—if that's what you truly believe. But don't be blind either, even for the sake of your own twisted theories."

Instead of lunging at me again, Willinger calmly squatted on the bed's edge and folded his arms across his chest. "You're just a young man," he huffed tiredly. "I don't expect you to appreciate my advice—not yet anyway. There are still many lessons that you must learn, Mr. Dayton. If you're ever hoping to become a successful reporter, take my word for it: walk away with what's left of your pride, while you still can walk away."

"I still have your daughter's account of what happened," I announced, believing that Belinda might rescue me from her father's carefully measured threats. But as my eyes veered to the girl, I watched her face melt in the heat like a stick of wax wavering beneath a candle's flame. As it now stood, my only evidence remained allegiant to her father.

"I'm sorry," she whispered across the room to me. "I can't help you now."

Suddenly I felt betrayed and hopelessly inadequate in the company I stood before. The anger that Willinger had sought to expose from within me now surfaced. "Stop lying to yourself. I beg you, don't turn your daughter into what you have become!"

Before I managed to embarrass myself any further, the guards detained me again. At Willinger's request, I was briskly escorted toward the door, but not before being subjected to the impact of a fist across the side of my nose. This blind-sided punch stunned me momentarily, but I quickly regained my senses at the sound of Belinda's timid voice.

"Wait," she called to me. "The stranger I told you about—I just remembered his name."

Willinger attempted to silence his daughter by smothering her lips with the palm of his hand. "Belinda," he raved, "Mr. Dayton doesn't need to be spoon fed any more nonsense. He's only trying to hurt you."

"Let her tell me," I insisted. Now furiously wrestling with the guards, I yelled, "She knows his name!"

"His name?" Willinger asked, shrugging his shoulders. He then pivoted toward his daughter with wild eyes and said, "What is this man talking about, Belinda?"

"Tell him," I pleaded, scrambling back toward the girl with both guards still latched onto my shirtsleeves. "Tell him the name of the man who saved your life."

Willinger stood up from the bed and pushed me back into the guards' arms. "Get this idiot out of my sight," he commanded, balling his fists to strike me again.

"I'll gladly leave," I conceded, "but first let Belinda tell me his name…"

My words were now muffled under the weight of two incensed men. A flurry of fists rained down upon my face and body with the force of hurled stones. Strangely, although I suspected that this beating drew blood from my flesh, I withstood the onslaught until Belinda's statement was heard by all.

"The stranger's name was Jonathan," she murmured. "I'm sure of it now. Jonathan saved my life."

At that moment I closed my eyes with satisfaction, but did not reopen them again until the sound of howling dogs disrupted my unintended sleep. Apparently Willinger's bullies had beaten me into submission. I awoke half buried in the squalid confines of a dumpsite somewhere near Camden's fishing docks. Fish guts and other indefinable waste covered my skin. I assumed that Willinger's penchant for violence was almost as fierce as his sermons against God. But no thrashing—short of one resulting in death—could've eradicated my remembrance of Belinda's confession.

Dejected but not yet defeated, I returned to South Port with Belinda's message firmly rooted in my mind. Despite Willinger's admonitions, I intended to report the facts to Jenkins as planned. But before I relayed the news to my boss, he greeted me with a glum expression. Willinger had already contacted Jenkins and threatened him with an abuse similar to my own if he chose to print a word of my story. After Jenkins inspected my wounds, he decided that Belinda's recovery—no matter how miraculous—simply didn't justify the cost of reconstructing his face.

In compensation for my anguish, Jenkins offered me another chance to write for his newspaper. Maybe I should've been grateful, but I felt cheated and bewildered by Jenkins's cowardice. Even so, I reluctantly returned to The Port Chronicle with a renewed sense of purpose. Publicly, my attempt to disclose Belinda's tale had ended, but my private intentions didn't easily fade away.

I planned to substantiate the connection that Belinda and I shared with this ambiguous man named Jonathan. As a result of my conviction, I no longer regarded myself as a reporter performing a job. I felt obligated to discover the unknown—whatever it may be, and at the price of my own sanity if necessary.

Jonathan consumed my every thought. I sensed him huddled beside me in the dark, like a scintillating energy that was invisible to all but a few fortunate souls. From this point forward, life's purpose became an ongoing search for me. My quest to unveil this stranger's identity, however, delivered me to uncharted levels of astonishment and pain—some of which will never be fully understood or appreciated in my own lifetime.

▼

CHAPTER THIRTEEN

SEARCHING FOR JONATHAN

On the following morning, Theodore turned his jeep into a gravel-surfaced parking lot adjacent to the Sunset Motel. Since moving to Wakeland, he had driven past this dilapidated landmark nearly every day without so much as offering it a glance or second thought. To some, the cedar-shake structure served as a humble reminder to Wakeland's roots. Most people, including Theodore, considered it a defect at an intersection of flourishing farmlands.

Once stepping outside his vehicle, Theodore gazed across the parking area with discontent. Empty bottles of brandy and crushed beer cans dotted the muddy landscape. An assortment of undesirable drifters had gradually transformed this motel and its reputation into a seedy playground. The rubbish marked the demise of a once-proud establishment, and reminded Theodore why he had purposely avoided it until now.

No trace of sunlight reflected in the sky today. Oil-colored clouds coiled in serpentine patterns across the region, squeezing the morning's delicate glow into submission. A dank chill hung in April's air. Storm clouds converged between the distant hills, just beyond a hedgerow of grain silos. In the farther distance, beyond the motel's decaying shadow, Theodore noticed the spire of Wakeland's church piercing the pending darkness.

Theodore reluctantly proceeded toward the motel, disregarding an impulse to make better use of his time. He almost regretted phoning Belinda Willinger to arrange this appointment, but Father Quinn's words had reverberated in his mind all evening. Maybe the old priest knew what Theodore needed after all.

As Theodore neared a crumbling, slate walkway, he detoured onto a wooden porch that wrapped around the motel's foundation. This platform, he surmised, had probably once served as a clandestine meeting place for a congregation of wandering hearts. Now, its rotted, unpainted woodwork swayed like an old ship on a squall-struck sea.

At the farthest end of the porch, an elder man sat motionless in a lawn chair. After looking at the man, Theodore presumed he was in his late sixties. Once their eyes met, the older man hoisted his plump backside out of the vinyl chair. He sported a wrinkled suit jacket, dark trousers, and red fishing cap. His face was covered in an unkempt beard. Most conspicuously, he held a folded comic book beneath his armpit. Obviously, he appeared to be waiting for the arrival of someone of great importance to him.

"Excuse me," Theodore announced to the codger while glancing at the napkin that he had tucked in his palm. "I'm looking for a woman by the name of Belinda Willinger. I'm supposed to meet her here this morning."

Twitching slightly, the older man hobbled closer to Theodore so that he could study his face. "You're Theodore Dayton?" he questioned.

"That's right," Theodore said. He then remembered that Belinda had mentioned another older man would be joining them. "You must be Mr. Gibbon."

The old man nodded his chin and extended his hand before saying, "Please, call me Danny. And thank you for responding to our invitation so promptly. Belinda was almost certain that you wouldn't come."

"Well," Theodore sighed, "I hope you're not wasting my time."

"Maybe we'd be more comfortable if we talked inside," Danny suggested, gesturing to the door behind him.

After following Danny inside, Theodore was immediately repulsed by the room's musty interior. The décor consisted of two single beds, one dressing table, and a small television propped up on an aluminum cart in the corner. A variety of paintings, depicting seascapes and forests, hid the cracked plaster on the olive-colored walls. At the room's far end, near the bathroom door, the light of a single lamp illuminated particles of dust and cobwebs rimming the ceiling and floors.

Theodore turned his attention to a blank-faced woman perched on a folding chair near the room's only window. Although she made no facial expression to display her satisfaction, Belinda was elated by Theodore's arrival. Still, both Danny and she had reservations about the man's identity; they wanted to be absolutely certain that he was who Father Quinn claimed him to be.

"I'm very sorry about the death of your father, Theodore," Danny started. "I hope that your mother is getting the support that she no doubt needs during this difficult time."

Theodore smirked before replying, "Well, since my mother has been dead for over thirty-five years, it'd be impossible for me to know."

Humbled by Theodore's frankness, Danny said, "Forgive me, Theodore. I didn't mean to offend you. Belinda and I just wanted to make sure that you are Lawrence's son."

"Believe me, Danny," Theodore huffed, "I wish I was lying. I'm sure Father Quinn already told you that Lawrence and I were practically strangers."

Danny bowed his head before crouching onto the bed's mattress. "I'm sure your estrangement was very complicated. Do you want to talk about that at all?"

Theodore's attention quickly diverted to Belinda. He noticed that she wore a black garment with a white-laced shawl wrapped around her shoulders. The old woman's frail wrists and ankles stuck out from beneath the dark layers of material.

While glaring at the woman, Theodore's anger and stress fused simultaneously. "You told me over the phone that you knew Lawrence Dayton," he snapped. "And I told you that I didn't want to make a big deal about our little chat here today. If you know anything about my father, now is the time to tell me, Miss Willinger."

Belinda peered at Theodore with sadness teeming from her dark eyes, for she didn't precisely know how to alleviate the man's anger at this moment. Fortunately, Danny learned to play the role of a mediator far better than his thus far silenced partner demonstrated.

"I realize that this is a confusing time for you," Danny said gently. "But if you settle down, I'm sure we'll be able to accomplish something worthwhile here this morning."

"I'm as settled as I'll ever be in regard to my father," Theodore grumbled. Even as Theodore uttered these words, he knew that he was not being honest with himself. He of course yearned to know more about Lawrence, but his inability to concede to this fact caused him to become increasingly hostile.

"Maybe we can begin by talking about a specific memory of your father," Danny suggested. "Surely, you must have some remembrance of him."

"No," Theodore answered, dispassionately lowering his head. "The man left my mother when I was still an infant. My mother rarely spoke about him when she was alive. To be honest, I don't know why he wanted to find me, other than a possibility that he knew he was dying and had nowhere else to turn."

"What I find interesting," Danny mused, "is your strong feelings toward Lawrence. Even though he abandoned you when you were still too young to know what a father was, you felt obligated to see that he received a proper burial. Why would you do that for a man who was no closer to your heart than a stranger?"

Theodore shrugged his shoulders before responding, "I'm not sure. Maybe I wanted to prove a point."

"To yourself or him?" Danny asked, curiously unrolling his comic book as he leaned forward on the bed.

Before Theodore examined his motives, Belinda used what remained of her vanishing strength by standing up from the chair. She reached out for Theodore like a blind person patting the air for obstructions. Then, once finding Theodore's hand, she gently rested her palm into his.

Theodore's initial reaction was to pull away from her uninvited touch, but he hesitated. Within seconds he sensed a warm energy exuding from Belinda's fingertips; it felt like a warm gush of water flowing over the coldness in his bones. Amazingly, the hostility that had already started to resurface within Theodore now began to dissipate.

Belinda's voice sounded as soothing as the energy that dispersed from her fingertips. "There's a lot of pain inside of you," she whispered, massaging her hands further along Theodore's forearms. "It's the sort of agony that often comes with unanswered questions."

"You don't know me well enough to assume anything," Theodore remarked.

"I don't blame you for being upset," Belinda continued, "but you should understand that your father wasn't an evil man—"

"He just didn't let anyone get too close to him," Danny interjected.

Theodore searched Danny's face for a hint of deceit or any visible expression that would have exposed his intentions. He then pivoted toward Belinda and analyzed her.

"Tell me," Theodore demanded, "why are you two so interested in my father's life?"

Belinda urged Theodore to ease down into the chair where she had previously sat. After pressing on his shoulder, she sensed his resistance. "We're here to help each other," Belinda said, "and I suppose we can only fairly do that by explaining our connection to your father."

"We don't expect you to believe us now," Danny noted. "All we want you to do is listen."

"This is getting too weird for me," Theodore said, staring at Belinda's crinkled face. He detected her eyes penetrating his own, and through the reflection of her pupils, he saw his own sorrow manifesting.

Sensing that Theodore was weakening to her request, Belinda grabbed both of his shoulders and asked, "Do you feel that, Theodore? Many years ago I experienced the presence of something miraculous. It is not a gift that can be bought, bargained for, or even wished upon. Yet it is this energy that has enabled me to continue, just as it had once allowed your father to continue his quest."

"I don't know what the hell you're talking about," Theodore said, trying to break free from Belinda's grasp.

"When I touch your skin, Theodore, I can feel that you're not yet a part of our connection. Your skin is cold, and so is your heart."

Belinda now stood quivering before Theodore, almost collapsing to the floorboards as the warmth emitting from her palms caused her hands to burn. "Okay, Miss Willinger," Theodore conceded, if only to spare the old woman a stroke. "What do you want from me?"

Realizing that Belinda was too overwrought with emotion to continue, Danny expounded upon what he deemed to be true. He paused in his thoughts while searching for the right words to convey his feelings.

"We are convinced that our lives have been significantly altered by a force that is not part of the world as you see and understand it."

"You're still not making any sense to me, Danny," Theodore complained. "How can I help you?"

Without responding to Theodore's question, Danny continued with his explanation. "When Belinda touched you a moment ago, Theodore, you felt something—didn't you?"

"I felt warm," Theodore admitted, now rubbing his fingers against his palm. "Is this some kind of trick?"

"It's no trick," Danny confessed. "It is an energy granted to those who have experienced a miracle in their lifetime. Belinda and your father have both been blessed by a messenger from God."

Theodore had hoped that their discourse didn't sway toward his own dismissal of God. He assumed that Father Quinn had persuaded the old couple to speak on his behalf. "Quinn doesn't know when to quit," he huffed. "Why can't that old man just leave me alone?"

"Theodore," Danny said, "Father Quinn didn't send us to you. We have come on our own freewill in hope that you can help us learn more about your father."

"Funny," Theodore cackled in disgust, "I came here under the impression that you knew more about the guy than I did."

Belinda's voice suddenly returned to conversation, this time a frenzied edge invaded her tone. "Don't you see?" she declared. "Our connection to Lawrence was only the beginning of something much more important. We're still on a quest to discover the truth."

"You've come to the wrong man," Theodore countered. "I don't have any idea of what you two are jabbering about."

"It is our opinion," Danny proclaimed, "that an angelic force dramatically influenced your father's choices throughout his lifetime. If this is true, then he may have had a direct impact on the quality of your life as well."

Theodore now speculated that this conference was an ill-timed joke. Undermining this theory, however, was the fact that neither of the would-be comedians showed a trace of mockery. Contrarily, their eyes remained fixated and their lips pressed together with outright dignity.

Theodore attempted to conceal his agitation with this response: "Look, you two seem like decent people, and your intentions are most likely harmless. But if you knew anything about my life, you'd realize that you're wasting your time."

"I was saved from death, as was your father," Belinda said in one breath.

Still unconvinced, Theodore hastened for the door. Before he managed to leave, Danny blurted out the incredible event that occurred to Lawrence in Pittsburgh when they were children. Theodore paused long enough in the doorway to listen to Danny's story, but was still indifferent to the matter.

Belinda's encounter in Camden when she was a teenager prompted Theodore to move back inside. Despite the serendipity that intertwined their lives with his father, Theodore heard no evidence to advance the notion that they had been healed by divine intervention.

"Do you think that Lawrence left something with me that may help you in your search?" As Theodore presented this question, he recalled the journal that Emily received on the day of Lawrence's funeral. Apparently, neither Danny nor Belinda had gotten close enough to Lawrence to intercept this memoir.

Danny took a moment to recollect his thoughts before continuing. "After Lawrence died, we asked the caretaker of this motel if he had noticed anything peculiar about Lawrence during his brief stay here. According to him, Lawrence spent many hours during his last weeks writing longhand in a notebook of some kind."

Theodore attempted to look surprised by this knowledge before saying, "Really? Maybe he was writing a novel?"

"Perhaps," Belinda said suspiciously, "but whatever project he devoted so much of his final days to has disappeared from his unclaimed possessions. We've checked with the caretaker, local authorities, and the coroner's office. Strangely, they haven't found anything that resembles a manuscript."

"I'm sorry," Theodore said, shaking his head with the lie. "I wish I could be more helpful."

"Are you certain that you haven't found anything, Theodore?" Danny asked.

"Danny, if my father really shared some kind of a connection with you and Miss Willinger, why do you think he had access to details regarding the whereabouts of whatever or whoever it is you're searching for?"

Danny lowered his voice to a whisper before saying, "Lawrence was ahead of us in his thoughts, Theodore. I don't have all the research complete, but I'm convinced that your father discovered a gateway to transcend the barrier that keeps most of us blind to our own spirituality. He knew things that no one else can answer—things that may very well change the fate of this world."

"Do you really expect me to believe this garbage?" Theodore chortled. The disgust now magnified in his eyes when he said, "You two have a lot of nerve coming to me with this crap."

"Why are you so afraid to see?" Belinda cried out to Theodore. "I understand your reservations," she went on, "but please don't stand here and laugh at us. We know that Jonathan once saved our lives, and he may be kind enough to one day save you from self-destruction."

"Who the hell is Jonathan?"

"That is what he called himself," Belinda revealed. "But he not really a part of mankind—not like you and me."

"It's a rather common name," Danny added, "but I suppose that's the point of it. Jonathan was an angel created in heaven, and never possessed a mortal soul."

"Come on," Theodore ranted. "Whatever happened in your past isn't worth talking about now. My father is dead, and I'm not so sorry that he is. Lawrence Dayton left my life forty-eight years ago. Even if I did believe in angels—and I don't—I doubt that one would ever choose to save my father's life."

Sensing that Theodore's composure was about to deteriorate, Belinda refrained from engaging in a heated debate with him. While gazing deeper into the man's eyes, she now understood that he had sustained far more than a loss of a father. The thoughts of her own childhood raced back into her mind, causing a tear to form in her eye.

"I'm afraid that we've come to a point where I must ask you a very personal question, Theodore," Belinda announced. She paused while Theodore paced back over to the door. She then asked, "Do you believe in God and heaven?"

A chill tapered across Theodore's spine as he fumbled for the words that might have relieved his feelings. Yet as he leaned against the doorway's frame, peering listlessly into the silvery horizon, he dreaded his own conclusion. Icy shivers combed the length of his extremities, numbing him to the bone. This coldness enveloped his thoughts as well, compelling him to retreat to a place within his mind where all faith in God and humanity had long since withered.

"I guess everybody's got a point where they stop believing in miracles," Theodore muttered, still looking at the dark clouds.

As Belinda stooped away from him, Theodore presumed that he had revealed enough about himself to ward her off forever. After a moment, she reclaimed her seat beside the bed and looked out the window through tear-stained eyes.

Though Belinda was almost resigned to letting Theodore leave, Danny was not yet finished. He expressed his concern to Theodore by saying, "Whether you believe in miracles or not, may I safely assume that you've at least read about angels?"

"Like you, I've read many fairy tales," Theodore answered. "But if you're claiming that an angel saved my father's life, then I'd say that you've lost your mind."

"Theodore, the angel that I speak of cannot be seen by everyone. I myself have never seen Jonathan, but that doesn't make me less any inclined to believe that he—and angels like him—may actually exist."

"It just doesn't sound logical," Theodore persisted. "Don't you understand what kind of a man my father was? He wasn't worthy of any good fortune."

"Why does it make you so angry to consider the thought that your father may have been in contact with a heavenly force?"

"This is crazy," Theodore cackled. "I wish you could hear how ridiculous you sound, Danny. It's almost embarrassing."

"There's no reason to be ashamed, Theodore," Danny said. "I wouldn't be telling you this right now unless I had facts about Lawrence's life to draw from."

Theodore could have simply walked away and disregarded everything that was unveiled to him this morning. Instead of leaving, he wandered outside onto the porch. A cool rain dropped from the clouds, peppering his forehead with refreshing moisture.

Danny permitted Theodore a moment to gather his composure before joining him on the porch. Once outside, Danny leered out across the muddy pastures in the direction where Theodore focused his eyes.

"Most of us have a limited understanding of angelic forces," Danny explained. "When I was a boy, I remember being as cynical as you are now."

"You still haven't told me why you think my father had communications with an angel."

"Before 1963, I had nothing to base my theory on," Danny admitted. "However, that was before I visited with your mother."

Theodore turned his head sharply toward Danny and asked, "What did my mother have to do with any of this?"

"She was married to Lawrence. Shortly before her death, I made it a point to go and see her."

"My mother never really knew that man," Theodore fumed.

"Oh, she knew him better than most people," Danny confirmed. "You see, Theodore, I never expected to become so involved with Lawrence's visions. But your mother's story changed my mind."

"What did she say to you?"

"As you know, your father left you and your mother in 1952, apparently while you were still an infant. What you may not know, however, is that Lawrence had been suffering from a series of inexplicable nightmares for months prior to his departure."

"Nightmares? Not as bad as mine, I bet."

"A week or so before that time," Danny continued, "Lawrence forced himself into becoming an insomniac. He was afraid to go to sleep. Your mother told me how he used to stand in front of the bathroom mirror for hours, literally without blinking his eyes."

"He left us with nothing," Theodore said, gritting his teeth. "How could any decent man do that to his own flesh and blood?"

"I can't respond to all of your father's motives," Danny said, "but I'm guessing that he was terrified of something—something that only he could comprehend."

"No," Theodore refuted. "He was just a selfish bastard."

"Though Lawrence left many of his intentions unanswered, he did leave one substantial message behind. According to your mother, he scrawled it in red lipstick upon the bathroom's mirror."

"Why would he do that?"

Danny shrugged his shoulders and hobbled closer to Theodore. "I can only presume that it was his way of describing his visions."

"You said it was a message. What did it say?"

"He wrote it backwards, but when reversed and read from left to right, it said: Isaiah 6:2."

Theodore repeated this in his mind before saying, "It sounds like a passage from the Bible—so what does that mean?"

"It's a reference from The Old Testament," Danny explained. "Those familiar with Scripture understand the relevance of this entry."

"Maybe you can help me figure out what it is you're talking about," Theodore said, withholding an urge to scream.

"The Bible speaks of numerous angels throughout the Old and New Testaments, but in the hierarchy of angelic forces, it is careful to cite the most powerful angels by a specific name only once."

"I'm afraid my Bible skills aren't what they used to be. You're still talking gibberish to me."

Danny exhaled a deep breath before presenting his next question. "Have you ever heard of the Seraphim?" After Theodore shook his head in bewilderment, Danny went on with his explanation. "In the second half of the eighth century BC, the prophet Isaiah recorded the emergence of six-winged angels. He is said to have witnessed these seraphs in a dazzling light in heaven. According to Scripture, these are the angels who sit closest to God; they preside over His kingdom. Such angels rarely intervene in human affairs."

As Danny spoke, Theodore's hands gradually raised against his own face. His fingers shivered with rage as he spoke. "What does any of this have to do with my father, Danny?"

"Don't you see, Theodore? Your father may have had a vision of a seraph. It is my belief that Jonathan may very well be this angel in question."

"You sure jump to conclusions, don't you?" Theodore grimaced. "Did you ever stop to think that Lawrence might've just written that jargon to get a rise out of people like you?"

"Your father wasn't an openly religious man," Danny said. "In fact, your mother had to drag him into church. Why would he write such a message at a time in his life when he seemed virtually incoherent?"

"I don't know," Theodore said, as he paced to the end of the porch. "But I think I've heard enough from you, Danny. Let's just forget we ever met—okay?"

As Theodore started off the porch, Belinda pulled herself away from her chair and joined Danny outside the motel. Rain dappled against her wrinkled cheeks as she called for Theodore's attention.

"Don't let God's light slip from your heart," she sobbed. "I've seen what can happen to a man who thinks as you do. My own father died with a bitter and broken soul. He resisted the truth until his dying breath. You deserve a better fate than that."

"I'm sorry, Miss Willinger," Theodore said without turning around. "We have nothing more to discuss."

A craving for seclusion now encompassed Theodore's thoughts. Whenever feeling cornered, he looked to Wakeland's rural roads for his peace. The emptiness of these winding trails sheltered him from reality for a while. Within moments after leaving the motel, he reclaimed a position behind the steering wheel inside his jeep.

Danny and Belinda watched quietly as the jeep sped off, serving up bits of gravel and mud in its bid to reclaim the open roads. While driving away, Theodore never glanced back to witness the Sunset Motel shrinking behind a shield of fog and rain.

"Do you think he'll be able to help us?" Danny asked Belinda.

"We'll give him another day or so," she replied, tilting her head toward the clouds. The rain fell more intensely now, but not hard enough to turn the old woman's face away from the sky. "He may be more like his father than he yet realizes."

Theodore still had two commitments to fulfill on this morning, one of which was unforeseen until this moment. As promised, he planned to accompany Regina and Emily to the hospital in Kindred Woods upon his return from the Sunset Motel. But now, with this most recent confrontation buzzing in his mind, he felt obligated to drive back to Wakeland's cemetery.

Despite the rain plummeting from the clouds in dime-sized droplets, Theodore stumbled through the muck and soggy pastures to reach the graveyard's wrought-iron gate. He shivered compulsively during these seconds, partly because of his drenched clothing, but mostly because of the tombstones that laid crumbled before his eyes.

Many of these granite markers had endured generations of decay. Theodore approached his wife's headstone with a sense of trepidation. Before Lawrence's funeral, he hadn't visited the graveyard in over six months. He bent over Claire's graveside and read the chiseled epitaph through trembling lips. With the storm's wind whirling in his ears, he dropped to his knees and pushed his hands through the soil and pale grass. Tears from his eyes mixed with the muddy puddles on the earth.

After Theodore pulled himself from this place, his eyes pivoted to the freshly turned dirt where his father had been planted. A flat stone plaque, bearing the inscription L.D. (1930-2000) was all that remained for this world to witness. Theodore edged closer to the grave, ignoring the mud that smothered his pants and shoes. While staring at the mound of soil, he saw something peculiar forging its way through the dirt.

To Theodore's amazement, a patch of white flowers had sprouted between pieces of rock and soil. An emergence of wild poppies wouldn't have seemed so astonishing to him, if it were not for the fact that no other flowers of any variety grew within this cemetery.

As Theodore stared more closely at the poppies, he suspected that they might have been a gift from Danny or Belinda. After wedging his fingers into the wet earth to undermine the flowers, however, he discovered something that he didn't expect to find—roots.

A cold wind still hammered the grounds, reminding Theodore that most fair-weather flowers couldn't withstand such harsh conditions. Maybe someone had taken time to plant these poppies. Or perhaps these blossoms had managed to defy nature and flourish on their own. Whatever the explanation, Theodore couldn't examine it with any seriousness now. He had other business to attend to on this morning.

Although Wakeland's cemetery was less than ten miles from the Dayton's home, rain had only just begun to deflect off the pine and maple trees on Theodore's property. Inside the house beneath the covered porch, Emily waited for her father to return.

Regina was kind enough to push Emily's wheelchair out onto the porch so that she had an unobstructed view of the hillside. Emily enjoyed watching the clouds creep across the hills. Sometimes she'd imagine the storm clouds transforming into waves; such formations reminded her of an undulating sea. Like breakers crashing against a shoreline, these clouds rammed against the verdant slopes before devouring it within a silvery mist.

Now consumed by these thoughts, Emily reached beneath her wheelchair and removed Lawrence's diary from a pouch. She opened the notebook to the crucifix, which marked her progress. As the storm drew nearer, she delved deeper into unraveling mystery set before her eyes.

CHAPTER FOURTEEN

▼

JOURNAL ENTRY EIGHT

DOVES AND DARKNESS

Over the years, I've studied virtually nothing to help me accurately distinguish between a dream and a nightmare, but the next phase of my life consisted of a series of images that pushed me to the brink of insanity. I have elected to describe these sleep-induced encounters as a way to rationalize my eventual choice to put an end to them.

These dreams of tranquility and turmoil meshed as one. Furthermore, I had difficulty separating the illusions from reality. The first vision occurred approximately six months after my encounter with Walter Willinger. Up until this time, I dreamt about nothing of particular substance. Sometimes

I'd see odd shapes or colors flashing behind my eyelids, but the details always eluded me upon awakening.

Initially I believed that my childhood illness had severely damaged an area within my brain that disallowed the remembrance of subconscious thought. But the night terrors that I now speak of marked an uninvited change within myself. Suddenly I began to sort through the vagaries and make sense out of what no one else could image to be real.

It was though a spiritual force had wrenched the soul from my sleeping body and deposited my thoughts into a surrealistic environment. A tunnel, churning with ribbons of blue and gold light, furnished a gateway toward the center of a vast timberland. I remember kneeling beneath the arched branches of hundreds of pine trees. The trunks and limbs of these wooden pillars shadowed the ground from which they grew.

After adjusting my thoughts to the forest's pristine environs, I heard a sound of wings fluttering in the air between the trees. Through the lower branches, nearly one hundred feet from where I knelt, I watched a drove of white-feathered birds' flit from tree to tree, as if waltzing with a tepid wind. These birds cooed gaily, like children reveling in play. I watched them in silence, never wishing to disturb their fancy flight into the unknown.

Once my presence was revealed, the birds descended to forest's floor and encircled me with a mirthful dance upon air. At close range, the plumage of each bird appeared whiter than billowy clouds. Though I didn't presume to be a specialist at identifying such species, I immediately labeled these birds as turtledoves.

For reasons yet unclear to me, I felt invigorated by these docile creatures. In flight they proved to be acrobatic adventurers, sensing that I wouldn't interfere while they glided within inches of my grasp. I wanted to touch their flickering wings, if only with a fingertip to satisfy my fascination with their fluid display of animation. Yet in spite of my curiosity, I didn't lift a hand or utter a word as the doves ascended skyward in tandem.

Before I had an opportunity to fully celebrate this moment, the tranquility of my retreat dissolved into darkness. A sudden wind whisked through the pine trees, inciting the doves to scatter aimlessly into air. These birds feared a force that I could not yet see or comprehend. Within seconds, a chill encompassed this woodland; this was followed by a presence of another form of unwelcome energy.

While squinting through a trail of wind and dust, I witnessed a jagged-winged apparition casting its shadow upon the pines. For lack of a better description, I've chosen to brand my mind's invader as a dark fiend. After entering the forest, it forwarded a demonic screech that caused the ground to quake. Though I sought to depict this wraith in physical terms, it possessed no constant features. Its eyes were like two columns of gray light; they pierced the summer foliage upon impact. Adding to the fiend's mysteriousness, it had the capacity to mutate its shape and blend with the smothering darkness now fixed before my eyes.

I cannot explain precisely why I dreamt of this entity. It sprang upon me so quickly, and seemed as inevitable as the moon interchanging with the sun. Although the better side of my mind vied to wish it away like a fomenting illness, the weaker part of me allowed it to fester and develop as voraciously as any cancer. I had truly become imperiled by my own concocted horrors. All I could do to remedy my madness was passively observe this filthy foe reign over all that was once clean.

Within seconds, I listened as the doves began to cry to one another. The sound of their sorrow filled my head with a forlorn melody. And then, the fiend descended from its place in the sky and disintegrated the forest's green canopy as swiftly as fire burning dry leaves. Now fully exposed to their nemesis, the doves dispersed into the sky's crimson glow. Their efforts to flee, however, proved to be a futile exercise. One by one, the white-winged creatures dropped languorously from the sky. A poison that I could not discern afflicted the doves. None of them survived.

I tried to help them, but the birds' demise could not be altered. I didn't possess the power to intervene or evade my own thoughts. Finally, after what seemed like hours of relentless torture, the doves' muffled cries became silent. Literally hundreds of these birds lay dead in the soil.

Though it was impossible for me to recite and exact method of execution, I knew that the shrouded fiend had destroyed these doves without regret.

For fifteen consecutive nights this identical scene unreeled in my mind with the consistency of a recording device stuck on replay. I strove to avoid sleep, thinking that depriving my body of its natural rhythms might encourage this dementia to dissolve or at least lapse into dormancy.

Typically, I'd awaken from these nightmares by forwarding a bellowing cry. Without fail, an icy sweat coated my brow, trickling its salty trail between my pursed lips. The bed sheets beneath my body often felt moist, too. Sometimes, while the darkness still lingered in my bedroom, I'd be too afraid to drag myself from bed in order to wash the stench from my flesh. Regrettably, I chose to wallow in my own filth rather than confront the blackness that separated me from the showering stall at the corridor's end.

As it was with most nightmares, the images gradually faded when morning's sunlight emerged through my window. Still, I shivered like I hadn't done since childhood. After several minutes of monitoring the rhythm of my heartbeat, I gradually regained ability to reason. Though the visions temporarily escaped me during daylight, I realized that there was more for me to do than simply wait for the next dream to occur.

Before the start of the sixteenth evening, I discovered the insidious answer to my restlessness. Ironically, it had been staring me in the face for weeks. I was just too blind to read between the lines until now. The truth made itself known to me in The Port Chronicle's headline. It read: 'Unexplained Deaths at Pine Grove Continue'. The relevance of these words changed my entire outlook. Everything that I had accomplished up until this moment seemed incredibly unimportant. With my new focus intact, I sought to put an end to the misery at large.

Pine Grove, a privately funded hospital for children, was located outside of the Pine Barrens in southern New Jersey. According to ongoing reports, the hospital had involuntarily established an infamous reputation for itself in the last year or so. Shockingly, this once-renowned facility had undergone a rash of unexplained deaths among its young patients. All total, twenty-eight children—all under the age of twelve—had died here in the last fifteen months. Initially, I was attracted to this story since the news first surfaced, but Jenkins promptly gave the assignment to another reporter.

Like many prone to skepticism, I wasn't completely satisfied with the answers that Pine Grove's personnel had offered to the public. The hospital dealt primarily with terminally diagnosed children, but it typically housed patients whose diseases had gone into remission. For example, before the recent spell of misfortune, Pine Grove had only averaged about four deaths per year. I believed that there was a hidden cause for this string of casualties, and it had nothing to do with the diseases.

Perhaps I let my nightmares get the best of me, but I sensed a connection between Pine Grove's fifteen months of decline and my equal number of nightmares. Out of all of the information thus far disclosed, two words registered in my mind as the most uncanny—Pine Grove. I impulsively thought of the trees in my dreams. Could it all be so simple? Had I been covertly summoned to Pine Grove through a tapestry of symbolic premonitions?

To a rational mind, my forthcoming analogy may have sounded absurd. Even if there was some odd coincidence between the location of the hospital and the setting of my visions, how did the doves and dark fiend fit into the framework of my resolutions? Admittedly, I had little else to base my theory upon but intuition; that still didn't make it any less true to me.

The doves in my dreams represented an innocence and vulnerability that could easily be linked to the children's plight at Pine Grove. Just as the birds had endured an unprovoked slaughter, the patients seemed equally prone to suffering at the hands of an unknown force. My most daunting task was to tie the children's deaths to something or someone within the confines of that hospital. Beside myself, no one had yet dared to fathom the likelihood of an immoral person being at the helm of this controversy. I believed that the tormentor, like the dark fiend in my nightmares, resided very close to those children's hearts. As you may remember, I had been trapped under the sinful watch of such a man before, and recognized the danger of confiding blindly in those who seemed most trustful.

Eventually I convinced myself that the only way to expose and stop the murdering was to visit Pine Grove. Of course I still had the unenviable chore of talking Jenkins into accepting my suspicions as sound judgment. Without any physical evidence to present, I didn't expect Jenkins to listen to me with any seriousness.

Jenkins was less than thrilled with the idea of me becoming even remotely involved in Pine Grove's troubles. He admonished me about the pitfalls that he and other notable newspapers encountered during their own investigations. Apparently the hospital was doing its best to conceal the dubious facts. I contended that the other reporters had failed because they sought information from the wrong people. If they really wanted to know the truth about what was happening in Pine Grove, they should have spoken to the primary source—the children.

I don't know if Jenkins really expected me to improve upon what had already been written, but he was willing to give me a second chance. I presumed that he was still brooding about my confrontation with Walter Willinger. For me, this particular matter had nothing to do with achieving professional accolades. It had become an entirely personal goal of mine to protect those children who were still alive.

Within a day after my conference with Jenkins, I was offered one train ticket to Pine Grove Hospital. Following my arrival at South Port's train station, I determined that I had another fear to conquer. Though I didn't dwell on its impact until seeing the train, a prospect of traveling by railroad terrified me. Suddenly, thoughts of my childhood transport to Pittsburgh caused me to tremble. The flashbacks of my uncertain destiny whirled through my mind.

Although it was the middle of winter, the train's passenger cabin was hot and crowded. Cigar smoke suspended in yellow spindles from the ceiling and redwood paneling. Stone-faced men and women sat shoulder to shoulder, scanning their magazines and dime-store novels with empty gazes. A few rambunctious children managed to open a section of square windows at the cart's rear. They showed enough common sense to poke their heads outside for a breath of January's crisp air.

I found my seat next to a female passenger. At that moment, I suspected it wasn't the train by itself that instigated my anxiety. She was a properly dressed lady, with auburn hair and green eyes. Yet despite her supple skin and dimpled cheeks, I couldn't help but to see the face of my mother through her expressions. I found her feminine ploys and voice grossly similar as well. While leering at her nubile features, I became gravely ill.

The woman smiled and offered me her hand as a greeting, but I extended no such formalities. Instead, I twitched at the touch of this stranger's knee against mine. I then imagined the cruel face of Lily Dayton taunting me with her indifference, just as she had exhibited during our trip to Pittsburgh when I was a boy. I silently cursed this woman. I despised the sweet scent of her perfume, and the way she smothered her lips beneath a gloss of seduction.

At this time, I realized that the scars inherited in childhood never truly dissolved with age. A beautiful woman sat beside me on this train, but I refused to embrace her advances. Sadly, I couldn't yet look beyond my haunted memories. Despite all the years of convincing myself that the past could never tarnish my future, I still lacked the most basic emotion that all good men cherished—the ability to love.

As the train chugged out of the station and made way northeast, the woman beside me gradually discovered that I wasn't in the mood for idle chatter. In a bid to redirect my concentration, I shifted my head toward the train's window. A cold, bosky landscape soon encompassed us in our travels. While peering wide-eyed across the snow-laden wilderness, a distinct serenity overwhelmed me. Fresh snow blanketed the leafless forests and surrounding pastures. I marveled at the sapphire sky and how unchallenged it appeared when matched against the grays of winter.

Apart from the steel rails gutting a rude path between this corridor of timber and rock, I sensed the natural world flourishing out here. It was if God's pulse grew stronger in the regions where men did not yet dare to tread. As the train neared the Pine Barrens, I beheld an age-old labyrinth of emerald spears jutting forth from the white cloaked earth.

It didn't seem likely that a hospital would've shared space alongside such pristine offerings, but as certain as blue skies fade to black, the field of evergreens eventually gave way to the shades of industrialization. In fairness to the artisans and architects, Pine Grove's exterior had been painstakingly crafted to blend into its chosen environment.

Working with the commitment to keep Pine Grove Hospital truly unattainable to outsiders, only one railroad led directly to the facility. No paved roads or highways were constructed near the hospital. The main structure, although contemporary in its A-frame design, cast an aesthetically satisfying shadow across the upland forests. As I exited the train, I noticed a caravan of jeeps and retired military vehicles lining the entire campus. Beside each of these vehicles, a duo of armed security guards awaited to escort would-be visitors to the hospital's registration center.

The hospital's front entrance was well within a stone's throw from the train station's platform, but confirmation from security proved to be a nonnegotiable procedure. One blue-uniformed guard directed me to a security den, where I was thoroughly frisked and then ushered between a passage of automatic doors.

Despite its rustic backdrop, Pine Grove was still a medical campus at its core. Upon entering its registration center, an antiseptic aroma ambushed my senses. I instantly felt the nausea that plagued me as a child. To further my discord, I found out very quickly that the staff at Pine Grove didn't enjoy playing host to inquiring reporters—especially under the circumstances at hand.

After gaining clearance into the hospital's main lobby, I was confronted by yet another unanticipated obstacle. This one came in the form of a gargantuan officer, who kept a steely-eyed vigil over the premises. His main function seemed to be dedicated to a nurse situated behind a desk at the center of the room. Judging by this woman's stone-cold gaze, I assumed that she was at the helm of all procedures from this point forward.

Her grim-visage stare reminded me of something akin to death. Bloodshot eyes blazed across the desk at me like scarlet darts. Her face, ravaged by age and sunlight, was framed in a fan of brittle white hair. Wrinkles cleaved deeply into her cheeks and protracted into a crusty ribbon of flesh beneath her chin.

I stood close enough to distinguish a badge pinned to her uniform. The tag read: Sara Venner, RN. After I offered her an introduction, Venner exercised the rancor of her personality. While scratching at her nose's pitted skin, she directed my attention toward a sign on the wall behind her desk. In bright red lettering, the sign read: No Visitors.

Since I realized that this nurse had most likely never disobeyed a rule in her life, I resorted to the art of persuasion. "Look, Nurse Venner," I said coyly, "I know you've probably had a fair share of reporters in here over the last few weeks, so I'm not gonna give you a hard time."

"Lucky me," Venner snorted with sarcasm. She then read my visitor pass before saying, "Let me explain something to you, Mr. Dayton. All visitors, especially those affiliated with the press, are not allowed on this hospital's premises without written approval."

"I know, I know," I stammered, "but I've come all the way from South Port. Can't you make an exception—just this once?"

Venner shook her head and returned her attention to the paperwork on the desk. When I refused to leave, her eyes slowly centered on me again. I remained persistent with my request. "Nurse, you've got to help me. I'm here to save this hospital's reputation. I just need to talk to the children. All I want is five minutes of their time."

"The children don't wish to speak with you," Venner sneered. "If you haven't guessed it by now, they are all very sick and in no condition to be badgered by a man like yourself."

Since Venner's tone bordered on blind arrogance, I surmised that she had more at stake in this hospital's operations than a timecard and a paycheck. As our discourse came to an end, I watched her raise one finger and point to the guard standing at her side. Without hesitating, the guard lumbered toward the desk with his thumbs stuck in either side of his belt loops. He appeared as intimidating as an amber-eyed tiger, but the nurse ordered him around like an insecure child.

"Marcus," Venner directed, "see to it that this gentleman finds the exit at once. I haven't got the time for this sort of nonsense right now."

The ursine-sized guard immediately turned toward me and grumbled, "Okay, Mister, you heard the nurse. It's time to leave."

Although Marcus was constrained by his duties, he seemed rather tame when compared to Venner's temperament. Still, I avoided the urge to test his ferocity by following him through the lobby without incident. Once outside of Venner's scornful watch, however, I decided to use the guard's malleable personality to my advantage.

"Marcus," I remarked, "you look like a man who knows what's going on around here."

"I do my best to keep my eyes peeled," he answered, momentarily basking in the recognition.

My voice dipped to a whisper before I continued. "I'm not trying to cause you any trouble, but I need your help."

Marcus paused before stuttering, "I—I don't if I can do that."

As we reached the main gate leading into the security den, I noticed a surplus of sweat gathering on Marcus's brow. He yanked a handkerchief from his hip pocket and sponged his forehead and neck dry. By this time, I already guessed that this guard knew more about the situation than I originally anticipated. Perspiration rarely flowed so amply from men encased in ignorance.

Marcus opened the gate and pointed me toward the exit. "You should go now," he advised, glancing back toward the lobby as if an unseen spy was following us. "I can't help you." His expression appeared tortured now, as if needles had been inserted into his saucer-shaped eyes.

"What are you so afraid of?" My own voice became hostile as fragments of my childhood rushed back into my head. Instead of walking away, I edged closer to Marcus and clasped my hand around his thick wrist. His muscles trembled at this gesture. I sensed cold sweat seeping heavily through his pores.

"I don't have to remind you what the right thing to do is," I said. "The children at this hospital are in jeopardy. You must help me help them."

While standing face to face (or at least face to chest) with this guard, I discerned a fear in him that seemed unreasonable for a man his size. His slouch at the shoulders hinted of an ill confidence, and his slurred words gave a false impression of stupidity. But Marcus wasn't a dumb man. He was clearly frightened by something. Scared of what or whom I did not yet know, but I was bound to uncover the truth. He had the facts stashed in his mind for far too long. I sensed frustration surfacing from behind his pleading eyes. A cry for help wasn't far off from my ears.

"It's gotten so damn crazy around here," Marcus murmured. "I don't even know who I can trust anymore, and that's the plumb truth."

"Trust me," I said. "Tell me what's going on."

Marcus glanced behind himself again before whispering, "It's all about the kids—they just don't seem right to me."

"You mean because they're sick?"

"No, no—it ain't like that. I've seen a lot of sick kids before, you know, and most right here at this hospital. But something has changed. Those kids in here now just don't laugh or smile anymore. It's like the life has been sucked right out of their eyeballs or something. I keep waiting for someone to pull their strings, cause they sure look like a bunch of puppets to me."

Though Marcus didn't suspect it yet, his words were extremely unsettling and revealing to me. As I listened to his explanation, my heartbeat quickened. I quickly launched into a rapid dialogue with him in order to gather as much information as possible.

"When did you first start to notice a change in the children's behavior?" I asked.

Marcus shrugged his shoulders and guessed, "Maybe a year ago, but I ain't sure."

"But one thing is sure, Marcus. The children who are now dying at an accelerated rate at this hospital have all shown some significant change in their personalities over the past twelve months. Can you give me a simple yes or no on that?"

"I'd agree with that," he answered, nodding his chin.

"Well, that makes our job a bit easier, Marcus, because now all we got to do is figure out what happened at this hospital that might've caused those kids to change into a band of puppets, as you called them."

After mulling over my words for a moment, Marcus stated, "I really don't know what to tell you, Mister. I do know that everything started to go haywire right after that new doctor got here."

"New doctor? You mean a replacement?"

"Yeah," Marcus said. "Strangest and saddest thing, too. The old doctor was a kind-hearted man. He really loved these kids. He treated them like a grandpa does his grandchildren. If that man had a negative bone in his body, I never saw or heard tell of it."

"Why did he leave Pine Grove?"

"He just cut out one day. And that wasn't like him. He worked in the children's ward for many years, and then one day he just left. That's when the new doc took over."

Feeling queasy in the midst of my next thought, I asked, "Who is the new doctor—what is his name?"

Marcus's lips tightened with the sound of my breathing. Evidently, the guard's memory betrayed him at a most inopportune time.

"You must know the doctor's name?" I asked again, this time more insistently.

Still Marcus remained mute. It was as though he was momentarily lost in his recollections. If I dared to know the name of the new doctor at Pine Grove, it would have to be pried from another source. If I didn't view cowardice as a vice against mankind, I might've had sense enough to leave. But being burdened by my own brand of hubris, I needed to know more than what Marcus had so graciously offered.

Nurse Venner possessed all the answers that had thus far eluded me. Without regard for consequence (and many would follow), I charged back through the lobby with Marcus in close pursuit. Before I managed to reach Venner's desk, she had already dialed an emergency code into her phone.

"You are now trespassing, Mr. Dayton," Venner admonished. She then glared across the room toward Marcus. He retreated to the corner of the room as if awaiting punishment.

I had already committed myself to stand ground. "I want to speak with the person in charge," I demanded.

"I manage all procedures," Venner exclaimed, standing up from her seat as if to defend herself. "As I already told you, you have no business here with us, Mr. Dayton."

"Let me see the children," I insisted. "You can't keep them locked up forever. Their thoughts need to be heard."

Instead of responding to my outburst, Venner calmly took her seat behind her computer and began to jab her fingers across the keyboard. Then, in a cleverly composed tone, she hissed, "Everything we do here is for the children. That is all I wish to say to you."

"You're hiding something," I prodded, still secretly supporting my dream's content as if it was based on more than conjecture. "Marcus told me everything—he knows that something is wrong at this hospital."

Nurse Venner didn't squander too much of her energy worrying about my next intention. Before I stammered through another word, a quartet of police officers assembled in the lobby with their guns drawn and aimed directly at me. Though I made no attempt to escape my inevitable arrest,

I wasn't sure if they'd squeeze the guns' triggers as hastily as they brandished them from their holsters.

Venner simpered at my predicament as if she had secured yet another victory for Pine Grove's clandestine deeds. She postured in the unlikely role of a distressed damsel as I became cast as the proverbial villain in the eyes of the law. As the officers approached in tandem, I saw a contrived look of terror locked in the nurse's eyes.

To worsen matters, Marcus, the only witness to my defense, had suddenly retreated toward the security den. I now stood alone at the mercy of these men, and judging by their scowls, I sensed that they wouldn't show much enthusiasm toward my version of the truth. Instead, they anxiously listened to Venner's rambling diatribe regarding my insubordination and trespass.

Before Venner finished relaying her concocted tale, the officers detained me. The idea of being shuttled off to jail didn't trouble me as much as I knew it would my boss. Presumably, Jenkins couldn't hack the embarrassment of another gaffe at the hands of a budding journalist. On this occasion, however, my incarceration was at least temporarily suspended by an improbable figure.

A tall man, garbed in an ashen-colored suit, sauntered through the revolving glass doors leading into the reception area. His hair and eyes were as black and glinting as the polish on his leather shoes. I immediately sensed that he was a proud and powerful person whose arrogance was only superseded by his allurement to women. He forwarded a closed-mouth grin at the officers and then gently wrapped his arm around Venner's shoulder. The old spinster nearly swooned under his feet on the spot.

"Please, officers," the man stated as he turned toward me. "I'm sure this is all just a little misunderstanding."

"Nurse Venner told us to take him out of here," one guard responded.

"Of course," the man replied in an amicable tone, "but this show of force is hardly necessary. Let him go."

Despite everything that I've described about this particular man, and the fact that he saved me from a trip to the county jail, I suddenly felt weary in his presence. As I looked at him, a visceral chill swept over my skin, causing my legs to buckle and heart to palpitate irregularly. After the officers released me, I stumbled forward and touched the floor with both of my knees. A spell of vertigo had momentarily encompassed all of my thoughts.

Sensing that my sanity was in jeopardy, I tried to confront that which had terrorized me. Before I recouped my balance, a pair of frigid hands clasped upon my shoulders and hoisted me off the floor. This man supported my weight effortlessly, as if I had the makings of a puppet affixed to a set of strings. As I dangled helplessly in his grasp, he glared at me with a tempered amusement. I then knew that we had met before.

Although years had passed since I last set eyes upon this image, I well remembered the face that had haunted me when I was just a boy. Even now the eyes of Dr. Kross burned an indelible imprint in the back of my mind. Yet despite the passage of time and my own maturation, the mark of age hadn't altered Kross's appearance. Remarkably, he still possessed the youthful glow of a man approaching his prime.

Was it possible that Kross had forgotten who I was? And if that was not true, then why—after all this time—had he elected to make himself known to me again? After reevaluating the horror that he had imposed upon the children in Pittsburgh, I made the necessary connection. Just as before, Kross continued his quest to slay the children of this world.

Hot venom surged into my blood while I glared at Kross's soulless eyes. Though I didn't yet fathom the complexities of this fiend's mind, I realized that he had to be stopped even if it meant subjecting myself to the perils now placed before me.

"Kross," I murmured. "You don't remember me, do you?"

The man shrugged his shoulders and released my arms. "I beg your pardon? By what name did you call me?"

"Doctor Kross," I repeated, this time with a sharp edge slicing into my voice. "We met once before—in Pittsburgh—when I was just a boy."

"I'm sorry," the man denied, "my name is Doctor Konrad, and I can't remember you at all."

"Think harder," I grimaced, nudging my face within an inch of this man's nose. "My name is Lawrence Dayton, and you were one of the doctor's assigned to treat my cancer."

"I'm afraid that's impossible," the man insisted, this time presenting his infectious smile to the nurse and officers. "I've never practiced medicine in Pittsburgh. You've obviously mistaken me for someone else."

By now Venner had rejoined the man and whispered something in his ear. She then directed a sneer at me and said, "I think this man may be insane, Doctor Konrad. We should let the police handle this from here."

Without consulting with the man, the officers concurred with Venner. They grabbed me and began to drag me away. I wasn't about to depart without at least trying to pry a confession from the fraud that stood before me.

"I'm not crazy," I said, wrestling with the officers. "Tell them who you really are, Kross! Tell them that you are a murderer of children!"

Venner now stood as a barrier between my tormentor and me. "Take this man out of here at once," she shouted. "He's endangering the welfare of everyone in this room."

"I'll leave peacefully once the truth is known," I said. The officers, however, proved to be too much for me. Within seconds, they swatted me to the floor with a few pelts from their truncheons. Then, while relishing in my agony, they knelt on my back and clasped my wrists in cuffs. In spite of my pain and humility, I refused to change my mind in regard to this matter in question.

I soon learned that Dr. Kross, a.k.a. Dr. Konrad, had established a legion of disciples for himself in his short time at this hospital. Unfortunately, I didn't have any evidence to validate my belief, so there wasn't cause to question his creditability. Despite my emotional tirade, as it was later termed by the authorities, the officers ushered me out of Pine Grove without resorting to further violence.

If Nurse Venner's request for prosecution had been honored, I would've been spending more time in New Jersey than initially planned. But I managed to escape jail because Dr. Konrad declined his right to press charges. The man's apparent tolerance for my behavior made no sense. I had intentionally accused him of being the perpetrator of horrible acts in front of his staff, yet he responded by letting me walk away. Why?

Complying with Konrad's specific directions, the police escorted me out of town under the condition that I promised never to return to Pine Grove Hospital. At the time, I truly believed that I had the upper hand in this situation, and was willing to agree with any term that might hasten my deliverance from this place.

In retrospect, I understand why this fiend permitted me to leave so easily. He knew that I'd eventually revisit Pine Grove, and I now know that he waited for this ill-fated day more than I did. As I returned to South Port, I suspected that my life's purpose had changed once again, and a crucial choice between preserving my humanity and humility loomed like a bending shadow in the crevices of my mind.

CHAPTER FIFTEEN

▼

JOURNAL ENTRY NINE

GREEN HAVEN'S SPLENDOR

Well before the train returned to South Port, I concluded that I'd be about as welcome as the pox at Jenkins's office. To be fair, Jenkins had shown a reasonable amount of faith in me, but I suspected that his reputation—as sordid as it was—still meant more to him than a would-be journalist's dreams.

I arrived at The Chronicle with a plan to redeem myself, but since my defense was solely based on the happenings in a series of nightmares, I didn't hold much hope of escaping this predicament unscathed. Adding to my undoing, Nurse Venner had already taken steps to ensure that I'd never confront her or Dr. Konrad again. Immediately following my departure from Pine Grove, Venner phoned my boss and threatened his newspaper with a lawsuit if he refused to terminate my position.

After Jenkins summoned me into his smoke-laden cubicle for a private chat, I predicted the inevitable outcome of our discourse.

"Firing me isn't going to stop the murders at Pine Grove," I said. "Come on, Artie, can't you see what's happening here? Those kids' lives are in danger, and that nurse is a big part of the problem."

Jenkins sensed the sincerity of my plea, but it wasn't enough for him to risk being sued for slander. "Kid," he said, still puffing smoke from his mouth like a factory's stack. "You've gone too far this time, and you've really given me no choice."

"I'm just trying to do the job that you hired me to do."

"I didn't hire you to make an ass out of me. I gave you a shot because I felt that you might be a decent writer some day. But if even half of what Nurse Venner described to me is true, then I'm gonna seriously reconsider my judgement."

"I know it sounds unbelievable on the surface," I said, "but you got to stay on top of this thing. I've done some research. In the last fifteen months, twenty-eight children have died at Pine Grove Hospital—that's more than five times as many in the previous eighteen months."

"Even hospitals have bad years," Jenkins said coolly. "What's your point?"

"Artie, the increase of deaths at Pine Grove began exactly when the new pediatrician, Doctor Konrad, arrived. I see him as the only possible cause."

At this point, Jenkins sprang from his wooden chair and approached me in a manner that I'd never seen before. In near rage, he jabbed his finger into my chest and shouted as if I'd lost my ability to hear.

"Do you think I'm running a tabloid here? This may all be a cute stunt to you, but I don't got time or money for lawsuits. According to Nurse Venner, Dr. Konrad is a phenomenal physician. He's helped sick children all across this country. What would possess you to call him a murderer?"

"You wouldn't believe me if I told you," I said. "For the record, though, Konrad isn't his real name—or at least not a permanent one. I knew that man many years ago, but he called himself Doctor Kross back then."

No doubt feeling insecure with my resolutions, Jenkins simply turned his back on me and waddled back toward his desk. He reacted to his stress the only way he knew how—by sparking up another cigarette. After he sucked down half a tube of tobacco, he grumbled something inaudible and plopped down into his chair. I detected him groaning inwardly as he glanced at a yellow notepad on the desktop. As he knotted his fingers across a pile of papers jotted with black ink, his demeanor became more passive.

"I didn't want to mention any of this," Jenkins started, "but that nurse thought it might be a good idea to check into your background. She wanted me to pay particular attention to your medical history."

"Okay," I said, briefly wondering how Venner gained access to my private records so quickly and without my consent. "I'm not gonna deny that I had some health problems in my past, but that doesn't change what I'm telling you now."

"Look, kid, I'm not criticizing you for being sick as a boy, but maybe you're not ready to deal with other kids who got similar problems. Maybe those memories of your own illness are clouding your logic and causing you to blame the wrong people."

"I'm not sick anymore. I've come a long way since those days in Pittsburgh. Until recently, I've managed to live without the memories. But if you really want to know more about my past, why not ask the man whom most likely remembers more than me? Konrad was there, too."

"You're not gonna let this rest, are you, kid?"

"He was there," I affirmed, trying to keep my tone as balanced as Jenkins's voice. "If you check the medical files from Pittsburgh's Children's Center in 1942, you'll discover a series of unexplained deaths among the patients quartered there—not unlike the circumstances that are currently taking place at Pine Grove. Whether he refers to himself as Kross or

Konrad, the connection is clear—he's killing the children he comes in contact with."

Jenkins cleared his throat before confirming my suspicion. "Nurse Venner also took the liberty to research Pittsburgh's medical archives. According to her, no doctor by the name of Kross has ever practiced pediatrics at the Children's Center. In fact they couldn't even confirm a Doctor Kross being licensed by the state of Pennsylvania in 1942."

"That nurse is obviously lying to you, Artie. I think she's protecting Konrad because she's become a part of his scheme."

Shaking his head, Jenkins rejected my theory once again. "I made the phone call myself, kid," he said, somewhat distressed. "I wanted to give you the benefit of the doubt. But as far as I can tell, a Doctor Kross never existed. In 1942, the physician in charge of pediatrics was Doctor Cain, and he's been dead for almost five years now."

The more I conversed with Jenkins, the more I suspected the workings of an elaborate cover-up. But why in God's good name would numerous doctors and medical personnel from different hospitals band together to refute the truth? Veiled somewhere within these distortions, someone beside myself knew that Dr. Kross had existed.

"What about all the other children with me at the time," I persisted, "doesn't the medical staff in Pittsburgh have some documentation that would verify what I'm telling you?"

"Unfortunately," Jenkins explained, "during the same year that Doctor Cain died, most of the Children's Centers records were destroyed in a fire. Just by luck, your file was salvaged from the wreckage."

"I'm not imagining all of this," I muttered, but my tone grew pathetically sullen, as if I suddenly debated the veracity of my own words. In the midst of this upheaval, Jenkins peered at me with a trace of sorrow slipping into his expression.

"I hate to send you away like this, but I'm willing to offer you some help. Nurse Venner was kind enough to give me the name of a doctor who specializes in treating people who've had brain injuries. You may find someone like this useful."

"I don't need a psychiatrist. I just want somebody to believe me. Why won't anyone listen?"

"Because it's too crazy, kid. Furthermore, it's downright unethical to vilify a man who has dedicated his life to saving children. A doctor doesn't intentionally murder his own patients—it defies common sense."

For whatever this aggravation was worth, I knew that my attempt to convince Jenkins to believe me had failed. I wasn't exactly persuaded by his suggestions either. In order for my words to have any meaning at all to Jenkins, I needed for him to rethink his preconceptions. On the surface, I contended, we all may have demonstrated noble attributes at times, but the true measure of Konrad's impurity resided beneath the flesh, where cold blood flowed like a stream of poison through the channels of an infected heart.

Perhaps fate alone couldn't adequately justify my termination from The Chronicle. As it turned out, I lost more than a petty salary and a crew of false friends. My once fervent appetite for journalism had left me utterly satiated. I no longer envisioned myself being part of this newspaper or anything remotely connected to writing. I imagined there had to be a less burdensome way for a man to leave his signature in this world.

With my heart depleted of its intensity, I exited Jenkins's office with no immediate destination guiding my footsteps. My decision to eventually leave South Port, however, wasn't premeditated. Regrettably, most of the choices I made from this point forth were impetuous. In hindsight, it might've been wiser for me to examine my actions more cautiously before leaping headlong into the unknown. But in my travels I've also concluded that this specific flaw in my character wasn't entirely tamable. For reasons beyond my present comprehension, I couldn't resist the fatal urges churning within my head.

Ultimately, every man must be held accountable for what he does and doesn't accomplish in life. Yet as I now understand it, there may be other factors to deliberate. What if certain emotional traits—desirable or not—were inherited and as genetically destined as one's skin, hair, or eye color? Was it conceivable to suggest that my parents, although long dead and buried, had somehow influenced the current turmoil surfacing within me?

I had already inadvertently displayed an impulse to shun women because of an estranged bond with my mother, but now my gravest weakness amplified. Memories of my father's proclivities toward the ordinary meandered back into my mind. Though I realized that comparing myself to this man was potentially stifling to any creative pursuits, I began to wonder if we indeed were more alike than I ever dared to fathom.

Samuel Dayton aimed to live his life with few impediments. Despite his reclusive nature and genuine disregard for anything or anyone not bound to nature, I once gazed upon that common fellow as an infallible figure. Being too young to conceive otherwise, I sought to mimic his habits. Sometimes I'd stomp around the woods in his big, sooty boots, digging at the ground with a pick or shovel. I even went as far as pretending to sip whiskey from his rusty flask.

As difficult as it is for me to record these thoughts now, these scant images represented the purest recollections of my father. At risk of saturating my point in sentiment, I wished to cleave to these untainted memories forever. But alas, I've since grown to understand that heroes only emerged from the pages of storybooks. And fathers, like the rest of us, prove to be humanly flawed in the end. Similar to Samuel Dayton's descent into mediocrity, my own decline became nothing more trivial than a process of maturity.

While wandering out into the cold streets of South Port on this day, I suddenly accepted my insignificance in mainstream society with a greater sense of awareness. But I didn't look back at my lost opportunities. I was now strangely content to surrender my dreams as listlessly as my father had relinquished his own.

I spent the next few weeks trying to decipher the images in my nightmares. Though I prayed nightly for the dark fiend to disappear, its presence became more vivid. I felt consumed by this madness. I remember looking into a mirror and literally watching myself age. The soft tissue beneath my eyes became crinkled and discolored, and my once-dark hair tapered with gray strands.

Adding to my dismay, the children at Pine Grove Hospital continued to die at an irregular rate. I briefly considered approaching another newspaper with my story, but without any tangible evidence to present, I'd surely be branded as a loon. Instead of confronting my nemesis on my own terms, I decided to turn my back on this tragedy and leave South Port behind. Truthfully, with my money nearly gone, I had little choice in the matter. My only chance for redemption was to escape to a setting far removed from the clamor of city streets.

Before the winter was done hurling its frosty breath upon the city, I collected my belongings into a leather knapsack and set out to find the nearest bus station. After boarding the bus, I instructed the driver to deliver me to a location where the trees and mountains outnumbered the buildings and cars. Inevitably, I returned to Pennsylvania's countryside.

Although I wasted precious years convincing myself that rural America had somehow hindered my potential for glory, I was now old enough to rectify this misconception. In truth, I simply wanted to live a clean life and be free from the expectations of others. While surrounded by the blustery wilderness, I felt at ease with my pastoral roots.

After trudging for hours along a snow-clustered trail, I came upon a woodland community crammed with homespun comforts. The town of Green Haven had been stealthily constructed between a fortress of bosky hills, where none but those who lived within its boundaries would have ever thought to find it. A forest of evergreens shielded its roads from the smoke and commotion of far-off cities. Adding to its obscurity, the three square miles of housing wasn't even charted on a map.

At first glance, I didn't see a single structure built over two stories high. Most of Green Haven's buildings were pieced together with slate or stone quarried by a neighboring miller. The streets, almost entirely absent of automobiles, remained unpaved and capped with layers of ice. I noticed a few residents peering at me from behind curtained windows; others nervously shuffled along the streets with brown sacks of groceries tucked in the crook of their arms.

With a population of just over three hundred, the townspeople here snuffed out a stranger from their ranks like prowling bloodhounds. I must've appeared strangely pathetic to them all. My thin coat barely insulated me from the wintry gusts, yet I walked without trying to look inconvenienced by the cold. By fortune or not, I didn't venture to this town in hope of conjuring sympathy from these folks. Of course with my pockets nearly emptied of cash and my face and hands blistered by raw winds, I had inevitably arrived at a stopping point.

Feeling famished from my travels, my eyes connected with a brick-veneered storefront in the center of town. A shingle stapled to a wood and glass door read: Cooper's Eatery. I figured I had at least enough change jingling in my trousers to purchase a bowl of hot soup and maybe a slice of buttered bread. Once inside, I straddled a vinyl swivel chair in front of the counter. An inviting sound of sizzling burgers and other delicacies flavored the air with fatty scents.

A pot-bellied cook, garbed in a grease-splattered apron, plunked a fork and spoon on the countertop in front of me. He proceeded by filling a mug to its brim with black coffee. I thanked the man before positioning my nose above the drink's curling steam. While swilling the hot coffee between my lips, I sensed the frost slowly thawing from my head and chest. Afterwards I commended the man for his prompt service and piled a handful of icy quarters and nickels beside my empty cup.

"It's mighty cold outside," the silver-bearded cook with tattooed arms remarked. "A bit too cold for walking, wouldn't you say?"

I nodded, but my gesture didn't satisfy his curiosity. After I ordered my intended meal, he asked, "Are you just passing through town, or do you plan on staying for a spell?"

"That depends," I shivered, removing my jacket and draping it over an adjacent stool. "At this point, I think I'm at a crossroad in my life."

"Ain't no such road in Green Haven," the man chortled. He then fetched me a bowl of chicken soup. I ate ravenously, pouring the golden broth into my mouth without the use of a spoon. Startled by my appetite, he ladled another portion of soup from a pot and refilled my bowl.

"I don't have much money," I announced, shoving the change toward him.

"Keep it," he replied. "Never said that Cooper doesn't like to help a fellow out when he can."

"Thank you, Mr. Cooper," I said, this time picking up my spoon. After consuming more than a fair amount of food at the expense of Cooper, I felt revitalized enough to resume my journey. Before I grabbed my coat, however, Cooper pulled a red and white sign out from underneath the counter. The sign read: Help Wanted.

"I don't want to hold you up," Cooper suggested, "but I'm kind of short on hands around this place. You interested?"

"Do I look like a need a job?" I said, swallowing my pride nearly as quickly as I did my supper.

Cooper glanced at my change before saying, "Call it a hunch on my part, but you seem to be lingering on that crossroad, you know what I mean?"

After scanning the eatery's interior and noticing that I was the sole patron, I wondered how much assistance Cooper really needed. "Thanks again," I said, "but I got a lot of walking ahead of me."

"Really?" Cooper questioned knowingly, sensing my dire straits better than I did. He proceeded to wipe the counter with a cloth as I started for the exit. "The next town is some thirty miles west," he called out. "I'd advise that you wait for the train."

I stopped and turned toward Cooper and said, "Did you say thirty miles?" After a pause to reconsider my options, I asked, "If I did take you up on your offer, just what kind of work would I be doing?"

"Typical chores: cooking, washing dishes, or anything else that I might need done."

Though I certainly wasn't proud of my present ambitions, Cooper's offer represented the best one that I've heard in weeks. Besides, maybe this was the sort of job I needed to cleanse my mind. In my most humble voice, I said, "When can I start?"

Cooper smiled and reached beneath the counter again to reveal a blue smock similar to the one he sported, save for the stains. He tossed it on the stool in front of me. Within an hour, my new boss had me scrambling eggs and frying sausage for a Sunday morning crowd. After finishing what Cooper considered a successful debut on my part, I explained to him that I needed a place to stay in Green Haven.

"I've already figured out that much," Cooper said. "I got a small room in the cellar of this joint that will serve your needs for now. Honestly, it ain't nothing special, but it'll at least keep the snow off your head until you can get on your feet."

I certainly was not ungrateful to Cooper's hospitality, but I did become slightly suspicious of his goodwill. After all, folks usually didn't try so hard to assist others, especially in my upbringing. Before accepting the room, I asked him one more question.

"Cooper, why are you going out of your way to help me so much?"

He simply shrugged his shoulders and replied, "It's not about charity, if that's what you're thinking. I just figured that you looked like an honest, hard working young fellow. Trust me, I got a keen sense about those sort of traits in people."

Without knowing how to respond, I accepted the accommodations. Cooper then guided me through a trapdoor framed into the kitchen's floor. After descending a precariously constructed staircase, we entered a dingy supply room. My eyes met with a shadowed maze of metal shelves stacked with canned goods, sacks of flour, and sugar. Cobwebs and dust fluttered in the dank air. Cooper had divided the concrete floor into sections by suspending a collection of ratty sheets over loosely tied fishing lines. In the basement's back corner, a military cot was propped next to a steel oil drum, which now doubled as a table.

"Well," Cooper simpered, "it sure ain't paradise, but it beats the streets."

"Yes it does," I agreed, trying to appear soothed by this environment. "It'll be fine for me, Mr. Cooper. I don't know how I'll ever repay you for your kindness."

"Oh, maybe in the spring I'll think of something," Cooper added.

"What happens in the spring?"

"Most of the snow will be melted by then," he responded with a childish grin. "That's when you'll really start earning your keep around here."

As it turned out, Cooper not only operated the only diner in town, he also inherited the duties of groundskeeper at the local cemetery. Since he had grown noticeably less nimble and hunchbacked in his middle age, Cooper could no longer perform the tasks necessary to upkeep a graveyard. He now sought a young man, much like myself, to tend to these strenuous tasks as soon as the cold weather subsided.

I was initially appalled by the prospect of toiling among Green Haven's tombstones in exchange for room and board. But by April, I had my fill of greasy meals and irate customers. I welcomed the chance to work outside and perhaps even bask in the tranquility of my new surroundings.

The cemetery was modestly set behind a brick-veneered church on a tree-lined vista. The mindless chores of clipping grass and planting flowers soon helped me reflect upon my past with a superb clarity. I marked those moments spent in Green Haven's graveyard as an exercise in self-discovery. For the first time in years, I began to examine my fears more closely.

Up until this time, I was truly frightened by the process of dying. But as I labored alone among those headstones, I accepted life's conclusion more openly. Although surrounded by the aftermath of death, I felt invigorated by nature's timelessness and mankind's mortality. In the midst of this awakening, my nightmares slowly faded into obscurity. For now I slept with sweeter dreams forming in my imagination.

By the summer of 1950, I had established an identity for myself that I never thought possible. The freedoms of privacy permitted me to observe Green Haven's residents from afar. During perhaps their frailest and most insecure moments, I watched them nudge bright flowers into the soil. Their gestures seemed so pure and unchained from the fetters of life. I learned to embrace their honesty and unvarying belief that somewhere between the sky and fields, their silent prayers sailed into the souls of those who died before them.

For months I tended to this graveyard without interfering with their affairs. Cooper wisely instructed me to avoid interacting with those who grieved. I managed to abide by his rule without incident until one Sunday morning in June. It was then that I first set eyes upon the woman that I yearned to hold. She alone caused me to cast all of my previous misconceptions about women into the tepid winds of summer.

I first saw her when she was not more than twenty years old. She habitually visited the cemetery on each Sunday after church services. Without fail, she arrived alone, carrying a bushel of wildflowers in her quivering hands. I'd often viewed her kneeling beside a headstone. Her white frock gently blew in the warm air, briefly exposing her muscled legs. A mane of chestnut hair spun its way to the small of her back. Her lips and cheeks were apple-red. As for her skin, I had never seen such a supple offering. Her flesh appeared untouched by sunlight—whiter than a sheath of melted pearls.

Even before we spoke, I knew that she embodied a charm that only a fortunate few can hold claim to. I watched it in her feminine gait, and in the delicate yet noble way she stared upon her father's grave. Without exception, she represented everything that I was searching for in a woman but was too afraid to recognize until this very moment.

Our first dialogue occurred on an overcast morning in July. Storm clouds hovered like thin, silver lace among the surrounding hillsides. No ray of sunlight shone upon the fields today, yet I imagined a sphere of light enveloping this lady. While gazing at her, the grayness and rain was at least delayed for a short time.

A white dress clung to her svelte figure. Inviting perfumes of rose and honeysuckle mixed refreshingly with the moist lawn she crouched upon.

She wore no sandals to cover her bare feet. Her soles and toes—like those of a farm girl's—were firm and half-coated with mud and grass. I viewed her as an unspoiled woman whose beauty was personified through wholesomeness. Even at close range, my first impression only intensified.

When I finally gathered enough nerve to approach her, I was pleasantly surprised to see that she was not startled by my advance. Instead of ignoring me, she pivoted her legs slightly away from the headstone and offered me a casual smile. I nervously returned the favor before stammering through the syllables of my name. Then, like a sunflower unfurling its petals toward the sky, she extended her right hand and placed her fingertips into my awaiting palm.

"It's nice to meet you, Lawrence. My name is Victoria."

After listening to her pronounce her name, I motioned to the grave she knelt beside and said, "I hope I'm not bothering you, Victoria. If I am, I can always come back later."

"You're not bothering me at all," she responded softly, turning back to the granite headstone with a handful of lilacs. "You know, Lawrence, I've been watching you watch me for several weeks now."

Now being slightly red-faced, I said, "Oh, I wasn't really watching you—"

"It's okay," she interrupted. "I was sort of afraid to approach you, too."

"Well, I'm glad you at least noticed me. But I really didn't intend to come down here until later on—you know, after you were done paying your respects."

"You're very considerate," she said, setting the flowers in the grass beside the headstone. "I've been coming here for a little over a year now—ever since my father passed away."

"I'm very sorry to know that, Victoria."

"He was a very special man. I wish I had the chance to tell him that—just once again."

As difficult as it was for me to believe, Victoria had remedied my ill regard for women with just a few sincere words. I sensed virtue in her voice. She intoxicated my every thought with expectations of kindness.

When she stood up, I stared into a pair of golden eyes that gleamed like the soft hues of twilight upon the hills. A small amount of dirt had sullied the hem of her dress, but she brushed it clean with a girlish grin that I've seldom seen or heard.

"You're not from Green Haven," she guessed. "So what brings you to this little hideaway?"

I hesitated before saying, "Maybe I'm looking for a change of scenery."

"Lawrence, are you hiding from something?"

"No," I said, laughing with her. "Just searching."

"I like that," she said coyly. "Searching is a good hobby, I suppose. Of course, that's providing you eventually find what it is you're searching for."

I barely contained my jubilation when our eyes connected. In a whisper, I responded, "Well, Victoria, I think I'm a whole lot closer to finding that than I was a few minutes ago."

For the remainder of that morning, I knelt beside Victoria in the grass and listened to her talk about life. Her recollections were as pure and candid as my intentions. During this time, I held her hand and caressed her fingers with my own. After a while, neither of us minded the rain that drenched our skin and clothes. Our faces gleamed with a splendor that no sun could have duplicated. While glancing at the gray sky, I wished that our rapture might endure as long and as often as the rain falling from above.

If a grander sensation than young love existed, I do not know of its source. This woman's company warmed my blood. Our nervous laughter, darting glances, and exchange of passions and dreams all marked the beginning of something that every man and woman yearned to embrace.

Although neither of us could have guessed where this day would eventually lead us, I will tell you now that I shared the love of only one woman in my lifetime. Victoria, the lady in white who had visited her father's grave, would one day be my beloved wife.

▼

CHAPTER SIXTEEN

IN KINDRED WOODS

At some point during her reading, Emily had asked Regina to assist her from the porch to the backyard of her home. Emily secretly wanted to leave her wheelchair behind today, but she wasn't strong enough to stand in front of the tulip garden for more than a few minutes. Before her balance failed, Regina retrieved the wheelchair and helped her sit down.

While waiting for her father to return home, Emily remembered that she hadn't been outside her bedroom all winter. She had been eagerly waiting to see the tulips for weeks. Before turning her attention toward the garden, she tucked Lawrence's journal underneath her wheelchair. Leaning carefully toward the garden's perimeter, she plucked a single stem from a cluster of budding flowers. She held the tear-dropped shaped blossom beneath her nose, hoping to breathe the sweet scent concealed within its petals.

During his drive home from the Sunset Motel, Theodore had almost forgotten that he promised to escort his daughter and Regina to the children's hospital in Kindred Woods. Though he tried to disencumber his thoughts from what Belinda and Danny had revealed, their confessions resonated in his mind like a dagger being drawn through an open wound.

Now wet and soiled from the passing rain, Theodore shivered behind the steering wheel as he pulled into his driveway. For a moment he sat motionless inside the jeep, peering across the yard as if the mood around his home had somehow changed with his thoughts. Although the entire region was now encompassed with storm clouds, the darkest colors in the sky lingered like a cauldron of burning ash above his home.

From across the lawn, Regina noticed Theodore stumbling from the vehicle like a common drunkard. She approached him cautiously, hoping not to detect a heavy haze of booze on his breath. She instead observed a frightened man huddled against the jeep's open door. Out of courtesy for his apparent distress, Regina immediately suggested that they postpone their trip to Kindred Woods.

"I'm okay," Theodore assured her, while inhaling a gulp of the dewy air. He then reached back inside the jeep and grabbed his leather jacket from the seat. As he slipped the coat over his damp shirt, Regina wondered how his hair and clothing became soiled with rain and mud.

"Maybe you should go inside and change into some dry clothing," she suggested.

Rather than respond to Regina's advice, Theodore massaged both of his temples with his palms. As he did this, Regina noticed the tiny gashes on his hands from the previous night. She decided not to mention the fact that he neglected to bandage his cuts. She thought it was better to remain silent and let him work out his frustration without interruption.

"I don't know what's happening lately, Regina," he sighed. He then paced across the driveway and noticed his daughter sitting in her wheelchair in the backyard. "Sometimes I feel like my whole life is falling apart. Nothing makes sense to me anymore."

From his position, Theodore saw Emily staring at the tulip garden, just as his wife had done so many years before. He recalled how proud Claire had been when she cultivated her first tulips from seedlings. The notion of

Emily adoring these flowers in the same manner filled him with happiness and sorrow.

"I don't know how she stays so brave," Theodore whispered. "It's as if she doesn't even know what's happening to her."

Regina joined Theodore near the driveway. They then walked across the front lawn toward the house. "She's a very special person," Regina added. "I think we have both learned a lot from her."

Theodore paused as Emily struggled to roll her wheelchair through the yellow grass. His voice suddenly deflated, as if punctured by a lurid memory. Though he tried to conceal his sadness, tears spilled across his cheeks and mixed with the moisture of a few raindrops. By this time, Regina comforted him by placing her hand upon his forearm, not fully realizing that she touched him like a mother soothing her wounded son.

"You know," he said, wiping his eyes. "For awhile, I thought that Emily was going to beat this thing. I don't know—maybe it was false hope or something, but I really wanted to believe that she was stronger than the rest—stronger than me."

"Theodore, your daughter is the most courageous and unselfish child I've ever met," Regina said. "Despite everything, she just wants what's best for you."

"I can't stand the thought of losing her," Theodore sobbed. "But I know that there's nothing else I can do. Nothing can save her."

"Maybe not," Regina replied listlessly. "But you still have the power to make whatever time she has left meaningful. Don't waste it. Be the father she needs you to be."

Regina had stood witness to many parents who expressed similar feelings of futility at the prospect of losing a child. In the past she recommended spiritual intervention, but she withheld this sentiment on this occasion. While gazing at Theodore in the mid-morning's grayness, she searched in vain for the words that would make his agony disappear. Sadly, there were none.

While still looking across the yard toward his daughter, Theodore decided to change the subject slightly. "Have you confirmed our appointment with Doctor Garrison in Kindred Woods, Regina?"

"I spoke to him last night. He said there shouldn't be any problem with our plans. I'm sure he's looking forward to seeing Emily again."

"Did Emily ever actually tell you why she wanted to go back to the hospital?" Theodore asked.

"Well, I think she wants to see some of the children there. At first I didn't know if she'd be strong enough to go, but she seems more spry than usual."

At that moment, Emily emerged from behind the house. As she neared an incline in the yard, Regina rushed across the lawn and grabbed her wheelchair's handles. After they coasted safely down onto the brick walkway, Regina noticed a red tulip clasped in the girl's hand.

"I picked this for you," Emily said, offering the flower to Regina.

Once realizing that Theodore witnessed this exchange, Regina appeared embarrassed. "It's very pretty," she said, cupping the bulb against her sweater. "I can't believe how quickly these tulips have grown. I was outside the other day and I didn't see any blossoms."

"These tulips are special," Emily declared. "They always bloom early."

Regina thanked Emily and proceeded to push her wheelchair toward the jeep. She sensed Theodore studying her gestures across the yard. Although it was probably nothing more than pangs of guilt, Regina imagined Theodore fixating his eyes upon the tulip in her hand. As she and Emily moved closer, she saw him looking tenderly at his daughter.

Emily greeted her father with a nervous smile before saying, "Is everything okay, Dad?"

Theodore nodded his chin and kissed Emily on the forehead. To her skin, his lips felt as if they were glazed with ice. She also noticed him twitching slightly. "I guess we should get going soon if you want to make it to Kindred Woods on time."

"Right," Regina agreed, trying to conceal the tulip in her hands. "It's at least a three hour drive."

Emily appeared content as she reached underneath her wheelchair and removed Lawrence's journal from a denim pouch. As Theodore helped his daughter from her chair and into the jeep's back seat, he noticed the burnished edge of a crucifix wedged between the journal's pages. He almost asked her about the diary, but decided to repress his curiosity for now.

After Emily was safely buckled inside the jeep, with her wheelchair folded in a rear compartment, Theodore closed the door and turned toward Regina. He noticed her still standing outside the vehicle, trembling slightly with the tulip in hand.

"Are you coming?" Theodore asked her.

"Yes," Regina replied, delaying her response slightly. Then she went on to say, "Theodore, I don't know if Emily thanked you yet, but I wanted to let you know how proud I am of you."

"Proud? Just for driving to Kindred Woods?"

"No, I mean for letting Emily read your father's diary before you had a chance to. Even though it's what Lawrence may have wanted, I know that it was a very difficult decision for you to make."

"Well," Theodore said, while getting in behind the jeep's steering wheel. "I know this may sound crazy, but I'm hoping that some benefit will come out of all of this."

Theodore's eyes were now centered on the tulip. As Regina entered the jeep on its passenger side, he recalled that the flowers had barely emerged from the soil on the previous day. When starting the jeep's engine, he noticed a new batch of storm clouds amassing the western sky.

"The rain isn't finished with us yet," Theodore grumbled, while watching Regina place the tulip on the dashboard. "Looks like we'll be heading right into the storm, too."

"A little rain isn't bad," Emily shouted from the backseat. "The flowers sure seem to like it."

"They certainly do," Theodore whispered as he glanced at the tulip again. "I suppose it can only make things grow faster."

As Theodore predicted, rain began to fall more heavily with each passing mile. The water deflected off the jeep, sounding like a drumming of steel pellets on an aluminum surface. Eventually, the storm's cadence lulled everyone—besides Theodore—to sleep. While driving, Theodore alleviated his boredom by watching a congregation of birds gather in the roadside grasslands.

Emily awoke from her nap sometime afterwards, alarmed by the rainwater peeling off the road from beneath the jeep's spinning tires. In the distance, just beyond where the birds had gathered for a feast, a lone crow perched upon a rotted, wormwood fence. From Emily's position inside the jeep, she only heard rain, but at the same time she sensed a frightening metamorphous occurring within herself.

The debilitating pain, which had wracked Emily's frail body for months without relent, vanished. The grinding discomfort in her bones gradually subsided and the knotted muscles inside her stomach unwound. For a few moments she breathed as any normal girl, savoring the illusions of immortality that so many children unknowingly harbored.

In a moment of clarity, Emily remembered reading in one of her medical books that some chronically sick people experienced brief periods of rapture. It provided them with a false sense of convalescence. She knew that her death was inevitable, but at least she could enjoy a reprieve from the ravages of her disease during these final hours.

Emily mentioned nothing of this revelation to her father or Regina. It served no purpose to share such knowledge now. Perhaps it was better to simply let Theodore watch the birds flit through the half-flooded fields. And Regina, who slept with renewed thoughts of hope, need not be saddened at this time. Emily had faced fear by herself on more than one occasion.

Before growing tired again, Emily lifted Lawrence's journal off the seat and opened it across her lap. She traced her fingers over the gold crucifix, admiring the significance of this piece like never before. She then set the cross aside to find her place upon the page. While reading, she listened to the rain.

No longer compelled by the frolicking birds, Theodore spied apprehensively upon his daughter through his rearview mirror.

CHAPTER SEVENTEEN

▼

JOURNAL ENTRY TEN

TO DREAM AND DESPAIR

A foolish man may try to pretend that he doesn't need the company of a good woman in his life in order to be fulfilled. But I have lived long enough to confess that every man must eventually concede to his yearnings. No matter what cruelties he has endured at the hands of those softer than his own, he must learn to caress the feminine kind, or be forever blind without her touch.

In the autumn of 1950, just three months after Victoria and I conversed in the shadow of her father's grave, I asked this gentlewoman to be my wife. She accepted my proposal without hesitation. Although we knew little about each other, our love had ripened like the leaves in Green

Haven's forests. While still immersed in the giddy waves of discovery, I welcomed her into my empty arms. I then believed that her hand would at last close the void of loneliness in my life.

Up until the time that I met Victoria, I didn't realize how withdrawn I had become. Of course, Victoria was an incredibly easy lady to adore. Her life, unlike mine, had few emotional disruptions. She lived in the same town since her birth, never once considering departing for more idyllic pastures. The daughter of a doctor and part-time antique dealer, she spent a good portion of her youth working in her father's store. After he died, she continued to devote her time to the business that she helped establish.

Before we married, Victoria made it a point to tell me about all of her infirmities. Though none were readily apparent as far as I was concerned, she felt obligated to divulge one bit of information. Evidently, due to a preadolescent malady, she was incapable of bearing children. This condition may have dissuaded other suitors in the past, but I was confident that we could live just as happily without children.

In regard to my past, I wasn't as forthright with my bride as she had been with me. I didn't think it was necessary for her to know about my childhood illness or prolonged bitterness, especially toward women. And perhaps most unfairly, I neglected to discuss the nightmares that had ultimately led me to Green Haven. If any of this matters, my deception was not done in malice. I simply didn't want to lose her affections to a more suitable man.

Besides, with Victoria in my life, my worries soon dissolved. I no longer dreamt of the dark fiend or any of the surreal visions that I have previously described. It was as though love had cured me of all my past contempt. I credited Victoria as being the healer to my once-weary heart.

On a brisk October afternoon in 1950, I, dressed in a borrowed suit of gray wool, was married to Victoria. Because Cooper had been such a genuine source of friendship since my arrival in Green Haven, I asked him to stand up for me at the wedding. As I expected, Cooper accepted my offer without reservation.

At Victoria's request, Reverend Keegan, a Protestant minister, presided over our ceremony. All the folks in Green Haven were invited to share in our special day, and I presumed that every one of them managed to attend church on that morning. In truth, the country church room was as undecorated as a Puritan prayer house. Unvarnished, wooden pews lined a hardwood floor on both sides of the preacher's podium. For this occasion, a worn, burgundy carpet split the center of the crowded room.

I was initially apprehensive about getting married in a church, especially since I hadn't bothered to attend a service since I was old enough to make my own choices. Victoria helped me understand the importance of reciting our vows in the proper environment. Keeping with tradition, she wore a white dress. A sheer veil covered her face. She pinned her long hair up in a spiral bun, revealing her cream-colored shoulders. In her hands she carried a bouquet of white lilies, save for a single red tulip set in the center of the arrangement.

I still recall standing before the altar, listening to Reverend Keegan recite verbatim from Genesis 2: 23-25. Though I saw his mouth move, I barely heard the words fall from his lips. At this hour, all of my focus had been lent to this beautiful woman at my side. The adoration in her eyes made me feel vulnerable and somehow spiritually inferior. Yet as Keegan symbolized our wedding rings as a never-ending union, I embraced the plan of morality that God designed for His creations.

Even as I grew older and less secure in my perceptions, I clung to this memory like none other. I still smelled the decaying oak and maple leaves permeating in the trees outside the church. The withered leaves spiraled to the grass in trails of gold, ocher, and red—like a stream of aimless butterflies in their final descent. When lending an eye to autumn's forests, I appreciated the splendor that must've inspired the poets and painters of yore, and what would continue to invigorate the admirers of nature's boldest season for generations to come. Perhaps it's just my mind redefining reality so that the poignant moments of yesterday were not lost with age.

Together, Victoria and I prepared to conquer the world's woes and relish in its rapture that blazed like the leaves of that October day.

Of course there were those who frowned upon our love. At my expense they muttered words of disapproval, especially since I had no financial means to support a wife. Still, Victoria accepted me for the man I was and invited me to share her home in Green Haven's pristine countryside. Her stone cottage stood slightly lopsided in the woods. A grove of oak trees obstructed the main pathway, affording us with a privacy that newly married couples cherished. Although the four-room dwelling was visibly time-worn, a spell of heartiness churned through its plaster walls.

When I first entered Victoria's house, I was overwhelmed by the care she had demonstrated toward me. Piles of laundered shirts and pressed slacks awaited me on a cherry-stained dresser top. She had provided me with shaving cream, colognes, toothbrushes, and black socks. I even had a suit jacket to call my own. Apparently my new bride wanted to pamper me with affection, and I, being starved for such care, welcomed her gifts like a boy basking in his mother's embrace.

Perhaps the best and most pleasurable of all her offerings, however, came after the dimming of our bedroom lights. Afterwards, with our love consummated, I nuzzled Victoria in my arms and reaffirmed my loyalty toward her. As she slept at my shoulder, I sensed her soft breath at my ear. At this hour I truly believed that our devotion toward one another would never wither.

In the beginning, our marriage was unspoiled and marked by simplicity. I fondly recalled those days and nights of doing nothing more than staring into the tepid glow of Victoria's eyes. We sat out under golden sunsets and watched the stars glimmer like pellets of salt sprinkled upon a black canvass. We talked openly about the meaning of life and our future together.

When not engaged in such pastimes, we successfully managed to conduct business at the antique store in town. Between her samplings of antiquity and my jobs at the eatery and cemetery, we earned enough to live comfortably according to the lifestyle we had grown accustomed to.

Of course at this current rate of income, neither one of us were aiming to become rich before the next century. This compromise enhanced the probability that we'd concentrate on more essential matters—each other.

Each Sunday Victoria awoke with the sun and readied herself for Reverend Keegan's morning sermon. This became a ritual, which if given the option, I may have been less inclined to participate. But once realizing that my company and tolerance for organized prayer meant so much to my wife, I submitted to her request. In time I learned to respect the church.

Just prior to the spring of 1951, only six months after we shared our vows, Victoria approached me in our home's living room. Although it was near mid-April by a calendar's count, the air in Green Haven was still unseasonably cold. I burned a fire constantly in our fireplace since the previous December, and often preferred to nap in front of the crackling flames until accompanying my wife in bed. On some occasions, Victoria joined me on the couch and we'd ward off winter's chill with our own brand of electricity.

On this particular evening, Victoria came to me attired in an ivory nightgown. When she stood before the mantle, silhouetted by the fire's orange glow, I distinguished her body's naked curves. She had just stepped from the shower so her brown hair framed her face and neck in wet strands. I smelled a clean scent of soap and a dash of lilac-flavored perfume mixing with embers of burning oak. At first I presumed she wanted to make love but something more urgent weighed heavily upon her mind.

After she sat down on the couch beside me, I watched her yellow eyes fog with tears. She then sobbed, "I want to talk to you about something important, Lawrence."

I immediately held her shoulder and stroked my fingers through her damp hair, smearing beads of cool water from her ears and neck. "What is it?" I asked, sitting up and looking directly in her eyes. "Is there anything wrong?"

Victoria cleared her eyes with her palms before responding. "Nothing is wrong," she clarified. "I just want you to know that I would never intentionally mislead you."

"I know," I said, eagerly hoping that she didn't prove me wrong. "So why do I feel that something is bothering you?"

"Well," she said, pausing to find the best words to convey her message. Then, after releasing a guttural sigh, she murmured, "Remember when I told you about my problems with fertility?"

I thought pensively for a moment before recalling such a conversation. Believing that Victoria was distressed about her infertility, I said, "Don't worry, honey. As I told you before we got married, it doesn't matter if we ever have a baby. We don't need a child to be happy."

Victoria smiled cautiously and petted my cheek with her warm fingers. "I don't think you understand, Lawrence. I don't know how to say this, but—by some miracle—I'm pregnant."

I felt my heart flutter in my chest, then a spasm snaked its way through my stomach. Victoria kept silent as I repeated her spoken words several times in my mind.

"Hold on a minute," I said. "Didn't the doctors tell you that it was impossible for you to get pregnant?"

"That's what they told me," she affirmed. "But the doctors are not always right."

While carefully examining my wife's expression, I sensed that she was as surprised as I was by her conception. But why—in the wake up such hopeful news—did she shed tears? Was this show of emotion a natural mark of her felicity? Or was, as I feared, she simply afraid of my reaction?

"Have you seen your doctor yet?" I asked, sliding my hand from her face to feel her slightly pouched belly.

"Yes. Doctor Avery can't believe it," Victoria sniffled. "He wants to keep a close eye on things, but as far as he can tell, everything seems to be normal. He doesn't think I'll have any problems carrying the baby."

Victoria paused after saying this, allowing a smile to illuminate her face like a lighthouse beckoning on a shadowed sea. While gazing into my eyes, she whispered, "It's just so unbelievable. I feel so strange."

As Victoria leaned into my arms, I needed no encouragement to look startled. After her moist lips pressed against mine, I sensed her warm teardrops trickling across my cheeks. "Please tell me that you're happy," she muttered. "I know we've never discussed raising a child, but I think we can do this together, don't you?"

"I think we can do anything," I answered, holding her tighter in my arms. She soon settled her head against my chest.

In the room's warmth, I watched the fire toss shadows upon the walls. Some of these images fluttered like birds' wings, caressing the darkness with a soothing animation. But other shapes flickered wildly between the room's crevices, like the forked tongues of serpents. While nearly entranced by these visions, I thought about my lovely wife and the seed that flourished within her womb. With her eyes dappled by the fire's glow, I sensed that nothing could tarnish this woman's desire to mother a child. Whatever my range of feelings, now was a time to share in her joy.

I softened my tone before saying, "I guess I'm so shocked right now that I don't know exactly how I feel. More than anything else, I want you to be happy, Victoria."

"I know, Lawrence. It's a blessing from heaven. It's like Reverend Keegan always told me— "

"What did he tell you?"

"Never stop believing in God's miracles—no matter what. He said that if I prayed long enough for a baby, then God would listen."

For the rest of that evening I sat with Victoria and watched the logs in the fireplace burn to ash. As our silence lingered in the air like the white smoke curling from the chimney's flue, she clasped her palm with mine. Perhaps she wanted to tame the uncertainty that unfurled within my mind. All the while I wondered what kind of a father I would be. Though my attachment to Victoria never faltered, I couldn't help but to question my ability to parent a child. In truth, I sought to be a kinder man than my father had been to me. Still, I remember quivering in the darkness, dreadfully afraid of my own inadequacies.

Within a month after discovering Victoria's pregnancy, I had involuntarily succumbed to my nightmares' calling. In order to combat my fears, I forced insomnia upon myself. Just when I believed that my life and mind were well again, I glimpsed into the channels of my gravest reflections and plucked out the evil as freely as if it had never gone.

When Victoria was seven months into her pregnancy, the dark fiend returned with a vengeance. I often huddled in the living room's corner, trying to conceal the chronic shivering and coldness that oozed from my pores. And even without the flames flaring beneath the fireplace's mantle, I imagined the shape of a winged creature twirling on the ceiling, taunting me with its relentless assault upon my senses.

Victoria did not know how to react to my collapse from sanity. She usually permitted me to muddle through these trances undisturbed. When my delusions became too impossible to ignore, she begged me to get some help. I refused, stating that my condition was just a passing phobia—nothing more. Regrettably, as much as I honored this woman, I couldn't bring myself to tell her about my nightmares. As a result of my stubbornness, I sensed her love slipping away from me.

One evening, only three days before Victoria went into labor, I sat down in Cooper's Eatery, hoping to offset another night's sleep by consuming enough coffee to enliven a dead man's limbs. Cooper, who always had a blunt way of presenting the truth, tried not to delve too deeply into my burdens. Because of his indifference toward my restlessness, I was more willing to trust him with the illogical details.

After consuming two cups of coffee, I told Cooper, "I suppose the worst part in all of this is being too afraid to tell Victoria about my nightmares. I thought we could talk about anything, but I guess I'm not ready to deal with it."

"That's sort of how you were when you first came to Green Haven," Cooper said, picking at his teeth with a soda straw.

"I remember," I pouted. "I had some problems back then."

"You still didn't fix them," Cooper reminded me. "I don't really care to know the specifics, but you ain't yet made peace with yourself."

"That's a pretty good guess," I commended. "How'd you ever get to be so wise?"

Cooper simpered knowingly and poured me another cup of coffee from a steel kettle. "You think that you're the first bloke who ever lumbered in here looking like he lost his best friend? Let me tell you something, Lawrence. I've brewed a lot of coffee in my days, and listened to a crap load of heartbreak between the perks. Whatever your story, I've probably heard a hundred like it?"

"Not like mine," I argued. "Everything has gotten so crazy, I don't even know if I can explain it."

Showing regard for my plight, Cooper leaned across the counter and folded his elbows in front of himself. When he did this, I noticed numerous tattoos on his forearms and biceps. Although many of the tattoos' ink had faded into a hodgepodge of artistic samplings, some of the designs were still graphically vivid. One tattoo in particular—located on the outside of his right forearm—was remarkably preserved. It depicted a white bird in flight, ascending into a backdrop of verdant trees. Ironically, the artwork reminded me of the same species of bird that inhabited my dreams.

Before he pulled his arms away, I asked, "When did you get that tattoo—the one of the bird?"

Cooper casually glanced at where I pointed on his arm and said, "Oh, that's a beauty, isn't it? Believe it or not, I got that put on me over in Paris, back during The Big One. For being over thirty years old, it's held its color pretty nicely."

"It looks like a dove," I said, peering closely at the tattoo's detail.

"Does it have any special meaning to you?"

Cooper shrugged his shoulders before saying, "I guess it might." He then gestured to the portion of the tattoo that represented the dove's head. "You can't really make out all the detail, but that bird once had an olive branch tucked in its beak. I guess I wanted to make a statement about peace back then, you know, like that story in the Bible with Noah."

"I know the one," I said.

Cooper appeared strangely numb when he replied, "Even the bravest of us were glad when the war was finally over. But that's water under the bridge, as they say. So, why the sudden interest in my tattoo?"

I don't know what compelled me to reveal the peculiarities of my dreams so willingly to Cooper, other than a desire to share my grief with someone who wouldn't judge me too harshly. "You're probably gonna think I'm nuts, Cooper, but I've seen that dove on your arm—and many like it—somewhere before."

"Hey, I never said it was one-of-a-kind," Cooper remarked, still ignorant to my confession.

"You don't understand, Cooper," I persisted. "I've seen doves flying in my nightmares. That's why I noticed your tattoo. No matter how I try, I can't get these images out of my mind."

Now believing that I was kidding, Cooper joked, "I always knew that you were a bird brain."

I responded to his humor in a sullen voice. "I know it sounds absurd, but this thing has been eating at me for a long time now—more than a year."

Cooper stopped laughing and said, "My god, you're serious, aren't you?"

"Take a good look at me, Cooper. I can't sleep at night. I can't even close my eyes during the day. Victoria thinks I've gone crazy, and I'm not so sure that she's wrong."

After studying my reaction for a moment, Cooper backed away from the counter. "I'm not trying to give you a hard time, Lawrence. I sure ain't an expert on this sort of stuff, but dreaming about doves—or any bird for that matter—doesn't sound too terrible to me."

"The doves in my nightmares aren't alone," I admitted, trembling as the words crossed my tongue. "Cooper, the doves in my dreams are dying. Something is killing them." The cup I held clattered against the saucer now, splattering hot coffee across my knuckles. I was currently numb to the scalding beverage's impact upon my flesh.

"Stop worrying so much," Cooper advised, yanking his undershirt's sleeve down to his wrist to conceal his arm. "If it makes you feel any better, I'll keep the damn bird covered from now on—okay?"

"Forget it, Cooper. It's not about the tattoo. I think my nightmares have been trying to signal a warning to me. Up until now, I've done my best to dodge the message, but it's reached a point where I'm forced to make a decision."

Humoring me, Cooper said, "You're talking miles above my head. Maybe you should save all this for Victoria. I'm sure she'd give you better advice, or at least the phone number of a good shrink."

I laughed, but merely as a defense to alleviate the disappointment that forged its way into my head. "You know, Cooper, you've known me long enough now to judge me as a sensible man. I just don't feel comfortable telling Victoria any of this, especially now that the baby is due."

Keeping a firm eye on my floundering mannerisms, Cooper sponged the spilled coffee of the counter with a dishrag. He then attempted to ease my consternation with some practical advice. "If it makes you feel any better, it's not uncommon for first-time fathers to get jittery. Maybe the thought of your wife having a baby is making you a little restless."

"I'd believe that," I replied, "if it weren't for the fact that I've been experiencing these dreams even before I met Victoria. Yet I will admit that the dreams have gotten more intense in the last six months."

"You see, Lawrence, it's like I've been trying to explain—you've got unresolved problems to work out. Every time you get worried or stressed, it results in a nightmare. I don't know why you're dreaming about dying birds, but it's nothing to get yourself sick over."

"Are you sure you're not a psychiatrist?" I asked, facetiously.

"If you keep strolling in here with stories like this, I might consider upping the price on coffee and rolls," Cooper chortled.

We laughed nervously for a moment, and I then became mute again. Despite Cooper's practical approach, I harbored fears about the meaning of my nightmares. Furthermore, I still hadn't informed him about the particulars of my most recent dream. I almost spared myself further embarrassment by not delving into it. But as Cooper bunched up his shirt's right sleeve again, my eyes were drawn back to the tattoo on his forearm. This time, I stared at the dove's design more intently.

After inspecting the tattoo's outline for several seconds, I said, "Cooper, you mentioned that a section of your tattoo had faded—the part with the olive branch."

Cooper confirmed my observation by nodding his chin. It was at that moment that I sprang from my seat and grabbed his wrist, holding his hand flat on the counter in the process.

"What are you doing now?" Cooper asked, clearly pestered by my sudden show of force.

"More than the branch has disappeared," I declared, nervously poking my finger at the dove's head. "You see—this dove doesn't have an eye. The bird's eye is gone!"

Cooper turned his arm so that he could study the tattoo as I did. "Oh, yeah," he said, somewhat dispassionately. "Well, I'm pretty sure it had an eye painted in there a long time ago. But, pardon my French, why the hell does that matter now?"

"This is a sign," I muttered, releasing his hand and reeling away from the counter. I felt dizzy and almost plunged to the floor. When I spoke again, my voice had reached a sheer level of dread.

"Last night, I dreamt of the doves again—only this dream was unlike all the others. These doves, just like your tattoo, were missing their eyes. I remember it so clearly now. The doves were blind. It's got to mean something, Cooper!"

"It means nothing," Cooper countered. "Look, Lawrence, I'm trying to keep an open mind about this stuff you're telling me, but I'm at my wits end here. This old tattoo doesn't have any meaning to you, and I hardly given it a thought in over twenty years."

Now exasperated with my efforts to convince Cooper, I decided to divulge nothing more to him at this time. My problem had grown too large for his comprehension. Feeling uneasy with the present situation, I excused myself. Cooper—always the persistent friend—didn't want me to leave the eatery without ensuring him that I'd return in a better frame of mind.

"Do yourself a favor," Cooper suggested, "go home and get some sleep. Talk to your wife, too. I think you'll feel a whole lot different about things once the baby is born."

"I wish it was all so easy as that," I said, listlessly. Then, feeling an urgent need to return home to my wife, I left the eatery in haste.

Sleep may have settled a man who was simply fatigued, but such an antidote couldn't remedy my present depression. When I arrived home later that evening, a rainstorm had just begun to dampen Green Haven's woodland. From my kitchen window, I watched random arms of lightning pulse through the gray clouds like crooked wands. In between these flashes, I made my way to the sink to fetch a cup of water.

I opened the cabinet above the stove in search of a glass. In the darkness, I fumbled to find one. Finally, I pulled a glass from the shelf. For a few moments I drank freely, refilling my glass several times before settling into a chair. The lightning stroked the room with shades of blue. During one such moment, my eyes scanned the glass I was holding. An emblem on the side of the cup caused my attention to peak. In small letters, I read the words 'Pine Grove Hospital Annual Fund.'

At that moment, the glass fell from my hand and shattered against the kitchen floor. How did this glass, bearing the words of Pine Grove, make its way into Victoria's possession? The connection wasn't clear to me until now, but I remembered that Victoria's father had been a doctor. I never thought to ask where he practiced medicine, but the answer was now in the palm of my hands.

I eventually made my way to the bedroom where Victoria slept. After undressing, I slunk my shivering body next to her. She shared her warmth by entwining her legs with mine. Her skin smelled of fresh linen as I nuzzled my face against her breasts. While listening to the clouds grumble with thunder, I set my hand upon her swollen belly and felt for the life thriving within her womb.

Though groggy, Victoria spoke to me. "I was worried that you wouldn't find your way home tonight."

"I'm okay," I answered, still thinking about my discovery in the kitchen. "How's the baby doing?"

"Fine. Doctor Avery said I'm due any day now."

I sighed and kissed my wife on her shoulder. "That's good," I sighed. "But I wanted to ask you something else, too."

"Right now?" she yawned, obviously agitated by my timing. "I'm kind of tired, you know?"

"I'm sorry, Victoria. This will only take a second."

Sensing the urgency in my voice, Victoria rubbed her eyes and sat upright in the bed. "Okay, Lawrence, what's bothering you now?"

"Maybe nothing," I said. "I just was wondering where your father worked before he died."

"What?" Victoria said, sounding perplexed. "Why are you asking me this question now?"

"Because I never thought to ask you before," I said. "Can you please tell me at what hospital he worked?"

Victoria paused for a moment before throwing her head back down upon her pillow. "He worked at many hospitals," she murmured. "What difference does this make to you—or to us—for that matter?"

"Just tell me where he last practiced, Victoria—that's all I need to know."

"He was working in New Jersey," she said, confirming my suspicion. "It was a private hospital. You've probably never even heard of the place."

"Was it Pine Grove Hospital?" I asked, knowingly.

At first, Victoria appeared surprised by my knowledge, but quickly attributed it to some stealthy investigation on my part. "I believe it was Pine Grove," she admitted. "Though I don't really see the relevance of any of this now, Lawrence."

"You're probably right, Victoria. Go back to sleep now."

Before closing her eyes, Victoria peered at me sadly. "Honestly, Lawrence, I wish you would tell me what's on your mind. I can't help you if you refuse to talk to me."

"Everything will be all right," I said, rubbing my hand against her shoulder. "I'm okay now."

Victoria rolled to her side and stared helplessly at the ceiling. As lightning illuminated our room, I watched her eyes spark with their own electricity. During this time, I almost told her about my nightmares and her father's unfortunate connection to the happenings at Pine Grove, but the words tangled on my tongue and dissolved in the back of my throat.

For now I'd be safer to let Victoria shut her eyes and fall asleep to the rain's drumming upon our home's roof. I simply gazed out the bedroom window, waiting for the moon and stars to reclaim their place in the sky. Although the rain dissipated into silence within an hour's time, the real storm—the one churning incessantly within my mind—had just begun to dampen all that I ever cherished.

CHAPTER EIGHTEEN

▼

A CURIOUS DEPARTURE

By the time Theodore's jeep reached the stone-pillared entrance to the hospital at Kindred Woods, rain had drenched the surrounding embankments and flooded into the main road. A glow of cherry-colored sirens pulsated from a convoy of police cars and ambulances. Emergency crews advised many of the intrepid travelers to turn around or lodge in nearby motels until the storm subsided.

The hospital's campus was set in the lower regions, secluded from the highway by a string of valley walls. Roads and businesses were closed throughout the area, but the driveway leading toward the hospital remained unobstructed. While staring at an endless clump of black clouds dangling over the neighboring hills, Theodore guessed that the storm hadn't yet culminated.

As Theodore slowed his jeep to a standstill along the road, he began to second-guess his decision to drive here today. But Emily, who had just stopped reading to investigate the delay firsthand, was not about to turn back now.

"The hospital is right down that road," Emily stated, pointing between the columns of stone bearing the hospital's name.

"Yes, I know, Emily," Theodore said, "but it looks like it's raining fairly hard in the valley. Maybe we should wait until this storm passes."

"No," Emily refuted. "I don't want to wait. I need to go today."

After Theodore's expression slipped between a mixture of sadness and guilt, Regina interjected with her own opinion. "We are very close, and the police haven't blocked the entrance yet. I don't think we'll have any problems."

Theodore nodded his chin before revising his initial thought. "We'd probably be okay on the way down, but if this rain picks up, it'll be a lot tougher getting back up the hill."

"So we might have to stay at the hospital an extra hour or so," Regina countered. "I'm sure Doctor Garrison won't mind."

Theodore expelled a disgruntled moan, and then glanced into the rearview mirror to monitor Emily's reaction. After noticing that she was content with Regina's suggestion, he turned the steering wheel and started to drive down the snakelike hill. In the process, he offered Regina a darting glance from across the seat.

"How'd you ever get to be so persuasive?" he asked, teasingly.

Regina shrugged her shoulders and coyly replied, "Maybe I learned it from the company I keep."

Theodore snickered and redirected his attention to the road. Five minutes later, they came upon a wire mesh fence blocking each side of the two-lane road. A guard, cloaked in a fluorescent yellow rain slicker, signaled for the jeep to stop. The guard demanded identification and confirmation of an appointment before he opened the gate.

Once inside, they were greeted by an endless track of high security fencing erected along the roadway. Had Theodore not been here before, he would have guessed that they were entering a prison camp rather than a facility designed to house sick children.

"I don't remember this place being so big," Theodore remarked, while gazing at the nearly fifty acres of woodland encompassing the parking lot.

"It looks like they're expanding," Regina said. "I didn't expect this."

Theodore slowed his jeep near the parking area overlooking a sloping plat. Cedar mulched gardens, soon to be overturned with a tapestry of golden tulips, flanked the south lawn. This vegetation eventually gave way to a limestone courtyard, replete with sculpted shrubbery and fountains of percolating water. Another patio, decked with black flagstone, served as a passage toward the hospital's reception center.

The facility itself stood like a monument of glass, white plaster, and brick. To the unsuspecting eye, it looked like a poorly misplaced hotel for the corporate elite. Although the fripperies of architecture were numerous, much of the facility's exterior was now under construction; scaffolding enclosed three floors on the hospital's north side.

"I can't believe all the changes they're making," Regina said. "Doctor Garrison didn't mention anything about this to me."

Though Regina seemed impressed with the hospital's ambitions, Theodore gazed at it all with a cynical eye. "I know one thing," he grumbled, "someone went to a heck of a lot of trouble putting this place together."

"It's for a good cause," Regina reminded him.

"Wouldn't this place fit better into a city? I mean—it's sort of an eyesore sitting out here in the country, don't you think?"

"The idea was to make the children from this area feel at home, Theodore. I think it's a good hospital. Besides, the land wasn't being used for anything—it had been vacated long before construction started."

"Vacated? You mean there was something here prior to this hospital?"

"A long time ago," Regina answered. "Apparently, this whole area used to be a mining town back in the early part of the 1900's. I was told that the town shut down sometime in the 1940's."

After leaning up from the back seat, Emily said, "That's very sad. I wondered what happened to all of the people who lived and worked here."

Regina shrugged her shoulders before attempting to guess. "Moved on, hopefully to make better lives for themselves. But that's all in the past now. At least something positive has come out of it."

As Theodore exited the jeep, he squinted between the raindrops dousing the adjoining hills. From afar these sloping peaks reminded him of tired sentinels, overseers to the ghosts of forgotten men and their families. He envisioned a scene long ago, whereupon these grassy knolls the once-weary inhabitants toiled at the earth's crust, praying to sustain themselves. What honor did these subterranean servants know? If only now, from their displaced or uncovered graves, these miners could have seen what had become of their homeland—what would they think? Would they believe that their lives had relevance? Or would they simply be disheartened by the demise of all that they once worked so diligently to preserve?

Theodore's reverie lasted only a minute. Emily then swung open the jeep's rear door. Much to the surprise of Theodore and Regina, she had unbuckled herself from her seat and attempted to exit the vehicle unassisted. When her father protested, Emily said, "I can do this by myself, Dad. Trust me, I haven't forgotten how to walk."

"I don't think this is the time to prove anything," Theodore reprimanded. "Let me at least help you get into your wheelchair."

Emily appeared agitated when she finally plopped both of her feet on the pavement. After mocking the simplicity of her accomplishment, she stretched her arms back behind her head and declared, "You see, there's nothing to it."

"Maybe you're pushing yourself a little too much," Regina admonished Emily. "I'd feel better if you were in your wheelchair."

"I want to walk on my own," Emily insisted. "It's not a big deal."

Of course Regina realized that walking was no daunting task for any healthy child, but she deemed that Emily was far too feeble and prone to injury at this point. One fall to the concrete could have easily shattered the girl's weakened bones.

"You don't have to be embarrassed about using a wheelchair," Regina reminded her. "Many of the children here need help getting around."

Emily persisted with her stubbornness by saying, "I don't need it today, Regina." She then reached beneath her seat for an umbrella.

"At least let one of us hold your hand," Theodore suggested, fetching for Emily's wrist.

With rain peppering the ground, Emily snapped open the nylon parasol and scampered ahead like a pony racing for a blue ribbon. "I can do this by myself," she hollered, wistfully. "Hey, Dad," she then called, "if you really want to hold hands with someone, Regina's palm is empty."

Trying to gracefully disregard the comment, Regina rolled her eyes and cleared her throat. Theodore didn't attempt to grab Regina's hand, but he did pick up the journal from the backseat and slipped it inside his leather jacket.

"Have you considered looking at it yet?" Regina questioned, motioning to the diary.

"Well," Theodore sighed, "if I get some extra time, I may take a glance at it—okay?"

Regina nodded with approval and said, "I'm going to make sure that you do."

Meanwhile, Emily continued to pace her steps so that she remained at least ten feet ahead of her father and Regina. She ignored Theodore's repeated request to slow down. Until this moment of freedom, Emily's physical activity had been reduced to almost nothing. She would gladly trade the chance of permanent fractures to sense the wind and rain whisking against her cheeks. An euphoric energy ignited within her soul. At last—and perhaps for the last time—she wanted to feel alive.

With umbrella in hand and water splashing over her shoes, Emily climbed a platform of limestone steps as merrily as if she had wings to catch the air. After mounting the top tread, she spun in a complete circle and giggled as the rain sprinkled against her face and body. She suddenly stopped her animated dance and tilted her head toward the gray sky. A flock of sparrows soared through the pervasive darkness overhead. In a state of bliss, her eyes followed the birds until they vanished behind a ribbon of verging hills.

Theodore and Regina managed to catch up with Emily, but both were breathless from their sprint up the stairs. While recouping his breath, a rare glow shimmered in Theodore's eyes, for he couldn't remember the last instance when he witnessed so much enthusiasm exuding from his daughter's face.

"What's gotten you so excited," Regina asked Emily. "It's like you've suddenly sprouted wings."

Emily glanced down the twenty stairs that she had just effortlessly vaulted and forwarded a smile toward Regina and her father. "I've been wanting to do that for a long time now," she said confidently.

Regina walked over to Emily and gently cupped her hand on the girl's shoulder. For a moment they stared at the immense structure in front of them together. "Are you ready to go inside?" asked Regina gently.

After expelling a deep sigh, Emily answered with a faint, "Yes."

Once navigating through a series of glass doors, they entered a cathedral-sized lobby, illuminated by a mixture of natural and artificial light. Theodore immediately frowned upon the hospital's lavish design. Perhaps green-veined marble flooring, brass-engirded moldings and contemporary furnishings would have swayed anyone besides him. The industrious interior also showcased mirrored alcoves, Oriental rugs, florid layouts of Italian tile, and walls of bleached stone.

Regina admitted that she had no knowledge of the hospital's plans to expand so quickly. Even she was somewhat taken aback by the hospital's decision to finance these needless luxuries.

"I can't believe how much this place has changed in the last six months," Regina remarked. She then started to look suspiciously at the numerous doctors and nurses shuffling through the lobby and adjacent corridors. Much to her surprise, she didn't recognize a single face.

As they wandered farther into the lobby, Theodore began to shiver uncontrollably. Regina guessed that the rain had chilled him, but Theodore wasn't as easily convinced. To him, no amount of gaudy masonry or garden terrariums could have concealed this hospital's attempt to enshroud the fact that somewhere behind the sterile gloss of this civilized palace, the lives of children hung in jeopardy.

Before Theodore's phobia became too distracting, one doctor excused himself from a circle of colleagues. He seemed more concerned with Emily's frail appearance as he approached.

"Hello," the whisker-chinned doctor said. "You people appear to be lost. May I be of some assistance?"

"We're looking for Doctor Garrison," Theodore said, gruffly.

The doctor cleared his throat and adjusted his plastic-framed eyeglasses against the bridge of his nose. Without immediately responding to Theodore's request, he introduced himself as Dr. Reed. Before exchanging another word, the doctor stooped over and peered at Emily. She stood beside Regina now, clinging to her shadow as a means of security.

Noticing that the child was visibly ill, Dr. Reed presented his next question gently. "Is this your first visit to Kindred Woods?"

Emily shook her head and replied, "I was here last October, but I don't like hospitals very much."

"Oh," Dr. Reed said, waving his hand as if swatting at a fly. "You've probably already noticed that our hospital isn't like all the others. The children here are very comfortable."

"Excuse me, Doctor," Regina politely interrupted. "I work at this hospital—or at least I used to. My name is Regina Hopewell. I made an appointment to visit with Doctor Garrison this afternoon."

"Which brings us back to my original question," Theodore added, "do you know where we can find him?"

Dr. Reed's bottom lip suddenly dipped into a frown, as if something tart had crossed his tongue. Judging by the doctor's reaction, Regina guessed that something was wrong. After the doctor tried to walk away, Regina grabbed the sleeve of his overcoat.

"Doctor," she said, suddenly perturbed by his avoidance of Theodore's question. "I don't mean to be rude, but will you help us find Doctor Garrison or not?"

"Are you members of Doctor Garrison's immediate family?"

"No," Regina said, becoming increasingly anxious by the tone of this conversation. "Doctor Garrison is the director of the children's ward here. I just spoke to him last night."

"From his home?" Dr. Reed asked, appearing as perplexed as Regina.

"No," Regina said. "I called him here at the hospital. He confirmed an appointment with Emily for today."

"I'm afraid that's impossible," Dr. Reed replied, scratching his earlobe. "Sadly, Doctor Garrison doesn't practice at this hospital anymore. He retired about five months ago."

"You must be mistaken," Regina insisted. "Doctor Garrison worked at this hospital since it opened over thirteen years ago. He wouldn't just walk away."

Dr. Reed shrugged his shoulders innocently before explaining. "I'm afraid the new management needed to make some changes. Unfortunately, Doctor Garrison didn't fit in with our hospital's future plans."

Regina turned toward Theodore with an expression of utter bewilderment. She didn't wish to become curt with Dr. Reed, but she believed that he was either lying or thoroughly mistaken. Being cautious to not intentionally upset Theodore or Emily, Regina asked if she could consult with Dr. Reed privately. He agreed and escorted her to an adjacent corridor, where they conferred at a much lower decibel.

"I don't want to take up too much of your time, Doctor Reed," Regina started, "but we must be having a breakdown in communication. As I said, I just spoke to Doctor Garrison last night from this hospital. His voice is very familiar to me. He was looking forward to seeing Emily again."

Dr. Reed tried to be empathetic to her plight when he said, "I'd like to tell you that I'm wrong, but the fact remains—Doctor Garrison is no longer associated with this hospital. If you're patient, I may be able to get you an address where he can be contacted."

Regina inhaled several gulps of air before pulling a handkerchief from her purse. While trying to reassess the situation, she blotted some perspiration from her forehead. Though normally cool-headed when faced with adversity, she sensed herself losing her self-control.

"If it wasn't Doctor Garrison, whom I spoke with," she thought aloud, "then whose voice was it?"

"This hospital employees over two hundred physicians," Dr. Reed explained. "It's unlikely that I'd ever be able to find out for sure."

"Who is in charge of the children's ward now?"

"That would be Doctor Kraven. He's the newest member here at Kindred Woods, but he's a truly remarkable man."

Regina repeated that name in her mind before asking, "Is Doctor Kraven here today?"

Dr. Reed nodded his chin and then attempted to excuse himself. Just prior to leaving, he assured Regina that he would relay their situation to Dr. Kraven. Feeling as though Dr. Reed had exhausted his bid to be helpful, she thanked him for his honesty and returned to Theodore. After reentering the lobby, Regina noticed that Emily was no longer standing next to her father. Theodore explained that Emily had gone to use the restroom.

"Did you get any more information from that doctor?" Theodore asked.

"More than I expected," Regina huffed. "None of this is making sense, Theodore. I'm positive that I spoke to Doctor Garrison."

"I didn't like the idea of coming here in the first place," Theodore murmured, "but now that we're here, I want to know what's going on."

"Maybe nothing is going on—I've obviously lost my mind."

"You know that's not true, Regina. There's got to be a reason why someone at this hospital would purposely mislead us."

"Can you think of one?"

Theodore paused momentarily before admitting, "Not right now, but I'm working on it."

Regina smiled and pushed her hands through her hair. "So am I," she uttered, while watching Dr. Reed return to conversation with the other doctors.

CHAPTER NINETEEN

▼

CALLING DOCTOR KRAVEN

Emily was in no hurry to reunite with Theodore and Regina on her way back from the bathroom. During her dawdling, she noticed a passageway leading into a miniature art exhibition. Although she recognized most of the paintings and sculptures as replications from the Renaissance Period, the seemingly misplaced gallery intrigued her. She paused in the blue stone tiled foyer and gazed upon some of these offerings.

Emily remembered reading about Raphael's paintings in the Vatican, and Leonardo da Vinci's contributions to humanistic beauty. But mostly, she was persuaded by the perfectionism and unrivaled resolve of Michaelangelo. His greatest work—his hallowed fresco of Creation painted upon the Sistine Chapel's ceiling—was represented here in a series of enlarged photographs. She spent several minutes focusing her eyes and imagination on the visual equivalent to the Bible's telling of Genesis.

Because Emily concentrated so intensely on this work, she neglected to hear the footsteps of an approaching figure. Had she redirected her vision slightly, she might have noticed this man watching her almost as piercingly as she studied the art. He chose not to disturb her at first by simply positioning himself at the room's far corner like a marble statue.

After several minutes, he discerned the telltale signs of disease in the child's face. In his judgement, she appeared too ill to be promenading the corridors alone. To avoid startling the child, he cautiously edged two paces farther into the foyer. As his shadow expanded across a wall of glass encasements like an ebony stain, Emily shifted away from the exhibit and cast a stare in his direction.

Though normally reserved when encountering a stranger, Emily was instantly attracted to this handsome, olive-skinned observer. He stood tall and lean, broadened by muscles at the shoulders, and complimented by an array of Romanesque-like features. Aside from his wavy black hair, he had a narrow nose, a cleft chin, and a tint of tenebrous simmering in his deep-set eyes. And when he finally spoke, his sonorous voice rebounded off the marble walls with a commanding display of virility.

"What do you think of our little collection?" he asked, referring to the print of Michaelangelo's masterpiece. "Every time I look at it, I can never find the words to quite express my feelings. Of course, the true merit of this creation cannot be fully appreciated until you've been to Rome and stared upon its craftsmanship firsthand."

Emily eyed the man carefully, all the while thinking that his whetted features would have been envied by Adonis. Although her attraction to the opposite sex was not yet fully developed, she would have had to been blind in order to overlook his physical prowess.

"Have you really been to Italy?" Emily asked him, staring at a laminated identification tag pinned to his tweed jacket. She then knew that he worked as a doctor at this hospital.

"I've been there more times than I can remember," he proudly claimed. "And I've always made it a point to visit the Vatican City. It's sort of second home to me now."

Emily smiled sheepishly before refocusing her attention on the wall in front of her. Though she enjoyed the man's company, she didn't want to talk to him for too long a period. She suddenly felt self-conscious about her illness, especially when considering her sickly appearance.

The doctor, of course, was astute enough to not mention anything that might upset the girl. He spoke to her as if he couldn't see any symptoms of her disease.

"Are you studying the works of Michaelangelo?" he asked, charmingly disregarding the child's age.

Not knowing how to judge the man's question, Emily chuckled. After stifling her giggle, she said, "I'm not in an advanced art class yet. We don't start learning about fine art until high school."

"Then you are not in high school yet?"

"No. I'm only thirteen. I've learned quite a bit on my own, though. I've always wanted to visit the Sistine Chapel, but I never made it farther than New York."

"What do you find most appealing about the Chapel's art?"

Emily studied the replica again, centering on the life-like textures and flesh tones of the mortal images of Eden. With her voice pinched to a whisper, she said, "I guess it's the artist's determination that I admire most. I read that it took Michaelangelo over three years to complete the ceiling."

"Indeed it did," the doctor affirmed. "For a girl who is only thirteen, you certainly seem to be well educated."

"Not really," Emily said, humbly. "I read a lot of books. It helps pass the time."

"I love books, too," the doctor declared. He then theatrically knelt to one knee and extended his open palm toward Emily's hand. After taking the girl's hand in his own, he said, "You look like a fan of the classics to me. Let me guess—I suppose you've read Milton in your spare time?"

"Well," Emily answered with a smile. "I've read 'Paradise Lost' at least twice."

The man then raised to his feet and released Emily's hand. "It's really quite refreshing to meet a girl your age who has such an avid interest in literature. Do you read poetry often?"

"Sometimes. I just finished reading a book of poetry by Emily Dickinson."

"I enjoy her poems myself," the doctor chimed. "What's your favorite poem written by her?"

Once recalling that Dickinson's poems had no specific titles, Emily remained silent in thought for a moment. Since the doctor didn't wish to confuse her with his request, he clarified himself by saying, "I've forgotten so much of what she's done for American Literature. Could you please freshen my memory by reciting a verse or two of her poetry for me."

"I don't know," Emily said shyly. "Do you really want me to?"

"I would be very grateful," the doctor said, brandishing an infectious smile. Emily closed her eyes momentarily. After tapping into a feigned thought, she stared directly into the doctor's eyes. Then, without stammering over a single syllable, she recited the selected verse perfectly.

"Hope is the thing with feathers—That perches in the soul—And sings the tune without the words—And never stops—at all."

After finishing her brief recital, Emily exhaled a breath. She felt invigorated by her utterance. Despite what her father may have debated, hope was something she never abandoned. Through all her agony, it was this comfort—this 'thing with feathers'—that permitted her dreams to soar.

Before the doctor congratulated the girl for her effort, he heard the footsteps of two people walking into the gallery. He stood upright, veering to spot Theodore and Regina pacing toward them. Emily suddenly remembered that she had been gone far longer than she originally promised.

"We thought you were lost," Regina said to Emily, taking a quick glance at the doctor standing beside her. "Have you been in here the whole time?"

"Yes," Emily answered, "I was just looking at this art." She then paused and motioned to the doctor before saying, "And I met this doctor."

The doctor stepped forward, grinning at Regina and Theodore like an old friend. "I didn't mean to keep your daughter detained too long," he apologized.

"I'm Emily's father," Theodore indicated. "This lady with me is my daughter's nurse, Regina Hopewell."

Regina smiled courteously at the doctor before reaching for Emily's hand.

The doctor tucked his hands in his pant's pockets and joked, "I certainly didn't mean to be presumptuous. Anyway, as this young lady already pointed out, we were simply admiring some of the achievements of the Renaissance, and a bit of poetry as well."

Theodore was terse with his next question to the doctor. "Who are you?"

The doctor properly introduced himself by extending his right hand and motioning to his identification tag. "My name is Doctor Kraven. I'm the new director of the children's ward here at Kindred Woods."

Emily seemed gladdened by the status of her new acquaintance. She quickly centered on each of Dr. Kraven's gestures as if they were intended solely for her viewing. After accidentally locating the one person who could supposedly assist them, Theodore and Regina both shook the doctor's hand and accepted an invitation to join him for a cup of coffee in the hospital's cafeteria.

While sipping coffee in a spacious, mosaic-floor café', Regina recounted the events that led them to Kindred Woods, including the mysterious phone conversation that she shared with someone masquerading as Dr. Garrison. Although Dr. Kraven maintained an empathetic tone, he seemed equally shocked by the circumstances.

"I can't imagine someone on our staff purposely misinforming you, Miss Hopewell," Dr. Kraven said, stirring his black, unsweetened coffee with a spoon. "But I'm afraid that Doctor Reed was correct with the information he gave you. Doctor Garrison hasn't practiced at this hospital in at least five months."

"So we drove out here this morning for nothing," Theodore huffed, grimacing as he pushed his chair away from the circular table. "Someone should take responsibility for this nonsense."

"I agree, Mr. Dayton," Dr. Kraven said. "But until this imposter is located, I'm afraid there's not much that I can do."

Being accustomed to hospital protocol, Regina knew that Dr. Kraven had the power to temporarily suspend the facility's strict visitation policy.

"I know this is against procedure, Doctor, but Emily really wanted to meet with some of the children here today. Isn't it possible for someone else to show her around the ward?"

"I truly want to help you, Miss Hopewell," Dr. Kraven replied, glancing tenderly across the table toward Emily. Emily smiled as she listened to the doctor speak. "She's really a bright child. But I am a little confused as to why she wants to visit the ward. Perhaps Emily can clear this up for me."

"I want to see the children," Emily said, sipping at her ice water.

"And then what?" Dr. Kraven asked.

"I'd also like to talk to them for a little while. I guess I really want to know how they're handling their diseases, especially while being confined in a hospital."

"You may be surprised to know, Emily," Dr. Kraven boasted, "that most of the children at Kindred Woods actually prefer staying here over their own homes. We pride ourselves on promoting a sort of camaraderie between the children. I think such relationships can serve as a medicine by itself."

Without saying so, Regina agreed with the doctor's philosophy, but Theodore never regretted letting Emily choose where she wanted to stay. But as he peered at his daughter's pale face, he wasn't sure if she knew what was best for her. Theodore believed that if Emily really sought to gain entrance into the children's ward, she would've have taken steps to be admitted long before now.

After finishing his coffee, Dr. Kraven excused himself from the table. After three minutes, he returned. At this point, he appeared eager to please his guests.

"I just spoke with security," Dr. Kraven said, scratching his left temple with his thumb. "It appears as though this storm isn't going to let up for a couple of hours."

"You're not gonna make us wait out in the rain, are you, Doctor?" Theodore asked, sardonically.

Dr. Kraven forced himself to laugh before saying, "I've come up with a better solution. Since I feel somewhat at fault for your predicament, I've decided to suspend ward policy."

"Does that mean I can go into the children's ward?" Emily asked, glancing at Theodore and Regina for support.

"Yes," Dr. Kraven replied, "but there are certain rules that I cannot ignore."

"Like what?" asked Theodore tiredly.

"Well, for starters, Emily would only be permitted into the children's ward while seated in a wheelchair. I've already arranged to have one sent to the lobby for her to use. Secondly, we don't allow adults into the ward, unless of course you're a staff member or a parent to a patient."

"I work here," Regina reminded the doctor. "I can go with her."

"Unfortunately, Miss Hopewell, since you have taken a sabbatical from your position, you don't qualify," Dr. Kraven explained.

"She can't go alone," Theodore remarked. "Who'll take her?"

Dr. Kraven cleared his throat and straightened his scarlet tie. "I'm not normally so gracious, Mr. Dayton, but since you have driven many miles and the weather is still quite bad, I've decided to assume the responsibility myself."

Theodore glanced at Emily for confirmation. "What do you think, Emily? Would you mind if Regina and I waited here while the doctor showed you around the ward?"

Emily suddenly liked this idea better than any alternative option. In a short period of time she had grown quite smitten by Dr. Kraven's charm and goodwill.

"I'd like to go with Doctor Kraven," she announced, beaming like a girl who'd just been asked on her first date.

Not unexpectedly, Theodore failed to recognize Emily's infatuation. He casually glanced across the table at Regina and asked, "I guess we can spare an extra hour or so—right?"

"Sure. I can always use another cup of coffee or two."

With this matter now negotiated, Theodore and Regina thanked the doctor for his favor. Dr. Kraven remained extremely humble while he departed to make arrangements with members of his staff. In a matter of minutes, a blue-suited medic pushed a wheelchair into the cafeteria. He approached Emily and positioned the wheelchair so that she could easily sit down. Dr. Kraven reemerged behind the medic, insisting that all the details have been formalized.

"You must have a lot of clout around here in order to get things done so quickly, Doctor," Theodore observed.

Still trying to sound reserved, Dr. Kraven said, "We try to help out one another when we can. It's a team effort, really."

Since Emily had been so adamant about leaving her own wheelchair in the jeep, Theodore couldn't help but to notice how eagerly she conformed to Dr. Kraven's demand.

"Why does she have to ride in a wheelchair?" Theodore asked, although he didn't necessarily disagree with the regulation.

"Strictly for insurance purposes," Dr. Kraven said. "Precaution is a top priority around here, Mr. Dayton."

"How long will you be gone?" Regina asked from her seat at the table. Dr. Kraven glimpsed at his watch and pursed his lips together as if exploring his appointment schedule via memory.

"No more than an hour," Dr. Kraven answered. "I think Emily will find out all she wants to know by then."

Emily agreed by nodding her chin. The medic then ushered her out of the dining area. From her seat in the wheelchair, Emily glanced back at her father and Regina, assuring them that she would be careful. As the wheelchair rolled across the tiled floor, Theodore winced at the sound of a piercing squeal. He motioned to the wheelchair, realizing that its worn, rubber-coated wheels were scraping against its metal axle.

Theodore directed Dr. Kraven's attention to the wheelchair's squeaking wheels before saying, "You should have someone get that thing fixed. It may be unsafe."

Dr. Kraven sighed and cupped his fingers on Theodore's shoulder. When he did this, Theodore inadvertently sensed coldness in the doctor's hands. "Everything is going to work out perfectly, Mr. Dayton. Your daughter is in safe hands now."

Theodore eased down into his chair without responding. Dr. Kraven then informed him that he planned to escort Emily through the newest addition to the children's ward. None of them had yet visited this section, which had been confidentially designed on the hospital's bottom floor. Up until this point, Theodore believed that they had entered the facility at ground level, but as Dr. Kraven indicated, another entire floor was constructed directly beneath where they now sat.

Although Regina was hesitant to question the decision to construct a ward beneath the ground, Theodore felt insecure about its practicality. After all, children—especially those stricken by terminal disease—appreciated sunlight. Why lodge them in a lair-like setting where they could only imagine the colors of day and night?

"Let me ask you something before you go," Theodore called to Dr. Kraven. "With all this space available, why did you feel the need to build a children's ward in the basement?"

"It's really not an issue with the children, Mr. Dayton. They've come to like their new dwelling," Dr. Kraven explained.

"It seems kind of cold," Theodore countered. "I can't imagine those kids feeling good about being cooped up underground."

"We've gone to painstaking lengths to create a healthy atmosphere for our children. In all due respect, Mr. Dayton, this is a business that I've had my hand in for many years. The children have learned to trust me."

Theodore considered asking Dr. Kraven more probing questions, but it would have served no purpose now. Emily had already chosen to stay at home, and he was well beyond the point of wondering where she may want to go next. After erasing his mind of many vague thoughts—including an unexplainable chill that tapered through his shoulder and neck—Theodore turned back toward Regina at the table and allowed the doctor to slip away without further comment.

Regina peered at Theodore with mixed emotions. She didn't know whether or not to reach for his hand or walk out of the room. Before objecting to his impolite behavior, her attention was drawn to the square bulge beneath his jacket. Once sensing where her eyes were trained, Theodore revealed the folder of paper. He casually tossed the journal on the table and enlaced his fingers.

Glancing at the notebook, Regina noticed the gold crucifix set as a marker between its pages.

"Go on," Theodore remarked, motioning toward the diary. "You want to read it, too, Regina."

"Not really," Regina lied. "I mean—not before you do, and Emily."

Theodore imagined himself opening the journal, but he couldn't stop his fingers from shaking. He allowed Regina to inspect his trembling hands. "You see," he said, knowingly. "I can't bring myself to do it. Can you believe it? I'm afraid to learn the truth about my own father—even after he's dead."

"But you brought the diary in here for a reason," Regina reminded him, while gently touching his white knuckles with her fingers. "Emily has read a good portion of it already. I don't think you should feel guilty any longer."

Theodore stared frightfully at the journal. While inching his fingers closer to its pages, he tried to recall some of the repressed memories from his own childhood. Nothing was clear to him before the age of five. No matter how long or fiercely he tried, he couldn't recall anything about his father. Now, with the answers shadowed beneath his fingertips, he wondered if it was wise to unveil the obscurities of his youth. Would such hidden knowledge make him a better man? Or would it simply—and finally—secure his aimlessness forever?

"I can't do it, Regina," he sighed. His hands sagged to each side of the table as if weighted with slabs of concrete. "Maybe that's why my father mailed his diary to Emily in the first place. He knew I was a coward at heart."

"We'll never know for sure unless you open that book and read it," Regina said. "I can't put myself in your place, but if there's a purpose to all of this emptiness you feel, I think you should try to understand it, no matter how much it hurts you."

"Read it for me," Theodore whispered. "I'm giving you my permission."

"You know I can't. You must interpret his words for yourself."

Theodore's eyes finally swayed toward Regina's face. Although she couldn't be certain, she thought that he might have tried to gaze into her eyes. After several minutes of controlled silence, he continued to speak in a hushed voice.

"I don't know if I've ever made this clear to you before, Regina, but you're the only person I trust now. I've given up almost everything in my life, but I still need your support on this one thing."

"Theodore, I—I can't—"

"Are you my friend, Regina?"

"You know I am. And as your friend, I'm trying to tell you the right thing to do."

"I need for you to help me," Theodore reemphasized, this time nearly shoving the journal into her lap. "I may or may not be able to make sense of my father's life, but I'd rather hear it in your words than his."

Regina reluctantly opened the notebook to where Emily had placed the crucifix. She glimpsed at the top of the page, cautiously reading the words. Before allowing her eyes to roam further down the sheet of paper, she halted and debated on whether or not to continue. Her voice was glum when she spoke. "I don't see the point in this, Theodore. It'd be so much easier if you'd just give yourself a chance to view it."

Theodore stood up from his chair, stretching his arms behind his back before walking hastily toward the lobby. Regina tried to stop him, but it was obvious to her that he was running away again—at least for a while.

"I'll be back later," he said. "Maybe while I'm gone, you'll find something written in that book worth talking about."

Regina turned her eyes back to the journal, searching for her starting point. After setting the crucifix on the table near her coffee, she began to read from where Emily had stopped.

CHAPTER TWENTY

▼

JOURNAL ENTRY ELEVEN

BLIND FAITH LOST

Each October there's an undesired space reserved in my memory for the harvest moon's pale glow. In 1951, while watching a full moon flash its rays between the trees outside my home, I sensed a familiar foe creeping its way back into my head. I couldn't bring myself to stare upon this moon as merely a beacon in the dark. It now triggered all of the hibernating fear lodged within my mind.

Victoria gave birth to our first and only child on this night. From outside our bedroom, I listened in dismay as my wife's screams echoed through the trees. It was an arduous sound, a strange blend of pain and anticipation coiled between breathless chants for mercy. No matter how many years or moons may have passed over Green Haven's pastures, I still can hear the shrieks of that woman's labor. I felt so helpless to stand aside without a given purpose, glancing pensively at the silver stars hovering in autumn's mist. Through all of this unrest, a doctor cradled a new life like a crystal doll between his hands.

Once hearing the first wail of my infant son, I succumbed to the joy and anxiety that every father must endure. I remember my wife's face beaming brighter than the amber globe that lingered in the sky. And when she nestled the boy against her naked breast, I felt completely at ease for the first time in a long while.

My son was born a seemingly healthy baby, possessing ten fingers and toes, sea-blue eyes, and a ruddy complexion. Judging by the timbre of his cry, I assessed his lungs and heart to be in prime condition as well. Victoria wanted to pay homage to her father by naming our son after him. I had no objections to the first name of Theodore. Despite the oddities of my ongoing nightmares and inability to function coherently, I now needed to forget the past and concentrate on being a good mentor to my son.

In Victoria's mind, a blueprint for happiness had now been grounded like the cornerstone of a foundation. Yet I suspected that our family's stability couldn't be fairly appraised until testing the land it was settled upon. If I—representing the bedrock of our union—became unbalanced, a collapse in our relationship would inevitably occur. As it turned out, not much stress was needed to buckle the earth beneath us. The trembling in my head had already begun. Something was wrong with me. But what drove me to this condition of madness? Why did I loathe what I still couldn't see beyond the obscure dimensions of sleep?

Three months after Theodore's birth, a grim reality took root and fastened itself upon the frailest element within our home. In the beginning we tried to pretend that nothing was unordinary with our son. He ate and slept well enough, and even cooed and gurgled at the sound of my wife's voice. Yet during certain periods in which I held the boy, I sensed that he didn't have an ability to look directly into my own eyes.

In addition to this peculiarity, I soon detected that Theodore couldn't focus on simple objects, or even discern the shadow of a hand crossing his face. In a bid to disprove my fear, I'd wiggle my fingers in front of his eyes, hoping that he'd blink or reveal some reaction to movement. But he only managed to stare blankly into space, as if searching for a familiar voice rather than a reflection of light.

Fearing for Theodore's health, Victoria summoned Dr. Avery to our home and relayed his symptoms as best as she could understand them. After a brief examination of our son's eyes, a grave-faced doctor sat us down by the fireplace in our living room and confirmed what we already suspected to be true.

"I'm afraid your son is blind," Dr. Avery announced. "It's impossible for me to tell how or when this happened. Barring any high fever or unfound sickness, I'm going to assume that he's had this condition since birth."

"He can't be completely blind," Victoria countered, if only as a mode of defense. "He smiles when I talk to him. I know he must see me."

"Victoria, I can't measure the extent of Theodore's blindness until he's older," Dr. Avery explained. "He may be able to detect some shadows, but I think that he's stimulated by your voice rather than what he can actually see."

"Are you saying that our son will never be able to see?" Victoria cried.

Dr. Avery peered at us helplessly. His eyes told a story of great sorrow, but this was not comparable to my own heartache. "I don't know what to say right now," the doctor told both of us. "I wish I had better news to report."

Of all the vices that a man must endure in a lifetime, none can be quite as devastating to his spirit than the birth of an imperfect child. The prospect of raising a blind boy was more than I could bear. Initially, I tried to be grateful for what my wife and I had achieved, but a secret conflict lingered in my thoughts. What if I had somehow failed this boy? What if his blindness made it impossible for me to distinguish between right and wrong?

As I hoped, Victoria stood up and confronted this infliction as if it was nothing more than a temporary setback. She would always be the stronger of us two, the true source behind whatever courage I claimed as my own.

Despite the irreversibility of Theodore's blindness, she sought to find an optimistic angle to our plight. I often heard her assuring the townspeople that we were lucky to have been blessed with a child. She went on to say that many children have overcome greater odds than our son would ever be inclined to face.

I wanted to convey gratitude to those who offered condolences, but I was consumed by my own bitterness. No matter how I tried to erase such feelings from my mind, I knew that so much in life depended upon the ability to see. Being born into a world of darkness seemed unjust. Every child should be permitted the chance to savor a sunset, or look upon the sky and hills with the wondrous glow of youth. How does a father explain the color green to a son who has only felt the cool grass fold beneath his toes? How does a star take shape in an eye that's never espied a shimmer of light?

When my depression became too debilitating to ignore, my wife, Cooper, and others members of the community suggested that I seek the guidance of a psychiatrist. I refused, opting instead to wallow in my self-pity. Soon enough, work became a constant distraction to my lamentations. After convincing myself that I was incapable of giving back the love to my son that I once promised, I retreated to the cemetery and spent my days in solitude.

As part of my evening routine, I surrendered all hope of falling asleep. Because of my insomnia, my physical appearance became unbearably haggard. I stopped showering for days at a time. The stink emitting from my flesh was almost too much for me to stand. My hair became knotted and greasy, dangling at my shoulders in gnarly strands.

I learned to avoid Victoria and the baby as if they had been the source to my uncleanness. After nearly two months of this unprovoked behavior, I sensed that my wife had finally grown repulsed by my antics. She began to neglect my emotional instability, and no longer asked or cared why I didn't join her in bed at night.

I often wasted these late hours by standing in front of a mirror, trying to spy upon the torturous visions that swirled behind my eyelids. During these periods, a mere shadow or flicker of light sent me into a near frenzy. Sometimes I'd lurch through the corridors with a knife in hand, wielding its blade at the demons that desecrated the walls of my home.

Every sound in my ears amplified to a maddening level. I heard things that most had learned to disregard. Even the slightest wind whirling between the trees sounded like the groans of dying creatures. A creak in the floorboards, or the simple ticking of a clock both seemed like invasions upon my senses. Even with my refusal to sleep, I knew that the dark fiend was winning the war being waged within my head.

I blamed this dark fiend for my son's handicap as well as my alienation from Victoria. But I had only myself to despise for what I had become, for no other face beside my own was cast in the mirror's reflection. It was never my intention to forfeit the love of my wife and child. I cherished them more than trite words could convey. Yet in spite of my noble efforts to become a better father to my son than my own was to me, I had transformed into a far more detestable man.

All of my inner-fear climaxed on a cold January evening in 1952. Though I didn't yet know it, this night would be the last time that I would spend with my wife and son in Green Haven. In the midst of one of my deepest meditations, I wandered into the bathroom of our home. It was after midnight, and I'd just returned from the confines of the graveyard.

It was a frightening prospect to gaze at myself in the mirror now. In addition to my questionable hygiene, I had become gaunt and woefully pale, perhaps no darker than the snowdrift layered upon the windowsill. The face I saw tonight might as well have been a stranger to my eyes. But I was compelled to set my sights into the glass and try to unlock the goodness that remained hidden behind the horror.

With a crescent moon providing a sole source of light through an adjacent window, I approached the marble-topped vanity and clasped my hands upon the suspended mirror. Warm electricity exuded from its surface. I felt a mild vibration sift into my fingertips and gradually seep inside my veins.

Although I couldn't be certain if I physically budged from where I stood, I felt myself rising off of the floor as if held aloft by an invisible hand.

Whether or not it was merely a hallucination, I imagined myself plunging headlong into the mirror's surface. It was as though the plane of glass had transformed into a glistening pool of liquid. Like a portal outstretching into another realm, I passed through this gateway and soared weightlessly between a cyclone of clouds. The light between these clouds—if that's what it truly was—shined bluer than the untainted skies of autumn and possessed the aroma of spring's rebirth.

Just beyond these vapors, I discerned the image of a land speckled with pine trees. They were poised like wooden steeples upon a flowered terrain. The tunnel that drew me closer to its center began to widen. I effortlessly descended into this pastel-colored woodland. Within this forest, I noticed a stream of sapphire water, and just past its run, I distinguished the magenta-colored formations of far-off clouds.

Adding to these phenomena, thousands of white doves sailed between the treetops. Unlike the cursed birds of my previous nightmares, these doves appeared to have nothing to dread within this paradise. They flitted like glittering darts above my head, gathering in masses and ascending into a gilded mist. While edging closer to the stream, I heard the faint flutter of wings blending soothingly with the sound of trickling water.

Before making a guess as to where I was or the purpose of my apparent journey, the sky began to shower me with white plumage. An endless deluge of feathers floated to the land as if plucked from the wings of each bird in flight. Within seconds the green field was sheathed in ivory. I stood my ground, hoping that whatever force had brought me here would let itself be seen at last. In these moments, I thought of my childhood. And as I watched a ribbon of light toss fallen feathers into the air, I felt the presence of a marvelous creation hovering at my side.

The light gradually subsided and revealed the image of another man standing in its hazy remnants. Contrary to everything else that I had thus far beheld, this man took definite form. He appeared to me with golden hair masking a face that was glazed with honey-brown whiskers. I remember his indigo eyes most vividly. As the feathers settled in place upon the grass and water, I realized that this man wasn't a stranger to me after all. I had encountered such a man before and once believed that I could find his hand again.

Though it was merely a dream that had delivered me to this moment, ten years had passed since I last gazed upon the face of my friend. I still only knew him as Jonathan. Only now I wasn't a boy struggling to survive cancer. Was it possible—after all this time—that Jonathan still remembered me? Could his blue eyes pierce the lines that furrowed through my colorless cheeks? Could he save me again from the blackness that seethed within my mind?

The longer I stared at Jonathan, the more I realized that he wasn't like me. For reasons I didn't yet fully understand, I knew that he was far different from any other person of flesh and blood. Unlike our first encounter, Jonathan offered me no words on this occasion. But through his silent gaze, I sensed that he was as troubled as I was by my present disposition. Though I must have shouted out his name for help, he did not move from his place upon the ground. As my eyes searched deeper into his expression, I spied a tear trickling down his cheek.

Had I been the source to Jonathan's sorrow? Did he cry for me in these moments, or was he simply afraid? I watched how his eyes carefully studied the feathers that lay upon the earth. And he held some of the broken feathers in his hand like a child mending a misused toy. I think Jonathan had come here to tell me something. Why else would he reveal himself to me again at this hour?

I was awakened from this dream by a sound of shattering glass. And then all of what I just described—including Jonathan's appearance—vanished behind a curtain of white fog. Once re-focusing my blurry vision, I was momentarily startled to see myself peering deeply into the mirror's reflection. Surprisingly, the mirror's glass remained intact. A cracked bottle of Victoria's perfume and some of her toiletries lying in the sink served as the source to my disruption.

When my eyes swayed back to the mirror, I noticed that I had scribbled a cryptic message on its surface with a tube of Victoria's lipstick. Though I didn't lend much attention to the word's meaning at the time, I have since determined that this was my way of leaving a message to my family. If I am to be accurate with my confession, I believe it was Jonathan's way of telling me who he was.

No matter what had transpired within that dream, I now understood where my heart would eventually lead me. Despite my affection for Victoria and my son, a time had come for me to leave Green Haven. I needed to return to the horror that Pine Grove Hospital had become and use the necessary force to put an end to Dr. Konrad's depraved scheme.

Leaving Victoria and Theodore behind wasn't an easy choice for me, though I knew it had to be done. Since the chance of failure loomed as a constant threat, I accepted this mission as my own. Admittedly, my choice to depart our home so abruptly was impulsive, but I never intended to see my family suffer. They only deserved love, and this was something that I was incapable of offering at this moment.

It may have been foolish of me to relinquish my position in the family in order to confront an individual that I didn't even completely understand. But what choice did I truly have? The children of this world deserved a better fate, and I was the one man who could give back to them what Konrad had taken—their faith.

Before leaving the house that evening, I packed a few essentials into a cloth knapsack. I selected a six-inch blade kitchen knife as a weapon, though I didn't suspect that I was bold enough to plunge it into another man. As for money, Victoria and I had stashed enough quarters in a jar above the refrigerator to at least purchase me one train ticket to Jersey. From there I'd make my way to Pine Grove either by railroad or foot. Other than that, I hadn't mapped out any definite course of action.

I would like to offer a firsthand account of my confrontation with Dr. Konrad, but somewhere between boarding a train in Green Haven and nearing the Pine Barrens, I abandoned my memory. I've chosen to describe this twenty-four hour period as a blackout, but I was still physically conscious and motivated by a distinct purpose. For the details regarding the forthcoming events in Pine Grove, I relied on the evidence presented to me by those who didn't view the world through the same set of dreams.

Chapter Twenty-One

▼

Journal Entry Twelve

Confronting the Fiend

I remember being consumed by a ray of light that shone with more intensity than the sun reflecting off a mirrored surface. Within this sphere of energy I saw the doves using this pocket of electricity as both their wind and shield to the world outside. They flew high enough so that the trees beneath their wings were dwarfed to the size of matchsticks. All seemed perfectly serene within their realm. Yet while gazing into the birds' curious eyes, I couldn't displace Jonathan's face and the tears sliding across his narrow cheeks.

Despite the doves' efforts to simply flutter and be free from the woes of sorrow and sacrifice, these creatures could not escape the trap that had been set for them. One after another, I watched these white phantoms crash into the pine trees. Upon impact with the earth, nothing remained but the remnants of their feathers.

I screamed at the dark fiend, imploring it to let me die in place of these innocent flyers. As my words echoed through the recesses of my mind, everything around me grew darker. I distinguished the muffled cries of children begging for their lives amidst the rain and wind. And then an encompassing silence overwhelmed me. The visions inside my head suddenly disappeared and I felt myself reposed in state of prolonged sleep.

At last—sleep—a forgotten but welcome friend. Apparently the nightmare was over. Maybe I had endured this battle after all. But just as I began to rest at ease, the mysterious light that first summoned me into this environment returned. My skin and eyes burned, as if being repeatedly jabbed with hot needles. Though I suspected this to be a product of my imagination, the pain I felt was real.

I awoke from this nightmare with a frenzied cry. I heard the name of my friend forming in my brain before it crossed my tongue. "Jonathan," I wailed, "Please help me, Jonathan!"

When my eyes came into focus again, I realized that I was no longer in a forest. To my surprise, I was lying on a bed somewhere, physically exhausted from reasons that I did not fathom. This wasn't my home. The room's ceiling was white, and crudely lit by scattered panels of fluorescent light. I slept upon soft, clean linen, but it hadn't the scent of my wife's skin. Like the room itself, the sheets smelled sterile and unfamiliar. With my eyes still burning with fatigue, I scanned the room's interior.

While trying to prop myself up in bed, I realized that my leg was heavily bandaged. I also had a wound to my abdomen. Of course I had no memory of such injuries, or who brought me to this place. At the thought of being abandoned in a strange hospital, I immediately started to shout for assistance. Within seconds the room's door swung open. At that moment, I noticed that my left wrist was handcuffed to the bed's metal frame.

"What's happening?" I demanded to know, looking toward the first person to enter through the door. A tall, square-jawed man remained stationary in the shadows at the room's far side. He wore a dark jacket with a wool scarf wrapped around his shoulders. His upper lip was masked behind a dark mustache. Judging by his scowl, I sensed that he had been waiting outside this room for a while. As he moved closer, I was certain that I'd never met him before.

"Where am I?" I asked, almost embarrassed by my ignorance. "And why am I handcuffed to this bed?"

The stranger didn't answer me right away. He dragged a wooden chair up beside my bed and straddled the seat. After shuffling through some pockets in his jacket, he removed a fountain pen and palm-sized pad of paper.

"Just relax, Mr. Dayton, everything is under control now," he said.

"What's going on?" I asked, this time urgently tugging on the cuff that bound my wrist. "Am I in some kind of trouble?"

The man scribbled something into his notepad before he spoke. "You really don't know?" he asked, shaking his head as if he didn't believe me. "Mr. Dayton, you are at Florence Memorial Hospital—just outside of Pine Grove."

"Pine Grove," I repeated listlessly, realizing that I couldn't recall anything after boarding the train in Green Haven. I then looked at my body's injuries more intently. The wound on my leg was severe enough so that I couldn't move it. "My god," I whispered. "What the hell has happened to me?"

The man glared at me strangely before saying, "You've been shot, Mr. Dayton. Can't you remember?"

"Shot? I've been shot?" I cried. I still had no memory of a single detail regarding my present circumstance. In a grave voice, I then asked, "Who shot me—was it you?"

Before responding to my question, the man felt compelled to introduce himself. "I'm Sergeant Larson from the Barren County Police. Before you say anything else, I'm required to inform you that you're under arrest."

"Arrest," I laughed nervously, but the man's grim expression did not flinch. After a moment, I asked, "Why would you want to arrest me?"

"Attempted murder, for starters," Larson replied without a trace of mockery. "Whether you can remember why you're here or not, Mr. Dayton, you tried to kill two people last night at Pine Grove Hospital."

"You're crazy! I would never do such a thing!"

Larson ignored my comment and stated, "Typically my officers aim to kill. You're very lucky to be alive."

While I pondered this information in perplexed agony, Larson summoned for two uniformed policemen. The officers entered the room carrying an assortment of manila envelopes. "I think I need to refresh your memory a bit," Larson said. He then took the envelopes from the officers and instructed them to wait outside. After they had gone, Larson opened one packet and displayed a collection of black and white photographs. After shuffling the photos between his fingers like a card dealer, he tossed them on the bed for me to observe.

With my unshackled hand, I picked up the photos and glanced at the images. I at first hoped this was the punchline to a bad joke, but what I saw in those photographs wasn't even remotely funny. To my horror, I saw myself sprawled out on a concrete walkway. A puddle of blood bloomed out from the right side of my body. Beside me, circled in red marker, a stained knife laid near my extended fingers. Much to my dismay, I wasn't the only victim. Another photo revealed a nurse lying on her back. Her white uniform was lathered in blood. As I stared closer at the woman's face, I realized that it was Nurse Venner.

"I—I couldn't have done this," I stammered. "This can't be real."

"It's very real," Larson assured me. "That nurse sustained multiple stab wounds to her chest and neck. Luckily for her, your aim is just as sloppy as your judgment."

As tears of either anguish or shame filtered through my eyes, I flipped to another photograph of a knife—the identical knife that I had taken with me before leaving Green Haven. But I never recalled brandishing this weapon, much less sticking into the flesh of another person.

"Sergeant," I tried to explain, "you have to believe me when I tell you that I didn't mean to hurt that woman."

"You know, Mr. Dayton, I don't need any excuses. I got over twenty people at the hospital who witnessed the assault. This of course doesn't include the fact that your bloody fingerprints are all over the weapon and victim's throat."

"I never wanted to hurt her," I insisted, still trying to wish this all away like another nightmare. "I don't have any reason to harm anyone."

"According to witnesses, you weren't after the nurse. She just got in your way."

"Who was I trying to harm?" As I finished my question, I already suspected that Dr. Konrad played some role in all of this. After Larson confirmed that Konrad was in fact my target, I knew that the person in the photographs could be no one other than me.

"Did I manage to stab him, too," I asked, almost in fiendish anticipation.

Larson shook his head and jotted something in his notes. "You managed to cut another guard," he explained, "but Doctor Konrad managed to escape your rampage unharmed."

At that moment I felt as if a heavy stone had been dropped upon my chest. My breathing became erratic. Whatever had transpired on the previous night now seemed entirely purposeless. I had failed in my attempt to stop Konrad, and lived to face the consequences of my stupidity. Without looking at Larson, I flipped the photographs back into his hands.

"I figured you wouldn't want to talk about the details of your little escapade right now," Larson continued. "I'd like to save us both a lot of time and trouble, though. He then removed a folded paper from his hip pocket and placed it on the bed.

"What's that?" I asked, referring to the paper.

"I'm gonna need a signed confession from you, Mr. Dayton. At this point, it's strictly procedural."

I glanced at the documents legal jargon before saying, "I'm not ready to sign anything just yet, Sergeant Larson."

"Here we go," Larson sighed wearily. "Look, I got enough evidence to put you away for fifteen years, maybe more. The best and only thing you got going for you right now is your willingness to cooperate with me. Don't push this thing anymore—there's no way out for you now."

"You don't understand," I murmured. "I won't sign anything until I can get a chance to clear up my head."

Larson's thus far repressed demeanor suddenly faltered. "You son of a bitch," he snarled, "I should've blown you away when I had the chance. Let me tell you something, Mr. Dayton, you may think that you're pretty bold by walking into my district and carving up a hospital's staff, but I think you're a coward."

"I'm just trying to protect my rights," I declared.

Larson crumbled the paper in his fist before continuing. "Of course you are. I suppose a man like you thinks he's entitled to rights. Heck, I've seen how your type can clog up the courts for years. Frankly, it's disgusting to watch worms like you wriggle their ways through loopholes."

"Sergeant, I think everything is a little out of control right now. I—I need to talk to someone who can help me. I really can't remember much of what you claimed I did."

"That's a lie and you know it. We all saw the look in your eyes, Mr. Dayton. You were very precise in what you wanted to do, otherwise you would've never gotten as far as you did."

"I know this sounds bizarre," I said lethargically. "But it's like I just awoke in the middle of a terrible nightmare. You must believe me, I simply can't remember what happened last night."

"Okay," Larson said, clearing his throat as he stood up from the chair. "How much time do you need before I can get some real answers?"

I shrugged my shoulders and replied, "Let me talk to someone first."

"Now we're getting to the heart of the matter," Larson simpered. "You want a lawyer, right?"

"No. I just want to talk to my wife. I need to let her know what happened."

"She already knows," Larson said. "In fact, your wife is the first person we called. She's waiting outside."

"Please, Sergeant, let me speak to her. She'll be able to help me."

Perhaps Larson looked at me with more pity than he gazed at most facing similar charges. I assumed that he had already conversed with Victoria, and she no doubt acknowledged my unreasonable behavior of late. Even with a suspicion of my emotional instability, it was Larson's duty to expose me as a lunatic who had premeditated an act of homicide. Whether I wanted to believe this or not, I think Larson was satisfied with the notion that I was far sicker than I could presently comprehend.

"It's a shame that you couldn't have treated your wife with a little more dignity," Larson scolded me. "For some unknown reason, I'm under the impression that she cared about you at one time."

I tried to ignore Larson's words as he slipped out of the room, but his statement lashed against my ears with the sting of a bullwhip. As I cringed at my own shortcomings, Victoria entered the room. She stood beside me in a sable skirt and blouse. Her smooth, uncolored skin appeared colder than the Arctic's tundra. Her eyes, once ablaze with love, were now almost imperceptible at the core. I did not presume to fully understand the feelings of betrayal that weighted this good woman's eyes into darkness.

Maybe I would have been better off to have never tried to love this lady. As I gazed at her now, I realized that she was suddenly as wayward as I was. How could I fault her for weeping as she approached my bedside? She had given me so much of her life, so much of her dignity, and all that remained of her womanhood. I selfishly indulged in it all like a child being handed sweet candy for his tooth. But in my mind I sensed that my secrets had somehow rendered me unworthy of her affections.

Victoria remained silent for a moment, hoping that I might offer some insight into the horrible stories that Larson and others must have already told her.

"How long have I been gone from you?" I asked, thinking that it could've been minutes or months since I last witnessed her pretty smile or felt her skin next to mine.

"Too long," she whispered. As she looked over my body, particularly the bandages on my leg and stomach, she brushed her hair off her shoulders and neck. "I guess what the police told me is true," she sobbed. "You really did hurt those people at the hospital, didn't you?"

"Victoria, it's not as simple as it may seem—"

"Just tell me why, Lawrence? Why would you want to kill anyone? You had so much to live for. Why would you risk it all now?"

"Please," I implored my wife, hoping that she might listen as I attempted to apologize for my actions. "I never wanted things to turn out this way. I love you and our son. Whatever I did or will do from this point forward won't ever change those facts."

I then extended my palm toward her and said, "Please, Victoria, take my hand for a moment."

Instead of holding my hand, she enlaced her fingers behind her back. I couldn't blame her for resisting. "I should've seen this coming," she cried. "You know, Lawrence, you were never the same man after I told you that I was pregnant. I saw the fear in your eyes just as clearly as I see it now."

"There are things about me—in my past—that you don't know about," I admitted, shamefully. "It's almost pointless for me to tell you this now, Victoria, because you probably wouldn't believe me."

"We all have a past life," Victoria sobbed. "For whatever reason, you were frightened by Theodore's blindness. I think that's what pushed you further away from us."

"I'm sorry. I wish you could understand how sorry I am."

"I made the mistake of thinking that you were different. Maybe some men are really more dangerous than they appear."

"I never posed a threat to you. I'd do anything to protect you—you know that."

"No I don't. I don't know you at all, Lawrence. I'm looking at a very confused man right now. And truthfully, I'm not sure how to react. The police are prepared to prosecute you, and I can't disapprove of that. I tried to get you some help, but you wouldn't listen."

"I listened," I said, "but I wasn't ready to do anything about it."

"But you still haven't told me why you wanted to kill a nurse and doctor," Victoria sobbed. "Why would you want to commit such a horrible act on innocent people?"

"They're not so innocent. Doctor Konrad is not the man he pretends to be. Your father knew as much. I only wish he was alive to help me prove it."

"Don't you dare mention my father now. He has nothing to do with your madness. You are in desperate need of therapy. I only wish I could've seen your dark side before now."

Once realizing that Victoria would never understand the burdens of my subconscious mind, I simply lowered my head in silence. There may have been a time when I could've mustered the courage to articulate the facts to her, but the moment was not right. I still struggled with my recollections and felt drained of any emotion regarding the welfare of Dr. Konrad and his dubious cohorts.

"I wouldn't blame you if you walked out of this room and never looked back," I said, tempting fate as only a fool would do.

"Is that what you really want—to be alone again?"

"Do I still have a choice?"

Victoria approached me with a scorn that I'd never seen before. I sensed the anger cutting through her eyes like a tempered blade tearing through flesh. She raised her hand to slap my face, but seeing that my cheeks were already bruised and swollen, she resisted her impulse to strike.

"Do you even care about the position that you put your family in?" she snapped. "I can handle my own humility, but it's Theodore that I'm concerned about. Sergeant Larson said that it's very likely that you're going to jail. And even if you don't, they won't let you live with us. You're a menace to your own family."

"I've already told you that you're safe with me."

"How can I trust anything that you say to me now? It's impossible for me to live with the worry that you'll do this again, maybe this time to someone you really care about."

"I haven't gone crazy," I said, though my denial was curiously subdued.

"Then what you've done was on purpose," Victoria countered. "What's more evil than that?"

"I tried to explain to the sergeant that I blacked out—"

"Before or after you arrived at Pine Grove?"

"Before. I feel foolish having to defend myself to you. I need your support, not an interrogation."

"I can't give you my support any longer," she declared. "This has all been so hard for me to deal with, but it's partly my own fault. I should've waited longer before accepting your proposal."

"It hurts me to hear you say those words, Victoria."

As our conversation continued, I sensed my wife refueling her emotions without resorting to tears as a primary vehicle. "Because we made a child together," she started, "we'll always be connected. But I can't make any promises to you about our future together as a married couple."

"So," I gasped, feeling as though the inevitable aim of her discourse had finally come into focus. "You really don't love me anymore?"

"I love you, Lawrence. That's why this is so difficult for me to confess to you. I don't see you living a normal life with us in Green Haven at any time in the near future. Maybe it's best if we stay apart for awhile."

"The courts will make certain of that," I sulked.

"Regardless what the law decides to do with you," she continued, "I need some peace of mind right now. If that means raising our son alone, then so be it."

By pleading for forgiveness, I might have eventually persuaded my wife to reconsider her hasty decision. But as a result of my guilt, the flow of our conversation became stagnant. Since I had no valid excuse for my deeds, only a woman as unstable as me would've been compelled to stand at my side. After all, there were finer men to choose from on every corner in Green Haven. Victoria was certainly still young and beautiful enough to find a warm hand to caress her at night. Perhaps that was my secret hope for her.

Before Victoria left the hospital, I asked her to kiss me one last time. At this hour I truly believed that our lips would not touch again for many years to come, nor would our eyes soon meet with the ardency that once brought us together. Though I wished for her lips to level against my own, she couldn't permit herself to connect intimately with a man accused of attempted murder.

"Some crimes," she explained, "can only be forgiven by God."

With those words, Victoria bowed her head and stepped backwards out of the room. I wanted to call out to her, but she drifted away from me like an empty bottle cast upon a dark current of water. From this moment forward, I knew that I was destined to live alone in this world. The sad and most telling aspect of this confession is that such knowledge did not surprise me. Somehow I always suspected that I would surrender my dignity just as my father had relinquished his own. It now seemed fruitless to combat my family's curse.

It was time to confront my nightmares in the confines of reality.

CHAPTER TWENTY-TWO

▼

REGINA'S ULTIMATUM

As Regina waited for Theodore to return to the café, she realized that she might have delved too deeply into Lawrence's diary. After a few more minutes passed, she reached for the crucifix on the table. While staring passively at the cross, she placed it between the journal's pages and closed the notebook against her chest.

Theodore's inability to see the love around him made sense to Regina. For the first time, she understood that he was still blind to the world. In addition, the diary helped her examine her own life with greater clarity. She was tempted to learn more, but one question loomed in her mind. Was it possible for Theodore to ever offer his love to a woman again?

Regina felt her heart quicken in her chest at the thought of curing Theodore of his disease. In many ways, his sickness had prevented him to live his life without regret. Never before this moment had she experienced such a potent urge to end her silent agony. It was time for her to bare her soul to Theodore and wipe the veil of fear away so that their eyes could finally penetrate the blackness of broken dreams.

Still quivering at the notion of her present intentions, Regina unwillingly relived the shame that had been methodically instilled in her as a young Catholic girl. She then recalled a time many years ago, where in her high school, she was taunted by a cruel nun with a penchant for leather whips. An instance of abuse stemmed from a kiss that Regina had welcomed from an altar boy. This beating, coupled with many others, eventually taught her that lusty thoughts about boys were impure and unnatural.

For many years afterwards, even while attending college, Regina avoided dating. In the few times that a man kissed her or attempted to fondle her in ways she considered inappropriate, she became repulsed by his advances. It was during such times that she felt the sting of Sister Catherine's whip slashing against her bare thighs in front of a room full of grimacing classmates. The raspy voice of that maniacal woman still rebounded in her head.

As she grew older and much less confident in her sexuality, Regina learned to suppress her desires by immersing herself in work. Until this moment, the penitence of her past barely seemed worth fretting over. But as she stood up from the chair and noticed her drab reflection in an adjacent panel of glass, she regretted her choice to be alone.

As Regina moved closer to the glass, she discerned the lines of age creeping into her skin. Her dark hair hung limply across her forehead, combed carelessly into her dull eyes. Not a trace of makeup touched her pale flesh. This was not the true image that Regina wanted for project. With her youth now gone, there was no more time to squander.

With her hands placed firmly against the mirrored panel, Regina neglected to distinguish Theodore's approaching footsteps. He had been standing at the back of the café for several seconds, watching her stare at herself with a sense of confusion. He then noticed the journal lying on the floor next to her feet. The crucifix gleamed against his eyes.

Theodore tried not to startle her when he asked, "Regina, is everything okay?"

Hearing the sound of his voice prompted Regina to turn around quickly. Once realizing that she had dropped the journal to the floor, she casually bent down to scoop it up in her arms.

"I'm fine," she insisted, while pushing the crucifix back inside the notebook.

"You look a little nervous," Theodore observed.

Regina's cheeks blushed as she placed the notebook on a marble-surfaced table. As Theodore edged closer, he suspected that something written within the diary had unnerved the woman. She appeared dazed as she hunkered into a nearby chair. After several seconds of silence, Theodore repeated his question. Still, she remained evasive at first.

"Sit down next to me," she said, almost beseechingly.

Theodore immediately knelt beside Regina's chair and clasped his hands together as if engaged in a prayer. "You've read something in my father's journal," he guessed. "Do you want to talk about it?"

"No," Regina answered. "I don't think that will help us right now."

"But you did read some of it—didn't you?"

"Some," she whispered. She then extended her hand and cupped her palm on Theodore's shoulder. She sensed his muscles in his neck and arms tighten. He glanced at her hand and slowly pivoted his face so that their eyes momentarily connected.

"Just look at me," said Regina softly. "I want to see your eyes."

"My eyes? Why the sudden interest in my eyes?"

With her other hand, Regina placed two fingers beneath Theodore's chin and pushed gently on his bowed head. Without resisting, he looked squarely at the woman. She stared into a pair of dark blue eyes that currently possessed the clarity of a storm swept sea. Yet just beyond the clouds of gray, she discovered a spark of faint light pulsating like an electric heartbeat. Somewhere within this storm, a field of hidden energy waited to be rekindled.

Theodore smiled tenderly at Regina before grabbing her hand with his own. As he peeled her fingers from his shoulder, he sensed the warmth from her palm seeping into his chilled flesh. Without uttering the words, they realized that the present circumstances had enabled them to connect in a way that made them both feel apologetic.

"I know I haven't been easy to live with over the last six months," Theodore confessed. "Sometimes I can't believe that you've given up your career to take care of my daughter."

"But I have a confession of my own to make," Regina said, probing deeper into Theodore's eyes with her own. "Of course you must know that I love Emily as if she was my own daughter, but I wouldn't be entirely truthful if I told you that she was the only reason I was staying in Wakeland."

Sensing where Regina was leading him, Theodore attempted to ease her thoughts. "Regina, you don't have to say this now—"

"I do, Theodore—I must tell you what's on my mind. I've never been this forward with any man before, but I want us to be together. I think we should try to—"

"To love," Theodore finished her thought. Regina's eyes fogged with tears as she watched him tremble with the proposition. He suddenly raised to his feet and breathed heavily, as if trying to recapture the air of inno-cence that had existed between them until this moment.

Theodore paced nervously around the table before saying, "You know, Emily thinks we should be together, too."

"I know," Regina said, blushing. "But this is something that we have to decide for ourselves. Don't you agree?"

Theodore glanced at Regina again and then let his eyes sway to the journal laying on the tabletop. Before he spoke another word, Regina had already uncovered the uncertainty in his expression. She sensed warmth trying to burst through his cold exterior, but it just wasn't enough. He wasn't ready to love again. His heart was still partially frozen. The prospect of a new beginning frightened him more than death itself.

"You still have a long way to go," Regina whispered to him, trying to contain her teardrops. Her tone then became more serious. "I didn't want to leave Wakeland without at least making my feelings known," she admitted.

Theodore seemed startled by Regina's announcement. "What are you talking about? When did you decide that you were going to leave?"

"Honestly, I've been thinking about it for a few weeks now. I just haven't found the right moment to tell Emily or you."

"Hold on a minute, Regina," Theodore fumed. "Is this an ultimatum or something?"

"I don't want it to sound that way. But you have to understand my situation, Theodore. I'm a nurse, and I have a duty here in Kindred Woods, providing that Doctor Kraven will allow me to have my job back."

"But what about Emily? She still needs you."

Regina hoped that he wouldn't hide behind his daughter's illness any longer. When he remained silent for a few seconds, she continued with her thought. "We both know that Emily is a strong girl. There's nothing more that I can do for her. You're the most important person in her life right now. She wants you to get better, even if she can't."

"Okay, maybe you're right," Theodore agreed, though visibly upset by Regina's frankness. "But would it be wrong for me to admit that I need you?"

"As a nurse for your daughter or as a woman?"

"I don't know—"

"I'll help you find another home nurse before I leave," Regina sighed, struggling to repress her disappointment.

"That's no good. I don't need another nurse. I've never trusted any woman as much as you since—"

"Please," Regina interrupted, "don't say her name. I know how you feel about your deceased wife, but I don't want to be compared to her any longer—especially after what I just told you."

"I need more time," Theodore countered. "I have strong feelings for you, Regina. Don't make me beg you to stay."

"This isn't only about you and Emily. I've finally realized that I need to do something for myself. I've offered my kindness to so many people for so long that I've forgotten how to care for my own needs. I guess I just don't want to be lonely anymore."

Had this conversation unwound in another time or place, Theodore might have mustered the fortitude to welcome Regina into his arms—not as a means of self-sacrifice—but as one of necessity. Yet he still couldn't displace the notion that Emily was gravely ill, and her sickness reminded him of the ongoing misery linked to his past.

Why did all the cherished things in Theodore's life either die or fade into nothing but a series of dark recollections? Was he truly cursed? Did all those who touch his hand or kiss his lips fall prey to the sinister forces at work? He could only guess the truth, but in his mind he suspected that the answers to many of his questions resided within the confessions of his father's journal.

Seeing that much of Theodore's attention was again diverted to the journal, Regina picked the notebook off the table and fanned its pages in front of his eyes. She didn't pretend to be appeased by Theodore's inability to convey his innermost feelings. If nothing else stood to be accomplished, perhaps he could finally develop the courage to look into his father's past before passing final judgment upon the dead.

"Do yourself a favor," Regina advised, "read this journal. No matter what happens between us, I think your father's words will help you understand more about yourself."

Without hesitating, Theodore accepted the journal. He then thanked Regina for her resolve on what had become a terribly awkward transition in thought for both of them. At first he considered opening the diary immediately, but eventually decided that he'd be more comfortable reading alone.

Before excusing himself from the café, he asked Regina to reconsider her decision on leaving Wakeland in haste. "I'm not asking you to stay another six months," he said. "Just promise me that you'll think things over for a couple of days before you go."

"I don't think we can prolong this much longer," Regina replied. "It's too complicated now, and the longer I stay, the more confusing it becomes."

"When do you plan to leave?"

"As soon as we leave the hospital. I can be back here in Kindred Woods by the end of the week."

"Regina, I still think we can work something out—"

"No, Theodore. I've made up my mind this time."

"Has living with Emily and me really been that painful to you?"

"It helps me understand the truth about life," Regina answered.

"Which is what?"

"No one has to be lonely in this world, Theodore, unless they're too blind to see what's right in front of their eyes."

Rather than try to dissuade Regina any longer, Theodore turned and left the café without glancing back. When Regina was alone again, she settled into her chair and wiped the tears from her eyes.

CHAPTER TWENTY-THREE

▼

IN THE MINION'S LAIR

In comparison to the rest of the hospital's amenities, Emily thought that the elevator ride leading into the children's ward was not as pleasant as it could have been. The elevator's hydraulics failed at least two times during their descent into the basement. The carriage rattled unexpectedly, causing Emily to grip the handles on her wheelchair a bit tighter than normal.

After several seconds of uncertainty, the contraption screeched to a halt some twenty feet beneath the ground. "Next time we'll use the stairs," Dr. Kraven promised, before taking hold of the wheelchair and guiding Emily into a dimly lit corridor.

Emily remained optimistic as Dr. Kraven progressed through a narrow passageway leading toward the children's ward. But she soon discovered that the concrete walls and hazy light had a negative effect upon her senses. No visible effort had been made on the part of the hospital to conceal the basement's drab surroundings. There were no windows to be found at anywhere on the floor and no colors to offset the looming shadows.

Twenty paces later, Dr. Kraven stopped the wheelchair in front of an iron gate, which separated them from the ward's only entrance.

"Why is this gate here?" Emily asked, the skepticism rising in her voice.

Dr. Kraven swiped a plastic key card through an electronic scanning device before explaining, "It's merely for security purposes."

"Are the children locked inside?"

"Not locked," Dr. Kraven corrected. "Safeguarded is the word I prefer." He then depressed an amber button located on the wall. The gate automatically divided on its sliding track, permitting them access into the ward. "It's a matter of keeping unauthorized people out."

"Are the kids allowed to go beyond this gate?" Emily asked.

"I needn't remind you, Emily, that this ward is designed for terminally ill children. Under normal circumstances, they have no reason to venture outside this area. As a matter of convenience, everything is brought to them."

"What about sunlight and fresh air?"

Now feeling distracted by Emily's questioning, Dr. Kraven knelt beside her wheelchair and peered directly into her inquisitive eyes. "I can assure you that these patients receive whatever they wish for—including recreation time outside the facility."

Emily smiled sheepishly before replying, "I don't mean to be so nosey, Doctor Kraven. I just don't like the idea of having a gate on the floor. It makes this place feel like a jail."

"I'm afraid that's one of the drawbacks of living in an unsafe society," Dr. Kraven explained. "But if it makes you feel any better, the children and their parents sleep easier knowing that only certain members of our staff have clearance for this particular ward."

"It seems odd to me," Emily sighed, "but I guess I'll take your word for it."

Once inside the ward, Emily noticed that several female nurses had abruptly paused in their duties to greet Dr. Kraven. Some of them flirted with the doctor brazenly, jawing at his prowess like a gaggle of giddy schoolgirls. They offered no word of encouragement to Emily. Instead, they shunned her as if the doctor was pushing an empty wheelchair.

After casually fending off their advances, Dr. Kraven ushered Emily down an adjoining hall that led to another locked gate. Beyond this barrier, the doctor noted, the children were kept for most of each day. When reaching the gate, Emily was permitted to get out of the wheelchair and walk inside, providing she still had the strength to do so.

Feeling confident at first, Emily lunged from her seat and ensured Dr. Kraven that she would need no further assistance. Within two steps, however, a heavy sweat lathered her brow and she suddenly sensed herself becoming woozy. After a moment of confusion, she stumbled and turned back toward the wheelchair. She then plopped down into the chair in a fit of frustration.

"I don't understand," she gasped. "I felt fine a couple of minutes ago."

"Yes," Dr. Kraven said, trying to sound empathetic. "But you're a very sick young lady. That's why I recommended the wheelchair for you in the first place."

"I'll be okay in a minute," Emily insisted, wiping the perspiration from her pale cheeks.

"We can do this another time," Dr. Kraven suggested. "Perhaps when you're feeling a bit better."

"I'll be okay," she repeated. "Besides, time is something I'm kind of short on, but I guess you knew that already."

Dr. Kraven remained silent as Emily exercised whatever resiliency she had left to regain her stamina. Within a minute, she appeared composed enough to enter the ward.

"I shouldn't be more than ten minutes," she told Dr. Kraven.

"Feel free to take your time, Emily, but I'd like to offer you a warning before you go inside. Many of the children in there have endured extensive treatments for their diseases. I realize that you've undergone similar therapies in the past, but you should be prepared to see some unpleasantness."

"I know what to expect," Emily said, trying to sound brave.

"Very well," Dr. Kraven remarked as he utilized his clearance card to unlock the steel gate.

After Emily's dizziness subsided, she again strove to disburden herself from the wheelchair. As she hoped, her willpower prevailed once again. Even Dr. Kraven was astounded by her ability to rebound so quickly from her near collapse. Rather than wait for a commendation from the doctor, she gingerly stepped through the gate's opening and set her eyes upon the ravaged victims at hand.

Until this moment, Emily had never imagined herself to appear so sickly. But after studying the other children—some who no doubt suffered from similar ailments—she recognized that her condition was no less serious or saddening.

For several seconds she stood slump-shouldered in the room's corner, glancing timidly from bed to bed. The children's beds were set in parallel rows across the tiled floor, reminding her of headstones in a churchyard. The interior walls were cracked and carelessly painted with a dull, beige acrylic. Despite the fifteen children lying side by side, this ward possessed an eerie hollowness. No one talked. Not even a curious whisper passed between their beds. Only the faint sound of discourse from members of the staff could be heard in a neighboring corridor. It was as though these children hadn't even the will to notice that a visitor had arrived.

In an effort to be more visible, Emily hobbled to the room's center. She ignored a spastic pain that wound her belly into a knot. Even in the midst of agony, she could plainly see that these children weren't sleeping. Their pale expressions seemed to be etched upon gray tablets. Thirty blackened eyes peered at her without a glimmer of hope. It was as though all their gleeful visions had been eroded or never fully realized. In spite of the tired hearts that still beat within this room, death's presence loomed like a shadow waiting to lunge upon a sliver of superficial light.

Had it always been this terrible in here? Emily of course remembered that all hospital's left an unnatural feeling surging through her bones. But she never before encountered an entire ward being so purely subdued. Even during her prior visit with Dr. Garrison, she never sensed such a profound and shared bitterness among a group of children.

Emily dealt with her distress better than most, but whatever kept her alive for these past two years wasn't sustained solely through medicine. She couldn't quite grasp the precise ingredients required to remedy her own sickness, but she guessed that an irreplaceable substance of hope was sorely missing from these surroundings. Surely once deprived of this basic need, the sick died sooner and with much unsought shame. A sorrow oozed from these children's pores. It made Emily want to reach out and embrace their brittle limbs, but at the same time, she felt overwhelmed by the despondency pervading through this room like a rancid wind.

Once it became fairly obvious that the children weren't in any mood to welcome Emily into the ward, she decided to initiate conversation with one patient. After viewing the occupants for several seconds, she approached the bedside of a tiny, whey-faced girl. Out of all of the children present, this girl with pumpkin-colored hair and olive-green eyes appeared the most inquisitive. Although she made no effort to converse with Emily, she seemed less lethargic than the rest.

Before Emily introduced herself, the bedridden girl noticed a distinct difference between her and the other children. In a voice almost as diminutive as her stature, the girl asked, "Where's your hospital gown?"

"Excuse me?" Emily replied.

"Your gown," the girl repeated, motioning toward Emily's jeans and sweater. "They don't let us wear regular clothes in here, you know."

"Oh, but I'm not a patient here."

The girl peered skeptically at Emily. Judging by Emily's frail appearance, the girl couldn't help but to think that she was fibbing. "You don't have to hide it," she remarked. "We're all sick in here."

"I didn't say I wasn't sick," Emily clarified. "I just said that I wasn't a patient at this hospital."

"Then why are you here?"

Emily hadn't fully rationalized the exact purpose of this venture. She estimated that her interest must've been a symptom of a progressing illness, coupled with the inspection of Lawrence's journal. Of course none of this really mattered to the girl who she now stood beside. In order to alleviate the girl's anxiety, Emily asked for her name and how long she had been at Kindred Woods.

"Why do you care?" the girl responded, curtly.

Emily shrugged her shoulders before saying, "Isn't this what people usually do when they first meet?"

"You haven't told me your name yet."

"I'm Emily Dayton. I live in Wakeland with my father."

"So what's wrong with you?"

"Well," Emily answered, "I've been ill for a couple of years now. In the beginning, I was very mad and upset. I wanted to blame someone, but I've since learned that it's nobody's fault, especially my own. Sometimes kids—like you and me—get sick for reasons that no one really understands."

After mulling over those words, the girl huffed out her name with less enthusiasm than Emily would've hoped for. "If it matters, and I don't think it does, my name is Colleen. I once lived in New Jersey, but now I spend most of my time in here—waiting."

"Waiting for what?"

Colleen rolled her eyes before expressing her agitation. "What do you think? Doctor Kraven told me that I've only got a couple of months left before I die."

"He told you that?"

"Of course," Colleen replied, sedately. "He tells all of us that."

"All of us? Meaning all of you kids in here?"

"He's just being honest," Colleen pouted, realizing that Emily was appalled by this information.

"Colleen, there's a big difference between being honest and cruel. Why would Doctor Kraven want to upset all of his patients?"

"Who said we're upset? Most of the kids in here know what's happening. We've been through all the failed operations and false hope. Trust me, we've seen all kinds of doctors and they've tried to prepare us as gently as they could. Doctor Kraven has a more direct way of doing things."

Emily permitted her eyes to dart around the room again. All of the children were now propped up in their beds like a discarded band of inanimate puppets waiting to have their strings tugged. They appeared
strangely content to let Colleen preach their grief. When no one chose to
protest Dr. Kraven's unorthodox methods, Emily became incensed. This
feeling of rage aggravated a burning sensation in her stomach's lining. By
now the other children plainly saw that Emily was in no better condition
than they were.

"Maybe you should lie down on a bed," Colleen suggested.

Emily clenched her teeth and waved off her spell of agony along with
Colleen's hasty opinion. "I don't need a bed in here," Emily groaned.
"This isn't where I wish to spend my last days." She then turned toward all
the children and declared, "You should make an effort to pull yourselves
up off of these beds and enjoy whatever time God has chosen to give you."

"God isn't alive," a young male voice echoed from behind Emily. She
then pivoted toward the boy and saw a bald-headed twelve-year-old with
indented cheeks peering at her through bloodshot eyes. He clamped a pillow between his bony knees, but even with this fluffy pad disguising his
torso, Emily sensed that he was frail enough to fracture a bone if he even
dared to separate himself from his mattress.

As a result of the boy's immobility, raw lesions tore through the back of
his arms and legs. Upon closer observation, Emily noticed that his teeth
had rotted and his skin appeared waxy and pale. Despite his sickly appearance, Emily only paid mind to what he had uttered. She prayed that her
ears had deceived her, but his words reverberated in her head like the
weight of stone mallets being repeatedly bashed against her temples.

After moving closer to the boy, Emily asked him, "Why would you ever
think such a horrible thing?"

The boy didn't feel inspired to answer. Colleen elected to respond on
his behalf. "He says what he does because it's true. None of us in here
believe in God anymore."

Emily turned back to Colleen before asking, "Why?"

"Isn't it obvious to you yet? What has God done for us so far? We may have once believed, but how long can we really be expected to accept the lies that so many healthy people preach?"

"But God isn't a lie," Emily cried. "He is real, realer than all of our sicknesses combined. He hasn't turned away from us, Colleen. Don't you understand, this is God's way of drawing us closer to Him—and to heaven."

"You're starting to sound like one of those priests that Doctor Garrison used to bring in here," Colleen scolded. "Why don't you just accept reality—we're dying, and there's nothing else to talk about."

"I think you and the other children are making a big mistake," Emily admonished. "I learned a long time ago that a person never really dies. The body may not live forever, but the spirit inside us lives on. That's the reality that faith offers to all people—at least to those who still believe in God."

"You're beginning to bore us," Colleen yawned. "We've heard such sermons a thousand times before. You're too late to make a difference."

As Emily pitched her gaze from bed to bed around the ward, she realized that some hideous infection had spread among these kids with more lethalness than an untamed virus. In a moment of frustration, she turned back to the boy who had first instigated this matter.

"Who told you that God isn't alive?" Emily asked. She trembled as the wicked pain inside her stomach intensified. The boy, who was now intimidated by Emily's forwardness, slumped down in his bed and cowered beneath the linen. "You're not going to tell me, are you?"

The frightened boy shook his head and looked to Colleen for reassurance. "Does it really matter?" Colleen interjected. "If you must know, Doctor Kraven helped us understand the truth about everything."

"He told you to stop believing in God?"

"Well, not exactly. He let us decide that part for ourselves."

"And you all came to the same conclusion?"

"We've decided that it doesn't serve any good to put our trusts in myths," Colleen explained, coolly. "If you want to believe in God—or the boogie man for that matter—we're sure not going to try and convince you otherwise. Why can't you just accept the way we feel and let it be?"

"Because I know you're all wrong," Emily countered. "But I also know that none of this is your fault. I now understand that Doctor Kraven has influenced you. Don't you get it, Colleen, he's taking advantage of the fact that you're all sick, and he's forcing you to give up your last shred of hope."

"That's not true," Colleen denied. "Doctor Kraven is the first honest doctor that I've ever met. He simply tells us what our parents and relatives are too afraid to admit. No god can save us. Take a look around you. Can't you see the suffering?"

"I see confusion more than anything else."

"You know, Emily, I've met a few kids like you before. They bounce in here from time to time, preaching about all the bliss that's in store for them after they die. But what's really blissful about dying? The answer is nothing, and that's exactly what you get when you tilt your head to the sky and start talking to the clouds."

While confronting the coerced depravity of this room's occupants, Emily suddenly found herself stammering to defend her religious convictions. Perhaps the wrenching pain carving into her belly had finally become too acute to ignore. Gritting her teeth, she buckled over with a whimper as Colleen and the other children looked on with stony glares.

"Maybe we should call for help," the quivering boy suggested. "She looks pretty sick."

"Why call a doctor for her?" asked Colleen snippily. "If she's so convinced that God's looking out for her, let her pray for help and see what good it brings her."

"I don't think we should be mean to her," another girl then added. "She never did anything to hurt us."

"Okay," Colleen conceded, reaching across her bed to depress an emergency button on the wall. "I wasn't really going to let her suffer. I was just trying to teach her a lesson."

By now Emily endured too much pain to immediately respond to their chatter. Despite her duress, she managed to crawl against a nearby wall and prop her back against the concrete blocks. Within seconds, Dr. Kraven rushed into the ward. He immediately noticed Emily huddled on the floor in a fetal position. Her face was partially hidden in her lap. After assuring the other children that he had control of the situation, Dr. Kraven approached Emily and bent down beside her.

He placed his hand upon her knee and felt a cool sweat seeping through her jeans. Before he uttered a word, Emily lifted her chin and shoved his arm away with her hand.

"It's okay now, Emily," Dr. Kraven insisted. "I'm here to help you."

Two seconds later, Emily had regained her presence of mind. She was now thoroughly convinced that Dr. Kraven had betrayed these children. "What's happening in this place?" she whispered, attempting to let her breath catch up with her flickering thoughts. "What are you doing to those children?"

"I'm afraid I don't know what you mean."

"Don't lie to me, Doctor Kraven. The children here are far sicker than I thought."

"Of course," Dr. Kraven concurred. "I tried to prepare you for the worst. The treatments can sometimes make their behavior quite unpredictable."

"I'm not talking about that," Emily sniveled, but her fury far surpassed any urge to cry. "I want to know why none of those kids believe in God. You've done something to their minds, haven't you?"

Before engaging in any further conversation, Dr. Kraven advised Emily to return to the wheelchair as quickly as possible. After staggering to reclaim a standing position, Emily reluctantly followed him outside the ward. Once settling into the wheelchair, Emily sensed her stomach muscles loosening. After a few minutes, she felt well enough to breathe at a normal rate.

"Apparently, you're not as tough as you'd like to believe," Dr. Kraven said, offering her a clean napkin to dry the perspiration from her face.

Emily refused his offering by swatting his hand. "I've obviously done something to upset you, Emily. How can I make it up to you?"

"You can start by answering my question," she huffed. "Why are all of those kids so convinced that God doesn't exist?"

Dr. Kraven's mouth frowned before replying, "That's a rather odd question to ask me. I'm their doctor, not their clergyman."

"They're vulnerable to whatever you say," Emily snapped. "I'll admit, you almost had me fooled as well. But I think I know what's going on here. You're poisoning their minds with hatred."

Dr. Kraven chuckled innocently and said, "Emily, that's quite an accusation. Of course it sounds foolish coming from a girl as bright as you."

"Just tell me why you're hurting them? Haven't they suffered enough? Must you steal their last shred of hope before they die?"

"I can't simply jump inside their heads and tell them what to believe or disbelieve—especially in matters of faith. The best I can do is keep them safe and comfortable."

Even before Dr. Kraven finished his denial, Emily sensed a burning sensation cutting into her abdomen again—this time gradually creeping its way toward her heart. With her respiration eclipsed by pain, she still managed to reaffirm her belief. "Why are you doing this to them, Doctor Kraven? I don't understand what you want to accomplish."

Seeing that Emily was conspicuously ill, Dr. Kraven attempted to calm her mood by offering medical assistance. Emily rejected his advance by kicking at his arms with her feet. "Keep away from me! Don't you dare touch me."

"Emily, you're very sick and confused. Please, either let me help you or I'll be forced to have you sedated."

"No," Emily grimaced, trying to push the wheelchair away from Dr. Kraven's grasp. "You want to put me in one of those deathbeds! I won't let you do to me what you've done to them!"

"Dear child, I wish you could hear how irrational you sound, but I realize that you may not be reasoning too clearly right now."

"I know what I'm saying. You can't lie to me! I don't want to hear you deny it any longer. Just tell me why you've decided to take God away from them at a time when they need Him most."

"You're making more out of this than is necessary. As I already explained, I don't preach to any child. Be it good or evil, they are each accountable for their own thoughts. Personally, I'm disappointed that you've formed such a low opinion of me. I thought we were well on the verge of becoming close friends."

"You're a liar, Doctor Kraven. You don't need me as a friend. All you really want to do is hurt me—hurt me in a way that no disease by itself could ever do. I won't let you steal God from my heart."

Dr. Kraven cackled freely before commenting, "You've got a lively imagination. I suspect that much of that creativity can be traced to your obsession with literature. However, you should never be blind to what is real and what is not."

At this point, Emily had heard enough from Dr. Kraven. She planned to escape from this ward, but the iron gates had already closed around her. She was far too feeble to remove herself from the wheelchair, and any scream she managed wouldn't have echoed beyond the elevator's shaft.

Left with no other option, Emily began to push herself in the wheelchair up the corridor. She called out for help to a passing nurse, but the woman seemed deaf to her plea. At this critical moment, Emily realized that Dr. Kraven wasn't the sole participant in the unwinding scheme at this hospital.

Now breathless and bewildered, Emily slouched over in the wheelchair. She could no longer deny or suspend the pain that wilted her body like a blossom caught in a winter frost. When she heard Dr. Kraven's footsteps approaching, she knew that it was too late to avoid him.

When Dr. Kraven neared the wheelchair, he simply shook his head as Emily plunged headlong from her seat, smacking her face against the concrete floor. While attempting to crawl toward the elevator, she groaned heavily. Finally, with Dr. Kraven standing over her, she stopped and placed her arms at each side.

"It really doesn't have to be so grueling, Emily," Dr. Kraven whispered. "You can feel the pain gnawing at your body's tissue much more intensely now. It's impossible for you to contain it any longer. Eventually, you'll be begging me to give you something to ease your agony."

"I don't need anything from you," Emily stammered. "Go away—leave me alone. You're nothing but an evil man!"

"Oh, come on. Now is not the time for you to be hurling insults at me. Frankly, I expected keener observations from a girl who has dabbled in the classics. Tell me, Emily, what would Dickinson say to you now if she could compose the words that best described your plight? Might she say: 'Because I could not stop for Death—He kindly stopped for me'?"

"Go away," Emily sobbed, this time hiding her face with her hands. "I want you to leave right now."

"I can't do that," Dr. Kraven said, his voice oozing with sarcasm. "I mean, how would it look if I left you to die in the basement of this hospital?" He then reached down and grabbed Emily's shoulder. After sliding his cold fingers over her back, he placed his fingers up near her neck and checked her pulse.

Emily cringed at his touch, but she wasn't agile enough to escape his frigid clutches. "I'm afraid it's worst than I thought," Dr. Kraven muttered. "Your heart is very tired. I sense the life ebbing away even as I speak to you now."

Emily used what remained of her strength by scooting over onto her backside. With her energy now depleted, she calmly gazed upward into the ceiling's fluorescent light. "God help you," she murmured.

Dr. Kraven responded with a sneer. "You haven't yet identified the facts about God, dear child. Isn't that why you truly came to Kindred Woods on this day—to at last discover what in your mind you already suspect to be true?"

"God is alive," Emily repeated, but her voice was wispy by now.

"Perhaps," Dr. Kraven chortled, "but He is not with you. Like so many other children who've slunk through these corridors, you will die a lonely death. There is no god who will answer your prayers. He doesn't even hear your cries for mercy. You and your kind are a detestable sight to His eyes—a mistake that must be first condemned and then eliminated."

"I—I knew you were a wicked man," Emily stuttered, "I felt it—"

"Your rage is misdirected. Despite what you may think of me in these moments, I am not your enemy. I've come to this hospital to let you and other children know that I am their friend. When death comes for you, I will be there to subdue your cries. I am the one who must collect the shattered pieces of broken lives and mend them together again. If it fills your mind with any sense of pleasure, then label me as a wicked man. But I will not mislead you, Emily. I will not stand before you and tell you that God cares."

"He does! He must!"

"Don't you see? Everything that you've been told about Him has been a lie. How much suffering are you willing to endure before you finally concede to the fact that God has abandoned you? To Him, you are no more vital to this Earth than the animals that rot in foreign fields. It's time for you to free yourself from His grasp, dear child. Reject Him, and you shall be live a better life beside the one true Lord."

Since Emily was too weak to respond, she simply closed her eyelids and allowed an irrepressible urge to sleep to overtake her mind. Within seconds, Dr. Kraven lifted the unconscious girl off the floor and set her body gently in the wheelchair. He then turned to see a nurse standing behind him.

The female nurse crossed her arms in front of her body while peering wide-eyed at Dr. Kraven. She flashed an expression of approval. "Is everything going as planned, Doctor?" she asked, moving toward the wheelchair.

"It's still too early to tell," Dr. Kraven said. "She has a much stronger will than the others."

"Then she must be the one," the nurse whispered, the tension mounting in her voice.

"See to it that she's admitted into the ward immediately," Dr. Kraven commanded.

"Do you want to put her in with the other children?"

"No. I want this patient to be placed into a private room."

"Of course," the nurse agreed. "But, Doctor, we still have her father and that home nurse waiting for her upstairs. How should we handle them?"

"Leave the details up to me," Dr. Kraven insisted. With those words, he paced down the hall and stepped into an awaiting elevator. As the doors slid shut, he appeared satisfied with his deed, but he also realized that his ultimate task was not yet finished.

Meanwhile, Theodore settled onto a plush leather couch in a vacant lounge. After opening Lawrence's journal on his lap, he flipped through the sheets of paper without bothering to read the handwritten words. Eventually, he reached a mark in the diary where Regina had placed the crucifix.

Now subdued by the room's silence, Theodore rubbed his fingers over the cross's beveled surface. Before allowing himself to delve too deeply into his own emotions, he turned the page and enveloped the cross in paper. Without further regard to Christ's image, he let the true thoughts of his father leap off the page and burrow within his mind.

CHAPTER TWENTY-FOUR

▼

JOURNAL ENTRY THIRTEEN

ASYLUM BY THE SEA

If nothing good can ever be achieved by the reading of this diary, let it at least be regarded as a blueprint to how abruptly a man's fate may change in this world. In my life, I have learned one absolute truth: Everything that God created—including the minds and hearts of all His creatures—will gradually succumb to destruction. There can be no set time allotted for any one life. There can be no clear division between the pure and impure. Lastly, there will be no recourse for a soul who has sacrificed the most fruitful years of his life by pursuing the illusions in a dream.

I would now like to introduce you to the next stage of my life. If I endured a graver or more desperate period, it has since escaped my memory.

In 1953, just three months after my twenty-third birthday, I was ushered
into a courthouse in New Jersey to face an irate judge and jury on the most
serious charge of attempted murder. Needless to say, my defense was as non-
existent as my silent prayers for acquittal.

Faces from the past filed into this steamy, maple-encrusted courtroom
to hear the sentence that would drastically eliminate my privilege of freedom. Victoria came in support, but only at the request of authorities. She
didn't bring our son. Cooper and Reverend Keegan also attended,
although they glared at me like two feral beasts that'd been betrayed by
their master's hand. No ambivalence existed here on this day. Everyone
knew wholeheartedly that I was guilty of the said charges. They just didn't
understand why. In this, they were not alone.

Prior to my inevitable conviction, an inexperienced public defender
proposed two strategies on my behalf. I greeted my options with little
enthusiasm. Firstly, I was instructed to stand before the jury with my posture slumped forward and eyes flitting about the ceiling as if I had no
sense of what was happening. My second choice was to approach the jury
as a sane man and convey to them what no one beside myself would have
the comprehension to appreciate.

By choosing the first option of insanity, I'd avoid prison and perhaps be
sentenced to a minimum stay at a low-security institution. If I confessed
to premeditating a murder plot, I may have been looking at twenty years
in prison. It seemed like an easy decision, but I was very hesitant to sign
away my sanity. By claiming mental derangement, I risked the likelihood
of being subjected to an asylum. This was no less threatening to my future
than the bars of a jail cell.

After carefully measuring the pros and cons, I decided that I wasn't prepared to squander twenty years of my life in prison. Rather than burden
you with the details of my legal tribulations, I will say that the outcome
went precisely as anticipated. The square-jawed judge handed down my
punishment without a trace of regret. Since I had already deemed myself
to be socially unfit, he sentenced me to spend an indefinite period of time

under the observation of a psychiatric team at Crestpoint Mental Institution in southern New Jersey.

Though my legal representative shook my hand as if we'd won some significant victory, I wasn't so giddy about the accommodations of my future residence. I fully understood that a stigma had been unfairly leveled upon those who were classified as mentally ill. Now that I had voluntarily surrendered my dignity, I wondered what chance I had at ever reclaiming my family's trust.

When the trial concluded, Victoria didn't waste too many tears crying over my predicament. I knew then that we would never love one another like we had before. As she approached me in the courthouse, I recalled that perfect moment when we first met. Just like today, an ivory dress clung to her narrow hips as she strode toward me. As always, her face was a perfect profile of womanhood. Her features were as natural and vibrant as the rarest and most beautiful gems. Still, a substance was blatantly absent from her lips. Was it merely a sampling of her ruby-colored lipstick, or was it something far more irreplaceable?

As Victoria moved closer towards me, I remembered what had drawn me to her side. She once possessed a smile that could make the heart of the coldest cynic melt like ice in the sun. But as she gazed at me today, I sensed that her joy had been washed away by a merciless tide. Judging by her disenchanted expression, I gathered that she had found the courage to impart some unhappy news to me.

Out of regard for our son's welfare, Victoria had decided to immediately return to Green Haven to raise our son. In the likely event of my prolonged departure from home, she suggested that Theodore never be told of my whereabouts. I could hardly disagree with her logic at this point. It wasn't until much later that I debated on whether or not Theodore needed to know the truth about his father.

Before being escorted away by the court officers, I had an opportunity to converse briefly with Victoria. I didn't know it then, but this exchange of dialogue represented our last spoken words together for many years to come.

"I can understand that you want to keep Theodore away from this madness," I said, "but can I count on you to at least bring him to see me occasionally?"

"Reverend Keegan thought it would be too much of a burden—"

"Forget about what he said. What do you feel is the right thing to do?"

Victoria glared at me as plainly as a stranger passing another on a crowded street did. In a voice no bigger than my shrinking ego, she responded, "I can't promise that I'll ever visit you, Lawrence. Too much has happened."

"Don't treat me like a common criminal. They may have the power to lock me up in a padded cell, but eventually they're going to learn what I already know."

"Stop it, Lawrence! I don't want to hear any more of this. I'm almost afraid to think what will become of you. Despite everything, I still want to see you recover."

"How can I hope to recover when everyone I know and loved has turned against me?"

"Maybe you've turned against yourself. Have you yet considered that?"

"Victoria, all I'm asking for you to do is to stay in contact with me. I think I deserve the opportunity to know how my son is doing, even if he doesn't know who I am."

"I'll write letters," she sighed, "and maybe send photographs."

"Do you think I wanted things to turn out like this? I never wanted to disappoint you. If you remember nothing else about me, please never forget that."

They had to drag me from the courthouse on that day. I remember latching onto the tables, weeping like an infant being plucked from his mother's breast. Though I ached for Victoria to call out to me, if only to offer a final word of encouragement, she did not. Instead, she peered at me with mirthless eyes, perhaps wishing that she could reclaim her innocence as simply as she turned for the door.

In light of my past shortcomings, I thought that my life couldn't possibly get any worst. As it turned out, Crestpoint had a darker and more devious history than my own. The pearl-colored, clapboard edifice looked like a clone to numerous beach resorts that popped up along New Jersey's seacoast. Aside from acres of barbwire fencing and steel-caged windows, the structure reminded me of one of those Victorian hideaways designed for the affluent urbanites vying for a suntan.

From the north side of a road leading into the institution, I saw beige-colored sand hugging the Atlantic Ocean. Sunlight reflected off the waves, and a briny mist lingered in the air. Seagulls hovered like stalled kites beside the shoreline, scouring for fallen crumbs as the ocean folded against the beach. The lapping water glimmered like a sheet of crystal. In these moments, I thought about the unrivaled power set before my eyes, and realized how easily water washed away the dreams of yesterday and replaced them with those of tomorrow.

I was blindly towed between the tides of time. I felt myself being consumed by the churning currents. The names of countless souls had been tagged and forgotten once encamped behind Crestpoint's walls. From the outside looking in, it all appeared innocuous, even quite tranquil. But the real danger—like the ocean itself—resided beneath its surface.

Crestpoint served as a depot for the unfit members of our human race. Murderers and lunatics commingled in a habitat that defied common sense. Upon entering the facility, the faint scent of saltwater gave way to a noxious odor. Despite all efforts to neutralize the air with disinfectants, I immediately identified the stench of unwashed occupants gathered upon the floors.

Crestpoint's patients had been collected like defected toys and strewn together in various stages of mental decay. Each man was issued a white jumpsuit, absent of all buttons and strings. A badge of black letters, embroidered to their backs, identified them as a number rather than a name. The majority of those I studied wore no shoes or socks, and each was bound at the ankles by steel fetters.

These tormented faces represented the forgotten sons and fathers of society. No one in here cared if they lived or died. I suppose the most shameful part to all this madness was that even with all their fragmented thoughts, these men realized that they were unloved by mankind long before they came to Crestpoint. Perhaps, in their own primitive way, they committed their crimes as a way to draw attention to themselves.

As I wandered through the ward, a room full of crazed eyes dissected my apprehension. Had it really come to this? Was I now seen through their eyes as being one of them? Though at times I sought to be compassionate to these cheerless loons, I could not forgive them for their sins. They had spilled the cold blood of men and women, and violated all laws of common decency. Though I stood among them, I did not view myself as part of their circle.

After a few weeks I learned that Crestpoint served to reinforce the agony of its patients on a daily basis. The psychiatrists who presided over this asylum never actually intended for me to walk away. Contrarily, the longer I remained living among these deranged men, the more clear to me it became that I'd never be dismissed from these premises alive. Whether I chose to concede to the fact of not, this institution had become a refuge with no viable exit.

Within a month after arriving at Crestpoint, I realized that I needed a transfer. Of course switching from this institution to another was about as likely as Victoria welcoming me back home. Part of the problem stemmed from a host of legal restrictions drafted by the state, but I was subjected to harsher standards than the other patients because of a report filed by Dr. Konrad. Apparently, he had provided Crestpoint's psychiatric team with an encyclopedic-sized evaluation of my paranoiac behavior. No one questioned the accuracy of Konrad's research, especially Dr. Blake, who was the shrink assigned to access my cognitive disability.

Dr. Blake wouldn't have been such a bad man if he didn't allow himself to be persuaded by Konrad so easily. He certainly wasn't the first man to embrace Konrad's perverted methods. Based on Blake's twenty years of practice in abnormal psychology, I may have bargained on him to notice Konrad's peculiar characteristics. During some of my private consultations with Dr. Blake, I'd often try to point out Konrad's less-than-favorable record. Despite my efforts, nothing in the way of an investigation was ever conducted.

Though it was impossible for me to verify my belief, I presumed that the murders at Pine Grove continued long after I became incarcerated at Crestpoint. Over time I slowly lost my will to care about the world outside, and retreated to my appointed cell in silent protest. For months I talked to no one other than my doctors. Those who ventured too far into my space or line of sight were physically brushed aside.

Six months after my arrival, the doctors warned me that I couldn't possibly expect to get better by sealing myself in a cubicle for twelve hours every day. Many of the self-appointed experts, particularly Dr. Blake, advised that I join the other patients in periodic meetings. At these "house chats," as they were called, patients strove to socialize and probe the various problems that may have triggered their abhorrent behavior. I leered upon these affairs with a critical eye, and soon began to perceive that they were all being displayed like freaks in an experimental circus.

By refusing to volunteer myself for this brand of manipulation, I unwittingly encouraged the doctors and other personnel to turn against me. In a short span of time, I was targeted for more one-on-one evaluation than any other patient quartered at Crestpoint. I can't say exactly why they disliked me, but I gathered that the doctors feared a man like me. This was not a result of any unique intelligence on my part. I simply attributed their worry to my unwillingness to adopt their procedures.

Well after it became obvious that my stay at Crestpoint would be much longer than I originally predicted, Dr. Blake summoned me into his office for a frank discussion about my supposed insanity. Since patients were normally restricted from leaving the main house without written approval from the entire psychiatric team, I was surprised by Dr. Blake's decision to see me alone. Yet with my hands and feet clasped in shackles, I figured not to be a threat.

Dr. Blake didn't loathe me as much as the others. In a peculiar way, he at times reminded me of my father. Though Dr. Blake had the benefit of an ivy-league education and expensive wardrobe, he demonstrated a posture and aloofness that could have belonged to a disheartened miner. All things considered, I at first despised this skinny, inquisitive man. Eventually, however, I acquired mixed feelings about his intentions.

Dr. Blake's office mimicked his personality. It was a bland room and simple in its outward design. The décor was a modest mixture of contemporary furnishings, coupled with soft hues of green and ivory carpeting. To his credit, Blake didn't attempt to impress me with his knowledge, and I appreciated his down-to-earth ethics when he wasn't under the vicious scrutiny of his peers. Had we met under different circumstances, I might've had a lot more to talk about than I was presently willing to share.

As I made myself as comfortable as possible on a vinyl chair in front of his desk, Blake revealed a mound of papers filed in manila folders. These documents, I discovered, all pertained to my past, present, and predicted maladies. Blake went to some trouble delving into my history, and in the process uncovered things about me that he that I had kept buried for years. Although I was initially startled by his tenacious research, I soon realized that he was fretting over nonessential information.

"We've been over this rubbish at least fifty times," I said, reclining in the chair as best I could with chains linked to my wrists. "I'm convinced that you're not going to be satisfied with what I say until I admit that I'm crazy."

Blake studied me with his squinty, gray eyes before saying, "You know, Lawrence, those among us who are truly mentally impaired never think of themselves as such. Much like yourself, they believe they are perfectly normal."

"Then why expend so much energy trying to convince them otherwise?"

"Let's talk about you for a moment," Blake suggested. "I can only measure the degree of your disability against the crime."

"What if I just had a bad day? Doesn't that count for anything?"

Blake shuffled his papers while gnawing nervously on the tip of his fountain pen. "You seem like a reasonably intelligent man and all of our cognitive tests haven't proven otherwise. So tell me, Lawrence, what's a man with a 165 IQ doing parading around a children's hospital with a kitchen knife?"

"I told you my story once already, Blake. Weren't you listening?"

"Maybe I need to hear it again."

"Come on," I sneered, "it's not going to change."

Blake now stared more closely at me. I watched his eyes widen behind the thick lenses of his eyeglasses. After a moment of contemplation, he scratched at the bone-white hair sprouting in a semicircle around his ears. While he spoke, I lent my attention to the mauve-colored warts that peppered his forehead.

"Your refusal to talk about your delusions makes you far more mysterious than the other patients. I can't force you to talk about what's really troubling you. If you refuse to let me help, how can I ever offer you a fair evaluation?"

"Like I told you before, Blake, I don't need to be evaluated. I'm not going to let you pick my brain apart. So why don't you just let me wait out my time in peace? Do you have to take what little pride I have left before I leave?"

"Lawrence, you're not ever going to leave here unless we can document some progress. As it stands now, you've shown us none."

"I'm not ready to share my story with a room full of loons who can't understand what the hell I'm talking about. How can I expect them to comprehend? You don't even believe me."

"It's not a matter of me believing you. I just need to determine whether or not you believe what you've proposed in these reports."

"It's all true," I sighed tiredly. "And I don't regret what I did. Konrad has to be stopped. If you really want to do a service for this community, Blake, you'll get that murderer out of Pine Grove."

At this point in our conversation I expelled a breath of frustration and jumped up from the chair like a boy in the midst of a tantrum. I felt Dr. Blake's eyes penetrating me as I lurched over to the office's window. While watching a sparrow fly from a nearby tree I uttered, "Despite what you and the rest of those shrinks think of me, I know that my dreams are real."

"Let's talk about those dreams again," Blake suggested, casually referring to the documents placed before him on his desk. "If I'm to understand you, upon coming here you told me that you were dreaming about doves—birds, am I right?"

I shook my head and sternly replied, "That's correct, but as I said before, these doves were not intended to be regarded as ordinary birds."

"That's right," Blake remembered, humoring me with his mellow voice. "You contended that the doves in your dreams were actually symbolic to the ill children at Pine Grove—"

"Right again," I declared, despondently. "That's where Doctor Konrad comes into play. He's also in my dreams—not as a bird, but as something closer to a shadow, like a winged creature."

"Something evil, perhaps?"

"Very evil," I agreed. "It's certainly not what it appears to be."

"This thing—or dark fiend as you initially referred to it—is somehow linked to Doctor Konrad? I may be able to understand your visions of doves being associated with children, but why do you draw the connection between a doctor and something bent on destroying young lives?"

I turned away from the window and smiled insincerely at the doctor. "No matter how many times we go through this, Blake, we always end up in the same place. Stop trying to analyze everything I say, and just listen."

"I'm listening," Blake assured me, "but what you're saying isn't reasonable. And it sounds even more absurd when you start talking about angels."

"I've only seen one angel," I corrected. "Let me make that clear."

"And how does this angel—this angel you named Jonathan—fit into all of this?"

"I don't have an answer for that yet. And to be honest, I don't think I'm ever going to get one. If I had to guess, I'd say that Jonathan wanted to tell me something important. Personally, I don't think either of us had a choice in the matter."

"Do you still see doves while you sleep, Lawrence?"

"I don't know—maybe, but everything is vague since I came to this place. I just wish none of this ever happened."

Before Dr. Blake could add any more to my upset, I asked to be returned to my cell. Feeling as though he had badgered me enough for one day, Blake agreed to my request. Later on, while I stewed in the silence between my walls, I thought about how odd I must've sounded to that doctor. I couldn't dislike him for suspecting that I was insane. After all, I presently had nothing to validate my theory regarding Dr. Konrad. If placed in Blake's position, I might've been equally cautious toward a man with such a reputation as my own.

I eventually convinced myself that any further information that I offered to Blake regarding Jonathan or the dark fiend would surely work against me at a future conference. Rather than subject myself to Blake's trickery, I clung to the imaginary notion that silence represented my best chance at obtaining freedom. I didn't want to spend my days at Crestpoint brooding over the significance of my dreams. Now more than anything else, I simply prayed to hear from Victoria so that I could see my son again, if only through the images of a photograph.

A year and six months after my arrival at Crestpoint, Victoria mailed her first letter to me. She enclosed six photographs of our son at various stages of his development. The boy, like his beautiful mother, was blessed with striking features, including eyes as lucid as a sun struck sea. In her three-page exposition, Victoria made no excuses for the eighteen months it took her to compile her thoughts into words. She did, however, relay the most encouraging news about our boy that I had heard in a long while.

Soon after returning to Green Haven, Victoria began to devote much of her idle time toward church functions. When she required a recess from mothering Theodore or tending to the antique shop, Reverend Keegan and other trusted members of the community assumed the responsibilities of fatherhood that I had forfeited. It was during one such occasion that Keegan noticed that my son was reacting to patterns of light. Soon thereafter, Dr. Avery confirmed that Theodore's vision was—by some unlikely miracle—gradually repairing itself.

I recited Victoria's words several times over in my mind, making certain that I hadn't mistook her message. Dr. Avery believed that Theodore's eyesight would be fully functional before his third birthday. I always knew—or at least hoped in my dearest prayers—that our son would not be forced to wander through his youth in darkness. Though my faith in God was currently muddled, I was thankful to Him for this chance he extended to my child.

In tears, I finished reading Victoria's letter, all the while scanning for the words where she would declare her loneliness in my absence. But this thought was no more part of the letter than I was of her heart. As I already surmised, Victoria had moved on with her ambitions. The loss of this woman—especially one so cherished—was a supreme sacrifice to my ego. For weeks I pondered the influences that might've led Victoria away from me. Was she in love with another man? I was almost afraid to know the answer.

If the truth were told, I had lost her affections long ago and left her with a burden of a blind infant cleaving to her shoulder. To think that her good fortune would in turn improve my own was a selfish and short-lived notion.

Three months following this initial correspondence, Victoria mailed me another package. This envelope contained all the paperwork necessary to finalize our divorce. Regrettably, I signed these documents without dissecting the legal jargon. In the process, I waived all parental rights in relation to my son's upbringing. In 1955, I wrote to Victoria at several intervals, begging her to reconsider her decision to keep Theodore away from Crestpoint. After weeks of anxiously waiting for a reply, my letters were returned unopened.

Complying with a divorce didn't mean that I was still agreeable to the idea of being estranged from my son. Now that Theodore was older and no longer hindered by blindness, I thought he might wish to meet with me, if only to supply a brief remedy for both of us. Dr. Blake recognized my desperation and forwarded numerous letters to Victoria's address, stating that a supervised visitation from family members was permissible—even advisable—during the process of recovery. I didn't pretend to know what deplorable thoughts had been whispered into Victoria's ear by now, but she never bothered to respond to these requests.

In December of 1955, I abandoned all hope that Victoria would ever try to contact me again. As a consequence of this realization, my depression quickly deepened. Dr. Blake became so protective in regard to my welfare that he—fearing I would hang myself—removed the sheets from my bed and assigned round-the-clock medics to watch over my shoulder. I can't say for certain if I plotted to end my life at this stage or not, but the prospect of dying no longer frightened me as it once did. In an odd way, while casually slipping into the routines of this asylum, I already felt partially dead.

While lying on the floor of my cell in absolute darkness, I listened to the cries of crazed men rebounding through the corridors. These blistering howls, which once filled my dreams with a sense of trepidation, slowly dissolved into my subconscious. Whether I wished to accept Crestpoint as my home or not, I inevitably became consumed by its maddening spell. The patients, who I once considered repulsive, had unwittingly become the products by which I measured my own sanity.

For years the names and faces of these deranged men remained primarily invisible to my eyes. In truth, we were all expendable to one another and to the rest of society. There were times when I wished that I had sooner understood the value of securing some recognition in this world. Every man, no matter how thoroughly depraved or inept, needed to know that his life was not lived in vain. In the cruel end to come, it didn't matter how we felt about ourselves. Ultimately, the opinions of others unfairly served as a reference to our worth.

However misdirected our motives might have been, society had branded us with its unrelenting terms. I likened this entire experience to being suspended in purgatory; only our wait for heaven or hell was eternal. Day after night I watched the sun and moon trade places in the sky, warring for their apportioned claim over light and darkness. Eventually, all sense of time and purpose faded into the nothingness of my unrealized dreams.

Despite Victoria's refusal to acknowledge my existence, I continued to send letters to her home in Green Haven for two more years. By 1957 I had collected over two hundred pieces of unopened mail. As a reminder of my ongoing quest to see my son, I stacked these envelopes exactly in the order I received them on a shelf in my room. Dr. Blake advised that I should have made better use of my time, but I wasn't prepared to join the other patients who so readily confessed their miseries.

If it were not for the kindness of the sole person who contacted me, I may have continued to squander postage on a woman who no longer cared for me. A friend from my past proved to be all the evidence I needed to determine that life had a vicious way of kicking a man between his eyes, especially while he lied close to the ground. Cooper, my one-time savior in this triangle of pain, replied to one of my letters in November of 1957. As always, his message was succinct and brutally honest.

Cooper's words explained that Victoria no longer resided in Green Haven. By the day I received this news, she had already been gone for twelve months. For reasons not fully specified in Cooper's letter, she chose to depart her pastoral community in haste, hoping to make a fresh beginning for herself and Theodore in Philadelphia. How ironic, I thought, that she would attempt to erase her past by seeking refuge in the same city where I first embarked. Although I viewed her decision quite peculiar, I at least gained confirmation as to why my letters went ignored. I could now put down my pen knowing that I tried to be a good father, albeit from afar.

It was during this same period that I realized that all life—like the Earth itself—revolved in one continuous circle, never stopping to turn back, yet always returning to where it once had been. Similarly, we were destined by the deeds of our past, and the people and places that we met and left behind eventually reveal themselves to us again. They may not come to us directly, but through fragmented memories we uncover the rights and wrongs of our yesterdays and reapply them to our tomorrows. Despite our purest strivings to keep the shadows of sorrow and joy at a safe distance, we inevitably sense them again through the eyes of faraway friends and nearby strangers.

CHAPTER TWENTY-FIVE

▼

JOURNAL ENTRY FOURTEEN

VICTORIA'S GIFT

While reflecting upon the events of a lifetime, I've elected to organize my memories through a series of decades. Such an arrangement of time enabled me to calculate precisely how I've changed over the years. I've already recounted my youth by following this plan, but now I must push my pen forward with greater uncertainty, for I sense my breath weakening as I remember all of the sorrow that has delivered me to this moment.

By 1961, I had wasted nearly an entire decade of my life wandering through the corridors of my seaside asylum. My youth had been frittered away because of pride and resentment. I despised the man I had become, but I loathed what surrounded me with even a greater indignation. In my own mind, I was far saner than those who tried to befriend me were.

Why was I made to reside in such mental squalor for so long? Couldn't the doctors sense that I was a genuinely coherent man? In spite of my past sins and misanthropic tendencies, as they called it, didn't they yet feel that I deserved a chance to live like a human being again?

Dr. Blake documented my complaints and often made it a point to confer with those who arbitrated my destiny. Since I still refused to admit my propensity toward violence, none of the doctors were resigned to offering me a second chance at a normal life. And so I returned to the wretched ranks in search of the truth about myself, all the while pondering over the unseen mysteries that had lowered me to this level of shame.

As the pages on the calendar continued to turn, I involuntarily learned to eat and bathe with these two-legged beasts. The house chats had taught me that they were all shrouded in a thin layer of mortal flesh. I listened to their tales of woe with no pity in my heart. Most of these patients blamed society's class system for their abnormalities. Others took umbrage at their parents' inadequacies. And the philosophers of the lot condemned the human race in general, insisting that their murderous deeds reflected an innate desire to maim, which of course we all unwittingly possessed.

Sadly, the sufferers amidst all of this lunacy were Victoria and our son. In spite of the passage of time, I still adored that woman like on the hour we first wed. I never favored the absurd notion that love could simply die. It may wither like a flower lacking moisture, but if given sufficient nourishment, it always stood a chance to flourish again. Though I hadn't heard from Victoria or my son in years, I prayed nightly for their welfare, for I wholeheartedly anticipated that we wouldn't depart from this world as the strangers we had become.

In the autumn of 1962, following my son's tenth birthday, I received a telegram in the mail that altered my life's journey once again. Immediately after interpreting the letter's postage mark, I became elated by Victoria's choice to write to me after years of silence. She stipulated that she wanted to see me again as soon as it could be arranged. I didn't yet understand the urgency of her tone, but I hoped that she'd finally realized my significance to our son's upbringing.

She was mindful enough to enclose three color photographs of Theodore, including one from his most recent birthday celebration. Much to my satisfaction, the boy had grown into a rather good-looking young man, mostly because he relied upon his mother's comeliness. Yet I remembered being especially charmed by the clarity of his eyes. It would've been improbable for anyone to presume that he had combated blindness as an infant. He appeared buoyant and carefree in his mannerisms, grinning as if he had discovered something about life that everyone else didn't perceive.

Although visibly older and a bit more ornery than his earlier years, Dr. Blake was still approachable regarding matters of visitation. My circumstance was particularly motivating for him, being that I hadn't had the benefit of a single visitor since arriving at Crestpoint. Normal procedures required all visitors to greet the patients in a stale recreation room situated among a throng of grim-faced guards. Fortunately, Dr. Blake permitted me to converse privately with Victoria in my cell. Since I hadn't even thought to ask for special accommodations, his gesture struck me as an honorable one.

Before Victoria's scheduled arrival, I reminisced about the few but special moments we shared together in Green Haven. My memory served me well in regard to her appearance. I made a firm point of forming a photograph of her loveliness in my mind. Her image solidified itself so thoroughly within my subconscious that all I needed to do was close my eyelids and permit her radiance to reemerge. Like a ray of sunlight severing dark tides, she'd light a path across the sea of agony for me to follow. During my gravest hours, I slumbered in peace for as long as her smile and soft glow turned to where I stood.

A man's memory was a gift unlike any other, especially in the way that it safeguarded him from the uncertainties of reality. Where else but within one's own recollections could a love affair last forever? My mental picture of Victoria had been preserved and sealed from the unclean air. I rehearsed the details of her beauty as if time was not a factor to her as it was to me. The passing of ten years seemed unimportant, for she would always be enchanting in my mind's eye. I once believed that she would have lived forever untouched and free from the burdens that ruined us all.

Yet when Victoria finally approached my cell, I clawed at my eyes as if blinded by some obscene vision. Indeed, a woman stood beside Dr. Blake, but this couldn't be the same person I immortalized. This lady was frail and puckered in the face like a wrinkled crone. Although she was not yet thirty-five, the youthful glow had been stripped from her flesh. Her eyes, once as splendid as a setting sun, now appeared half-sunken in their sockets and darkened by ashen-colored bags. And her lips looked cracked and as bloodless as flaking skin.

I only needed a moment to determine that something had gone afoul with Victoria's health. Time and reality had combined to steal the memory of her loveliness from me. Some insidious disease had devoured her figure. She no longer had hips or breasts to hold the shape of her black dress. The drab material hung over her shoulders like a tarpaulin fallen across a lamp-post. Adding to these ravages, her once-glorious hair of chestnut-colored locks was now cropped up around her ears and thinned to near transparency against her skull.

Victoria's voice had surrendered its sweetness as well. She sounded feeble and disorientated. Even so, she must have noticed the grief magnifying in my eyes. At this moment, all that I prayed for seemed pointless. I thought to blame myself for her agony. Never before now had I felt so utterly helpless in the presence of such spoiled grace. I sought to curse someone from my past, but I hadn't the resolve to do anything but stare at her with the pity that I could never quite summon for myself.

Before Dr. Blake left us alone, he brought two folding chairs into my cell. Since I had often praised Victoria's beauty in the past, I sensed him gauging my distress as he set the chairs beside a small table in the room's corner. After kindly assisting Victoria, who was armed with a packet of papers, to a chair, Blake politely excused himself from our company.

While watching Victoria crouch tentatively into the chair, I felt obligated to mention her sickness, but I didn't want to seem harsh. For several seconds, I tamed an urge to cry. In the meantime, she eased into conversation with me as nonchalantly as possible.

"I know it's been a long time since we've seen each other, Lawrence," she started. "It doesn't serve much purpose now for me to say this to you, but I wish I hadn't waited so long."

"Tell me what's wrong," I cried out, no longer trying to stifle my sorrow. "What has happened to you, Victoria?"

Victoria flattened her hands to her side and sighed laboriously. Her humor sounded woefully rehearsed when she remarked, "So you noticed. Well, I guess I can't hide this thing much longer, can I?"

"Please, tell me what's wrong?"

Her voice lowered to nearly a whisper when she replied, "It's cancer, Lawrence." She then paused momentarily, trying to coach the bravery back into her tone. "They think it started in my breasts, but it really doesn't matter at this point."

My voice shuddered when I spoke again. "Why didn't you come to me sooner?"

"I don't mean to sound cruel, but I don't think I would be here right now if I wasn't sick."

By this early point in our discourse, I had almost forgotten everything I wanted to ask Victoria. So much time was mislaid between us, but now I understood how trivial all of my brooding and self-pity had been. All thoughts of my son instantly faded from my mind. Suddenly, the only thing that mattered to me was Victoria's welfare.

"There must be something that they can do for you," I offered, desperately searching my intellect for information and technology that didn't yet exist. "They can't just let you die—"

"No one is letting me die," Victoria sobbed. "It's taken me six months to admit this, but I'm really dying. There's nobody to blame. People die—sometimes much too soon."

Not knowing exactly how to react, I hung my head and muttered the condolence she had no doubt heard countless times before. "I wish there was something that I could do."

"There's nothing anyone can do," she replied, reaching out her hand to caress my shivering hand with her fingers. Her touch warmed my skin instantly. "It's probably unfair of me to unload all of this on you right now, Lawrence. You've got your own problems to work out."

"My problems don't matter now. I want to help you in any way I can."

"You know, when I found out that you were still in this place, I felt conflicted. Trust me, I didn't come here to pass on any guilt. However, there are some matters that I must talk to you about before I die."

My voice was suddenly fueled by rage. While saying the words, I felt my hand slamming down upon the table. "I can't believe this is happening. Why must the innocent always suffer?"

"Don't make me out to be an innocent woman. I'm not proud of all the choices I've made in my lifetime."

"You've never done anything to hurt anyone in your entire life."

"Don't be so sure," she corrected me. "I did keep your son away from you all of these years."

"Because you're a caring mother," I said through clenched teeth. "I don't blame you for trying to protect him—especially from this environment."

Before tempering my lament with any more of her humbleness, Victoria reached for the packet that she had brought with her. She opened the folder on the table, spreading out numerous photographs of our son and hand-scrawled papers.

Victoria took a moment to dry her eyes with a handkerchief before murmuring, "I've spent quite a bit of time trying to figure out how I was going to get through this conversation without offending you, Lawrence."

"I don't understand—how would you offend me?"

"We need to talk about Theodore's future," she answered.

My eyes were now trained on the photographs of our son. "Okay," I huffed, still emotionally torn by the gravity of her illness. "He's still just a boy. If you die, who'll take care of him?"

"Everything has been arranged," Victoria declared. She then displayed a brochure, advertising a large brownstone building on its facing flap. I scanned the pamphlet and its enclosed literature briefly while listening to Victoria's explanation. "That's Riverside Christian Boarding School, about twenty miles north of Philadelphia. Theodore will be living there until he's finished with his education."

"Since when does a boarding school keep children year round?"

"They normally don't, but I've made special arrangements with Father Jordan, the headmaster at Riverside. He's aware of my situation and he's promised to look after Theodore."

"How does Theodore feel about this?"

"Well," Victoria wept, "he's very glum right now, and maybe a bit angry, too."

"Did you tell him that you're dying?"

"I did," she replied meekly, "but I don't think he's ready to accept it yet. I can't really blame the boy, you know. He's extremely withdrawn."

I felt the urge to tempt fate by asking, "What about me, Victoria? Did he ever ask about the whereabouts of his father?"

"A couple of times," Victoria admitted, "but I didn't have the courage to tell him that you were locked up in a mental institution."

"You must've told him something—"

Victoria's voice hushed when she said, "Yes, I did. At the advice of Reverend Keegan, I told him that you disappeared. I know it was an easy way out for me, but I didn't have any other option."

"The truth would've been better," I grimaced. "He can't think very highly of me now."

"You're right, Lawrence, but I'm not apologizing for my choice. I still want to set things right with you, though."

"Then return to Philadelphia and tell him where I really am. He's old enough now to decide on whether or not he wants to see me."

"I won't do that. Both Father Jordan and I agreed that exposing Theodore to you at this point would be far too detrimental for him. He's not ready for any more stress. I won't do anything to jeopardize my son's future."

"What about my future?" I pleaded. "I know it's been a long time since we had a chance to love each other, Victoria, but you must feel some compassion for me. Don't I deserve an opportunity to earn our son's trust, too?"

Victoria directed my attention to a key on the table that was mixed between the photographs. "I'm here to offer you something that you didn't give to me, Lawrence—a choice."

I then took the silver key in my hand and asked, "With this?"

"More than anything else, you need to find the willpower to get out of this place. You've grown too comfortable here, and I think you're afraid to leave. Dr. Blake says that you're not trying to communicate with the others, but I'm hoping that you'll get better. That's why I'm leaving this key with you."

"What doors will it open for me now?" I asked, feeling pathetically inept.

"There's a safe deposit box at my bank in Philadelphia," she stated. "The bank's address and box number is printed on that key's tag. I've arranged to have twenty thousand dollars in insurance policies to be placed in that box upon my passing. These policies are in your name, Lawrence, and only you may cash them. It's not a lot of money, but it's enough to help you get started once you leave Crestpoint."

"I don't know, Victoria," I debated. "Is twenty thousand dollars enough money to buy my son's love and respect?"

"That part remains entirely up to you," Victoria answered. "I can't say for certain where Theodore will be when and if you ever get out of this place. Right now I know he's at Riverside, and he'll most likely remain there for the next seven years or so. If you can get yourself together by then, there will be nothing to prevent you from visiting your son and telling him everything that you think is necessary for him to know."

"I guess you worked out the details as best as you could," I said, placing the key back down on the table. I then asked, "What comes next for you? Where do you plan to go from here?"

"I'm going back to Philadelphia for a short time, mostly to say goodbye to my friends, and of course Theodore. After that, I'm returning to Green Haven—this time for good."

"What's there for you now, Victoria?"

"I want to be buried next to my father," she said with the confidence rising in her tone.

When Victoria expressed this notion to me, I reminisced of the day when our eyes first connected. I fondly recalled her stooping alongside her father's headstone, with her summer frock moistened by the rain. I savored this memory because it signified a perfect moment in my life. I now wished that we could go backward in time together to plant the seeds that would permit our love to grow fresh again.

Yet in the midst of this recollection, a strangely bitter thought entered my mind. It suddenly occurred to me that Victoria had never truly left her father in Green Haven's cemetery. In her mind, he was still haunting her, watching her with the critical gaze that only a father could muster.

Maybe it was for the benefit of both of us that our conversation didn't linger on any longer. I had my share of anger to vent, but it now seemed grossly malicious to brandish such rage at Victoria. I decided to let her go quietly, all the while being grateful that she thought enough of me to leave a generous piece of her wealth in my possession.

Before departing from my company forever, Victoria reached out her thin hand and clasped my palm into her own for one final touch. As our fingers enlaced, I sensed an absence of strength in her delicate joints. She barely managed to squeeze my hand with enough pressure to let me sense her diminishing life. During these seconds, I peered deeply into her cool eyes. The twilight of vitality seemed to be submerging in darkness.

Victoria wasn't an ordinary lady by any account. She represented a full diagram of femininity. She was a mother, a daughter, a leader, and a wife.

I reacted to her wisdom in complete resignation, as if finally freed from the grip of a beguiling spell. I let her walk away, moving as silently as a bird's shadow sliding across the face of a cloud.

In the end, Victoria made me feel as though I had something left to offer to this world—and to our son. Even if no one else entrusted a shred of faith in me, she did not lose hope. For this reserved vote of confidence, I will always be thankful that we once walked as one.

Five months following Victoria's visit to Crestpoint, I received another telegram from Cooper in Green Haven. He informed me that Victoria had died peacefully, while sleeping in her bed. Her wish to be planted beside her father had at last come to fruition. She was at home now, but my journey was not yet done.

CHAPTER TWENTY-SIX

▼

THE LIGHT REVEALED

As Lawrence's memoirs resonated in Theodore's mind, he sensed tears welling in his eyes like a flow of lava. In an unguarded moment, when he could no longer contain the emotional eruption that surged within his head, the scorching drops spilt across his cheeks. He did not wipe the tears from his face until they slid between his parched lips and dribbled into his mouth. Some of his tears splattered on the journal's pages, causing the ink to smear. After another moment, he placed the crucifix on the page where he stopped reading and closed the journal, blending the mark of his sorrow with that of his father's.

Many questions filtered through Theodore's mind now. After all those lost years, had he truly misinterpreted his father's intentions? Was Lawrence's quest to meet with him really hindered by a set of uncontrollable circumstances? Theodore was also mortified to learn that he was afflicted by blindness as a child. If this was true, how much damage had this condition already done to his eyes? He wondered if the darkness still existed in some state of dormancy within his mind.

Before Theodore had an opportunity to contemplate these mysteries at length, he heard Regina shouting for him from outside the lounge. Once sensing the urgency in her tone, Theodore leapt to his feet and bounded into the corridor. He still cradled the journal against his chest. Prior to uttering a word to Regina, he suspected that something had happened to Emily.

"Tell me what's going on!" he commanded, clutching Regina by her shoulders. This spontaneous reaction caused the journal to slip from his grasp and fall to the floor.

"I'm not sure," Regina answered, trying to catch her breath. "I was searching all over this hospital for you—"

"Just tell me what happened!"

"It's Emily."

One second after Regina responded, Dr. Reed paced into the adjoining corridor. He greeted Regina and Theodore in the hallway. When Theodore noticed Dr. Reed fidgeting with his clipboard, he pivoted away from Regina and rushed in front of him.

"Doctor, what the hell is going on? Where's Emily?"

"Please, Mr. Dayton," Dr. Reed insisted. "I need for you to calm down."

"Don't tell me what to do," Theodore snapped. "Just tell me where my daughter is?"

"We've had a bit of a problem," Dr. Reed sighed, but before he could finish his thought, Theodore grabbed him by his scrub suit.

"Tell me where she is," Theodore insisted.

"She's with Doctor Kraven," Dr. Reed replied, apologetically as possible. "I'm afraid she's very ill."

Theodore felt his hands trembling when he barked out, "What are you trying to say to me?"

At this point, Regina stepped forward and placed her hand on Theodore's shoulder. "Emily's unconscious," she clarified. "Doctor Reed just told me a few minutes ago."

Feeling woozy but not entirely unprepared for such news, Theodore hobbled away from the doctor and raised his hands to both sides of his temples. He rubbed at his head as if trying to ward off a throbbing sensation building within his brain.

When Theodore felt well enough to speak again, his voice was very sullen. He turned his attention back to Dr. Reed and muttered, "When did this happen?"

"Just fifteen minutes ago."

"Take me to her, Doctor Reed," Theodore demanded.

"Of course, Mr. Dayton. You should be aware that Doctor Kraven has already admitted your daughter into a private room."

"They're still in the children's ward, aren't they?" Theodore asked.

Dr. Reed nodded his chin and instructed Regina to take hold of Theodore's hand. Once she did, Dr. Reed said, "I don't have all of the details for you yet, but Doctor Kraven will do his best to clear everything up."

Before they dashed out of the hallway and into a nearby elevator, Regina picked the journal off of the floor. She then assisted Theodore into the elevator beside Dr. Reed. Well before the elevator began its descent toward the basement, Theodore sensed a convulsion overcoming his mind and body. He barely heard Regina's consoling words as he stooped forward, bracing himself against the handrail as if all life was being methodically siphoned from his veins.

When the elevator halted, Theodore's face appeared pale. He mumbled some gibberish at Dr. Reed before Regina helped him assume a standing position. As the elevator's doors opened, a young nurse greeted Dr. Reed with a smile. This woman seemed unfazed by the sight of Theodore and Regina.

"Follow me," she directed, pointing toward a corridor, sporadically lined with fluorescent light. She then looked at Dr. Reed and whispered, "We just moved the new child into B-Ward."

"B-Ward—what the hell is that?" Theodore shouted.

"Relax, Mr. Dayton," Dr. Reed explained. "B-Ward is a private section in our care center down here. She'll be away from the other children—at least for a while."

"Why must she be kept separate from the other patients?" asked Regina worriedly.

Dr. Reed shrugged his shoulders and glanced at the nurse for an explanation. In a stoic voice, she replied, "We always isolate the children when they first come in here."

"Since when?" Regina asked.

"Since Doctor Kraven arrived, of course," the nurse tittered. "As I'm sure you've noticed by now, he's made quite a few changes at Kindred Woods in the last six months."

Neither Regina nor Theodore felt motivated enough to respond to the nurse. They simply remained silent while traversing the sprawling passageway. As Theodore edged closer to the ward, he felt himself growing sicker with each step. As he already suspected, the hallway's end marked the beginning of further torment. He didn't try to imagine the extent of Emily's relapse, but he feared the outcome.

After another minute, they reached a steel gate. A sign posted on a wall closest to Theodore read: 'B-Ward—Authorized Personnel Only'. In a fit of frustration, Theodore clamped his hands around the gate's iron bars and rattled it. This disturbance roused the attention of two medics on the opposite side of the gate.

"Open up this damn thing now," Theodore screamed. "Why the hell is this gate blocking the entrance?"

At first the medics appeared confused, but Dr. Reed was approaching from behind to clear the air. "It's okay," he ensured the medics, motioning for them to unlatch the gate's lock. "Please inform Doctor Kraven that we've located Mr. Dayton. He's ready to see his daughter now."

Dr. Reed then turned back toward Theodore and reminded him to maintain self-control. Theodore reluctantly released his hands from the gate and inhaled deeply. After expelling at least one breath of nervous energy, he assured the doctor that he would oblige by his instructions.

Within a few seconds, the medics unlocked the gate. As the doors slid open, Dr. Kraven appeared from between the gate's bending shadows. To both Theodore's and Regina's astonishment, he appeared composed and visibly untroubled by Emily's circumstances. And though Theodore couldn't be absolutely certain, he thought that the glib-faced doctor was smirking at them from afar.

Theodore was still quivering when he greeted Dr. Kraven. "Where's my daughter? I want to see her right now." He managed to squeeze himself past both medics to get closer to Dr. Kraven. "Are you going to take me to her or not?"

Dr. Kraven fastened the top button on his shirt before saying, "Mr. Dayton, I'm sure you know that we're doing everything to accommodate your daughter."

"Why won't you just let me see her?" Theodore questioned, disregarding Dr. Kraven's casual gesticulations.

Once recognizing Theodore's discontent, Dr. Kraven wrapped his arm around the man's shoulder. When their skin touched, Theodore sensed a chill sweeping over his body. Then Dr. Kraven simpered and replied, "I don't think you really want to burst into Emily's room in your state of mind. Why don't you take a moment to settle down."

"I want to see her now," Theodore persisted.

Before Dr. Kraven responded, Regina intervened again, all the while trying to dissuade Theodore from doing something irrational. She attempted to comfort him with the same comments that a doctor may have used, but he wasn't listening. After breaking away from Dr. Kraven's grip, his eyes scanned the ward for a lone room with a light gleaming upon the concrete floor. Without hesitating, he bounded forward into the ward. Dr. Reed followed in his steps, but was immediately stopped by Dr. Kraven's voice.

"Let him go—after all, the child is his daughter."

"Doctor Kraven," Regina implored, "What's wrong with Emily?"

"Miss Hopewell, you were once a nurse here, isn't that correct?" Dr. Kraven inquired.

"I was—"

"Then the gravity of that child's illness should already be fairly obvious to you."

"I was hoping you could be a little more specific."

"Yes, of course, Miss Hopewell," Dr. Kraven said, folding his arms in front of himself. "Rest easy, Miss Hopewell, a full report shall be filled out by me before morning. In the meantime, I suggest that we wait for Mr. Dayton to rejoin us. I'm sure he'll have quite a few questions of his own."

When Theodore initially bolted into the room, he expected to see his daughter linked to an array of life-saving equipment. He cringed at the wicked thought of watching Emily being subjected to infusion pumps, I.V. fluids, and monitors. But as his eyes adjusted to the room's encompassing shadows, his apprehension shifted to confusion.

Emily was lying unconscious on a steel bed in the center of the room. There were no medical apparatuses of any kind positioned around her bed. In fact, all supply carts and wall-mounted oxygen connections had either been removed or uninstalled. She was reposed in bed, with her legs partially blanketed by one piece of white linen.

When nearing her bedside, Theodore distinguished a soft scent of Emily's hair pervading in the air. Her skin looked paler than he remembered, and the expanding shadows that looped beneath her eyes had darkened through her cheeks like pools of oil. Her clothes had been removed and replaced by a standard hospital gown. She rested peacefully, but her eyes flickered behind their tightened lids, as if she was trying to escape from an abyss with no conceivable exit.

With tears once again emerging from Theodore's eyes, he bent to one knee and pressed his lips against Emily's forehead. He shuddered at the coldness exuding from her skin. As a ribbon of his teardrops spread upon Emily's sunken cheeks, he wondered when his heartache would end.

After Theodore raised to his feet, he whispered a few words to Emily, while wondering to himself if she would ever have another chance to respond to his voice. He felt helpless to combat the hallucination of this forthcoming death. And suddenly, as sweat thickened on his brow, he no longer saw Emily's body lying limply on the bed. To his dismay, he now imagined his wife's petrified expression of pain.

Claire's lifeless image appeared to him in a blood-soaked hospital gown, exactly how she looked on her deathbed. A final scream for mercy was etched upon her face. She did not want to die and leave behind the beautiful creation that blossomed within her womb. Yet she no longer twitched a muscle. Her fixated eyes stared into the surgical lamps' evasive glare.

He remembered being dragged from Claire's bedside, pleading for the panicky obstetricians to help her. But he then knew that something had gone terribly wrong. He saw fear glistening in the doctors' eyes like burning embers. He clearly heard his own cries echoing through the hospital's corridors, but he couldn't control the guilt that ravaged his heart. The glares of saddened faces soon encompassed him, but no one offered the words he most wanted to hear.

After closing his eyes and reopening them again, Theodore realized that Emily was still lying in the bed. The mirage had faded for now, but he believed that the memories of his wife's death would continue to ferment in his imagination forever. Although it was nearly impossible for him to rationalize his illness until this very moment, he now understood that he couldn't expect to survive much longer while immersed in the misery of such moments.

As Emily neared death, Theodore's failures seemed to magnify and his feelings of regret churned within his brain with greater intensity. After finally admitting to himself that there was nothing else he could do for her, he slunk quietly away from her bedside. When he exited the room, Regina was waiting directly outside the door.

Theodore stared at Regina uneasily as he leaned against the frame of the door. "How long have you been standing there?"

"Just a few seconds," Regina replied. "Is Emily responding to your voice at all?"

Theodore lowered his eyes and answered, "No, she's not doing anything."

Regina wiped her nose and face with a handkerchief before offering Theodore a fresh cloth to dry his own eyes. "I think Doctor Kraven has a few papers for you to sign," she sniffled, pointing to an open door on the opposite side of the hallway. "He's waiting for you in his office."

"What kind of papers?"

"I'm guessing, but I think it's about admitting Emily into this hospital."

"I never agreed to that," Theodore huffed.

"Well, realistically, Theodore, I don't think we have a choice any longer."

"Regina, you know how Emily feels about hospitals. She doesn't want to die in here—not like this."

Though Regina sensed the antagonism building in Theodore's voice again, she wasn't prepared to back down so timidly. "Look, Theodore, we've done all we can for her at home. Maybe it's best that we came here today. Emily needs more treatment than I can give her at home. You know it's the right thing to do."

"I'm still not signing any damn papers," Theodore said smugly. "One way or another, I plan on getting Emily out of this place."

"At least talk to Doctor. Kraven first," Regina recommended. "He's willing to help us. We should be grateful."

"Should we?" Theodore said, sarcastically.

Rather than volley adversarial remarks with Theodore, Regina retreated to Emily's bedside. She insisted on sitting beside Emily for a short while, praying that some friendly company might help rejuvenate her.

In the meantime, Theodore steered his attention toward Dr. Kraven's office. As he approached the doorway, he smelled a sweet fragrance of lavender and sage candles wafting in the air. Inside, seated behind a black-lacquered desk, Dr. Kraven reclined comfortably in a leather chair. Once distinguishing Theodore standing in the hallway, he snickered gaily and stood up from his chair.

"Theodore," Dr. Kraven called in a pleasant voice, "please come in. I've been waiting for you to join me."

Theodore stepped wearily into Dr. Kraven's office. Similar to the rest of the hospital's ambiance, this room was obviously designed to be an indulgent extension of its occupant's personality. The floor was tiled in white and black onyx, while the walls were painted in dull pewter. Most of the trim around the windows and doors was finished in polished brass. Other than the candlelight shimmering in the room's corners, no other source of illumination permeated the interior.

Beside the desk in the center of the room, two chairs, covered in red velvet, were positioned beneath the lone window. The rest of the room remained empty. Theodore listened to his own footsteps as they echoed off the marble tiles. Instead of commenting on Dr. Kraven's peculiar setting, Theodore eased down into a chair without offering his opinion.

Dr. Kraven had already gone to the trouble of preparing a cup full of steaming coffee for his guest. He amused himself by watching Theodore suspiciously eyeball his surroundings.

"I know it's a rather plain setting," Dr. Kraven declared in reference to his colorless domain. "The simplicity helps keep me focused on what's truly important around here."

"Nothing is simple about this place," Theodore mumbled. "You've obviously gone out of your way trying to help my daughter."

"Believe me, Theodore, I was extremely unnerved by her condition. She should have been admitted to a hospital long before today."

"It's her choice. Emily doesn't want to be here, and I plan to take her out of here as soon as she wakes up."

"I see," Dr. Kraven said, reaching in his desk's drawer to gather some forms. "Miss Hopewell did mention to me that you've developed a phobia for hospitals…"

"Like I said," Theodore interrupted, "it's not my decision."

"I respect your devotion to honor Emily's request, but now is the time to put your emotions and silly fears on hold. If we review this situation from a practical point of view, I'm sure you'll agree that she's in far safer hands with us."

"Don't give me that crap," Theodore contested. "Before I brought her to this place, she was doing fine—or at least a whole lot better than I've seen her in a long time."

"We both know how gravely ill your daughter is," Dr. Kraven countered. "I'm not saying we perform miracles in here, but at least I can assure you that she'll be kept as comfortable as possible."

"Is that all you can offer me now? What's the difference if she dies quietly at home or lingers on in this place for a few more weeks? I don't want to watch her suffer anymore. She's been through too much pain, more than any kid should ever have to experience."

"I agree," Dr. Kraven said, shuffling the paperwork in his hands. "But I'm afraid society has conditioned us to believe that the quality of a human life is categorically linked to a quantity of years. Of course we realize that this premise becomes illogical once a terminal disease strikes a child."

Now feeling anxious, Theodore reached across the desk and grabbed the cup of coffee. He put the cup's brim beneath his nose for a moment before taking a sip. "So what do you suggest I do—let her stay alive in here as long as possible, even though she's in constant agony most of the time?"

"You know I can't make that decision for you, but you've already begun the process, haven't you?"

"What process?"

"Well," Dr. Kraven said diplomatically, "I'm sure Emily's doctors informed you of her prognosis for well over two years now. In the beginning, I'm betting that they didn't think she'd survive for more than five years."

"Up until six months ago, she was getting better," Theodore said, withholding an urge to holler. "Her leukemia went into remission."

"Yes, I've read the files that Doctor Garrison left behind. We both understand that treatment usually pauses such cancers."

"What are you trying to tell me?"

"Like most caring parents, Theodore, you selected the quantity of life over the quality. I'm certainly in no position to second-guess your decision at this time."

Theodore finished drinking the cup of coffee before saying, "Don't put this on my shoulders." He then placed the cup on the desk and stood up, avoiding the papers that Dr. Kraven attempted to hand him. "I'm not about to sign anything until I can speak to my daughter."

"In all due respect, if she is fortunate enough to awaken, what do you expect her to say to you?"

Theodore shrugged his shoulders and replied, "Maybe she'll want me to take her home—maybe not. But I'll tell you this, for the last six months Emily has refused to go to the hospital. There were times when Regina and I thought about bringing her in here, but Emily insisted that she didn't want to die in a hospital."

"And do still truly believe that keeping her at home is best solution?"

"I don't know," Theodore sighed, "maybe it's a matter of stubbornness on my part, too. I may not be able to save my daughter's life, but seeing that she is at peace is the only thing I have left to cling to."

Without replying to Theodore's words, Dr. Kraven collected the admittance papers and returned them to his desk's drawer. He then stood up from his chair and paced toward the room's left corner. For a moment, he stood next to one of the wall-mounted candles, inhaling traces of the candle smoke. Now feeling reinvigorated, he turned to face Theodore again, with his eyes shining like wet coal in sunlight.

"Perhaps this isn't an appropriate moment for me to bring this up," Dr. Kraven started, "but Emily gave me a distinct impression that she was avoiding the hospital to protect you. Could there be any truth to this?"

Theodore appeared insulted and perplexed before denying, "Emily didn't say that. It's always been her choice. She never needed to protect me."

Dr. Kraven folded his fingers together in a prayer-like gesture as he sidled closer to Theodore. In a hushed tone, he asked, "Would I be wrong to assume that you've had a rather traumatic experience at a hospital in the past?"

"I don't think that's important for us to discuss," Theodore sneered.

The doctor's voice lowered to a whisper when he responded again. "Emily told me how her mother died, Theodore. I realize how hurtful that moment must've been for you."

Theodore immediately sprang forward, knocking a chair to its side upon the floor. "How dare you mention my wife to me now! You had no right to ask my daughter about her mother's death. Who the hell do you think you are?"

"Emily volunteered this information to me. If the truth must be told, Theodore, your daughter's been worried about you ever since Claire died."

"I'm warning you," Theodore said, pointing his finger in Dr. Kraven's face. "You didn't have any right to remind Emily about that horrible ordeal."

"I'm reminding you," Dr. Kraven exclaimed. "Although I emphasize with your loss, I also understand that you've inadvertently subjected your daughter to your own fears."

"What are you babbling about? Emily isn't afraid of me."

"No, she's afraid for you. She knows what happened to her mother in that labor room, and she sees you unwilling to let go of the woman you loved."

"Emily couldn't have told you that."

"She did indeed," Dr. Kraven confirmed. "However, it should comfort you to know that Emily still loves you very much, enough that she's willing to suffer through her disease at home so you don't have to endure the trauma of watching her die in a hospital like you did your wife."

Theodore gritted his teeth before sobbing, "That's impossible for her to know. I never told Emily that I actually witnessed her mother's death."

"But it's painfully obvious to her," Dr. Kraven said, gazing into Theodore's reddened eyes. He then raised both of his hands and placed them gently upon Theodore's shoulders. He felt the man's body shivering. "Your fear is not irrational. You must realize that Claire's death has nothing to do with your daughter's disease. Emily must be free to make her own choices, without the thought of how they in turn hurt you."

A feeling of wooziness suddenly overcame Theodore, and he lunged for the toppled chair to prevent himself from falling down. He stared wearily into the room's shadows, listening to a steady vibration that now surged within his mind. After a few moments, he realized that this mysterious sound was identical to a ticking clock.

After swallowing several deep breaths, the maddening rhythm soon dissipated in Theodore's head. The rage that he felt only a few seconds before had instantly faded. When he resumed conversation with the doctor, his voice was subdued.

"What do you suggest I do now?"

"At the very least, keep your daughter here until morning. If she regains consciousness by then, simply ask her what she wants to do. I certainly won't detain her in this ward if she really wants to go home. However, if she chooses to stay, I would recommend that you give her your blessing."

Theodore nodded his chin once and said, "I guess that's all I can do right now, isn't it?"

Without waiting for a reply, Theodore straightened his posture and turned to leave the office. Dr. Kraven made no attempt to stop the disillusioned man at this point. When Theodore entered the hallway, he stood silently near Emily's room, contemplating his shortcomings with greater clarity.

After several seconds, Theodore felt stable enough to peer into his daughter's room again. When he did, he saw Regina sitting quietly beside Emily's bed. She was combing her fingers through the girl's flaxen hair. A smile formed on Theodore's lips as he tried to imagine what Regina was thinking during these seconds. Regina removed her hand from Emily's forehead and placed it back into her own lap.

Regina now turned her attention to the journal, where Theodore had stopped reading. As the crucifix's polished gold gleamed against her hand, she removed it from the notebook's binding and stuffed it beneath Emily's bed pillow. The smile soon faded from Theodore's mouth as Regina's eyes scanned the journal's pages. But he didn't want to disturb her now—at least not until he could find the courage to fully discover the truth about his father's life for himself.

CHAPTER TWENTY-SEVEN

▼

JOURNAL ENTRY FIFTEEN

FAREWELL TO INSANITY

When I entered Crestpoint Mental Institution in 1953, I never imagined that I'd sacrifice nearly eighteen years of my life trying to persuade a colony of psychiatrists into believing that I was a normal man. In spite of my persistence, these doctors pried and tinkered with my mind for years. I don't even think they knew what they were searching for.

Although it may be deemed as a rather meager victory in comparison to lost time, I had at least maintained my independence of thought. No matter how many years may have passed, they couldn't change me. In hindsight, I would've been released from the asylum inside of twelve months had I simply confessed to being a lunatic. But even after years of silence, and no recent encounters from either Jonathan or the dark fiend, I held my principles intact without ever feeling obligated to share them upon request.

Much to my satisfaction, Crestpoint succumbed to the insistence of modern times before I did. In 1971, the governor of New Jersey ordered the facility to be closed indefinitely. A mandatory report found numerous violations, some of which specified inadequate knowledge in current trends in psychotherapy. Most of the quartered patients were being relocated to another institution, but I, by some strange twist in fortune, received my official dismissal alongside half the doctors who treated me for nearly two decades.

On the summer morning before my discharge, Dr. Blake, who now neared retirement, visited me on a concrete terrace overlooking the Atlantic Ocean. For some reason, I studied the ocean's power more closely on this day than ever before. I marveled at the waves and how they jutted into the beach in a series of synchronized explosions.

Just as when I first arrived here, saltwater breezes churned with scents of seaweed. The seagulls soared between the tepid winds, blending ceaselessly with the sun-streaked surf. In these moments, I wished that I could join these creatures in their dance upon air and water, if only to amuse myself in the rapture of the unknown.

Now hampered by arthritis in both knees, Dr. Blake hobbled up beside me. He wasn't nearly the same man whom I met in 1953. The white hair that still clung to his skull had turned gray, and nickel-sized warts crept across his eyelids and spread over his nose. Furthermore, as an advocate to the mentally ill, his voice had curdled like rancid milk. Most of his opinions were suddenly as pessimistic as my own.

"I guess it's time for us to finally say our farewells," Blake mumbled, his voice barely perceptible above the gulls' piercing cries.

"Yeah," I chuckled, still gazing at the ocean. "Farewell to insanity. To be honest with you, Blake, it's more like good riddance."

"You never were one to take our research seriously, Lawrence. But no matter what you think of Crestpoint, you're going to be a free man again.

You've been given a second chance—that's something most of us don't get in life."

"I guess I should be grateful that they finally decided to close this place," I huffed. "You and I might not be having this conversation otherwise."

"No matter what you believe, you've always controlled your own destiny in here."

Now perturbed, I pivoted my body so that I faced the hunchbacked doctor. "Let's face it," I sneered. "No one in this place ever had any intention of letting me go. Like you, I might've been in here until I was too old to do anything else."

"We were only trying to help you. I wish you could at least accept that."

"You've only succeeded in stealing my youth from me, Blake. I can't shake your hand in good faith, especially now that I'm a stranger to my own son."

Dr. Blake lowered his head in shame, as if my words had shredded his heart. For a moment, he scurried through his tangled thoughts, searching for a tender way to tell me something I needed to hear before leaving Crestpoint. He first reminded me of the time I asked him to check into Dr. Konrad's medical records at Pine Grove. He then apologized for ignoring my request.

"But there's more to this story," I surmised. "Did you finally look into Konrad's record?"

Dr. Blake brushed off my statement with a huff before replying, "Pine Grove Hospital closed in 1967. But before they shut down, I paid a visit to their staff."

"So what I said about Konrad must've had some impact on you, huh?"

"I can't verify the stories you've told me about that man," Blake clarified, "but I did meet with the children under Doctor Konrad's direct supervision. Some of them demonstrated extremely irregular behavior patterns before they died."

"You're not surprising me," I groaned.

"Well," Blake whispered, "I was shocked—even ashamed of what I witnessed in my short time there. The children were certainly apathetic."

"But it was more than apathy, wasn't it, Blake?" I surmised. "Those kids had lost something far more precious than their lives. They surrendered their faith. After that was gone, there was nothing left to take."

Instead of denying my theory any longer, Dr. Blake nodded his chin in agreement. "I never thought I'd hear myself admit this, but I was not unhappy to see Pine Grove shut down. Ironically, I feel that many young lives were saved as a result of that decision."

"But it doesn't change the fact that Konrad is still out there, perhaps assuming a new identity at another unsuspecting hospital. He won't stop killing those children. He's not like you or me. For that matter, he's not like any man."

"Well," Blake murmured glumly, "I suppose we'll never know for sure. Anyway, considering our options, maybe it's best that we don't."

With my frustration momentarily restrained, I turned my eyes back toward the ocean. After several seconds, I realized that Blake was gazing out across the blue horizon alongside me.

"You know," Blake said, breaking the mood of silence that slowly developed between us. "In light of what we just discussed, I think there's something else that I should mention to you."

"More good news, I hope."

"Well, it's more like strange news. I've been mulling over this for a few years now, and I was curious if you could help me make some sense of it."

Dr. Blake's tone sounded urgent, so I went against my instinct and lent him my attention for another minute. "A few months before Pine Grove closed in 1967, a couple of children, a boy and a girl, were brought to me for a psychological evaluation. I was told they were both terminally ill when they arrived at Pine Grove five weeks prior to our meeting. By coincidence of not, these children had experienced the same level of despondency as the other patients under Dr. Konrad's supervision."

"At least you're starting to make the connection," I stated. "I only wish that you could've done your homework a little sooner. You would've saved us both a lot of time and aggravation."

"Let me finish," Blake insisted. "As I said, these children were initially given absolutely no hope for survival. Yet within three weeks after arriving at Pine Grove, their illnesses simply vanished. Even under the most scrutinizing standards, they're bodies were completely free from disease."

I smiled to myself before shifting toward Blake again. Then I asked in a somber voice, "Why do I feel that Konrad had nothing to do with this miracle?"

Dr. Blake paused and nudged his eyeglasses against the bridge of his nose. He appeared bewildered when he finally responded. "No one ever had the chance to ask Doctor Konrad's opinion. He disappeared shortly before the hospital closed."

"But you did speak to the children," I said knowingly.

"I did," Blake confessed, "and like you, they attributed their recoveries to a single man—or someone who appeared to them as a man—named Jonathan."

"I guess you're finally ready to believe me now, aren't you?"

Of course Blake couldn't answer me directly. I supposed it would have compromised his integrity as a doctor to admit that he'd been wrong about me. Secretly, I was pleased to know that Jonathan had finally stopped what I had failed to accomplish in Pine Grove. After I selected to turn away from Blake again, I think he realized that I wasn't enthusiastic about obtaining his friendship or goodwill. Yet the old doctor persisted with his issues until I felt compelled to answer him with a visual that he could understand.

"It's all very amazing isn't it?" I asked, pointing out across the ocean.

Blake squinted to the space where I directed my index finger and said, "What is?"

"All of it," I exclaimed excitedly, sweeping my hand out in front of the picturesque beachfront. "You know, the ocean's power always makes me pause in wonder. No one could ever recreate something as magnificent as our Earth's oceans. It's a shame that we all take it for granted."

"Some of us don't," Blake argued. "The water is a source of beauty to many people."

"On the other hand, Blake, it serves as reminder to our inability to duplicate the miracles happening all around us. If you really think about it, we're here on these shores at the mercy of tides. At any moment, those waves could leap from their boundaries and wash our cities and towns away like grains of sand."

"Yes, of course, Lawrence. I suppose we are all complacent to our vulnerabilities at times."

"But what great force stirs the water, Blake? If it is not something science can explain or predict with any accuracy, can't we view it as being the product created by a far more superior power?"

"Like what—God? Is that what this idea is all about?"

I remained silent, if only to allow Blake a moment to absorb the syllables of his own statement. After a moment of contemplation, he offered, "I'm a practical man, Lawrence. It's not good enough for me to get overly romantic about the sea when people's lives depend upon research and scientific advancements."

"What did you expect me to tell you—the whereabouts of Jonathan?"

"That would be a good start."

"I wish I knew," I sulked. "But I haven't seen my angel friend in many years."

"I wish you would stop referring to him as an angel," Blake grumbled. "It makes me wonder why I signed your discharge papers to begin with."

"I'm sorry," I said lowly. "I don't have anything else to offer you, Blake. You're fishing in the wrong pond."

"So you're just going to walk away from here and disappear from the rest of society forever?"

"That's not a terrible idea, but I have some obligations to take care of in Philadelphia before I make any other commitments."

"Your son, of course," Blake remembered. "Do you really think you'll find him after all of these years?"

"I don't know, but I owe to myself—and him—to at least try."

Dr. Blake staid beside me for a few more minutes on that morning, watching the ocean gradually recede from the beach. Though I don't know what became of Blake after this day, I prayed that he would one day realize that miracles weren't merely a byproduct of a man's imagination—they were the everlasting source behind it.

Though I was at first eager to revisit Philadelphia, my prolonged absence from society had placed me at a disadvantage in its ever-changing surroundings. In 1971, while navigating through these avenues, I felt almost infantile in my pursuit to blend into the masses. A maze of traffic-littered trails and towering buildings all seemed threatening to my eyes. And what I fondly remembered about the city of old was now smothered by a hoard of disenchanted faces.

This city's occupants were not the same as I remembered. Strangers no longer looked in my eyes when I passed them on the road. They rambled along with exaggerated paces, forwarding unsteady glances at the pavement and sky. While it was true that we were piled together like matchsticks in a box, we seemed oblivious to one another. These streets reminded me of Crestpoint, only here, the would-be patients had fewer restrictions.

As I slunk invisibly along the crowded sidewalks, the sights and smells of a crumbling civilization became far more unsettling. In entire neighborhoods, store and tenement facades had been desecrated with neon paints and archaic symbols. Other structures stood vacant, with metal curtains drawn across their windows and doors. Vagrants drifted between the alleyways, begging the well-dressed merchants for spare change. In addition to this unpleasantness, sirens and taxicab horns competed with the roar of an elevated subway. Truly, the sounds mixed in a symphony orchestrated for the insane.

I wondered how Victoria had ever persuaded herself into leaving our son in the middle of all this chaos. Though I never inquired, I couldn't understand why she didn't take him back to Green Haven with her before she died. He would've been safer growing up in the country, and—from my point of view—certainly much easier to find.

My search to find Theodore began at Riverside Christian Boarding School. Despite its name, I failed to come across a single waterway in the vicinity of its cubed premises. The school was situated in the city's outskirts on a sixty-acre expanse. Surprisingly, this spacious campus, replete with English gardens and flower-laden pathways, afforded me with a refreshing change of scenery.

It was summer and an aromatic scent of rosebuds swirled in the afternoon breezes. As I approached the school's front lawn, I glanced skyward to admire a golden crucifix affixed to a slanted roof. With the sun shining behind it, the cross cast a shadow over a grassy knoll. I likened its emergence to a compass guiding a beleaguered traveler back home.

Father Jordan presided over this landscape like a groundskeeper rather than a headmaster with nearly fifty years of service under his collar. He was a remarkably pleasant and articulate priest, more so than I expected from a man of seventy-plus years. His cobalt-blue eyes were clearer than my own, and I think I had at least as much gray as him twisting through my hair.

As we previously agreed by way of phone, I met Father Jordan in the campus's garden and explained to him who I was and my present ambitions. Without hesitating, he remembered my son, as well as Victoria by name. Unfortunately for me, Theodore was already nineteen years old by this date, and no longer the academy's legal responsibility. Jordan informed me that Theodore had left Riverside following his seventeenth birthday. According to the priest, he left no forwarding address or intended destination.

"I just wish that I could've gotten here a little sooner," I said. "I think he would've liked to known that I was still alive."

"Yes, I'm sure of that," Jordan said.

"Why didn't you ever tell him where I was, Father?"

"I made a promise to his mother," Jordan told me. "When Victoria first came to me, I didn't know if I'd be able to help Theodore. In many ways, the boy seemed lost. I couldn't subject him to any more pain."

"But as he grew older," I debated, "didn't he ever wonder about me? You must've said something to ease his mind."

Jordan bowed his head to his chest before confessing, "Oddly enough, the boy never asked me too many questions. At the time, I was thankful that he kept to himself, because I simply didn't know if you still cared or possessed the mental capacity to function as a father."

"So he left nothing behind—not even an address where he might be staying?"

"I'm sorry," Jordan answered. "The best I can tell you is that he may still be residing in Philadelphia."

"What about college—did he have any interest in school?"

"Not really, Mr. Dayton. I think living in a dormitory for so long soured his taste for academics."

After realizing that the priest had only vague speculations to offer in regard to my son's whereabouts, I thanked him for his time and decided to resume my quest elsewhere. Before leaving the garden, however, Jordan invited me back to the boy's dormitory to show me where my son had lived for over seven years. At this point, any potential clues in relation to my son's interests were helpful. I immediately accepted Jordan's offer.

During this brief tour, Jordan recalled that he had stored some mementos that may have had some value to me. He pulled them from an old sea chest that he kept in the rectory's office.

"Victoria sent numerous letters to our academy before she died," Jordan explained. "Most of these writings were addressed to Theodore or me, but she also forwarded a collection of postcards that were delivered to her home in Green Haven by a couple who seemed quite adamant about meeting you."

"That's odd," I muttered, staring at a pile of the neatly bound post-cards. "Why didn't she just have those postcards mailed directly to me?"

"Maybe she didn't want these people to contact you," Jordan suggested.

I then picked a handful of postcards off the table and read the signa-tures aloud. To my astonishment, the names of Danny Gibbon and Belinda Willinger were scrawled on most of the unread mail. After my ini-tial shock subsided, I began to read their observations more intently. Up until the time of Victoria's death in 1963, my acquaintances from the past had been searching for me.

Apparently they were on a spiritual quest of some nature and had col-lected testimony from numerous people who claimed to be the recipients of a miracle during a critical stage in their lives. All of these people, regard-less of age or religious background, attributed the miracles to a stranger, who only identified himself to them as Jonathan.

Since I had no intention of revisiting this part of my life again, the postcards triggered a bit of paranoia in me. Admittedly, I was afraid to communicate with Jonathan again. With this notion piloting my thoughts, I tossed the postcards back on the desk.

"I won't be needing these," I announced, my voice now trembling.

Jordan promptly gathered the postcards and flipped them in a trashcan. "I regret that I can't be more helpful," he said. "Had I known that you were truly detained for all those years, I would've insisted that Theodore leave me an address where he could be reached."

"In the event that my son does come back to see you, Father, will prom-ise me that you'll tell him I was here."

"Of course. Will you be staying in Philadelphia for long?"

"I'm not sure," I responded faintly, almost humiliated by the fact that I had no immediate desire to do anything outside of finding my son. "I'll be here for a few weeks."

Jordan then took a pen in hand and wrote something on a piece of blue paper. I took the paper from him and read the words aloud, "Father Jason Halloway—Our Lady of Hope Church."

"He's a friend of my in the city," Jordan explained. "If you find yourself in the vicinity of South Boulevard, please stop in his church and see him."

"No offense, but why would I want to see him?"

"Father Halloway has been known to help out newcomers in the past, and I also tried to persuade your son to go see him."

I left Father Jordan on that day with a bitter sensation boiling in the depths of my stomach. By merely spending a few minutes with me, I suspected that Jordan recognized that I had deliberately drifted away from God in recent years. Although most of what I had envisioned was still unclear to me, I felt undeserving to be burdened by the appearance of Jonathan. On more than one occasion I often wondered why I was chosen to bear witness to the wickedness that was inflicted upon the children. More than anything, I wanted to live a normal life and dream about the superficial pleasures that lulled others to sleep when darkness touched their eyes.

CHAPTER TWENTY-EIGHT

▼

JOURNAL ENTRY SIXTEEN

OUR LADY OF HOPE

Before the tangerine hues of dawn brushed against the cityscape, I returned to Philadelphia's streets. After traveling between the city's avenues and slumbering among drunken hobos and harlots, fatigue and hunger reminded me that a man must yield to his body's temporal demands. I decided that now would be an appropriate time to pursue Victoria's gift.

With relatively few directions in hand, I easily found the bank located in the city's downtown section. Luckily, I hadn't misplaced the key to the safe deposit box. Within this box, just as Victoria had promised, I claimed the documents that instantly enabled me to salvage a sense of dignity.

Whoever said that money couldn't buy happiness was never made to compete with vermin for scraps of food.

Victoria's generosity enabled me to afford nutritious meals, adequate shelter, and a decent suit of clothes. Within a week, I had set up a temporary residence for myself in the business district. My modestly equipped room came with a bed, a toilet and bathtub. I didn't make an honest attempt to befriend anyone at this time. In a way, I was almost afraid to mingle in the crowds outside.

A feverish energy smoldered in these summer streets. I sensed it searing through my windows at the crack of daybreak. On the first Sunday in August, however, I managed to step outside of my room for the first time in nearly three days. Once I lost myself within the crowd, I began to wonder what I was searching for.

Undoubtedly, the early 70's socially scarred the people of Philadelphia. I suspected that war and poverty had impacted us all. In my opinion, the young people felt the aftermath of the previous decade most severely. A huge majority of these denim-clad youths had united in rebellious packs and chanted for peace. As I looked into their glazed eyes, I saw no depth, only the clarity of their fears. Secretly, I too was afraid of what was happening to us.

When I passed by the churchyards or watched as mothers wept in the shadows of recruiting stations, I realized that Father Jordan had frowned upon all of this long before me. Without further provocation, I found myself being summoned to the address that Jordan had provided me with. As I approached South Boulevard, I was attracted to the sparrows that flitted between the rooftops. Without exaggeration, Our Lady of Hope's desert-yellow brick and limestone exterior combined to make the most impressive church that I had yet gazed upon. For a moment, I stood in admiration beneath the structure's consecrated formations.

For perhaps the first time in my life, I absorbed all of the church's architecture with a sense of reverence. When I opened the church's doors, a fragrance of sweet incense enveloped my body. Now invigorated by a holiness that I had rarely felt before, I glanced ahead toward the altar's elevated steps. A scarlet carpet unfurled beneath my feet, flowing like a current of blood toward the massive crucifix hanging on the gold- embroidered walls.

As I stepped farther into the church's rectangular hall, my ears were immediately drawn to a melodious sound. I aimed my stare toward the altar's steps, where a young female soothed my heart with Christian songs. The woman faced the pews, but I caught a glimpse of her flaxen hair and ivory gown shining in the colored prisms cast from the church room's windows.

After I edged closer to the girl, a pale-faced altar boy emerged from behind the confessional. He was garbed in a white vestment, holding a hymnbook snugly against his chest. The boy looked uncomfortable with my ragged appearance. Maybe he thought I belonged in the streets, quibbling with the rest of those who were too afraid or disillusioned to come inside.

He politely attempted to direct me to one of the pews, but I was still intrigued by the girl's voice. "Tell me," I asked, pointing to the altar. "Who is that girl singing?"

"She's in the choir," the boy answered, as if it should have been obvious to me. "As far as Father Halloway is concerned, she's the best singer he's ever heard."

"I don't think you'd get many people to disagree with him," I said, bracing my hands against the oak pew in front of me.

"The morning liturgy is about to begin," the boy said, expelling a sigh as he peered distressfully upon the nearly empty pews.

I then remembered that it was Sunday morning, but the church was almost vacant. Only a handful of glum-faced parishioners had managed to turn out for the pending services. Pretending that I was ignorant to the spiritual detachment at large, I asked the altar boy where everyone was. He explained that most of the people usually waited until evening to join in prayer, if they bothered to come at all.

"I guess I shouldn't be so shocked," I admitted. "I haven't stepped inside of a church myself since I was a boy, maybe younger than you."

"Well, you're here today," the boy simpered, "and it is never to late to come back."

I grinned at the boy's forced optimism before saying, "I think you may have a point there."

Without further comment, I took my place among those still hoping for goodness. In here, while encompassed by the ballads and prayers of two thousands years past, I sensed myself glowing with a vibrancy that I hadn't felt since childhood. Though I couldn't quite recall the prayers that the congregation murmured, it comforted me to know that we all hadn't surrendered our faith. Whatever circumstances had brought us together, they would not be worsened at this hour—at least for as long as the girl sang her tunes of grace in perfect harmony.

After services, I left the church without any further information on my son's whereabouts. Still, I did not view this as wasted time. The sun beat hotter against my forehead as I glided into the streets. The avenues were laden with folks engaged in the rituals of life. I wondered if any of them sensed how pure I felt about myself during these seconds. In an attempt to prolong my mood, I gazed beyond the foot traffic to find children playing games in the street. Some of them ran in tandem along the sidewalks, dodging between parked cars as they rushed by. Though I don't know what games they played, I envied the energy and innocence that they lent to such simple pleasures.

While walking deeper into the scowling masses, I came upon a group of youths that had formed themselves into a circle alongside the sidewalk. They had assembled together in white, satin robes, with silky regalia. Garlands of ivy and oak leaves were looped around their heads. The majority wore no shoes or socks, only sandals to shield their feet from the scorching pavement.

They had apparently assembled to partake in the ravings of a gaunt, bible-thumping preacher. He gathered them into a circle in the road and began to shout with an ardency I've seldom heard. Whether I was curious about his message or not, he summoned me into the crowd as easily as the rest of his followers. When I moved closer to him, I noticed that he was dressed in a flowing satin robe, bound at the waist with a chain of rosary beads. He clenched an open Bible in his hand, and he pounded it in beat with the inflection of his voice.

"The time has almost come for all us sinners," he barked, his eyes now directly centered on me. "We must stand together now!"

When his stare refused to break away from mine, I looked around myself to see if anyone else was listening to his admonition. Strangely, the glassy-eyed spectators were seemingly oblivious to my position among them. It was as if a paralyzing force had momentarily desensitized the entire clan.

With my heart thrusting faster, I turned my eyes back to the preacher. He then sidled through the crowd toward me, pushing the young and woman aside with gentle strokes of his hands. A mischievous spark ignited in his bright eyes before he whispered to me, "You have come to stop the pain, haven't you?"

"What are you talking about?" I shivered, still trying unsuccessfully to pivot my eyes away from his.

"You know the beast is coming," he cringed. "You've seen it—"

"You're crazy."

The preacher smirked knowingly as he dragged his thumb across the Bible's pages, turning them to a section in The New Testament that he read verbatim. Though I at first couldn't recall the chapter and verse he recited, I later identified the passage as 13: 4, from The Book of Revelation.

"Why do you say these words to me?" I cried, grabbing hold of his arm as if the same forces that once entranced me had inspired him. "Please—if you know anything, tell me now!"

In a steady but somber voice the preacher replied, "The Great Tribulation is coming, my friend. Who will stand to stop the pain?"

"I don't know what you mean. What pain?"

With a numb glare creeping into his expression, the preacher slunk away from me. He did not take a moment to look at me again. The robed men and women beside me now began to circulate freely again, as if loosened from their trances. They now gazed cautiously upon me, but one young female, who wasn't much older than sixteen, pawed at my arms and shouted, "Join us, dear friend—let's stop the pain."

Hastened by fear, I returned to my room and recounted the preacher's words repeatedly. Before long, I found myself flipping through the pages of the Bible, searching for a passage that might have enlightened me. Admittedly, I hadn't studied The New Testament in decades, especially the prophetic visions that St. John recorded in the final book.

As far as the preacher was concerned, I never saw him after this day. Was he merely a false prophet taking advantage of the drug-induced adherents of his day, or did his admonition really mean something? With little else to do, I lied down on my bed with the intent to remain there until my tension eased. I don't exactly know what instigated my anxiety. Perhaps I was trying to keep myself sheltered from reality once again.

When the afternoon edged into twilight, my eyes began to sting from exhaustion. I dozed off for several hours. Just as it had been for the last ten years or so, my sleep was uneventful. At this point in my life I had grown content to forget my dreams before awakening. Though I at first didn't regret my inability to recall such thoughts, I gradually sensed that it was a symptom of my prolonged consternation.

On this night, I awoke to the sound of pealing sirens. I steered my eyes to an alarm clock's red glow. The clock's neon display flashed: 12:00 A. M. As the sirens whirled outside my window with urgency, I pulled myself from bed and staggered over to investigate the disturbance. While looking out into the street, I smelled a faint odor of smoke wafting in the evening's humid air. A fire was raging in close proximity to my room. I saw black plumes of smoke rising between the buildings. Its wild flames lit up the ebony sky like a volcanic eruption. The sirens grew louder, too, inciting people to assemble in the streets to serve as witnesses to the pending tragedy.

Though I didn't yet know what had caught fire, my curiosity prompted me to follow the smoke. I of course had no experience in combating fires, and possessed no desire to be entertained by the heroics of those who did. Yet while hurrying through the streets toward South Boulevard, I sensed myself becoming dominated by a gruesome thought.

In my mind I recalled the singing of an incredibly enchanting voice. This feminine cry rebounded inside my head as I approached the mobbed street corner leading onto South Boulevard. Between the assembling fire trucks and emergency vehicles, I witnessed the fiery end to this trail. To my dismay, flames and charcoal-colored smoke had devoured much of the church that I had visited only hours ago. By the time of my arrival, the fire had become too intense to combat.

Although the flames singed my eyes as I scurried past a police barricade, I felt as though I needed to get closer to Our Lady of Hope, for a young girl still screamed from within its crumbling walls. Couldn't anyone hear her cries for mercy? Or was this sound merely an echo swirling within my brain?

Several firemen and paramedics stood by the mayhem helplessly, fixating their eyes on the engulfed structure. I watched anxiously as exhausted firefighters hunkered by the roadside, dirtied with soot and blood. Charred victims squirmed on the pavement. Their dead or dying bodies lay blistered beyond recognition.

The church had exploded into an inferno during Sunday evening's Mass. Half of the thirty parishioners managed to escape unharmed, but those seated nearest to the altar were not as fortunate. Within seconds, I learned that Father Halloway was still inside the church, alongside the young woman who had telepathically summoned me to this scene.

I approached the disgruntled firemen frantically, demanding to know what was being done to spare those folks who were trapped inside the church. Through the combined commotion of crackling flames and whistling sirens, I still heard the screeches from people burning to death. One fireman, although tearfully apologetic, insisted that there was nothing more they could do to save them.

"But they're burning alive!" I shrieked, before breaking through the crowd and dashing toward the stairs leading to the church's doors. Several policemen chased me until the fierce heat and lung-singing smoke repelled them. I ignored their commands to halt and stormed blindly through the funnels of black mist and fire.

As I bounded the church's steps, I stumbled over a smoldering body. The man's petrified face was as gray as gravel and his eyes were completely dissolved from his skull. Despite the carnage, I pressed onward. Without proper thought for my own welfare, I sprang into the church and braved the flames' wicked lashes. Once inside, I lost my ability to see. Nothing could penetrate the smoke. I dared not inhale a breath of the poison fumes. My lungs would have surely melted within my chest had I swallowed a single gulp.

I continued down the church's center aisle. Never before now had I experienced such punishment, yet I refused to submit to the fire's wrath. In my heart, I knew it would be wrong to fail the woman who remained somewhere within this cavern of flames. As blades of fire lapped against the church's walls and engulfed the pews in a field of orange light, I pressed onward. By now, I could barely discern the altar's steps. Yet behind the altar, I quivered at the sight of the crucifix's blazing icon. The face and body of Christ was swaddled in a ribbon of fire.

Despite the insurmountable odds of recovering a single life from this wreckage, I crouched to the floor and crawled upon my hands and knees toward the altar's steps. Even with my face pressed against the carpeting, I nearly suffocated in the pathway. Soon thereafter, my lungs betrayed me. I felt the torrid smoke shredding my esophagus as it siphoned through my body. Suspecting that my opportunity to escape had already passed, I edged closer—until I felt the decimated loins of fallen worshippers oozing between the weight of my fingers.

Upon the altar's steps, with a Bible burning to ash in his withered hands, Father Halloway lay lifeless. As if in prayer, his fissured lips were still parted. His eyes were open, too, but bulged grotesquely from their sockets as the pulpy flesh dissolved into pools of blood around his head. Fearing the worst for all, I focused my attention on the white-gowned lady at his side. She had collapsed adjacent to the priest, but had not yet been fully incinerated. Though she may have already been asphyxiated, I vowed to carry her out of this church for as long as I still had the strength to move.

After I rolled the woman on her backside, I realized that this fire hadn't been selective when claiming its victims. A portion of her face and chest had already become stripped of its vital skin. Her blonde hair was shorn against her scalp on the right side of her head. Though I didn't fully inspect the extent of her wounds, I knew that she was still alive. I noticed her torso heaving slightly, almost as if an unseen but deadly pressure was constricting her chest.

Without offering further consideration to the task in front of me, I stood up and hoisted her unconscious body onto my shoulder. Though I have no explanation in regard to my stamina, I carried her effortlessly. Perhaps it was a strength that we all fostered within our souls in times of crisis. Once my legs were set in motion, I realized that my route leading away from the altar had disappeared. The fire suddenly erupted on all sides of me, waggling its frenzied arms like forked tongues.

During these seconds, the ceiling's wooden rafters plummeted to the floor like flaming battering rams, exploding into hundreds of splinters upon impact. At that same moment, pressurized water shot through the church's windows, fragmenting the ornate windows into shards of rain-bow-colored glass.

Breathlessly, I forged through this fire's dreadful heart like a man obsessed. When it seemed as though my entire body was entombed in flames, I sensed the exit in front of me. The fire trucks' sirens allowed me to fumble my way through the smoke. Miraculously, I emerged from the church with the woman still cradled against my shoulder. Firemen and paramedics set upon me in seconds, with oxygen masks and first-aid kits in tow. Before I reached the steps, I lowered the injured woman to the platform. I then fainted from exhaustion and tumbled headlong down the flight of stairs.

Those onlookers watched me flip like a rubber doll over the blue stone treads. They must've assumed that I was dead by the time my face impacted against the street. But after allowing myself a few moments to recuperate, I stood up again. Now the medics surrounded me so that I didn't have any alternative but to submit to their treatment.

"I'm okay," I kept telling the medics, "just take care of that girl—don't let her die."

Minutes later, I found myself pinned on a gurney in the business end of an ambulance. A young paramedic had linked an oxygen mask up to my nose as a precaution, but I tore the plastic apparatus from my face and—without gagging—insisted that I needed no additional air.

"I don't know how the heck you made it out of that church alive," the paramedic said, his voice teeming with bewilderment.

"That makes two of us," I huffed, sitting upright on the gurney. Then, after seeing a host of firemen walking toward me, I asked, "Where's the girl? What happened to the girl?"

"Relax, she's on her way to the hospital. She's burned up pretty badly, though."

"Will she survive?"

As the medic shrugged his shoulders, a squad chief, decked out in full fire gear, peeked his head inside the ambulance. He stared at me for a minute and seemed amazed that I had no visible injuries. The flames hadn't even touched my skin.

"You know," the fire chief complained, "you're either an extremely lucky or pathetically stupid man to do what you did."

"I was trying to help," I answered sheepishly.

"Next time, help by keeping your ass out of the way. I got enough bodies to deal with here tonight without adding your name to the list."

"I understand. I'm sorry if I caused any trouble."

The chief asked, "Did you even know that girl?"

"No," I declared, shaking my head. "I never met her before—not really, anyway."

The chief then glared at the paramedic and said, "You got a name on this guy yet?"

"I don't know," the medic replied. "He won't tell me. He says he wants to keep his name out of the newspapers."

The chief smirked knowingly before pulling his head out of the ambulance. He then paced away without offering me another glance. The medic tried to defend the chief's behavior by saying, "He's under a lot of pressure tonight. That's the second church this year to burn down in his jurisdiction."

"I'm sorry to know that," I groaned. "I just want you to make sure that that girl doesn't die—can you do that for me?"

"Well," the medic sighed, "I'm sure the doctors will do everything possible to save her, but I think it's important that you take some credit for risking your life to save her. Why don't you go talk to the media?"

"No thanks," I refused. "I didn't come here tonight to become a hero." I then climbed out of the ambulance and lost myself in the restless crowd.

Perhaps it was a miscalculation on my part for wanting to keep my name out of the press. In all likelihood, some widespread publicity might've alerted my son to the fact that I was still alive. But I simply didn't feel comfortable with the prospect of playing the role of a humanitarian. The notion of strangers approaching me with praise for good deeds seemed rather disingenuous. If they were truly searching for something to feel good about, I could've aimed them in a different direction. For the life of me, I didn't understand what had happened, or how I managed to avoid perishing in the fire that claimed so many other lives on that dreadful night.

It wasn't until the following dawn that I fully comprehended the fire's ghastly impact upon the public. I turned to page three of my local newspaper to locate the story that involved me. Suddenly, I was known as the 'mysterious drifter'. Although I rarely considered myself mysterious, the phrase had an ear-catching ring to it that I couldn't deny.

At any rate, the choirgirl in question had sustained severe burns over one-third of her body. Despite the hardship that no doubt awaited this young woman, at least she was not marked to die. For a moment, I felt certain that I had accomplished something worth savoring—if only in solitude.

The newspaper provided a succinct profile on this woman. She was tragically orphaned at the age of five, and had since been fostered and schooled by nuns in an abbey near Philadelphia. Apparently, she was a college-bound upstart, with a solid Christian background and a virtuoso in music and art. Her forte, as I could avow, was singing hymns and serving as an organist at church functions. As best as I can remember, the paper only identified her as Claire—a modest yet magnificent person who would only grow more pertinent to my quest as time passed by.

CHAPTER TWENTY-NINE

▼

RECOLLECTIONS OF CLAIRE

After Regina reviewed these words several times, her eyes fogged with tears. At that moment, she realized that it was improper for her to read through Lawrence's journal without permission from the man who wrote it. Since that notion of approval was not possible, she put the diary down on the floor, with the intention of never picking it up again.

Regina did not understand why she was so unnerved by Lawrence's confessions, but then she recalled the photograph of Claire that Theodore had destroyed on the previous night. She remembered the unsightly scars overlapping the woman's skin, and then a serendipitous thought filled her mind with a sense of wonder.

Was it truly conceivable that Lawrence had saved his son's future wife from a premature death—without suspecting that they would one day meet? If this scenario was so, Theodore had no way of knowing that his father had actually participated in his short-lived happiness, albeit in the guise of a mysterious drifter from afar.

As Regina debated this possibility in silence, she turned toward the room's doorway and noticed that Theodore had been studying her. Without speaking, he walked into the room. After briefly looking to the bed where Emily lay, he slouched down into a chair beside Regina. He appeared as though he would burst into tears at any second.

Theodore paused for a moment before saying, "I don't know what it is about this place that bothers me, Regina, but I feel as if I don't have any control in here." He then let his eyes center on his unconscious daughter for a second. "Maybe it's the way everyone acts around that doctor," he continued. "They all seem like they're afraid of him or something, don't they?"

Regina cleared her throat and replied, "I don't want to sound like I'm defending Doctor Kraven, but he is in charge of this hospital. I think he needs to have that authority."

Without responding to Regina's observation, Theodore pushed his chair closer to Emily's bedside. He set his hand on her forehead and felt her body's temperature. Sensing that her skin was freezing, he pulled back his hand and stared at Regina with a perplexed expression. "She's so cold," he quivered.

Regina placed her hand on Emily's cheek and remarked, "She does feel extremely cold."

"Is that normal?"

"I can't be sure, Theodore."

"You see, Doctor Kraven doesn't even know why she's unconscious, but I don't think it has anything to do with her disease."

Regina then cupped her hand on Theodore's trembling arm. She felt a frigid perspiration exuding from his pores. "My god," she cried, "you're almost as cold as Emily. You should get some rest. It's not doing us any good to deny what we know is happening to Emily. We've done everything possible."

"No," Theodore screamed, gritting his teeth. "It's not going to end like this—not in here. She's going to wake up, Regina...and—"

"And what?"

Theodore's voice shrunk to a whisper as he murmured, "And come home with me. She doesn't want to die in here. I promised her that I wouldn't leave her in a hospital."

"You can't control everything now," Regina emphasized, trying not to sound too domineering. "Whether we do it today or wait until tomorrow, we're eventually going to have to let go of her."

Theodore slouched deeper into his chair. During the awkwardness of this moment, he observed his father's journal lying on the floor next to the bed. He looked at the notebook briefly before pivoting his eyes back toward Regina. Recognizing that the crucifix was now missing from the notebook, he extended his hand beneath Emily's pillow and removed the gold cross from the bed. Regina watched him peer at the cross, as if he was trying to utter a prayer without moving his lips.

Regina eased back into her seat and caressed Theodore's shoulders. He allowed her to massage the knotted muscles in his back for a few seconds before saying, "I saw you put this cross beneath Emily's pillow. Why did you do that?"

"I didn't mean to offend you. I did it for Emily."

Theodore tossed the crucifix on top of the journal and rolled his eyes in a fit of disapproval. "I see that you were also peeking into my father's writings again," he continued. "I hope you're learning something worthwhile from it all."

"I was wrong to read the journal," Regina confessed shamefully. "I just thought that it might help me understand you a little better—"

"Me? Why am I such a puzzle to you all of a sudden?"

"I'd rather not say," Regina sighed. "But there are some entries in Lawrence's journal that you should take the time to read."

Theodore chuckled insincerely and remarked, "Do you really think that anything my father says now can affect me? I've already learned to live with my imperfections. You know what's really strange, though? It's the feeling that I'm the only person in the world who can't find any peace."

"But you're starting to understand your fears," Regina offered. "I'll be the first one to admit that you can't change what has happened to your family, but maybe you can do something to change yourself."

Theodore wiped a tear away from his eye as he glanced at Emily's pale face. In a muted voice, he sighed, "I don't know if that would even be fair."

"Try to forget what you're afraid of and focus on what you once loved about life." Regina grabbed his arm tighter now and pulled her body closer to his. "I know I've tried to ignore the fact that you were in love with your wife, but I think it's important for you to talk about Claire now."

Theodore sat passively for several seconds, relishing the memories of his youth that flipped through his mind like an unfurling scrapbook. A small but reluctant smile brushed against his lips as he organized his thoughts into words. He became so absorbed by his recollections that he didn't even notice Regina grinning at him with compassion.

"I suppose you're not in the mood for a long-winded love story," Theodore said to Regina. "Besides, I wouldn't even know where to begin."

"Why not start at the beginning?" Regina suggested. "Where did you meet her?"

"Ironically enough," Theodore snickered, "I think it was in a church in Philadelphia. She used to sing in the choir."

"Is that the kind of woman you were attracted to?"

"I don't know," Theodore sighed, rubbing his forehead with his palms. "I just remember that she was a beautiful woman, with an equally beautiful voice." As he uttered these words, Regina watched his fingers stroke through his daughter's hair, tracing her cheek and earlobe like a butterfly dancing on the edge of a flower.

"So you married her right away?"

"Not exactly. It took me two years to muster up the courage. But I never regretted my oath to her. True love does strange things to a man's eyes, Regina. He starts looking at everything differently, even himself."

Regina felt inclined to mention that love affected a woman's vision in a similar way, but she repressed her feelings for now. Despite the bitterness that presently existed within Theodore's mind, she also perceived the decency of his soul—the soul that desperately tried to fight its way through the dark passages of reality.

"When did you decide to move out of Philadelphia?" Regina asked, hoping that Theodore hadn't grown bored with her inquiry.

"I guess it was in the spring of 1986," Theodore replied. "Claire got this crazy idea to refurbish a creaky, old farmhouse. She wanted to live out on a farm, overlooking a pasture of cows and horses."

"And that's when you came to Wakeland?"

"Yeah, after a few stops along the way."

Regina then trained her eyes on Emily and asked, "So you decided to have a child together. Do you want to talk about that at all?"

"That's another story in itself, and one that's very personal to me."

"I'd like to hear it, if you don't mind."

Theodore exhaled and stood up from his chair. While speaking, he paced nervously throughout the room, no longer focusing his eyes on his daughter's face. "Regina, this is going to sound strange to you, but I think that Claire and I knew the exact moment in which Emily was conceived."

"I've heard people say this to me before, but I've never been lucky enough to understand it," Regina said. "What were you were both feeling at the time?"

"I don't know if I can put the feeling into words, but it had something to do with the ocean."

"Now I'm confused. What does the ocean have to do with anything in relation to Claire's pregnancy?"

"It's where we were when it happened. In the summer of 1986, Claire and I took a trip to Cape May, New Jersey. I never much cared about the beach before we went there, but Claire turned me on to it. She always was going to more trouble than necessary to make me happy. On this occasion, she even brought along her camera."

As Theodore recounted this memory, Regina remembered the photograph of Claire in Emily's bedroom back home. She also connected this image to the picture that Theodore had destroyed on the previous night. With grief mounting in her heart, she listened as he recounted the incident in a monotone voice.

"I remember how brilliantly Claire's eyes shone in the moonlight on that night. She hinted that mine were glowing, too. Anyway, while lying on the beach, we were both gazing up at the stars. We never realized how many stars were scattered in the sky. It seemed as though you could simply reach out your hand and snatch a handful of these glittering gems from midair."

Regina listened as Theodore shifted from place to place across the floor. "We stared at the sky for a long time that night," he started again. "At some point, Claire started to talk about God. I listened, and truly believed that she would be protected, you know, because her faith was so pure."

"She must have sensed some of that purity in you as well," Regina said. "Maybe you can find your faith again."

Theodore's eyes now filled with tears when he sobbed, "You don't understand. That night on the beach was a perfect time for us—a time when I was sure that we'd be together forever. It was there, while looking at those stars, that Claire told me she was pregnant."

"It must have been a wonderful feeling for both of you."

"So wonderful that I wanted to preserve the moment," Theodore said, smirking at his own reflection in the window. "I suggested that I take a photograph of her."

"Like the photograph in your bedroom?" Theodore stopped pacing the floor and lowered into a chair again. Regina spoke in a soft voice now. "Why did you destroy that photo of your wife? I don't understand why you would want to ruin that memory."

Theodore grimaced as his eyes fixated on the crucifix again. He then leaned over Emily's bedside and lightly touched his daughter's foot with his hand. "It was all a lie," he muttered. "No one loved God more than Claire. After returning to our hotel room that night, I remember placing my hand on her stomach. We whispered about the miracle of life, and I joined her in church to show God my thanks."

"Do you really think God lied to you?" Regina asked.

Theodore's voice was fractured by sorrow when he uttered, "Before Emily was born, Claire and I made a promise to each other that we'd raise our daughter as a Christian child. After Claire died, I tried to make good on that promise..."

"But you didn't—Instead, you abandoned your faith."

"It seemed like my only choice. Once Emily got sick, I stopped caring about everything. It was like a white spark fizzling out in the back of my mind, and for the first time I realized how alone I really was."

"I wish you weren't so stubborn," Regina said. "Neither you nor your daughter has to be alone, for as long as you don't turn your back on God. He is still with you, and He'll stay there for as long as you let Him."

Theodore sensed his anger subsiding as he stood in front of Regina. Then, after peering hesitantly into her eyes, he edged one step closer toward her. In great anticipation, Regina reached out her fingers, fetching for his embrace like the gentle leader of a sightless boy. For a second, the bloody memories of Claire's botched delivery raced through his thoughts.

Theodore stumbled forward and clutched Regina in his arms like he never had before. Her body felt warm and soft against his skin, but he couldn't conceal the cold sweat dripping from his flesh like pellets of ice. It frightened him to know that his lips were pressed against the dark hair surrounding Regina's neck. When she turned her head to focus both eyes on his face, their mouths nearly joined.

"It was selfish of me to think that you could stay in Wakeland forever," Theodore wept. "I understand that you need to find happiness, too. For what it's worth, I'll always be grateful for what you've done for Emily."

Regina raised her hand and stroked the matted hair off his forehead. She then studied his darkening eyes more intensely, trying to communicate her affection through a single gaze. While holding Theodore closer against her chest, she sensed his heart thumping with an uneven cadence, as if each ensuing breath was a struggle. She thought to kiss him in these seconds, but then subdued her desire.

As always, the urge to join together seemed to fade from their hearts. Together but now apart, they slumped in the chairs beside Emily's bed. Now content to let Theodore rest his head on her shoulder, Regina gazed at Emily's closed eyelids.

In the meantime, Theodore gradually closed his own eyes and drifted into sleep. Though Regina tried not to be intrusive, she couldn't resist an urge to dwell on the information she discovered in Lawrence's journal. How many more answers did those pages hold? At one level, she was satisfied with the notion that Lawrence had in fact saved Claire's life, but guilt surfaced within her thoughts, too, for she now knew something about Theodore's past that he would have never anticipated.

Although tempted to open the notebook again, Regina decided to curtail her curiosity for now. Instead of reaching for the journal, she picked the crucifix off the floor. When she grasped the metal cross, it felt as frigid as Theodore's flesh. She rubbed the gold between her hands for a few minutes before returning it to the journal's creased pages. Then, feeling quite fatigued, she shut her eyes and leaned her head against Theodore's shoulder.

Regina slept soundly for the remainder of this night, dreaming about the ocean and the suspended stars that cast a glow upon the ocean's dark tides so many years ago.

CHAPTER THIRTY

▼

EMILY'S NEW VISION

Emily opened her eyes on the following morning and noticed her father and Regina slumped together on folding chairs beside her bed. She did not attempt to awake them. Although the pain carving into her lower abdomen had faded, her head still felt as if it was weighted to her pillow with a sack full of stones. After inspecting the room's surroundings and her change of clothing, she realized that she had never left Kindred Woods.

Now embarrassed by her current predicament, Emily glimpsed at her gaunt body as if she had been violated. Her nearly transparent hospital gown seemed to have been tossed over her shoulders in haste. After sensing no conspicuous injuries to herself other than a headache, she sat upright in the bed, leaning her back against the headboard for support.

Emily waited in silence for fifteen minutes, watching her father shift uncomfortably in his sleep like a man strapped to a slab of needles. Contrarily, Regina slept as inanimate as a doll in her seat, but her expression had slowly slipped into a frown.

Before long, as if telepathically awakened by his daughter's stare, Theodore jumped to his feet like a toy mounted to a coiled spring. He rubbed the sleep from his eyes with both hands before realizing that Emily was no longer unconscious. A surge of adrenaline pushed him toward Emily's bedside. She sat motionless as he entwined his fingers with her own. Though he wanted to shout out as if had won some meager victory, he softened his voice so that his daughter wouldn't be startled.

"It's okay, Emily, you're safe now."

Emily nodded her chin, but did not utter a word. Instead, she gestured to a stainless steel sink in the adjacent bathroom. She then pointed to her mouth, indicating that she desired a drink of water. While her father fetched the water from the sink, Regina also awoke. Her reaction was similar to Theodore's.

Regina asked groggily, "Emily, how long have you been awake?"

In a raspy voice Emily said, "Not very long." Before she attempted to say anything more, she quickly took the cup of water from her father's hand and guzzled it down her throat. In the meantime, Regina rushed out into the hallway to find Dr. Kraven.

"Try to stay still until Regina gets back with the doctor," Theodore advised his daughter. He then sat on the edge of the bed and stroked Emily's cheek. "I was so afraid that you weren't going to wake up," he sobbed.

"Dad," Emily stated, but her voice was clearly unsympathetic to her father's concern. "I'm not ready to die just yet."

Theodore grabbed the paper cup from Emily's hand before asking, "Do you need anything else? When Emily didn't immediately respond, he pressed his hand across her forehead. He sensed that her body temperature was still abnormally cold. "You're freezing," he cringed, looking around the room for a spare blanket.

Emily turned her head so that her father's hand slipped away. She insisted that she felt no pain. "I was only sleeping," she insisted.

"But Doctor Kraven told us that you blacked out. We couldn't wake you up."

"That's impossible," Emily denied. "When did this happen?"

Theodore's face twisted with perplexity as he cried, "You really don't remember?"

Emily closed her eyes momentarily, desperately scanning her memory for the details of the previous night. After several seconds, she reopened her eyes and said to her father, "Since coming to the hospital yesterday, I can't remember anything too clearly."

"Don't worry about it, honey," Theodore assured her. "We don't have to talk about that right now."

Still dissatisfied with her mental block, Emily clasped her hands behind her neck and looked toward the room's ceiling. She then glanced at her father and asked, "Who put me in this room?"

"Doctor Kraven, I think."

Emily repeated this name in her thoughts before stating, "I don't know who that is. What happened to Doctor Garrison?"

Now suspecting that Emily had sustained some memory loss when falling unconscious, Theodore swept his hand through her hair. "Maybe you hit your head on the floor," he said. "Does your head hurt?"

"No, Dad," Emily groaned.

"Let's wait and see what the doctor thinks."

Before Theodore finished his thought, Regina reentered the room. One other uniformed nurse was at her side, but neither had located Dr. Kraven. When Theodore noticed that the doctor wasn't present, he lashed out at the nurse. "We need a doctor in here. Where is Doctor Kraven?"

"He'll be in momentarily," the RN replied, pacing to Emily's bedside. The nurse flashed a penlight into Emily's face to check the clarity of her eyes. "Eyes seem a bit glassy," she observed.

"She can't remember anything," Theodore snapped at the RN. "How the hell do you explain that?"

Regina stepped behind Theodore and pressed lightly on his shoulder with her fingertips. She then explained in a calm voice, "I've seen these sort of things happen before. Let's give her a little time to get her thoughts together."

Theodore almost offered his opinion, but his attention was drawn to another figure standing outside the room. Dr. Kraven stood in the door's entrance, casually loosening his scarlet tie as he walked inside. Theodore's anxiety was extremely visible at this point, but the doctor peered over his shoulder—focusing on Emily with greater intent.

After noticing that Emily was sitting upright on the bed with her eyes half-open, Dr. Kraven smiled. Emily gladly returned his gesture, though she was at first uncertain of his identity.

"Hello again, Emily," Dr. Kraven said, touching her leg. Emily may have not fully remembered her earlier encounter with this doctor, but it only took a second for her to become enamored by his handsome face.

"You're Doctor Kraven?" she asked, somewhat startled by his youthful appearance. "I thought you'd be a lot older."

"Well, I'm much older than I look," he smirked. After Dr. Kraven briefly checked her vital signs, he removed a clipboard from the front of her bed's frame and scribbled a few notes on a medical chart. In the meantime, in response to Dr. Kraven's subtle request, the RN excused herself from the room.

Emily then asked Dr. Kraven, "Are you going to take care of me from now on?"

Dr. Kraven's eyes drifted to Theodore before he replied, "That depends. I'm certainly going to try my best."

Theodore was too busy watching his daughter's expression to offer a response. Before exchanging any promises, he stepped between the doctor and Emily and said, "I think we've all had enough of this hospital, Doctor, and that includes Emily."

"Really?" Dr. Kraven chimed, glancing at Regina for a reaction. After she looked away in embarrassment, he pivoted toward Theodore. "I'm not in any position to prevent you from leaving here with your daughter today, Mr. Dayton, but shouldn't we think this over a bit?"

"I've already made up my mind," Theodore fumed. "I can tell you what Emily wants just as well as she can."

"Well, that's awfully diplomatic of you," Dr. Kraven declared, "but if it's not too much of a burden, I'd prefer to hear Emily tell me what she wants to do for herself."

Theodore paused momentarily before saying, "Since my daughter can't remember too much about her circumstances right now, I think this should be my decision." He motioned to Regina for verbal support, but she didn't know what to suggest at this stage. Emily, however, proved to be coherent enough to offer her own response.

"I may be sick," Emily complained to her father, "but I can still think for myself."

"Okay, honey," Theodore agreed, clasping her hand with his own. "Tell Doctor Kraven that you want to go home now." When Emily didn't respond immediately, Theodore's confidence began to wither. "I don't understand," he grumbled. "Don't you want to go back to your own bedroom?"

Emily swallowed hard before admitting, "I'm not sure what I want to do right now." While she spoke, her eyes focused directly into Dr. Kraven's dark eyes. "I need some time to think. Maybe I don't want to go back home right away."

"You're just a little frightened by what happened yesterday," Regina said, trying to offer a sensible explanation for the child's sudden change of heart.

"This isn't about fear," Theodore snapped. "Emily's never been afraid of anything—especially in regard to her home."

"I'm not afraid," Emily said matter-of-factly. "I just feel that it might be better for me to stay in the hospital right now."

Theodore turned angrily toward Dr. Kraven and yelled, "This is unbelievable!"

"Not at all," Dr. Kraven interrupted. "Your daughter is displaying a great deal of common sense, despite her amnesia. She'll be under constant supervision here."

"That's not going to happen," Theodore said, but he wasn't quite sure why Emily's decision caused him to feel so apprehensive. "This is all some kind of twisted game, isn't it?"

"Please, Mr. Dayton," Dr. Kraven tittered, "do I strike you as the type of man who participates in games—especially those that might involve the welfare of children?"

With his defense submerging faster than a torpedoed vessel, Theodore turned to Regina for an explanation. "Help me out here, Regina—I don't know what to do."

"I shouldn't get involved in this decision," Regina said, trying to remain indifferent.

After listening to the bickering for several seconds, Emily attempted to ease the tension. "I don't see the point in fighting over this," she said. "I didn't think it would be such a big deal. I thought I'd be making life easier for everyone by staying here."

Theodore plopped down on the side of the bed and exhaled a breath. In a rigid voice, he demanded, "I need to be alone with my daughter for a few minutes."

Dr. Kraven instantly complied with Theodore's request by inviting Regina to join him for a cup of coffee in the café. Regina politely refused the doctor, stating that she'd rather remain beside Theodore and Emily.

"I think I need to speak with Emily alone," Theodore then said to Regina. "Are you sure?"

Theodore nodded his chin once as Regina made her way toward the door with Dr. Kraven. After they had gone, Theodore leaned forward in his chair so that his face was only a few inches away from Emily's shoulder. The both kept quiet for a few seconds, studying one another as if they hadn't spoken in months. In the back of his mind, Theodore heard a strange ticking reverberating—like the sound of a clock. Yet when searching the room for a nearby source, he realized that there was no clock to be found on the walls.

Theodore rubbed at his temples with his palms before asking, "I guess we have a problem, don't we, Emily?"

"I don't want to make a big deal about staying here."

"This has always mattered to you before—"

"Well, not now—I've changed my mind. Now that I'm here, I don't understand why you want me to go home so badly."

"It's just so sudden," Theodore murmured. "I wouldn't normally be worried, but a lot of crazy things have happened."

"Dad," Emily said, staring at her father with darkening eyes. "There's really no point in bringing me back to Wakeland now. Doctor Kraven seems like a kind man. He'll take good care of me for whatever time I have left."

"Maybe I don't want him to do that. I don't trust that man."

Emily rolled her eyes and said, "Stop trying to protect me, Dad. It's not doing either one of us any good."

Theodore zeroed his eyes on his daughter's frigid expression. He felt as though she suddenly appeared detached from everything. His heart quickened in his chest when he asked, "Has Doctor Kraven done something to you?"

"What are you talking about?"

"Just tell me the truth, Emily—did he give you any drugs to make you go to sleep?"

Emily tossed her hands up in a bewildered gesture, before explaining to her father that she had no memory of anything that Dr. Kraven may have done to harm her. However, she did consider it peculiar for him to make such an accusation.

"Dr. Kraven wouldn't hurt me," she said, forcing her lips into a half-smile. "He's here to help us children, isn't he?"

Theodore might have had an easier time answering this question before last night, but now he wasn't convinced that Emily truly believed what she was saying. In a bid to test her memory, he picked up the journal lying on the floor beside the bed. He held the notebook in front of Emily to see how she reacted.

Emily simply shrugged her shoulders and asked, "What's that?"

"You really don't know?" Theodore cringed, flipping through the sheets of paper.

"I've never seen it before," Emily insisted.

"My father mailed you this journal before he died. You've spent quite a bit of time reading through it over the last day or so."

"That's strange, because I can't remember reading a word of it."

"You must at least remember my father's name."

Emily squeezed her eyelids shut, attempting to ram the lost details through the clogged channels of her brain. Finally, she opened both her eyes and shook her head. "I'm sorry," she sulked, "my memory is still pretty foggy."

Theodore continued turning the notebook's pages until he reached a section in it where Regina had set the crucifix as a marker. As his fingers brushed against the gold cross, he purposely flicked it out of the note-book's binding. It landed on the bed's mattress near Emily's right hand. Emily and Theodore stared at this icon without blinking. Normally, Emily would have revealed an emotion of fondness toward the crucifix, but she did nothing more than glare at it with the same forlorn gaze as her father.

"Why don't you hold it?" Theodore asked her, with his voice slightly raised above a whisper.

Emily peered at her father coldly and remarked, "I don't think that's a good idea right now."

"Why not?"

Her voice became increasingly irritated when she continued. "What's the point of it all, Dad—right? It's just a stupid cross. It doesn't mean any-thing to me."

Now suspecting that Emily had surrendered more than her memory, Theodore cautiously asked, "What are you trying to say to me, Emily?"

Emily looked at her father and said innocently, "You're the one who taught me that God doesn't really exist—except in our imaginations. You know, Dad, for the longest time, I had a hard time believing you, but I now understand why you lost your faith. It makes it easier for me to do the same thing."

"I never wanted you to think like me."

"Admit it, you didn't want me to believe in God. It's okay, though, because I'm not blaming you for trying to set me straight."

"Maybe you ought to talk this over with Regina," Theodore advised. "She'll be able to help you."

"I don't need Regina's help," Emily sneered. "I know what I feel."

"I don't believe you."

Realizing that her father wouldn't concede to her change of mind, Emily batted the crucifix to the floor with a swipe of her clenched fist. Stunned by this action, Theodore watched the cross slide across the tile near his feet. Without knowing how to react to her defiance, he simply looked at her with sorrow flaring in his pupils.

"What has happened to you?" Theodore quivered, standing up from the bed.

"I just want to prove that it's over. I don't need to live this lie any longer—not even for another minute. Let's face it, if there ever was a god, I don't think he's looking over my shoulder."

When Emily shifted her eyes toward Theodore again, she noticed tears forming in the corner of his eyes. She remained callous to this display of sensitivity. "Stop crying," she demanded. "Of all people, Dad, you should be thankful. You've finally got what you wished for."

"I never wished for you to be like this!"

"It's like looking in a mirror, isn't it? Sometimes we can't stand the sight of ourselves, but I'm much happier now. This hospital is the only thing that makes sense to me now. At least I know where the end really is in here."

Emily's bitter words snapped off her tongue like the lash of a whip. Theodore could almost feel the sting against his flesh as he recoiled from the bedside. Though he never expected to feel so utterly disillusioned in Emily's presence, he knew that he had surrendered his authority over her beliefs long before this hour. And the worst part of knowing this was the fact that he couldn't do anything to change her opinion now, for his own heart pounded with the same rhythms of faithlessness.

Dejected by his daughter's words, Theodore bent to the floor and picked up the crucifix. He held the shining metal in his hand momentarily, and then stuffed it back into the journal's open binder. Emily sensed her father stalling, as if he hadn't finished with all that he needed to say. During these seconds, the ticking sound reached a crescendo in his mind. He staggered in front of Emily like a drunkard, holding his left hand to his head, while feeling for the walls with the other.

"Don't you hear that?" he asked Emily. He then propped up against the door's frame to maintain his balance. "It's a clock—it's ticking—"

Emily still refused to respond to her father's terrified voice.

"Please tell me that you hear that sound?" Theodore cried.

Finally, after he had nearly collapsed to the floor in a stupor, Emily said quite calmly, "I don't hear anything. Maybe you hit your head, too."

"No," Theodore insisted, "this sound is real—I know it is."

Once realizing that he was enduring agony, Emily suggested, "Just keep still and shut your eyes. It's all inside your mind."

Instead of listening to his daughter, Theodore lowered his body upon the floor and scurried out of the room on his hands and knees with the journal still in his possession. Once in the hallway, the noise stopped. He glanced behind himself again and noticed that Emily's eyes were shut. Within seconds, she had fallen back to sleep. He shouted into the room, but she didn't respond.

Theodore's scream may not have been loud enough to awaken Emily, but it did catch Regina's ear. She scrambled down the corridor in response to his cry. When reaching him, she noticed a thick perspiration exuding from every pore in his face and neck.

"My god," she cried, glancing into the room at Emily. "What happened?"

Theodore didn't answer Regina until he moved twenty paces down the neighboring corridor. In a muted voice, he said, "Leave me alone for now, Regina. I need to think."

"Why are you so upset?"

"I'm not sure," Theodore whispered, wiping the sweat from his brow. He then glanced at the journal in his hands, this time clutching it with both hands as he rose to his feet. Without offering an explanation to his disposition, he ran off into the corridor. Regina almost chased after him, but she turned toward Emily's room instead. As Regina started to walk inside, she was halted by Dr. Kraven's command.

"Let her be for now, Miss Hopewell."

Regina glared at the doctor before saying, "But she's unconscious again. She may need our help."

Dr. Kraven paced over to Regina and gently brushed his fingers against the side of her cheek. She shivered as their skin connected. Dr. Kraven declared, "I think you realize that there's not much more that we can do for that young lady. Perhaps it's best if we let her sleep for now."

"I'm uncomfortable standing here and doing nothing."

"Oh, don't be so dramatic. You've expended too much of your good energy worrying about that child. It's easy for me to see that you've become too close to your patient."

Regina nudged the doctor's hand away from her face. Without understanding why, she peered into the inky texture of his eyes. She sensed her mind weakening as her breathing increased.

Dr. Kraven spoke softly into her ear. "Don't resist me, Miss Hopewell." His strong hands latched on to her hips with a firmness that she found difficult to disfavor. "Free that child from your mind," Dr. Kraven continued. His lips now eased closer to her own. "And let that hapless man walk away from you as well."

Regina's pure thoughts now betrayed her. Dr. Kraven's authority actually aroused her senses. And although she didn't confess her desires, she moistened her mouth with her tongue, as if waiting—and hoping—for a kiss from this beautiful man. Tiny beads of sweat formed on her upper lip, and the nape of her neck became moist. Did she really want this man to press himself against her trembling body? Or was this just a lecherous spell dripping into her mind like a poison?

In a moment of clarity, Regina pushed Dr. Kraven away. She no longer stared into his throbbing, black eyes when she quivered, "I can't do this. I need to be alone."

"No one needs to be alone," Dr. Kraven said, folding his arms across his chest. "You're getting older now, Miss Hopewell. I sense that you want a man beside you now."

"Not just any man—"

"Forgive me for being so blunt with you, but you've already wasted so much time. Theodore will never change into the lover you hope he can one day be. He's a lost and empty soul, and he's dragging you down with him."

"You don't even know him," Regina said, now glancing into the doctor's eyes again.

"I've known men like him my entire life," Dr. Kraven declared. "Trust me—he'll never be able to offer you what I can." He now edged closer to Regina, forcing his mouth over her parted lips. She struggled for a moment, but then felt her body submitting to the hot sensations pulsating through her veins. After several seconds, he released Regina, leaving her to stagger against the room's door.

She was breathless with desire and anticipation when she said, "You had no right to do that. Don't come near me again."

"As you wish, but don't scorn me for merely trying to enlighten you to the pleasures that you dream about."

Still ashamed for partially enjoying the kiss, Regina wiped her mouth with her hand and quivered, "I never wanted a man like you. You repulse me."

"Now, Now, Miss Hopewell," Dr. Kraven smirked, "we both know that you're lying. I don't blame you for being hesitant toward my advances, so why don't you let me prove my affection to you? Join me and I'll see to it that you're never cold or lonely at night again."

"Stop it," Regina cried. "Just get away from me."

Dr. Kraven clasped his hands behind his back and peered over Regina's shoulder. After he noticed that Emily was sleeping, his smile widened and his black eyes gleamed as if they were glazed with a rich polish. "Can't you sense it in your heart? It's almost over now, and there's nothing you can do to stop it."

Now too sickened to say anything else to Dr. Kraven, Regina spun away from him and rejoined Emily's bedside. Within moments of sitting down, she clasped her face with both her hands and began to sob uncontrollably. Dr. Kraven shook his head in mock pity, before casually striding away from the door.

In the meantime, Theodore had rambled aimlessly through the corridors until reaching the locked gate. He pressed his face up against the gate's steel bars, while slowly bending to the floor. As he knelt upon the concrete, he tried closing his eyes to think, but his thoughts became snarled in a dark mist.

When Theodore finally opened his eyes, he peered at the journal resting beside him on the floor. The crucifix gleamed in the corridor's florescent light. For an inexplicable reason, Theodore reached for it. After touching the cross with his fingers, he sensed his own iciness. In dismay, he jerked his hand away. With this motion, the journal opened itself, as if its pages had been exposed to a wind. The sound of fluttering paper reminded him of the flapping of birds' wings.

Without further provocation, Theodore lowered his eyes upon the page and started to read his father's journal with a revitalized energy.

CHAPTER THIRTY-ONE

▼

JOURNAL ENTRY SEVENTEEN

THE LARK'S TRIBULATION

As the decade of the 70's neared its conclusion, I almost surrendered all hope of ever locating my son in Philadelphia. If Theodore was still living within the city's boundaries since his departure from Riverside, I assumed he would have at least attempted to contact Father Jordan. My frequent telegrams to Jordan always left me feeling frustrated and guilty. If any measure of success had been gained from my persistence, it may have stemmed from the casual association that Jordan and I now shared. After the passage of many years, I sensed that this priest was as distraught over Theodore's disappearance as I was.

During this time, my sanity had eroded to a degree where I sometimes considered suicide as a remedy to my strife. Perhaps I should've sought Jordan's guidance in regard to this matter, but shame kept me from revealing my depression. In the process of my breakdown, I experienced another series of obscure premonitions. Up until now, I felt confident that I could repress the illusions that once drove me to the point of madness. But by 1982, at the age of fifty-two, I found it nearly impossible to resist the surreal images fermenting within my mind.

To be accurate, all of my forthcoming visions were not menacing. In fact, some of my dreams actually afforded me with a much-needed reprieve from reality. At times, I imagined pastel-colored rainbows arching over verdant landscapes. Doves soared through the sky, too, and the sweet scent of wild roses wafted in the swirling zephyrs. But such images were only fleeting reminders of my instability. Soon enough I'd be compelled to revisit the darkness that resided within my brain.

Up until now, the evil had appeared to me in the formation of a mortal man. Whether he referred to himself as Kross or Konrad, I still sensed his possession over my soul. The dark fiend would soon appear to me in all of his God-defying fury.

By the summer of 1984 I was wasting most of my days away on the port docks outside of Philadelphia. I didn't wander here for any specific purpose, except maybe a chance to be near the water again—even if it was only among a fleet of rusty fishing boats and briny-skinned merchants. One day an amiable captain offered me a job as a deckhand aboard his fishing vessel—The Queen Lark. Though I knew virtually nothing about fishing, the mere prospect of sailing out into the water compelled me to accept his offer.

I boarded The Queen Lark with few serious reservations and gradually became acquainted with a crew of young seamen. According to these fellows, netting hoards of tuna and bluefish was a craft reserved for the most spirited among us. They wasted many unproductive hours assuring me that this industry relied on them more than they needed it. In spite of their failed attempts to impress me with their seafaring yarns, I appreciated their sense of brotherhood.

While toiling beside these men on several uneventful excursions, I learned to gaze at the ocean's swaying waves in awe and fear. Had I known that the Atlantic's tides were so variable, I may have opted to survey its beauty from a distance. At its worst, the ocean never stopped to weep for those who fell prey to its currents. At any time it could have easily swallowed ten thousand souls with one slap of its pulsating surface.

Considering the ocean's ever-present danger, it may be difficult to understand why men dared to challenge its ferocity on a daily basis. Yet as ugly and untamed as this water may have been, it was carefully counterbalanced by a far greater eminence. At its best, the seawater appeared like a mirrored plain into paradise. In the morning, sunlight poured from the heavens and reflected a tapestry of prisms for endless miles. At dawn, thousands of tiny waves rippled like golden dust, and at twilight, the horizon flared with hues of purple and orange. Under full moonlight, the black surface possessed an ominous sheen as well, as if it was layered in a sheath of cellophane.

In my logged hours aboard The Queen Lark we had braved storms choppy enough to rattle the nerves of our most seasoned men. But never had the ocean looked as dreadfully dark and wild than on the night of my premonition. An hour before reaching port, an unexpected squall flanked the eastern coastline. Within minutes, a silvery fog and wind consumed our ship's course. Unable to navigate, the captain stalled the Lark's engines and signaled a distress call to the coastguard in Cape May, New Jersey.

By now, six-foot breakers pummeled the ship's starboard, sending us reeling across the ocean's surface. For a while, the water spilt amply onto the ship's decks, flushing a handful of shrieking crewmembers to their watery graves. The less fortunate—like me—stood near the stern, waiting to be smothered by the frothing waves. But for whatever reason, the ocean did not consume me at first. I dropped to my knees and clasped my hands in front of myself, praying for the agony to end. For me, however, the torment was only beginning.

Between the mist and wind, the tides rolled over as the sea broke into sections. In this instance, a repulsive odor permeated the air. It was the smell of fire amid the storm. As the ocean percolated and curdled with smoke, a monstrous figure emerged from its depths. This hideous form ascended from the water like a writhing serpent. It waggled seven horned heads upon its shoulders. The centermost head claimed three spikes and a mouth full of fangs.

I could do nothing more than stare at this foul beast with pure uncertainty. Was it real? Or had my imagination created this? For confirmation, I turned to the other crewmen, but they had been methodically washed overboard and lost in the chaos. Now alone and utterly confounded, I pivoted back toward this infernal creation and swore to slay it with my bare fists.

Instead of concentrating its rage upon me, the beast unleashed a multitude of groans that sounded like the cries of suffering children. It then spewed fireballs upon the ocean from its mouths, forming a wall of flames around its snake-like torso. Its sickly yellow eyes pinched into vertical slots as black excrement belched from its seven cavernous jaws. Within seconds, the ship's hull slipped beneath the sea, and I now wallowed helplessly within this filthy inferno.

Though I commanded this demon to destroy me, it did not permit me to drown as easily as the rest of the crew. Instead, I was forced to witness its frightening wrath. The sky overhead blazed and stars shot toward the water like pellets of hail. Mixed within these fading orbs, I noticed hundreds of white doves diving toward the beast's jaws. Just as the stars collided with the sea, the doves streamed into the burning mist. And then, before my fate was fully realized, a brilliant energy enveloped my body. Almost magically, I sensed myself rising from the ocean as the beast hissed and submerged into the darkness.

I must have lost consciousness somewhere thereafter, because I don't recall being plucked from the water by the coastguard. In any event, when

I awakened, I way lying on another ship's deck encircled by uniformed officers. My body was wrapped in a blanket and bright lights shone in my eyes. Now shivering and disorientated, I wondered why these men appeared so composed in the aftermath of what I had just witnessed.

"You're safe now," an officer assured me, "We got you out of that water just in time."

"Where are the others?" I cried, looking around at the officers' glum expressions. "I wasn't alone out there—they were with me."

"Not anymore," the officer responded gravely. "That storm was pretty severe. You're the only survivor."

Petrified with remorse, I leaned my head back against the deck and stared at the black sky. At least for now, the stars had taken their rightful place along the horizon. The ocean revealed no evidence of commotion under the moonlight's pale glow. Before the dreadful thought escaped my mind, I asked the officers in a panicky voice, "Didn't you see it?"

"See what?" another guardsman asked.

If this beast's presence wasn't obvious to them, I knew that we hadn't shared the same visions. Evidently, the storm and the sinking of The Queen Lark were genuine events, but no one besides me had seen the monster that soaked this water in fire. I decided not to speak of my illusion at this time.

My rescuers didn't neglect to remind me of how privileged I had been to avoid drowning with the rest of my crew. Most men, they determined, would have been dead long before they managed to penetrate the wind and rain. Despite their observations, I didn't feel fortunate or even remotely grateful for averting death at this stage in life.

Though I hardly knew the men aboard The Queen Lark, I was saddened by the senselessness of their deaths. In my mind, it wasn't the storm itself that claimed the lives of those fishermen—it was the bane of my existence. This incessant curse, which I carried upon my back like an iron tomb, had now struck innocent strangers. Once again I stood alone, wondering why I had been chosen to endure such tragedy.

Shortly following the boating disaster, I returned to Philadelphia as a dejected soul. Unable to work, sleep, or participate in life's basic pleasures, I shut myself up in my room for what I prayed would be until I died. I felt terribly dirty and afraid during these hours of solitude. Had I died in this place, no one would have searched for me.

Three weeks passed before I managed to lurch back onto the streets to face daylight again. For the most part, my search for Theodore had ended years ago, but I wasn't done living yet. In these moments, I suspected that something appalling was happening to our world. I still confided in one person, and I believed that he would assist me with my hallucinations in some way.

After forwarding a letter to Father Jordan explaining my most recent encounter with the dark fiend, I revisited Riverside for the first time in many years. Admittedly, I didn't think Jordan would rank anything I expressed to him as sound evidence. He knew too much about my past for that to occur. Maybe I just needed to unload the forthcoming speculations to a man who wouldn't condemn my frailties. Besides, if anyone was capable of believing in what I viewed, a Christian-minded man may have been my only hope.

Understanding that I had several problems to sort out, Jordan greeted me with his Bible in hand. He waited pensively behind a white oak desk, garbed in full uniform, which included satin vestments typically reserved for Mass.

Though we had willingly corresponded with each other for years by way of mail, I peered at him as I would at any stranger on this afternoon. Maybe our awkwardness served as an asset for the discourse yet to come. After he invited me to sit down, I immediately informed the Jordan that I sought full privileges of confidentiality.

"Perhaps you'd be more at ease in confessional," Jordan suggested.

"No, Father," I countered. "I'd like to keep our conversation as informal as possible."

"Very well," Jordan conceded. He then reached into his desk drawer and displayed the letter that I wrote. He had taken some time to highlight numerous sections with yellow marker. To an untrained eye, it appeared as though I had failed one of his theological exams. He went on to say, "As you can plainly see, Lawrence, I've given your letter a great deal of my attention in the past week."

"Please don't tell me that I'm crazy. I've already lived through that diagnosis once."

"I didn't meet with you today to make any accusations. But I'd like to start by asking you about your knowledge of the Bible, especially what you may have studied before the accident you experienced at sea last month."

I tentatively watched Jordan open his Bible before saying, "I'm not going to lie to you, Father. I don't consider myself to be an extremely religious man."

Jordan continued to flip through the Bible's pages until reaching the last book in the New Testament. "I didn't ask you about your faith," Jordan emphasized. "I was merely trying to assess your knowledge on the Bible, particularly with The Book of Revelation."

"I've glimpsed at it a few times, but I've had a hard time with some of its ideas."

"That's not an unusual response," Jordan said. "Every generation since the first century has attempted to interpret St. John's prophetic visions—some better than others, I might add."

"I appreciate the information, but how does that explain what's wrong with me?"

"First off, Lawrence, there's nothing wrong with you, outside of an overactive imagination. You're certainly not the first man to be influenced by the symbolism in Revelation. "

"My dreams must mean something. Is there anything in that book that explains what I'm experiencing?"

"Of course," Jordan replied confidently, before putting on his eyeglasses and turning three pages forward in his Bible. He then explained,

"In Revelation, Chapter 13, Verse 1, John describes a beast—one which came straight out of the sea." Jordan then referred to the letter I had written and said, "I've spotted numerous similarities between what you've claimed to envision and what has been recorded and debated within this passage for almost two thousand years."

"Does that make what I've seen any less real?"

"No, but it does lend credence to the probability that you've been harboring repressed fears about this particular event. Perhaps you read the story as a boy, and its images have reemerged in your subconscious."

"Come on, Father, I've heard all this psychobabble before. You've got to do better than that."

"Listen," Jordan sighed, "many Christians and God-fearing men have reviewed Revelation like a doomsday manual. I suppose it's entertaining to take a story from this book out of context, but I don't think St. John intended his visions to be read as literal happenings."

"Maybe he knew something about our world's future that we don't want to admit," I suggested. "I mean, hypothetically speaking, if you envisioned what I did, how would you react?"

"Exactly as I am right now."

"Then you really don't believe what's written in the Bible—do you, Father Jordan?"

"Of course I do. I believe that there are good and evil forces stirring among us, and they may manifest into various formations within our minds. I cannot in good faith, however, tell you that Revelation is the sole guide to mankind's destiny. After all, it's nearly 1985, and the Great Tribulation has never occurred."

As I listened to Jordan speak, my memory flashed back to an earlier time. I couldn't at first remember precisely where or from whom I heard such words before. But then, as my heart began to pulsate, I asked the priest, "What is the Great Tribulation?"

"It's sort of an ultimate trial," Jordan answered, again directing my attention to the Bible as a primary reference. "In Chapter 13, Verse 5, St.

John foretold of a power. 'And power was given unto him to continue forty and two months.'"

"Power to whom?"

"The antichrist, presumably," Jordan said with a placid stare. "According to St. John, this beast shall have free reign over this Earth and all men for three and a half years—or forty-two months."

A burning sensation engulfed my abdomen as I buckled over in my chair. In a voice laced with pain, I asked, "When was all of this supposed to have taken place?"

Jordan simpered quietly at my ignorance before saying, "That's the vague part of the prophecy, Lawrence. Theologians have debated the exact date, but those who refer to this as the Great Tribulation predict that this period will come at an age of severe persecution for Christians—happening sometime around Christ's return."

"Then this period may still come to be."

"I wouldn't put too much faith into it."

"But you're a priest," I cried, somewhat disheartened by Jordan's flexibility in regard to this matter. "People come to you for guidance—for hope. If you're not pure in your own spiritual thoughts, then what does that mean for the rest of us?"

"Everyone must make their own peace with God. Live and pray clean, and obey the wisdom, as it is unveiled in the Gospels. If you follow this plan, you'll have nothing to fear come judgement day."

Without seeking Jordan's permission, I placed both of my hands on his desk and snatched the Bible from under his nose. After scanning several chapters in Revelation, I glanced up at the priest with a frightful thought. "You must be afraid for us, Father," I said. "Look what's happening to our society—to our world."

"I'm hopeful that things will get better," he replied. "I don't wish to preach pessimism. That's not the function of my school or the Church."

I then slid the Bible back in front of Jordan's flustered eyes, pointing with my finger to the passage cited in Revelation 20: 3. Jordan recited a portion of it aloud "...'Till the thousand years should be fulfilled: and after that he must be loosed a little season.'"

"Maybe our time has almost expired," I suggested.

"It all depends on how you wish to interpret it. I could find you twenty scholars who would disagree avidly with St. John's prophecies."

"But it is still possible that Satan will rise again, isn't it?"

Jordan released a disgruntled sigh before closing his Bible. He then removed his eyeglasses and reclined away from the desk. "You're certainly not making this easy for me."

"Just answer me this question," I persisted. "Do you deny the possibility that there are battles yet to be fought between the forces of heaven and hell?"

"I don't know," Jordan confessed. "I've seen so much horror over the last fifty years that I'm almost inclined to believe that mankind has waged an eternal war against himself."

"So where do we go from here? Isn't there anything we can do to save ourselves?"

"I suppose we can all spend more time concentrating on what is good about our world. God is out there, Lawrence, and he wants us to embrace His word. I'm afraid we have a tendency to see only what is easy, while ignoring what we truly need to observe."

For a moment, I said nothing. Instead, I focused my attention upon a mural of Christian icons behind Father Jordan's desk. I then determined that Jordan—although a benevolent man—could not be expected to solve the riddles of my life. Before departing Riverside, I was mindful to thank him for the knowledge he imparted on this occasion.

"Are you going back to Philadelphia?" Jordan asked.

"I won't be staying there much longer."

"Will you continue to write me?"

Before leaving Jordan's rectory, I turned back toward him and replied, "If there's anything else for us to discuss, Father, I know where to find you."

Jordan nodded his head once and forwarded a disconcerted stare at me. As I stepped outside, I heard him utter softly, "May God be in your company, Lawrence Dayton."

Now more than ever before in my lifetime, I needed to believe that He was.

CHAPTER THIRTY-TWO

▼

JOURNAL ENTRY EIGHTEEN

REVISITING OREFIELD

Growing old will never be a graceful journey for a man who cannot review his past with any sense of achievement. By 1985, I had squandered enough time to thoroughly contemplate my shortcomings, but the most obvious deficiency was one that I refused to recognize until now. Through my trials, I learned that regret and fear can be as detrimental to a man's health as any malignancy. Rather than brood over my frailties, I should've found the courage to change long before this moment.

Although I lived plainly since residing in Philadelphia, my limited savings, coupled with my inability to sustain employment, gradually left me destitute. In the winter of 1985, I was promptly evicted from my room above the hardware store in favor of someone who paid his rent on time. I soon took to the cold streets again, stuffing my life's possessions into a knapsack and two denim pockets.

For months I coexisted with exiled dreamers and drunken vagrants. Being poor most of my adult life had at least prepared me how to tolerate stale bread and meatless stew. What I couldn't adjust to, however, was the scowling glares from strangers. Sometimes, while scrounging for food and silver change among the working class, I became humiliated by my lack of ambition. Had I paused to gaze at my reflection in a pane of glass along the city's avenues, I would've surely spied into the face of failure.

In the spring of 1986, I set out on foot toward the country to rekindle my memories of nature's pastures. I didn't know exactly where my travels would lead me, but I sensed this expedition would be far more gratifying than the unforgiving fields of concrete from which I came. A destination wasn't essential in the beginning, so as long as each morning came packaged with creation's simplicities.

In the heat of summer afternoons, I remember sitting beside dusty trails beneath the shade of pine trees. Beyond where my eyes could see, songbirds whistled their melodies in the thicket. I watched rabbits and squirrels scamper across lush meadows, and deer lap water from timber-lined ponds. The purity of such scenery permitted me to feel the goodness in this earth again.

While drifting farther into the countryside, I ventured upon several rural communities that weren't even drafted on a map. The nameless folks residing within these towns restored some of my faith that I had lost in my fellow kind. I sensed the families living out here still trusted and cared for one another.

In my frequent stops along the wooded pathways, I'd often participate in their daily rituals. Some of these strangers offered me food, temporary housing, and clothing in exchange for manual labor on their farmlands. I worked diligently to ready their crops for the forthcoming harvest, if for no other reason than to prove to myself that I could still be a productive member of society.

By the autumn of 1986, I had invested nearly five months meandering through the rural footpaths of Pennsylvania's wilderness. During my progress, I forged homes in makeshift tents. On occasion, when the weather permitted, I slept on the cool pastures. For the first time in many years, I felt at ease with my pursuit into the unknown, and treasured the environment in ways that no city dweller could ever hope to fathom.

Though I wanted to believe that I could hide out here forever, I knew that my journey had an ultimate destination. Such a realization came to me unexpectedly in the winter of 1986. After enduring weeks of frigid temperatures, I came upon the debris of a deserted town that appeared vaguely familiar to my eyes. According to the maps, I had been advancing westward through the mountainous regions.

I couldn't understand why this town's ghostly remnants caused me to tremble. Then, while hiking down between the barren underbrush, I gazed upon the sagging hillsides and remembered a time from my past. I had in fact walked on this ground before. This land was once my boyhood home of Orefield.

I surveyed the landscape with sorrowful eyes, trying to envision the bending roads and shanties as they appeared over forty years ago. But my memory failed me, perhaps because I no longer desired to revisit this part of my dark history. Sadly, the boy inside me had withered long before this day.

I never anticipated Orefield to prosper once the mines closed. With the industry becoming too costly to operate, and most of the intrepid but ignorant engineers either dead or dying from their lung ailments, I predicted that this town's future would appear as bleak and desolate as it now did. What shocked me, however, was the displacement of the town's cemetery. I searched for many hours along the frozen embankments for my parents' gravesites, but to no avail. Their tombstones, along with at least two hundred other forgotten souls, had vanished within piles of clutter.

Following my inspection of the entire valley, I determined that there was nothing supernatural in relation to the removal of these graves. Apparently, the acreage was recently auctioned to a development company. They planned to construct a huge complex on these grounds in the near future. Those who were unfortunate enough to be buried here were treated with same discourtesy that afflicted them throughout their lives. Their headstones had been plowed over like worthless rocks and cast beneath pyramids of splintered wood.

It was more than likely that no one cared about these corpses. I had only stumbled upon this place by accident, but I couldn't help but to look at this scene as a subtle premonition to my own fate. It suddenly dawned upon me that I would perish in a similar fashion.

In an effort to conceal this irredeemable crime, the tombstones had been deliberately pummeled into bits. I crouched to the soil, combing my fingers through frozen mud and particles of granite. Didn't it matter that people once prayed over these stones? Ironically, even in death, they couldn't escape the despicable deeds of the living.

While brooding over the callousness of this act, I became distracted by a spell of fatigue. I stooped forward so that my body was reclined on the ground. Though I grappled at the rubble in an effort to pull myself upright, my legs and arms tingled and grew numb.

While gazing overhead, I became awestricken by the clouds. The sky glowed brighter than a hundred suns and the earth beneath me quaked. A light then trekked through the firmament like a glittering vapor trail. It rotated toward the ground in a cyclone of wind. Finally, the spiraling illumination gave way to a single ray of fire. This flaming blade sliced across the heavens in a parallel line, carving a fissure into atmosphere. Within seconds, the dirt around me sparkled as I had been entombed in crystal sand.

While staring into the light, a flock of doves spreading over the sky like a white-capped wave. Just as in my previous visions, these birds soared in formation, before settling upon the valley's floor with their eyes centered directly upon me. Following behind the doves' approach, a sphere of energy descended from the air. From within this orb an angel emerged.

Six wings kept him aloft. Two of these wings shielded his face from mine; two more concealed his torso, and the remaining pair was attached to his legs. He possessed an aura of fire around his entire body, and brandished a saber that simmered with golden smoke. I knew this angel from my past. It was the seraph who called himself Jonathan.

Prior to settling on the soil beside me, Jonathan fanned his wings and the particles of dust scattered. During these seconds, the doves vanished as well. I now peered at the seraph with a sense of astonishment, for I barely remembered how magnificent his appearance was after so many years.

Jonathan simply stared at me in silence, as though he was calculating my thoughts faster than I could form them.

"Jonathan," I hollered, "Why have you chosen to reveal yourself to me again?" As I uttered these words, the seraph hovered closer. As his wings expanded, a perfumed wind filled the valley. His golden hair flowed freely at his shoulders, appearing like a cape of translucent light.

Jonathan then said to me, "I've come to you with a message, Lawrence. We have reached a turning point in our trials. The archangels can no longer hold on to heaven. That is why you must be strong now."

"Me? I can't do anything to help you, Jonathan. Look at me," I cried, still struggling to rise to my feet. "I never asked to be cursed by the nightmares. I am just a man—nothing more."

"But you are a man who sees the truth," Jonathan replied. "You know that the children of this Earth are suffering in the grip of darkness."

"No one believes me—"

"God believes you, and that is why I've come to you at this hour. Throughout the years, we have relied on your strengths, as well as your weaknesses. Now you should know your part in this affair."

"Why does God send me His message now? It's too late for me—I've already lost everything."

"Not everything. You still possess what no angel can ever hope to own—a soul. It is this power that God bestowed onto each man in His domain. But I'm afraid that your kind doesn't recognize how invaluable a single soul can be."

Jonathan raised his fiery sword and waved it in a circular motion above his head. With this movement, the seraph created a hoop of light. "There is a dome of energy that divides heaven from hell," he explained. "Since the onset of time, such a shield has protected our region from the spell of evil. We once believed that God's kingdom would be impervious to the Devil's wrath, but mankind has proved us wrong."

"Why do you blame us?" I asked.

"The energy that I refer to can only be generated from your souls. It is for this reason that each life on Earth is valuable, for as long as they return to God with their faith intact."

In disbelief, I uttered, "God needs our souls?"

"Only the pure ones. In order to keep our barrier strong we must distribute mankind's energy upon the dome. Those who perish without their faith, however, cannot protect us. Their souls are devoured by the archfiend and they are then cast into darkness beyond heaven's gate."

"Why should I believe you now, Jonathan?"

"You've already begun to suspect the truth. In your mind, you realize that Earth's time is almost at its end. The spirits are weak now, and easy prey for the malevolence that stews among you."

"I've already tried to stop the evil," I said in disgust, clawing my fingers into the dirt. "God should have known better than to put His trust in our kind. In the end, we always come up short."

"Don't underestimate your kind, Lawrence. God still reserves hope for His creations. All is not yet lost. With the assistance of the angelic armies, we've kept the archfiend's legions at bay for thousands of years. For the last ten centuries, he has been contained, but I'm certain that his next uprising will devastate the sanctity of heaven."

"Fight the Devil yourself, Jonathan. If you defeated him once, why not do it again?"

"It is no longer our battle to win," Jonathan answered. "The dome protecting heaven has already been fractured. At the turn of the last century, a crack was discovered on its surface. It is through this fracture, I fear, that the archfiend will guide his minions upon his loosening."

"And you are powerless to repair this fracture?"

"As I told you, only mankind's pure energy can renew the shield. But as you plainly know, faith is not what it once was. Over the last hundred years, more men than ever before have died and gone the Devil's way. Because of this, the dome's crack has expanded. I'm afraid the scents of hell have already begun to sift through our hallowed grounds."

"But there must be something you can do to stop it."

Jonathan shook his head and lowered his sword. He then declared, "The hope that remains for heaven and earth does not rest with me."

"Won't God help us?"

"He already has. Though God is saddened by what has become of your kind, He refuses to surrender your souls. A plan has been devised in order to counteract the archfiend's approach, and it is one that will decide your fate as well as mine. In the year 1987, roughly fourteen years before the new millennium, a female child shall be conceived on this Earth. This child will be blessed with a soul that harnesses the purity of an army of God's worshippers. It is this child's soul that will be needed to repair the dome and repel the archfiend's fury."

"Then we will be saved—saved by a child."

"All is not in order," Jonathan advised. "Since the child will be born of flesh and blood, she'll possess the freewill that all humans share. God cannot make her spirit impenetrable to sin. Her purity will be tested and God cannot intervene."

"But this child will not fail us. She can't."

"Don't be so certain," Jonathan warned. "The archfiend does not play by the same set of rules. In his effort to secure the dome's penetration, he has sent thousands of his minions to Earth to corrupt the minds of children. The child in question will be their foremost prey."

"Then you must warn the children, Jonathan. Go to them—as you once came to me! How can God expect them to fight something they can't understand?"

"I wish I could tell you more, but God has forbade me to do so. I can only reveal to you that a great deal of suffering will be endured by those connected to the chosen child. In the end, she may prove to be the strongest link, but you, Lawrence Dayton, must go and find the weakest."

I lunged forward at the seraph now, hoping to hold onto him for another second. But my body passed right through the apparition. At this time, the hoop of energy dissolved and the seraph took to the sky again. Though I screamed out to Jonathan, he did not answer me. In another instance, his image faded into the sky. My cries echoed softly against the surrounding hillsides.

I stood upon this soil for several hours afterwards, praying for another sign to appear. But in my heart I knew that Jonathan would not revisit me on this day. He had delivered God's word. The rest of this mystery was mine to solve.

In reference to my most recent encounter with Jonathan, I'd like to declare that I realized my purpose in life. But once the seraph was gone, I resumed my aimless wanderings through the countryside for another three months. In some respects, I credited this retreat into nature as a remedy to my strife. Perhaps this time of isolation helped me to reflect upon the notion that a man was not truly created to live apart from his fellow kind.

No matter how cruelly society had treated me in the past, I suspected that loneliness was an instrument orchestrated by evil incarnate. When a man can speak to no one other than his subconscious, he may become influenced by a variety of voices. With this consideration in mind, I returned to Riverside in the spring of 1987 to renew my faith in God through the only mediator who knew that I was still alive.

Upon greeting Father Jordan for the first time in two years, he appeared pleasantly shocked. After I explained to him that I had embarked on a quest to nowhere, he simply smiled and shook my hand. Judging by the glint in the old priest's eyes, I sensed that he finally had some good news to share. I followed him back to his rectory, where he soon revealed a collection of letters from his sea chest. Without procrastinating, he handed these papers to me.

"I really didn't think that I'd ever see you again," Jordan said. "But now that you're here, I think I should tell you that I've been in contact with your son."

My mouth must have hung open like a busted door. For several seconds I uttered nothing. Jordan waited until I sat down before he continued. "Theodore is a married man now," he announced.

"Married?" I echoed, staring at the handwritten letters more curiously. "When did this happen?"

"A few years ago."

"Is he still living with his wife in Philadelphia?"

"Until last year," Jordan answered. "According to his letters, Claire wanted to move out into the country—"

"Claire?" I repeated, almost breathlessly.

"His wife, of course," Jordan clarified.

I swallowed hard and nearly bit my tongue before whispering my next question. "Did he send you any photographs of himself or his wife, Father?"

"I don't believe he did."

Without responding, I pressed my hands to my face and felt my eyes swelling with tears. Call it intuition, but I had no doubt in my mind that this was the same woman who I rescued from that church fire many years ago. Though Jordan may have deserved to know more about my brief encounter with Claire, I didn't want to burden him with my troubles.

After wiping my eyes, I said to Jordan, "Father, I know that I've been gone for a long time now, but did you mention my name to Theodore in any of your letters since I last spoke with you?"

Jordan shuffled in place and cleared his throat before admitting, "I couldn't bring myself to do it, Lawrence. I'm sorry."

"But he is my son, and you knew I was searching for him."

"Yes, I did, and maybe that's what bothered me."

"Why?"

"When you last left me, I wasn't sure what would become of you," Jordan explained. "You were raving about some prophecies in the Bible, and frankly, I just didn't want to upset him. We can't ignore the fact that your son hasn't heard from you in over thirty-five years."

I tried to rationalize with Jordan's logic, but I still felt slighted by his decision. "I wish there was a way you could have told him," I said.

"There's more to consider now than there was before," Jordan said, directing my attention to the most recently postmarked envelope on his desk. "Theodore last wrote to me three weeks ago. He mentioned that his wife is with child."

A sense of urgency crept into my tone when I asked, "When is this baby due to be born?"

"Ironically enough, any day now," Jordan said. He then went on to say, "I realize that you're eager to meet your son. Of course you must understand that Theodore has made a home for himself that doesn't necessarily include you at this stage. It would be wise for you to wait until after the baby is born and they're settled before you attempt to contact him."

"Where is he living now?"

"In a farming community in Pennsylvania. I believe the town is called Wakeland."

"Okay," I murmured, reciting the town's name several times over in my mind. I exhaled a series of breaths before thanking Jordan for his belated assistance.

Jordan peered at me in silence as I made my way toward the door. Perhaps he noticed the glow on my face as I started to leave. "Where are you going now?" he called to me.

"A long walk," I muttered, feeling thoroughly refreshed by my new-found knowledge.

"To Wakeland, no doubt," Jordan mused.

I paused in the doorway, tilting my head toward the sky outside. A flock of sparrows soared toward the northern hills. Then, feeling invigorated by the pervading scents of this season, I turned my back and offered Jordan a gracious wave of my hand. The priest followed my progress outside and asked, "What do you really hope to find in Wakeland, Lawrence?"

"I suppose just a missing piece from my past," I announced with no regret.

"But do you even know where Wakeland is located?"

"No," I said, pointing my finger at the ascending sparrows, "but they do."

I left Father Jordan standing along the flower-encrusted banks of Riverside. My mind and heart raced with pleasant visions as I tracked toward the foothills once again. Before leaving Riverside, I bent down beside a garden of red tulips. Literally hundreds of these crimson bulbs had bloomed, sending a sweet aroma swirling across the landscape. I picked one of these flowers and cupped its delicate petals in my left hand. With my senses empowered, I marched off into the countryside once again.

CHAPTER THIRTY-THREE

▼

THE LEGACY FORETOLD

Theodore clamped the journal shut against his torso and stared at the ceiling's light. Though he wanted to shift his legs, he felt paralyzed by a latent fear. His heartbeat slammed against his chest with a spasmodic rhythm, causing him to convulse as if a lethal poison had contaminated the air. The ticking sound inside his head recurred, too, inciting him to clamp his hands to his ears and froth at the mouth like a rabid animal.

Now, sweating profusely, Theodore placed his quivering hand upon the crucifix that remained at his side. The metal cross still felt icy next to his flesh, but he couldn't think of anything other than his father's diary. Whether he believed what Lawrence had written or not, an eruption of adrenaline deluged his senses. Seconds later, every muscle in his body knotted. Then, another sound vibrated within the recesses of his brain.

The light around Theodore faded to gray. In an effort to return to his daughter's bedside, he attempted to crawl forward, but before making headway, he collapsed face-first onto the floor. With his nose squashed against the concrete, he emitted a faint grunt and passed out. Somewhere within the throes of unconsciousness, he visualized the concrete floor breaking into pieces. Without further warning, he plunged into a vast crevice.

As Theodore's body descended into this pit, he observed the dismantled skeletons of men and women sticking out of the craggy earth. When his momentum finally stopped, he couldn't breathe. Only the sound of his rapid heartbeat assured him that he was not yet dead. His lungs gradually inflated with air. And then his eyes peeled open to survey the encompassing darkness.

"I'm dreaming," Theodore thought, while brushing the black soot from his clothes and face. He then examined both of his legs and arms, making certain no bones had fractured. After concluding that he was uninjured, he stood up and searched for an avenue of escape. Unfortunately, the only way out of this cavern was through the elevated fissure that he had already discovered.

Without adequate illumination, Theodore's progress slowed to a near standstill. But even if he could see, it would have been impossible for him to scale the piled tombstones spread out on all sides of the pit. As he edged closer to these gray stones, he noticed that the slabs were marked with epitaphs. It then occurred to him that this subterranean land was once a graveyard. At that moment, Theodore realized that he hadn't stumbled upon any discarded cemetery—this den of waste was all that remained of his father's boyhood home of Orefield.

In an effort to confirm his grief, Theodore bent over and brushed his fingers over the face of one headstone. Although hundreds of similar markers were strewn over the grounds, one of them had been engraved with a name that caused Theodore to shiver. He positioned his head within one inch of its surface to read the inscription aloud: "Samuel Dayton."

Theodore's eyes widened with confusion when he uttered, "What does this mean?" Now clearly reduced to tears, he knelt beside the tombstone. His voice was more enraged when he shouted into the air, "What is happening to me?"

Under normal circumstances, Theodore would have awakened from his sleep before now. This, however, was not a typical dream for him, because at some level—buried deep within his brain's pathways—he realized that this was not a dream. It was truly happening—not in a physical sense, but in a way that he could identify by simply concentrating on what Lawrence had revealed in his journal. Most importantly, he understood that whatever had happened to his father in the past had returned to haunt him as well. The only question that remained unanswered was why? Why his family? What sin against God did they commit to deserve such anguish?

Before Theodore had time to contemplate a reasonable explanation, a luminous light enveloped the cavern's walls. This energy descended upon him in seconds. From within this illumination—just as it had been described in his father's journal—he watched a single image materialize. Had he not remembered his father's words, he might've been in awe of the six-winged angel that now hovered in the dwelling beside him.

Theodore stared into the seraph's eyes without flinching. In a bold voice, he shouted, "You're the one who calls himself Jonathan." When the seraph did not respond, Theodore pointed to the gravestone and asked, "What does this name mean? Who is Samuel Dayton?"

Hearing those words, Jonathan lowered himself upon the soil. Instead of a saber in his hands, he petted the plumage of a white dove. Then, in voice that only Theodore discerned, the seraph responded, "The answer should be clear to you now."

Theodore bowed his head in silence, still trying to understand why this tombstone was essential for him to see. Gradually, a compartment opened in his mind. The seraph's energy provided him with a mental picture of one particular mining disaster. In his imagination, Theodore saw the walls of rock collapsing onto a man; he knew this fellow to be Samuel Dayton.

"Why are you doing this to me?" Theodore sobbed. "Are you here to tell me something about my past?"

The light encompassing Jonathan had dissipated and he appeared to Theodore as a common man. Only a faint trace of illumination framed the seraph's figure as he released the dove from his hands. Within seconds, the dove fluttered off into the darkness.

"Just tell me why?" Theodore murmured. "If all of what you revealed to my father is true, then there must have been a reason why my family was made to suffer."

"The sin in this family has an origin," Jonathan said, directing Theodore's attention to the engraved headstone at his side. "They begin with the father before your own—Samuel Dayton."

"What sin did he commit?"

Jonathan probed deeper into Theodore's eyes, penetrating his mind with yet another scene from long ago. This image revealed Samuel Dayton using his pickax to hack away the support columns in the mine's walls, thereby instigating a cave-in that claimed his life.

"What does this mean to me?" Theodore asked.

"Your grandfather, Samuel Dayton, descended into Orefield's shafts for one eternal visit," Jonathan explained. "His death was deemed an accident, but as I have just revealed to you, this man did not perish because of a mishap. Samuel wanted to die on that day, and he arranged his death in such a way so he wouldn't be thought of as a coward by those who sat in judgment of his remains."

"Suicide," Theodore whispered in dismay. He then kneeled to the ground and brushed his fingers through the black soot. "He may have killed himself in here, Jonathan, but I am not to blame for it, and neither was my father."

"In your eyes you may be correct, but in God's eyes you and your descendents have been selected to serve a higher purpose."

"Why would God choose my family for anything? Suicide is a sign of weakness—not of strength."

"That is precisely why I've appeared to you now, Theodore. God understands that the truest test for His creations resides in a man who has abandoned his faith—not just in God—but in himself."

"So this is our punishment? Because Samuel killed himself, my father and I must bear the brunt of God's rage."

"It's not about God's anger. It's about your own."

For a moment, Theodore appeared as hardened as the surrounding tombstones. He now realized that he had been used in an ancestral prophecy. "Is this what my blood is good for? Does my family mean nothing more to you than a sacrifice to God?"

"You must learn to see it another way," Jonathan admonished.

"And what way is that? Look at what has happened to my family, Jonathan—look at my father, who now lies dead in a grave of his own. What consolation has God offered him?"

"Since I do not share the assorted emotions that you do, I cannot fully understand the grief that your father encountered. But I know that you and Lawrence have lost many cherished things. The death of a wife isn't an easy burden to bear. And as I stand before you now, I know the most irreparable loss is the one that still awaits you in the hours ahead."

Theodore's eyes reddened as he uttered, "My daughter."

"Yes," Jonathan affirmed. "Emily is the child whose life and death we must now consider. By now you know what Emily's spirit represents to us. She is the final hope for heaven and the last hope for this world. But her soul—like yours—is in peril as we speak."

"Do you think I'm pleased to know that my daughter has been used by God? Is that what games are played by those who guard our souls?"

"You have obviously not found your faith yet."

"You mean I actually have a choice?" Theodore cried until he tumbled over onto the dark ground in a fit of bewilderment. He remained prostrate on the soot for several seconds, pounding at the tombstone with his blackened fists.

Jonathan broke his tantrum with the sound of his voice. "Don't you trust what your father wrote in his journal?" he asked, but Theodore did not respond. "You must understand that we are near the end of this prophecy. The threat of annihilation looms closer. As the new millennium nears, the archfiend grows stronger. Before long, he will pounce upon our region and infect all that was once pure."

"You don't need me to make a difference," Theodore groaned, defiantly thrashing his arms at the light projecting above his head. "Why not go to my daughter yourself? Tell her that her life doesn't mean anything here— that she is being sacrificed by God as a harness against evil."

"Theodore, I can't command you to respect God's judgement. But you mustn't let your daughter's soul wither in the company of darkness. God knows that it takes a strong man to undertake this task, and it is one that you must not forgo. Our nemesis has appointed a minion to do his bidding. Such a fallen angel tormented your father for his entire life. This dark fiend has come to steal the children's souls, and his energy is more potent than before."

"Why now? Why me?"

"Your daughter's faith was pure until you brought her to this place."

Theodore now recognized that the fiend in question had taken the form of Doctor Kraven. Without looking at the seraph, Theodore whispered, "Do away with the evil yourself, Jonathan. If God truly values my daughter's soul, why doesn't he send you to her side? As you can see, I can't save her now."

"You know what must be done," Jonathan persisted. Though you lack faith in these moments, God still exists within you."

Now torn between the uncertainties in his mind, Theodore admitted, "Even if I wanted to stop Kraven, how would I do it alone? What difference can one man really make?"

"The dark fiend is nourished by such poison thoughts. The longer you permitted your faithlessness to fester, the easier it became for him to contaminate your daughter's devotion in God. This evil relishes your hatred and thrives on your apathetic nature. Don't let him destroy our last hope."

"But how do I stop him from corrupting Emily?"

"Purify your thoughts," Jonathan said. "It's a simple as adopting God's wisdom."

"It's so hard for me to forget all the pain," Theodore shivered. "I felt so helpless for all this time. How do I know if God really cares for me?"

"Make your peace with Him and the questions will no longer be asked."

In another instance, the seraph ascended into a sphere of light. Theodore reached for the angel's shadow and implored, "Don't leave me, Jonathan. I still need your help."

"Go to your daughter now," Jonathan said. "Her soul depends on you."

"I don't know if I can do it—"

"There is little time to waste, Theodore. If there is still a chance for us, you must act now. But heed this warning: the dark fiend will not release Emily from his spell without a fight. He knows of her infirmity as well as he senses your own. If you should confront him without your faith intact, he will dissect your impurities and consume your soul."

"But how do I fight him?"

"With your heart."

These were the final words Theodore heard from the seraph. Immediately following Jonathan's ascent into the clouds, Theodore was hoisted back out of the pit by an invisible energy. After opening his eyes, he realized that he was staring at his own reflection in a puddle of blood. Some of his blood had dried in a burgundy paste around his lips and nose. In a near panic, he reached for the crucifix that had fallen somewhere at his side. By the time he placed his hand upon the cross, he distinguished Regina's frantic voice. He wasn't dreaming anymore.

Once seeing that Theodore had fallen and injured himself, Regina rushed to his side and gasped, "What has happened to you?"

Theodore shifted over onto his back and stammered, "I—I must've passed out or something."

Regina then glanced at the floor. After retrieving the journal from the pool of blood, she noticed the crucifix clasped in Theodore's hand. "What are you doing out here? I don't want you to leave me alone with that doctor again—do you understand me?"

"He's not a doctor," Theodore sighed woefully, while standing to his feet with the cross still clenched in his blood-streaked hand. After exhaling a stunted breath he said, "Regina, whatever happens to me from this point forward, I don't want you to follow me back into Emily's room."

"Why are you saying this to me, Theodore? I want to help you—"

"Then stay away. That's the best thing you can do for me right now."

When Theodore tried to push his way past Regina, she stood in front of him with her hands held against his chest. She could plainly see that his nose was still bleeding. "I want you to tell me what's going on," she demanded.

"I'm not sure, but I must go to Emily now."

"She's unconscious again. There's nothing you can do for her now."

"Until a few minutes ago, that's what I thought," Theodore said. His eyes then swayed to the journal in Regina's hands.

"Please don't keep secrets from me," Regina pleaded. "I've learned things about your father's life, too. I know what you're feeling inside."

"This isn't about my father," Theodore huffed, before moving forward against Regina's resistance. His eyes weren't even focused as he bounded closer to Emily's room.

"Why are you acting like this?" Regina cried, sensing his warm blood trickling over her palms. "Tell me what's happening!"

Theodore stopped and grabbed his temples as an unbearable sound amplified inside his head. He swayed momentarily, almost toppling to the concrete again. Regina took hold of his arm and held him upright. When she did this, Theodore spun away from her grasp and stumbled forward. "I don't have much time left to save her," he said.

When it became obvious that Theodore couldn't be persuaded to stop, Regina let him go forward. By the time Theodore reached Emily's room, she had slumped down in the corridor with the journal pressed against her chest.

Theodore entered Emily's room cautiously. From his position beside her bed, he saw that she was lying still. A single blanket covered her body. As he stepped closer to her bedside, he sensed the crucifix gradually warming in his hand.

CHAPTER THIRTY-FOUR

▼

THE SOUL'S SALVATION

Though Emily's was near death at this hour, Theodore did not view her as merely a victim of disease. He now believed that he had somehow failed his daughter for dishonoring her reverence toward God. He also understood a lesson his father had learned a long time ago. No matter how much heartache a man may endure, he must appreciate the miracle of life, and he must also strive to recognize the glory achieved by those who die with faith.

Theodore washed the blood from his face and hands before returning to Emily's bedside. After noticing that Emily was still sleeping, he balanced the crucifix on the girl's fingertips and softly murmured what he remembered of a prayer. Now, with the ticking sensation within his mind subdued, he breathed easier while waiting for Kraven to return.

"I won't ever leave you, Emily," Theodore whispered in her ear. Before this thought escaped his mind, Kraven appeared in the doorway. His eyes shone like flecks of burning coal. When he peered at Theodore, a slight grin crossed his lips.

In silence, Theodore watched Kraven walk into the room. After assessing the situation, the doctor snickered and noticed droplets of blood trailing into the adjacent bathroom. "We must do something to improve the cleaning procedures around here," Kraven said in jest. He then bent down to the floor and sopped up some of the blood on his fingertip.

Kraven smeared the blood between his thumb and index finger before saying, "I sense a coldness pervading in this room, Theodore."

"Your deeds are finished here, Kraven," Theodore replied, trying to keep his distance. "I know what you're doing and I've come to stop you."

Kraven stood upright and paced over to Theodore. His voice was still calm when he declared, "I suppose it was only a matter of time before you discovered the truth about your destiny. But I must remind you, Theodore, you are no different than I am."

As Kraven sidled closer to Emily's bedside, Theodore stood in front of him. "I was wrong to think as I did. But I'm a far different man now—I know what is right."

"Oh, do I really have to listen to all this righteousness?" Kraven sighed with sarcasm. "I have a bit of work yet to do."

"Stop it!" Theodore shouted. "As I said, your work here is done. You can't take my daughter from me."

"I don't need to take her," Kraven noted with confidence. "The child has already become a product for my master. No angel in heaven—or even God himself—can save her soul now. Emily has succumbed to the very sin that has destroyed you. Because of her, the legions shall rise together and burn heaven to ashes."

"I won't let you corrupt her soul, Kraven. I'll be dead before that happens."

"Now that," Kraven smirked, "is a challenge I'm well prepared to accept. "Do you think by reading a few sentiments scribbled in your father's memoirs will reverse the fact that you have soured your daughter's mind with hatred?"

"I'm here to save her now—"

"Don't misunderstand me," Kraven continued. "I don't fault the detest you must feel for God. With just cause, you've lashed out against the misdeeds He delivered onto your family."

"You still fear God," Theodore countered. "I didn't think that I could embrace His word again, but I can—I will."

Kraven snickered defiantly and edged closer to Theodore. His eyes now blazed with scarlet flames. "It must be rather convenient for you to turn your faith on and off like a switch on the wall. But your blood is tainted, Theodore. Your confessions hold little weight in the balance of things."

"I'm speaking the truth," Theodore affirmed without flinching. "Despite my past, I am still a man of God. I may have sinned for not sensing my duty before now, but I know that He still loves me. He still loves all of us who possess a soul—and that includes my daughter."

"You lie," Kraven hissed. "You love God like I know the light of heaven—it has all vanished from your soul. I sense your depravities. God sees through your shallow pledge as well, and He will severely punish you for your blasphemy."

"My faith is real!"

"Then there is a test," Kraven snarled. "Lend me your hand, Theodore, and let me sense the godlessness in your grip."

"What does touching my hand prove?"

"The pure soul is always warm and radiates from the flesh until the body dies," Kraven explained. "But the impure soul—like your own—remains cold. When I touched you before, I felt the coolness in your skin. I then knew that your spirit was cursed."

Theodore pushed his hands into Kraven's chest, allowing their bodies to connect for a brief instance. "Feel the change for yourself," Theodore said. Kraven clasped Theodore's wrists with his hands and glared into his eyes. Within seconds, the smile faded from Kraven's face, for he now felt the tepid energy flowing through Theodore's veins.

Sensing his dismay, Theodore shouted, "Never doubt me. My word is good."

Kraven released his grip and turned away from Emily's bedside. He then paced across the floor, but he wasn't prepared to admit defeat. "It is clear to me that you've been visited by an angel of God," he grumbled. "Even God suspected that you couldn't do this on your own."

"You've already underestimated me once, Kraven. I may surprise you again."

"What do you hope to accomplish by confronting me? Like you, I am merely a pawn in this vicious game. It's now just a matter of deciding which side of the board you wish to stand."

"I told you where I stand."

"And that's the part which is so baffling to me. If God had done the things to me that he has to you, I would think twice before fetching for his hand. Is it fair to condemn my master for the punishment that God has inflicted upon your family? In truth, you were treated with no more regard than vermin in His eyes. How can you tell me that your heart does not hold contempt for the one who has treated you as an insignificant creation?"

Now trembling, Theodore still refused to listen to Kraven's words. In the meantime, Emily began to stir in the bed. Without pivoting his eyes away from Kraven, Theodore said, "You can't get inside my head. I understand what Jonathan has told me."

"Your stupidity is unprecedented. Can't you see that your god wants the same as mine? They both yearn for power, but heaven is given all the glory. Now consider my poor master's plight. What was his real sin? As an angel, he may have been envious of your souls, but all he truly desired was a share of the throne. And for this exhibition of vanity, he was cast out from the world of light and made to exist in darkness."

"Say what you wish, Kraven, but I will never turn my back on God again—no matter what happens today."

"Wasn't it enough that you were born blind?" Kraven sneered, sensing the quiver in Theodore's voice. "Did you need to be reminded of your sins through your mother's hideous death? If you had witnessed her agony firsthand, you may have become a heathen long before you did."

"Stop it, Kraven!"

"But we're just getting started here, aren't we, Theodore? Perhaps knowledge of your father's misery is more relevant to you." Kraven still searched for the chink in Theodore's newly discovered shield when he said, "Your father was an idiotic man. He wandered alone through this world, begging in the streets and living among those with damaged brains."

"I'm not listening to you," Theodore cried. "You speak lies!"

"Deny me if you dare, but hear me out before you submit to God's spell again. Revisit the memory where your wife lay in the hospital. Remember her womb—and how it was shredded beyond recognition. Do you even care how excruciating it was for that woman to have a life cleaved from her ruptured body?"

Theodore now clenched his fists and screamed, "Stop it!"

"Remember your rage," Kraven continued, "remember the futility of watching that good woman bleed dry into the white linen. Remember her torturous screams—the unanswered prayers to God rushing over her shivering, pale lips."

"I'm warning you, Kraven, stop it!"

"That's right," Kraven goaded. "I feel your anger, too. But I was not responsible for such doings. This was all part of God's plan—a plan so that he may reign forever on a plain higher than all others."

Theodore thought about striking Kraven with his fist, but he knew that such an outburst would have only fueled the fiend with the power needed to pollute his mind. Rather than engage Kraven in a brawl that couldn't be won, Theodore sat down beside Emily's bed in silence. He then placed his hand over the crucifix, which was still balanced on his daughter's fingers.

Kraven became more incensed as Emily's eyelids began to flutter. He knew that she would awaken again. Now sensing that Theodore's faith was purer than initially anticipated, he continued his assault on his senses. "We have reached a critical stage. It is time that you seek your revenge against the God who has permitted your daughter's suffering."

Theodore grasped Emily's hand tighter and said, "I don't want revenge."

"But look at your daughter," Kraven sighed, motioning to the girl's frail limbs. "Didn't she deserve a better life than what was dealt to her? What child deserves to endure such misery? I know you have asked this question to yourself before, Theodore. It burns in your mind at this hour."

"She'll be with God soon."

"And what comfort does that offer you? Do you believe that her soul will always be invaluable to heaven? Her presence beside the angels will only delay the inevitable. We are too powerful now. Her energy cannot endure forever."

"I trust God can save us," Theodore insisted.

Before Kraven responded, Emily opened her eyes. She first glanced at Kraven, but then realized that her father was sitting beside her bed. Though visibly groggy, she sensed the weight of Theodore's hand stroking her fingers. She then saw the crucifix glimmering beneath the warmth of his palm.

"What is happening here, Dad?" she asked wearily.

Theodore leaned forward and smiled warmly at his daughter. He could see the light in her eyes was dim. As he pressed his lips against her forehead, Emily quivered. "It's okay, sweetheart," he whispered. "You're going to be safe from now on."

Emily shifted her eyes to notice Kraven hovering above them. He approached her bedside and said, "It's almost over, Emily. Tell your father to let you rest for now."

"I'm staying right here," Theodore assured his daughter. "I'm never going to leave you again. Do you understand what I'm telling you?"

"I think so," Emily uttered, but confusion was still evident in her voice.

At this moment, Kraven rushed forward and extended his hand toward Emily. "Take my hand now, dear child," he beseeched her. "Tell your father that you no longer hear God's word."

"Don't listen to him," Theodore countered. He then said, "Emily, I've thought some awful things about God over the past couple years. I'm sorry for not believing in you, but my worst regret was leaving you when you needed me to be strong."

"Leaving me?" Emily questioned as her fingers tightened around the crucifix. "You never left me, Dad."

"I did," Theodore sobbed. "After you became ill, I abandoned everyone. For the longest time I couldn't understand why you didn't feel the rage that I did. I now know that you were purer than that."

With his hand still extended in front of Emily's bed, Kraven implored her to redirect her thoughts. "If you can't trust your father, Emily, then who is there left to believe in?"

"Shut your mouth, Kraven! This is out of your control," Theodore said.

"What's this all about, Dad?"

"Tell her," Kraven demanded. "If she is to die, let her at least be put to rest knowing that she was betrayed by God."

Theodore again cautioned Emily by pointing to Kraven and saying, "This man isn't your friend. He's only trying to lure your spirit astray. Don't let him do it."

Though weakened by disease, Emily collected the energy to prop up in the bed. She then lowered her eyes upon the crucifix and traced her hand lightly over the symbol's burnished edges. Theodore did not speak as his daughter set the cross on the bed.

"Dad," she uttered, "do you really have faith in God again?"

Theodore placed both of his hands on Emily's face and held them gently in place. "Can you feel that?" he asked as a warmth emitted from his fingertips. "I've seen the truth today, Emily, and I'm sorry for ever doubting you. I can be strong again—like you."

Kraven sprang forward and snapped his hands down on the bed near Emily's legs. "There is no reason for you to accept his word now. He doesn't have the ability to speak the truth." Kraven then raised his palm and reached for Emily's fingers. "My hand is open to your embrace as well. Come with me, Emily, and the wrongs of the past will finally be righted."

"Why do you promise me such things?" Emily whispered.

"I promise you what no one else can. Let us not disremember the heartache that you've endured. What has the promise of heaven done for your soul? Too much is made of the lighted realm. All life flourishes in darkness, sheltered from the glare of reality. In darkness, like the womb itself, the seed of life is incubated from the terror that lies beyond its sheath. Together, as a part of my world, we can hibernate from what has caused you so much pain."

Emily nestled her fingers into Theodore's hands and said, "I have no more pain." She then gazed into her father's eyes and sighed, "We're together again."

Theodore's tension eased, for he now felt his daughter's love seeping into his flesh. From its place upon the bed, the crucifix shimmered as if had been bathed in sunlight. Realizing his failure, Kraven lowered his hands to his side.

"Why do you hold onto Him?" Kraven sulked, staring at the cross with slanted eyes. "This is your last chance to join us, Emily."

"She has already given you her answer, Kraven," Theodore said, his confidence now restored. "I think it's time you leave this place."

"You can't simply wish me away," Kraven raved. "I have been summoned here to collect the souls of children."

"But you have failed to possess my daughter's soul. Despite all your evil, it cannot erase God from the hearts of these children. They will all soon know exactly what you are."

Emily did not need to add anything to what Theodore stated. The presence of God shone clearly in her eyes. Kraven then knew that it would be impossible to steal her spirit. He conceded to her faith by nodding his chin once and stepping away from the bed.

Before exiting the room, Kraven turned toward Theodore and whispered a final admonition into his ear. "All is done for now, Theodore Dayton, and you shall stand as the victor for awhile. But mark this moment in your memory—when the hour of death ticks for your soul, I will be nearby—waiting to cup the coldness that stews in your twisted heart."

Theodore did not speak another word to the dark fiend. He let him retreat in silence. Once Kraven was gone, he set his head on the pillow next to Emily. When gazing tearfully into his daughter's diseased eyes, he knew that she was closer to what he had once feared. Though a victory had been gained in these past minutes, an irretrievable loss awaited in the moments ahead.

"I always knew that you would come back to God, Dad," Emily said, but her voice was audibly weak.

Theodore forced a smile to his lips and said softly, "I owe everything to you, Emily."

"What really changed your mind?"

Theodore thought to mention Jonathan, but he figured that Emily would know the answer to her question very soon. "Just rest for now, honey," he whispered. "But don't ever forget how much I love you—and how much God loves you."

Emily reached down to hold the crucifix in her hand before saying, "You know, Dad, I know why I needed to come here today." She then raised the cross and nudged the glowing metal against her father's chest. "It never was about me—"

Emily closed her eyes and reached for Theodore's hand. In these seconds, she sensed incredible warmth surging into her body. When she spoke again, her voice was trembling and her eyes reopened. "We've really done it—"

"We have," Theodore agreed, his voice cracking with sorrow.

"Maybe it's not too late for us after all—"

With those words, Emily released a short breath and closed her eyes one last time. Theodore sensed her heartbeat softening and then the slow, easy release of her tiny fingers from his own. Within another second, she was lying still on the bed. And then, from within the room's confines, Theodore imagined the sound of fluttering wings stirring on all sides of the bed. He lowered his head and cried for several minutes. As the sound dissipated, his mind filled with wonder. He stood upright and swept his fingers through his daughter's blonde hair. After kissing her once on the cheek, he knew that it was time to leave.

"You're safe now, Emily. God will take care of you from now on."

Theodore emerged from the room with the crucifix in hand. Regina greeted him in the corridor. She monitored his sorrow from afar. But something less painful had worked its way into his expression as well. She almost didn't recognize the emotion at first, but then she understood that Theodore had reclaimed a part of himself in that room that he had surrendered many years ago.

Theodore and Regina embraced without speaking a word, for nothing could convey the grief that they shared in these moments. After parting, Theodore trained his eyes directly into Regina's. While looking at the woman, he whispered, "We can go home now, Regina. Everything will work itself out."

Regina felt his hand slip into her own and tighten. After sensing his warmth, she smiled and replied, "I believe in you, Theodore."

As they walked up the corridor leading toward the elevator, the locked gates automatically opened. Several nurses and doctors tried to comfort Theodore, but he insisted that they had already done enough. When reaching the elevator, Regina noticed Dr. Reed leaning against the wall near a stairwell. His hair was drenched in perspiration, and his eyes were sprinkled with bewilderment. He held a gray suit jacket in his shivering hands.

"Doctor Reed?" Regina questioned, "is there something wrong?"

Dr. Reed shook his head and wiped his brow before stammering, "I…I just saw something unbelievable—"

Theodore examined the suit jacket and said knowingly, "This isn't your coat, is it?"

"No," Reed said, puzzled. "It's Doctor Kraven's—I think."

"Then why are you so frightened?" Regina asked.

"Because he was wearing it only a second ago—and then he was gone."

Regina shrugged his shoulders and glanced at Theodore, "Gone? Where do you think he went?"

"He just disappeared," Reed quivered. "Right before my eyes—"

Regina touched the doctor's shoulder and advised him to sit down. When he refused to comply, Theodore tried to lesson Reed's anxiety. "I'm sure everything will make sense to you before long." Theodore then took the jacket from Reed's hands and tossed it into a nearby trash pail. "I don't think Kraven will be coming back for that."

"Is this some kind of trick or something, Mr. Dayton?"

"It's no trick, but it's definitely something."

At that instance, Dr. Reed heard the sound of children giggling from inside the ward. He, along with Theodore and Regina, rushed into the ward to see the kids standing beside their beds. Some of them were playing, tossing bed pillows, and generally acting in the silly manner that children sometimes do.

"This is amazing," Reed sighed, his face brightening. "I've never seen them behave like this before."

"Well, see to it that it doesn't stop," Theodore suggested, before pacing out of the ward with Regina close at his side. They returned to the elevator and were greeted by a nurse. She held Lawrence's journal in her hands.

"I found this back on the floor near your daughter's room," she announced. "Do you want it?"

Theodore hesitated, but eventually accepted his father's journal by tucking it under his arm. With the notebook secure, he stepped inside the elevator with Regina. As the elevator's doors slid shut, Regina motioned to the journal and asked, "Are you going to read anymore of that?"

"I don't need to, Regina. I've read enough."

"Me, too," Regina agreed, while resting her head against Theodore's shoulder.

When they departed Kindred Woods on that day, the rain had stopped and sunlight reflected upon the hillsides again. As Theodore tilted his head toward the clearing sky, a flock of sparrows soared through the shadows cast from the hospital. "It's a better day out here today," he shouted, raising his hands to the air. "Can't you feel it, Regina?"

Regina inhaled the fresh air, savoring the grasslands. Though she could-n't deny the presence of spring, the real change exuded from the man whom she loved. "I can feel it," she declared, looking into Theodore's eyes. "I finally can."

Rain moistened the earth of Wakeland's cemetery on the morning of Emily's funeral. Despite the steady drizzle, sparrows had flown from their nests and assembled in formation on the grassy embankments. Though the sky was lathered in gray, it was easy to sense the rebirth of nature out here today.

Father Quinn stood atop the churchyard. His shadow cast across the white casket that held Emily's body. As he read the eulogy, he was pleased to see that nearly all the townspeople had gathered to honor Theodore's daughter. As they walked beside her coffin, some tossed rose petals onto the casket. Theodore and Regina made their offerings with red tulips.

After the prayers had been read and the crowd departed, Theodore approached Father Quinn and thanked him for his friendship. He added, "I'm hoping to come back to church soon, Father."

"I've always known that you'd return to us to us," Quinn said. He then grinned at Regina before saying, "So if you don't mind me asking, what are your plans for the future?"

When Quinn presented this question, Regina realized that he was referring to her relationship with Theodore. "I'm going to stay in Wakeland for now," Regina said, clasping Theodore's hand. "We have much to think about."

"Well, I'm certain that you'll both make the right decision," Quinn beamed, extending his hand to Theodore's shoulder. "I have a good feeling that we'll be seeing quite a bit more of each other."

With those words of encouragement, Quinn excused himself and hob-bled down the hill toward his car. Theodore then turned to face his daugh-ter's grave. Just as before, he noticed a patch of white poppies flourishing near his father's headstone. Only now, these flowers had spread over to Claire's plot, too. Soon, Theodore believed these poppies would decorate the soil around Emily's grave as well—uniting them as one within the soil of Wakeland's cemetery.

Seeing that Theodore was engrossed in thought, Regina spoke quietly into his ear. "We can stay for as long as you need." Theodore pulled Regina closer to his body, partially shielding her face from the rain.

"We can go now," he muttered.

As they descended the hillside, Theodore noticed Danny and Belinda waiting for them near his jeep. After offering Theodore their condolences, Danny practically implored him to help continue their search for Jonathan. At this point, Theodore was willing to oblige with their request, but not without stating his opinion.

"I thought I'd be seeing you two here today," Theodore said while opening the door to the jeep so that Regina could get inside. Once Regina entered the vehicle, he instructed her to hand him the notebook that he stashed underneath the passenger's seat. She followed his instructions without question.

With the journal in hand, Theodore walked over to Danny and said, "I wasn't entirely honest with you the other day. Before my father died, he left this behind."

Danny's face brightened as Theodore gave him the journal. "Is this what I think it is?" he teemed with excitement.

"It's his story," Theodore confirmed. "And in a way, it's Jonathan's story, too."

"You mean it's really true?" Belinda interjected. "Lawrence was truly visited by a seraph?"

"I'll let you make up your own minds," Theodore replied. "But don't forget, it's only one man's vision."

"Yes," Danny agreed, "but that single glimpse may be all we need to change people."

"Is that what you're trying to do, Danny—change the world?"

"That's not such a bad agenda, is it?" Belinda asked.

Theodore paced over to Belinda and lowered his eyes so that they were centered with her own. "Maybe not," he said. "I hope you find what you're looking for. I know I did."

Rather than prolong this discussion, Theodore decided to leave the cemetery for now. Once seated behind the steering wheel of his jeep, he glanced across the seat and smiled at Regina.

"Are you sure you want to leave that journal with them?" Regina asked, while watching the old man and woman putter away.

"They earned it. You'll have to trust me on that one."

"But you didn't even finish reading it."

"No, I think there was one entry left unread."

"Aren't you even a little curious about what happened to him?"

Theodore motioned to his tombstone on the hillside and said, "I know what happened, Regina. Maybe it's best to keep some of the mysteries in life intact. That's what keeps us dreaming—right?"

Regina demonstrated her approval by lightly touching Theodore's hand. He then started the jeep and drove away. As the vehicle turned onto the main road leading back to Theodore's home, Regina noticed that the gray clouds had dissolved from the sky.

"I can see the sun," Regina remarked, gesturing toward the horizon. "Maybe it's going to be a nice day after all."

Theodore observed the sky, too. Between the traces of blue etching into the heavens, he saw a single white dove ascending into the slivers of sunlight. His eyes intensified with color when he declared, "I'm sure you're right, Regina."

Once the jeep was clearly out of view, Danny and Belinda stopped and sat on a wooden bench. Danny was about to open the journal when Belinda said, "Do you think Theodore was trying to warn us?" she asked, somewhat disconcerted.

"Belinda, we've been searching for over thirty years for something like this. I'm sure Lawrence wrote everything he knew about Jonathan in this journal."

"That's the thing, Danny—I mean, do we really want to know everything?"

"This quest has kept me alive. You don't really want to give it up now." As Danny spoke these words, the notebook slipped from his shaking hands. It tumbled to the turf and opened on its binding. After he picked it off the ground, he realized that the journal's pages revealed the last chapter of Lawrence's memoirs. Feeling as though this may have been a sign, he conceded to Belinda's thought.

"What harm could it do to glance at a tiny portion of this?" Danny suggested, shrugging his shoulders in a bid to justify his curiosity. "Don't we at least deserve that much satisfaction?"

Belinda recognized the journal's entry number before saying, "I think this is the end of the diary. Shouldn't we start from the beginning?"

Danny smirked as he began to read. He then chuckled, "What's the point of being conventional at this point, Belinda?"

While the sparrows soared into the sky, Danny and Belinda reviewed the last words written in Lawrence Dayton's journal.

CHAPTER THIRTY-FIVE

▼

JOURNAL ENTRY NINETEEN

A VISIT WITH THE KEEPER

Before the autumn leaves drifted upon the pastures, I entered Wakeland with a renewed hope and sense of responsibility. The year was 1987, and I finally felt obligated to greet my son and recount our lost days together. Yet, soon after arriving in town, some local residents informed me that Claire Dayton had recently died while giving birth to her child. Theodore was left with the task of raising a daughter without a mother. Though I knew my son wouldn't fail as miserably I had, I feared that it wasn't the right moment for me to interrupt his grieving.

Perhaps this was just an inadequate excuse for retreating from Wakeland unannounced, but I never claimed to be a courageous man when facing rejection. In truth, my most agonizing struggle in life was to avoid loneliness. Though I regretted my decision, I waited another twelve years before returning to Wakeland. By now I had more than just one reason to venture back here, and I expected—and perhaps even deserved—the scorn from my son.

One month before I sat down to compose this journal, I knocked on the door of Theodore's farmhouse. When staring into the man's dull eyes, I sensed that I had arrived too late to resurrect his faith. Coldness flashed from his expression that could've turned the most staunchly determined man away in shivers.

With my quest clearly defined, however, I realized that I hadn't come to Wakeland solely to seek his forgiveness. In a letter that preceded my arrival, I informed Theodore that I sought burial in the town's cemetery upon my death. Obviously, I anticipated some resistance on the part of my son, but he agreed to my request without bickering over the basis of my decision.

"You could've come to me sooner," Theodore said to me. "Do you know how long I've been waiting?"

"I do," I said, awkwardly. "And I'm sorry that I couldn't face you before today. But since neither of us can correct the past, let's focus on the future."

"The future?" Theodore sobbed. "Is that why you've come here, Lawrence?"

I glanced beyond my son for a moment, concentrating briefly on his home's interior. Even before I uttered the words, he sensed that I wanted to see his daughter.

"She's very sick, you know," Theodore muttered.

"I have a feeling that she's well enough to see me."

"What makes you so certain that she'll even want to meet you?"

"It's more of a matter of me wanting to meet her."

Theodore gritted his teeth before saying, "But you don't even know my daughter."

"Let me see her, Theodore. Though it may seem unimportant to you now, I need to see that child's face."

"What about my face? Don't you owe me an explanation—or something?"

"I don't have all the answers for you now, but I promise you, Theodore, you'll understand everything one day soon."

For whatever reason, Theodore did not push me away from his doorway. Instead, he permitted me to enter his house as if he had been waiting for me like an overdue companion. Although we exchanged few words on this occasion, I didn't think anything that I said to him would curtail his disappointment. Rather than prolong our discomfort, I asked him to point me in the direction of his daughter's bedroom.

"She's upstairs," he whispered. "Look for a closed door at the end of the hallway."

Without pause, I bounded upstairs as swiftly as my old legs could propel me. As I neared Emily's bedroom, my pace slowed to almost a standstill. I had no real reason to hesitate at this stage in my journey, for I knew what vision would strike my eyes once I opened the door and peered inside. Theodore had most likely prepared Emily for my arrival, so the possibility of startling the child seemed doubtful.

My hand shook on the door's brass knob. I couldn't displace the fact that this child was different from all others. Though we had never met or spoken, I felt as though we were far closer than most people were. When I first looked at Emily, I wanted to be sad for her. She, like the mother she never knew, was enchanting. Disease could not shield her beauty from my eyes.

After my sorrow faded, I was content to sit down in a wooden chair beside her closet. Since she was sleeping when I first entered the room, I made no attempt to disrupt her. When ten minutes passed, she opened her eyes and cast a perplexed glance toward me. It took her a moment to figure out who I might be.

"My dad told me you were coming here today," she yawned, sitting upright in her bed. After studying my face, she declared, "You do look a little bit like him, you know."

"And you have your mother's blonde hair," I said, partially amused by her observation. "I'm sorry for waking you, Emily."

"It's okay," she assured me. "I know it sounds strange, but all this sleep is making me tired." She then grimaced at her window. The frost of March was still caked on the outside glass. "I want to get out of this bed," she complained. "But Regina won't let that happen."

"Regina is your nurse?"

"Yeah, but I like to think of her as my mother. By the way, how did you know that my mother had blonde hair?"

Reviewing my thoughts hastily, I said, "Your father mentioned it."

"He still misses her," Emily sulked. "I once thought this was a good thing, but now I'm not so sure."

"It's a difficult time for everyone," I murmured. "Maybe that's why I wanted to see you today."

"That still doesn't make sense to me. I don't even know what to call you."

"If it makes you comfortable, call me Lawrence. I can live with that."

"Okay, Lawrence," Emily sighed. "Explain to me why you wanted to come here."

Perhaps I didn't desire anything more or less than to simply sit beside this child for a few minutes, if only to confirm that she was protected from the dark fiend's infernal spells. Seeing the Bible positioned next to her night table, I assumed that she had not surrendered her spirit. I then took notice of her collection of books covering her bedroom's shelving.

"Have you really read all those books," I asked, amazed by her determination.

"Mostly," she replied before returning to her original concern. "Lawrence, I like the fact that you've come to see me, but my dad is the one you should be talking to. He has a lot of things to ask you."

"I don't want to answer any questions now. Besides, I already assured your father that he would know everything in time. But if I am to speak the truth, I'm not nearly as important to your father as you are."

"What do you mean?"

"He's going to need you to save him, and that person can't be me. My words alone won't mean anything to him right now."

"But you've never even tried."

"I know what I know, Emily."

"You still haven't told me why you've come here," Emily reminded me. "What do you want from me?"

Disregarding the girl's question, I dragged my chair closer to her bed. I then extended my hand and asked permission to hold her hand. "That is all I want. Is that too much to ask?"

"Why do you want to hold my hand?"

"No specific reason," I answered. "Let's call it a gesture of friendship."

Emily reluctantly placed her fingertips into mine before admitting, "Lawrence, I don't know if I'm ready to think of you as a friend yet." As she spoke, I felt a fluid warmth building in the center of my palm and gradually gliding upward through my forearm. Unwittingly, I grasped the child's hand tighter than I intended. She responded by tugging her hand free from mine. At this point, I retreated in my chair and watched her study me for several seconds.

"You didn't come to my house to just hold my hand," she surmised. "What do you really want?"

"Nothing," I insisted. "I just wanted to spend some time with you before I died."

"Are you dying, too?" Emily asked me, her voice now softened.

"We're all dying, Emily."

"Tell that to my father. He needs to know that he can't get mad about things that aren't in his control—like my sickness."

"Just see to it that he doesn't slip too far away from God's reach."

"Maybe it's already too late for that," Emily told me.

At this point, I stood up from the chair and moved next to Emily's night table. After centering my stare upon her Bible, I picked up the book and flipped through the pages of The New Testament. "There's much you need to know about yourself," I said to her, while finding a place of reference in The Book of Matthew. "I'm going to leave you with a story."

"From the Bible?"

"Yes," I answered, referring to the Scripture. "It's a familiar passage, but I think it's appropriate. It's from Matthew 18: 1."

"I think I remember this one," Emily said.

"It concerns the disciples of Jesus," I went on. "They once came to him with a question that had been baffling them for some time."

"What did they want to know?"

"They wanted to know who had the greatest importance in heaven. Some believed it was the rich—others said it must be the poor. And then there were those who insisted that only those who prayed most devoutly to God would be valued as supreme."

"How did Jesus answer them?"

"After many conferences, not a single disciple could guess the right answer. In order to undo their curiosity, Jesus summoned a child from the crowd. He then said something that I think most of us have forgotten."

"What did he tell them?"

"Jesus put that child in front of him and said, 'I assure you all, unless you change and become like little children, you will not enter the kingdom of God.' I'll let figure the rest out for yourself."

"But what about my dad, Lawrence? Do you know how I can help save him?"

After closing the Bible, I told her, "It's not easy being a father. I would like to help my son, but your safety has clouded his judgement. He needs to know that you will be safe with God—only then will he embrace what you already know to be true."

I left Emily on that day with the sunlight spilling between the sheer curtains of her window. Soon the frost on her window's sill would melt and the tulips would burst through the soil to thrive once again. After our meeting, I said good-bye to my son with the full knowledge that I'd never see him again—at least on this ground. He didn't beg me to stay. I suppose the pain of seeing me was too much for him to bear at that time.

I soon returned to the Sunset Motel to record my memories in this journal. So there won't be any future misunderstanding, it was my intention to mail this diary to Emily before my death. With this wish fulfilled, she shall know the truth as I saw it and then pass it on to those who need it.

I won't presume to prophesize the fate of our kind in this writing. But before I put my pen to rest, let me offer a few words of gratitude toward the suffering children of this Earth. After gazing into their curious eyes, I have uncovered a reflection of purity that still shines. Through the storms of humanity, these young souls are the ones we embrace to keep us afloat. They prevent us from submerging into the depths of despair. In the end, when the light fades from our eyes, I hope that we may discover the one true pathway to God. For those of us still searching, it shall be found hitched to the children's spirits as they return to live in harmony beside the keeper of the doves.

ABOUT THE AUTHOR

Michael Ciardi lives in Bethlehem, PA with his wife, Laura, and their two daughters, Brittney and Alyssa. Michael is a graduate of Montclair State University, in NJ, where he earned a degree in English. *Keeper of the Doves* is his first novel.

CPSIA information can be obtained at www.ICGtesting.com
Printed in the USA
BVOW07s2338051214

378188BV00005B/446/P